The warm afternoon sun was a blanket over the houses on River Street. Titus, deep in his sagging wicker chair, bowed his head and felt the heat flow through him.

'I know you're not asleep. You don't have to pretend you are.'

The Sheriff's eyes fluttered open. 'How are you, Miss Ballou?' The words were pitched only above a whisper, but there was no drowsiness in Semple's glance. It darted over her.

'Did you have me fired from the café?' With an effort Lane kept her body relaxed, leaning her back against the square piller, one foot dangling negligently. She would not come to Titus tightly strung and furious – that was the way he would want her. She sensed this.

'Well, now –' Titus played with one of the pearl buttons on his shirt. '– there wasn't anything really personal in it, you understand.'

'It's personal to me if I don't eat or have a place to sleep . . . but I'm not going to run, Sheriff Semple, I'm not going to go. I've been booted around for too long. I want to stay in Truro. I'm not going to go, do you hear?'

Semple's eyes were closed. His chest heaved with a sigh. 'I'd sure advise you to, Miss Ballou. I sure enough would.'

Robert Wilder

Flamingo Road

CORGI BOOKS

FLAMINGO ROAD

A CORGI BOOK 0 552 11848 6

First publication in Great Britain

PRINTING HISTORY
Corgi edition published 1961
Corgi edition reprinted 1962
Corgi edition reissued 1970
Corgi edition reissued 1981
Corgi edition reprinted 1983

This book is set in 9 on 9½pt Times

Corgi Books are published by Transworld Publishers Ltd.,
Century House, 61-63 Uxbridge Road, Ealing, London, W5 5SA
Made and printed in Great Britain by
Hunt Barnard Printing Ltd., Aylesbury, Bucks.

To my sister, Jean
This little for so much

Aside from the fact that in 1929 a former governor of Florida was indicted by a Federal Grand Jury in that state on charges of aiding and abetting a counterfeiting ring this book is fiction and the characters and incidents imaginary.

R.W.

CHAPTER ONE

IN THE CENTER OF A STUMP-DOTTED CLEARING WEST
of the railroad tracks, the patched and weather-yellow canvas
of the Great Coyne Traveling Exhibition sagged dejectedly in
the uncertain light of late afternoon. Along a scraggly path,
rutted and ridged with mounds and wire grass, the sideshow
banners fell in mottled folds, the figures in their faded paint
twisted and tortured into fantastic grotesques.

A rough board platform built over unsteady sawhorses
spanned the width before the main tent. Along it an excited
and inquisitive squirrel raced to leap triumphantly upon a
ticket box canted against a worn flight of steps. The little
animal posed there for a moment, its tail twitching with
nervous suspicion. Then, on some impulse, it streaked for the
tangled brush and disappeared. High in the silent trees a light
wind crept through the branches, sending a scattered shower
of copper-brown pine needles to the ground. They fell lightly
and without sound, some of them clinging to the drab, figured
entrances of the half-dozen exhibits, which gaped with the
blank and empty slackness of an idiot's mouth. Desolation,
poverty, and pitiful defeat ringed the lot.

Scattered pines and palmetto scrub pressed against the flat,
and the damp chill of Florida's early October was heavy in
the air. The tents seemed to huddle together against it. The
wind, coming from a distant river, winnowed through the
encircling woods, tugging at the bellying canvas and swinging
guy lines in a limp and regular cadence.

There was an uneasy and compelling quiet about the place.
Field Carlisle tramping through the clinging brush that daily
inched upon the clearing felt it. He paused on the edge and
kicked a heavily booted foot at a thick palmetto root. His
lips pursed in a tuneless whistle as his eyes searched the
abandoned acre.

Field had a feeling he was on a fool's errand and one which
interfered with the fishing he had planned. Instead of hooking
into a bass at this moment he was running a useless chore for
old pus-gut Semple. His being a deputy sheriff didn't make
much sense to begin with. It was crazier still when he was
sent out on something like this. Titus Semple could rest his
fat behind in a chair on the Palmer House porch, scratch his

7

belly with a lazy hand, and order his assistant to chase a carnival that had already left town.

Field lifted his head and sniffed hungrily at the moist, piny smell of the flat and decided he was complaining only because he thought he should. He liked the woods, the fresh, sweet smell of them and the feel of the ground beneath his feet. This carnival, though, made them stink. It was a dirty blot, noisome and unhealthy, and nothing short of a good fire would clean it up. This shallow stand of pine would go like a pitch knot if a match was set to it.

He gazed around the clearing. Everything was still here. Now he could go back and tell Titus. Titus did a mighty lot of unnecessary worrying, it seemed, for a fat man. Maybe that was why he had to have himself a deputy. Field grinned suddenly as he always did when he thought of himself as a deputy sheriff, a deputy to Titus Semple, who took the office about as seriously as he did the wart on the back of his neck. Now and then he'd get a silly notion like this one, and Field would be prodded into carrying it out. Titus, he imagined, just liked to give him something to do. Well, he could fish tomorrow or the next day or the day after. The knowledge pleased him, and he whistled with ragged unconcern.

The sound fluted strangely shrill and startled into silence a woodpecker drilling near by. Field walked slowly toward the tents, and his whistle died away, muted by the shoddy despair of the scene. It depressed him. He hesitated and then poked a finger upward at the brim of his large, soft hat, tilting it back on his head.

"I sure don't know"—he spoke wonderingly—"why anyone would want to claim this."

Someone was claiming the tents and the hauling wagons though. Semple had called to him from the porch of the Palmer House as he was strolling down River Street.

"Take yo'sef a run down to the circus lot, bub," Titus waved genially. "See that Coyne nor none of his men ain't took anything away. There's an attachment against the stuff that's got to be satisfied."

The effort of the order to his deputy so exhausted the Sheriff that he sank limply back into the wicker chair and panted. This was something new. Field was puzzled. Titus had long ago given up paying any attention to such things as attachments.

He waited to see if there was a joker hidden somewhere in the order, but Titus had dismissed him. His eyes were closed, and his face was a glistening benign pink moon, bagging at the jowls. Field peevishly abandoned the idea of fishing and started for the carnival location.

He heard about the attachment against Coyne when he left his car at Weaver's for a grease job. Lanlight, the feed and grain dealer who had given Coyne credit for years, suddenly became skittish about his money and brought the action to settle a bill of long standing. He knew, as did everyone else, Coyne was broke. For as long as the town of Truro could remember, old Tom Coyne had taken his bob-tailed, rattle-can caravan up and down the state. He was a Florida institution like the sulphur-water springs and Spanish moss. Fifteen years ago—Field's mind raced back—he used to work out passes to the sideshows by delivering handbills for Tom Coyne. The old man always waited for him to come around. He had been twelve then and a hard worker who really passed out the flimsy sheets and didn't cram them down the big hole in the first privy he came to.

Fifteen years ago the Great Coyne Traveling Exhibition had been an annual event in Truro. The crimson wagons splashed with gold, the sobbing, noisy calliope, the medicine man and his Indian helper, the performers and tasseled horses made a bright parade down River Street on the way to the lot. The Great Coyne was known from Jacksonville to Tampa. The years, however, knotted the show, and it seemed to shrink within itself. The red and gold cracked and peeled. The horses grew leaner, the exhibits smaller. One by one the old, familiar performers abandoned the troupe. The movies and the automobile had done for Coyne. People grew up and were no longer amused by a Hawaiian dancing act and a fake freak or two.

Coyne pleaded helplessly when the writ had been served. He stood in Lanlight's dusty office and ran his fingers around and around the napless brim of a once gray top hat.

"There really ain't nothin' worth attachin'," he argued. "You leave me go on down around Sanford, maybe into Plant City, an' I'll sure get some nigger business. I'll pay off every cent that way. Otherwise, nobody ain't goin' to be able to get themselves so much as a penny on the dollar."

Everyone who knew about it felt sorry for Tom Coyne, but Lanlight—the boys at City Hall said he must be having his period—wouldn't listen.

"I want that show closed," he yelled. "Throw those people out of Truro. A show like that don't do nothin' but take good money out of the town while the women with it go whorin' around the streets at night settin' up the home boys. I know my rights, an' I want the thing attached."

It was funny, Field mused, as he took in the few tents, how a man could get like Lanlight. It was one thing to refuse Coyne more credit and another to take his living this way.

Earlier in the afternoon Coyne and his people had dragged away from the lot in the direction of the Coast Line depot. Those who had it dug down for money and bought day coach tickets on Number 40 for Jacksonville, waiting in troubled silence on the platform for the train. The others scattered along the highway, hopeful of encountering a friendly truck driver who would give them a lift north. It was a shabby, tight-lipped little pilgrimage, and behind it now only this false-face of carnival remained to mark its passing.

Evening was spreading itself over the lot. Tents and trees began to lose shape merging into each other, and the scrub was cast in a peculiar greenish haze. Field was about to turn away, thinking wistfully of the fishing he had missed, when a faint yellow blob appeared on the canvas of the largest tent. Against it he could see a formless shadow move. It seemed to hunch itself, gnomelike, close to the ground. Someone had stayed behind after all. Maybe Coyne had come back to gather up a few things he could carry.

Field sighed. The hell with it. If he had left five minutes sooner he wouldn't have to do anything.

"Hey," he called without spirit and waited for a reply. "Hey, you there in the tent. Come on out now."

He thought he saw the shadow start but couldn't be sure. Whoever was inside didn't answer, and after a moment he walked over to the steps leading to the platform, crossed the trembling boards, pulled away the flap, and looked inside.

Seated on a battered crate, a smoking lantern between her feet, a girl leaned over the flickering light, rubbing her fingers in the timid heat. At the sound of his step she raised her head and regarded him impassively. With a deliberate movement of her hand she pushed back the straight black hair which fell over one eye and held it against her cheek while they stared at each other.

"What"—Field knew he sounded more curious than official —"what you doing here with that lantern?"

The girl dropped her hand, and the curtain of hair slanted across her face, half obscuring it. Her fingers spread out again over the lantern's top, groping for warmth.

The open insolence angered him. "Didn't you hear me? What are you doing here?"

10

"Holdin' a barbecue."

He could have sworn that she laughed although her face was without expression. It was just the way she had said it, a movement of the lips. This was sure a hell of a note. Why couldn't everyone have been gone the way they were supposed to? He was ill at ease and to cover his embarrassment stepped cautiously from the platform.

The glow of the lantern made a moving pool on the ground around him. He had a better look at her now. She was wearing a short blue skirt topped by a shapeless middy blouse. The canvas, rubber-soled sneakers on her feet were frayed, and their toe caps worn. Her slim legs were brown and sleek, bare of stockings and patterned by the light spreading out from the lantern's smoke-blackened chimney. Field was surprised. She looked like a youngster.

Whatever her age she was old enough to treat his presence with indifference. Ignoring him she reached down and gently chafed her toes. She did this slowly, methodically, one toe at a time.

"You belong with Coyne's show?" The sound of his voice almost startled Field. He hadn't meant it to be so loud.

The girl moved her hand to the left foot and worked across its narrow width.

"What's your name, anyhow?" Field was sure he had to say something.

She finished her massage and leaned back, raising her eyes to his. "Well"—she spoke thoughtfully as if trying to remember something—"sometimes I'm Seminole Annie. Other times I'm the Princess Kalina, siren of the Pacific. Once I was a jewel from a Sultan's harem, spirited away at great cost from a life of shame in the marble temples. Right now my name's Lane Balou. What's yours?"

Field was possessed by the uncomfortable feeling that in some manner he had been put on the defensive. After all, it was up to the girl to do the explaining.

"I'm the deputy sheriff of Truro." With an effort he kept his face straight.

The girl's eyebrows flicked upward. It was a gesture of deliberate impudence. "You don't look much like a sheriff," she concluded after a moment. "You look more like Buffalo Bill with that hat on."

She did laugh then, the tip of her tongue between her teeth, her face mobile and alive. The abruptness of the change in expression took Field by surprise. He found himself grinning back at her.

11

"All sheriffs have got to wear hats like this," he confided, "otherwise no one would know for sure they were the law."

The rising wind slapped at the tent flaps, and its breath caught the lantern's flame, bending it toward the already blackened chimney. The girl shivered and drew her arms across her breasts, hugging herself.

"Well"—she speculated on his tall, ranging height and solemn features—"take a chair then, Sheriff. Set by the fire a spell." She indicated the lantern with a nod of her head.

Field hesitated. This wasn't the way things should be going at all. A man lost some of his authority when he sat down. The girl should have been on her way with the others, and it was his business to tell her so. At least, he guessed that was his business.

"You work for Coyne?" He temporized with the question.

"I guess you could say that I *did* work for him." She emphasized the word accusingly. "If throwing my hip around in a grass skirt comes under the heading of work. Didn't you see me; or, maybe, you don't go to carnivals."

Field could understand her better now. She wasn't sore, not really, just sort of joking around halfway between. He looked about the tent and finally hooked a packing case out with his foot and sat upon it, facing her across the lantern. To cover his indecision he rolled a cigarette, licked carefully along the joint, and was about to put it in his mouth when he saw the hungry look in her eyes. He passed it over, and she took it without comment. After his second cigarette had been made and lighted, they smoked in companionable silence for a moment.

"You know," he said casually, "I'm supposed to throw you or anybody else here off the lot. Coyne lost his show this morning."

Smoke curled from the girl's small nostrils and mouth, drifting scarflike across her face. She inhaled deeply and emitted the draft in fine spurts from between her teeth.

"I figured that was what you were here for."

It was a calm acceptance of fact and made Field feel helpless. "Why didn't you go with the others? They all got rides or took the train. You should have gone with them." He wanted to put the blame where it belonged.

"I could have gone with Coyne. He offered to take me, only I decided that I'd been running long enough. Even a rabbit can get tired of being chased although the dog still thinks it's a lot of fun. I'm that rabbit."

"That doesn't make any sense."

"It does to me." She turned the limp cigarette between her fingers, examining it carefully. "After awhile you get tired of being pushed from town to town, sleeping in moldy tents, eating greasy food until you want to vomit from the smell of it. You get sick of knowing you're cheap and having people look at you as though you were a half-dollar hooker every time you step off the lot."

The words had a harsh, ugly sound and made Field uneasy. He wondered what he was going to do.

"Well"—he hesitated—"you can't stay here like this. You know that. Even if you could Truro isn't a good town for a girl to be alone in."

As if realizing she was making things difficult for him, she smiled again, a wistful, almost tender expression.

"No town is good to be alone in, is it?"

She rose from the crate, and Field saw she was taller than he had suspected. She stood straight, slim-bodied, arms at her sides, head tilted back as though she were listening for something. The lantern's light spotted her worn sneakers, accenting their pathetic condition. Finally she turned to face him; her small hands were clenched.

"They can't make me go away, can they?" she asked desperately. "I mean, if I don't want to go, there isn't anyone who will say I must. Folks can't just be batted about because a town doesn't want them, can they?"

Field stood up. This was sure enough a hell of a note. Damn Titus and his nonsense.

"No," he admitted, "I guess no one would want to do that, but"—his voice was sympathetic—"don't you reckon you'd be better off with the others?"

"They're not going any place. They're just running, too." She made the statement, not wearily, but with simple conviction.

He fumbled for words. "Anyhow, they're folks you know. They're more likely to help than any others."

Lane Ballou gathered the hair at the back of her neck with one hand and fastened it there with a small clip fished from the blouse pocket. The effect was startling. Shorn of the wild look of loose hair her face was a clear, dusky oval, vivid and arresting. The transformation was so complete, Field could only stare.

"I've had two years of that kind of help," she answered. "It got me hungry, dirty, and tired. I've damn near been killed by that kind of kindness. Now, maybe, I'll try it a different

13

way with strangers. It might as well be in Truro as any place else."

She walked in a tight little circle around the tent, her eyes steadfastly on the ground. Finally she halted and looked at him again.

"I don't suppose," she almost whispered, "you could go away and forget I was here for the night. I can sleep here. In the morning I can figure out something to do. Don't you see, it would give me a little time to—to straighten myself out."

Without waiting for a reply she went over to the tent's opening and, standing on the small flight of steps, stared up into the sky. The stars were out, scatterings of silver powder in a deep well, and the wind in the pines soughed faintly. She breathed deeply of the woods and then, still holding to the canvas flaps, turned her body half around to find Carlisle gazing at her.

"Well?" she asked again.

Field didn't know what to say. It sure wasn't the job of a deputy to send a girl out on the road alone, not in Truro.

"Haven't you any money at all?"

She came back inside the tent. "Sure, three dollars. That's a lot if you knew how many times I didn't have three dollars."

"All right." Field made up his mind with a rush. To hell with Lanlight and his attachment. The girl couldn't do him any harm sleeping in the tent one more night if she wanted to. "If you're not afraid to be out here alone, I guess you can stay until tomorrow or, maybe, until they come for the tents and things and find you. I won't say anything."

She smiled gratefully, and Field was ashamed of the little he was offering. It was a pretty pompous way to talk to a girl who was down to a pair of rubber sneakers and three dollars.

"Listen"—he wanted to get it over with—"I can see you get a room uptown. I can fix it for you all right. I wouldn't feel right knowing you were here by yourself."

She shook her head. "No, honest, I really want to stay. Maybe it sounds crazy, but I do."

Field was provoked by her stubbornness. "All right, sleep here then." He was on the point of leaving when something in her face caused him to stay, "Listen"—he tried to be friendly—"you will have to get something to eat. Come on along uptown with me. We'll take supper together."

Her surprise was a fleeting thing, tripping for a moment in her eyes. He saw it there. Then it vanished, and she watched him thoughtfully, her mouth twisted into a contemplative quirk. Field was restless beneath her study. He felt she was silently accusing him of something, he didn't know what. Her face cleared.

"That's pretty nice of you. I don't want to load on to your wagon. Anyhow, I don't feel much like eating."

If he had any sense, Field thought, he'd stop talking right now and go on about his business. His eyes ran again over her nondescript clothing, the dirty and worn sneakers. He'd make a hell of a picture walking up River Street with that. Surprised, he heard himself repeating the invitation.

"You'd better come along anyhow. You'll sleep better after a meal."

As though he had communicated his unspoken thoughts to her, the girl pulled at the hem of her blouse and ran a quick, smoothing hand over her skirt.

"I've got other clothes." The words were actually shy. She dropped to her knees and threw back the top of a wicker suitcase and from the packed clothing drew out a soft, gray skirt, light yellow sweater, and a pair of brown, low-heeled shoes. She closed the lid and spread the articles on its top. Turning from them she looked up at him. "If you still want to take me with you, I'll be glad to go."

He nodded, and at this sign she pulled the middy blouse over her head, and then the skirt dropped from her slim hips to the ground. She stood for a moment clad in only a brief cotton slip.

"It won't take me but a minute." Her voice was eager.

Field thought this was the damnedest thing he ever heard of, a girl undressing in front of a stranger as though he wasn't there. He might as well not have been there for all the attention she gave his presence. With a twisting movement she was in to the sweater, straightening it with a few sure tugs until it was snugly molding her high, youthful breasts. A moment later she had kicked out of the crumpled blue skirt and was snapping the band of the gray one around her waist. She had performed these operations without affectation or coquetry. He drew his breath sharply.

To cover his surprise Field began talking. "Lane," he said aimlessly, "is a funny name for a girl. It sounds more like a man's name."

"Yep"—she was busy with her shoes—"'most everyone says the same things at one time or another." She drew herself erect again, unconscious of the compelling picture she made, ran a broken piece of comb through her hair, then refastened it at the back. "I often thought about it. I guess maybe in the beginning it was something fancier like Elaine. I never did know my folks to ask them. People just called me Lane, so I never bothered much."

She had a peculiar trick of slurring some words, and the effect was an indefinite accent. Field tried to place it. He was about to ask her where she came from when she turned and faced him. In the fresh clothing she was lithe and cleanly beautiful. The astonishment he felt appeared in his eyes as he looked at her.

"Better?" It was more a statement of fact than a question.

At Field's nod a pleased flush brushed her cheeks.

"These"—she indicated the gray skirt with a touch of her finger—"were my getaway clothes. The others were for sleeping in tonight."

"You ought to be able to go a far piece in getting-away clothes like those." Field was amazed at himself. A few minutes ago he had been on the point of chasing her. Now he was passing words back and forth as though they were old friends. There was a directness about her, a calm acceptance of things as they were which made him feel they had known each other a long time. He was a little disturbed and puzzled over it.

She pointed to the lantern. "We'd better put that out, don't you think?"

Field picked up the light, pressed the wire lever lifting the chimney, and the flame snapped away beneath his breath. In the sudden darkness they groped toward the tent opening.

"I guess I should have let you go out first," Field apologized.

"Wait a minute." She moved ahead of him and reached back to find his hand. "I'm used to these steps. They take a lot of stumbling over before you can call them by their first names."

She pulled him forward confidently, up the steps and out on the platform. The night had closed over the flat, blotting out the low stumps and seared pines, wrapping it in a black cloak. The woods were almost without sound. Only the evening wind was in the trees, and it hunted there with a lonely and gentle call.

When their eyes had focused to the darkness, they left the platform and made their way along the tracked path.

"I always thought the law carried flashlights," Lane gasped as she stumbled in a hidden rut.

Field chuckled. "When I'm sheriff," he assured her solemnly, "I'll get me one. Right now I'm only a deputy."

"Next time"—her giggle was audible—"next time I'll get myself taken in by the head man, 'specially if it's after dark."

The woods thinned and finally dropped away altogether at the side of a broad, unpaved road. Pale street lights, high on bare yellow pine poles, dotted the way. At the far end, marking the beginning of River Street, they thickened into a shimmering cluster and lost their identity.

Lane sighed with open relief as her foot touched the highway and bent down to brush away the assorted twigs her skirt had caught in the brush. When she lifted her eyes suddenly and caught Field studying her, she met his gaze steadily.

"You know," she said softly, "you don't have to do this; take me in to town with you, I mean. Even if you wanted to back out now, I'd understand. You live around here, and I know what most people think about carnival folks."

"I wasn't thinkin' that," Field assured her gravely. "I was just thinkin' you looked mighty pretty. Too pretty," he added thoughtfully, "to be alone in Truro."

She wrinkled her nose distastefully. "I've been in lots worse places than Truro"—her tone was level—"and behaved myself in them too."

Field shrugged his broad shoulders. "I wouldn't be surprised. Truro, though, is maybe a little different."

They walked slowly, pausing once on the side of the road to allow a loaded bus to roar past. When it had swept by, Field pulled out papers and a half-filled sack of tobacco and carefully rolled two more cigarettes.

"I'll get some ready-mades in town," he said. "I don't care much for these either. I just like to make them."

"I wondered about that." Field knew that she was laughing now although her mouth was straight. "I thought it might have something to do with being a deputy sheriff or looking like Buffalo Bill."

She took one of the cigarettes and waited for his match.

They picked their way across eight sets of railroad tracks. Long, silent lines of freight cars banked the sidings, and far down the rails the tracks branched and widened to run alongside loading platforms and warehouses. There was a shadowy immensity to the yards, and the glow from the open fireboxes of a couple of switch engines lighted it evilly.

"That's a lot of railroad, it seems to me, for a town the size of Truro." Lane was plainly surprised.

"It's a junction now." Field waved a hand at the yard. "Lines sort of fan out from here all over the state."

They reached the sidewalk marking the town's improved limits. Field felt her hand upon his arm.

17

"You never did tell me your name." She tilted her face to him. "I don't just call you Sheriff, do I?"

He shook his head. "Nope. My name's Field Carlisle."

"Field? That's a funny name for a man." She mimicked his earlier comment with deadly accuracy and tucked her hand beneath his arm.

He laughed with her in a ready expression of understanding. "It's really Fielding, but everyone calls me Field."

"It's a nice name."

They walked without talking for awhile along the sidewalk bordered by white picket fences and hedged with honeysuckle, flame vine, and Cherokee rose. Half-concealed trim cottages were set back behind oaks, bootjack palmettoes, and dim magnolia trees, and the night air was scented with the fresh perfume of green and growing things. Now and then, as they passed along, Field lifted his hat and called a soft good evening to indistinguishable figures rocking silently in porch chairs.

Lane sensed rather than saw the occupants of the seats lean forward in an effort to identify the Deputy Sheriff's companion as they replied. An inexpressible feeling of loneliness possessed her, and her fingers closed tightly upon Carlisle's arm.

CHAPTER TWO

LEFT TO ITSELF TRURO WOULD HAVE BEEN SATISFIED to drowse through the years, sprawling indolently beneath a warm sun on the shelving bank of a dark and melancholy river, which felt its way from the tangled reaches of the cypress swamps to the sea.

That was how it had been in the beginning, for the needs of the community were small and easily satisfied. The early settlers fished the broad waters and hunted through the handy woods for their tables. They built homes along the shore, splitting into lumber the towering pines that had to be felled to clear a site. Truck gardens flourished in every back yard, and farther away, in the rich, black soil, larger farms spread and their owners prospered. If there was little actual money in the village in those days, it made not much difference since there was nothing on which to spend it.

18

The tides of immigration, creeping slowly upon Florida at the turn of the century, touched Truro only briefly at first. They divided and swept around her to the seaboards on the east and west, but they were not to be denied. The river was too close, and traffic moved upon it. Truro had to stir despite itself.

Shallow-draft, paddle-wheel steamers found the village a convenient stopover as they moved out from the interior. Docks, at first, and then larger piers stretched broader and longer from the shore. From the back country flowed the lumber, rosin, potato, and celery crops. The cotton, sugar, and citrus fruits moved in crates, barrels, bales, and sacks upon Truro for transshipment. Warehouses had to be built to store them, and men came in to handle the loads. New houses were starkly bare in fresh clearings, and River Street grew too narrow for the unexpected burdens thrust upon it. Then, the railroad laid a spur line from the east coast, and what was once Truro all but disappeared.

Twice daily, trains shuttled across the flat lands, hauling freight and passengers, and along the way Negroes maintained stacks of fat pine chunks for the refueling of the small engines. With the spur came new faces and strange accents. Men and their families moved in and upon Truro, seeking homes and farms. The restless and the aging, tourist and indigent, some with a little money, others with a great deal, and still others with none, filled the dirty plush seats in narrow-gauge cars. With the spur went the river's cargoes. The trains were faster and more reliable. The docks rotted, planking falling away with the years until only bare, slime-wrapped piles stood in naked and irregular lines out into the current. Now and then a steamer worked its way past the town, but its decks were no longer burdened with freight, and it made no stop, for the steamer was only something to catch the tourist's eye and became scenery. The matted shade of an earlier day crept upon the river bank.

Truro prospered, though. The merchants, commission men, warehouse owners, builders, and contractors grew wealthy, for if the railroad raped the river it paid handsomely for the deed.

Part of the state's inexhaustible resources poured into the town to be shipped from there to Jacksonville and eventually to the north. One by one the homes along River Street were abandoned to make way for restaurants, boarding-houses, hotels, drugstores, pool halls, barbershops, meat and grocery markets. The residents who once delighted in their nearness to the river moved hastily out of the path of commerce. Some

19

families went back into the still untouched woods and built new houses, preferring this semi-isolation to the rowdy brawl of the main street. Others, with more money to spend, moved into a recently cleared tract on a ridge. There, along Flamingo Road, rose fine, broad-porched dwellings or small, neat cottages. Well-tended lawns sloped to newly laid sidewalks, flowers and shrubs bloomed in vivid splendor, and the way was lined with ancient oaks, gray and mossladen. As residence on River Street impressed its mark of caste upon those who still dwelt there, so also did the families along Flamingo Road come to stand a little apart from their old-time neighbors who had moved to the other side of town or clung determinedly to the river shore.

Then the railroad wrought a second miracle. Instead of feeding the single-tracked spur, Truro was to become a junction point for the two coastal lines serving the state. Into it, from Jacksonville, trooped the workmen. Rails spread wider and wider, and upon them the passenger and freight cars, switching and traffic engines worked and banged. Homes for the laborers, maintenance men, and crews sprouted in precise rows of small, one-story buildings. The roundhouse, an enormous bastion of red brick, and the great, soot-covered shops dominated the yard with gloomy ferocity. The district was never silent.

With the railroad came people strange to Florida. Broad-faced Slavs from the mill and tool towns of Pennsylvania, Yankees from Connecticut and New York labored in the shops. Roaring Irishmen with the brogue still on their tongues manned the freights. The overflow of a dozen nationalities packed itself in among Truro's soft-spoken families. The newcomers jammed the steaming restaurants on River Street of an evening. They sat on stools, hunching over their food with savage concentration. They spoke with thick or rasping accents, shouldering their way along the narrow sidewalks, crowding into the poolrooms and the one motion picture house, and scrambling the length of the town on payday. Some brought their families, gray women, timid and amazed at the sight of open country, sunshine, trees, and growing things. Raucous, incredibly filthy-mouthed children roamed with predatory eagerness through the yards of the company's cottages near the tracks. Truro spread without plan. It ran to mean streets and slatternly houses; from the gaudy, noisy vigor of River Street to dark and evil districts along the tracks and the aloof precincts of Flamingo Road.

Truro grew hard, for the newcomers put their stamp upon

20

it. Brothels—pitifully wretched cribs in front of which the girls sat wearily on folding camp stools, to the elaborate establishment of Lute-Mae Sanders—thrived on the yards. By night the streets in the neighborhood of the tracks were populated by the eager and restless men who roamed them in search of women of all color.

Before the enactment of prohibition, Truro had supported two dozen liquor stores, for open saloons were forbidden in the county. In the rear of each store, however, there was a large room where the customers could take their bottles. With the Eighteenth Amendment smoke from still fires and the sour odor of mash was in the surrounding woods, and the fiery, colorless 'shine could be bought on almost every corner.

If Flamingo Road figuratively touched its nose delicately with a handkerchief at the mention of the yards, the district, and even sometimes at Truro itself, those who lived there were careful in their comment. Flamingo Road lived by the rentals, the trade, and the existence of the yards. They built homes, sent young sons and daughters to college, and paid for the automobiles. Flamingo Road took the breath of its life from all of the interlocking enterprises which had made a hoarse-voiced bawd out of Truro.

Flamingo Road had its own particular conceit. It liked to make dreamy reference to "the South," though it never had a part in the romantic pageantry implied by the expression and small connection with the gentry of a fantastic period. There were fine families to be found on the street. Solid, honest, prosperous, and well-reared families; the Morrells, the Davidsons, the Weldons, and Carlisles, descendants of Truro's first settlers. They had come from humble surroundings, from southern Georgia, Tennessee, Alabama, Ohio, and Kentucky, to prosper and multiply in a sun-washed land. There were also families not so solid and of dubious antecedents who by devious methods finally arrived on Flamingo Road. But, because the social scope was limited, they all clung together, a little envious, sometimes suspicious, or simply tolerant of each other, and made a common front.

Field Carlisle had been born on River Street in a low-flung rambling house of silver-gray shingles. As a youngster he had been able to take a few short steps from the porch and dive from the shore into the river. He hunted, fished, and played hooky along the lazy, big stream and paddled his awkward, flat-bottomed rowboat over its surface. When he was ten River Street was already changing, and his father, Judge Carlisle, decided to move.

"I sure hate to leave here, son," he confided gloomily one afternoon. "My father built this house. I was born in it, an' so were you. Your mother died in it. A whole hell of a lot of memories are stored under its roof."

They stood together, father and son, beneath a moss-strung oak in the back yard. Through the trees the rubbed-lead surface of the river glinted softly. Not knowing what reply to make or even if one was expected of him, Field remained silent. He picked an acorn from the ground and cracked the shell in his teeth. It tasted bitter as he knew it would. When he glanced hesitantly up at his father, he saw the man staring out over the trees, lost in his reverie.

Judge Carlisle—it was an honorary title—was as much a part of Truro as the river. To his musty old offices above the Farmers' Bank came all of the local legal business and some from the county. Everything considered, he should have been a prosperous man but wasn't. He had small regard for money, and little cash was ever to be seen around the house or found in his account. Now and then he would turn loose a threat to have the law on those persons who owed him money and wouldn't pay, but they were as empty as he meant them to be. He voiced the warnings only to convince himself he wasn't a bad businessman—anyhow, not as bad as his accounts proved—and that he could be happily solvent if he wanted to be hard about such matters. As a result, some of Field's earliest recollections were concerned with unpaid butcher bills and demands for the settlement of credits extended by Truro's merchants. Somehow the Judge always managed to dig up a few dollars when the situation became acute.

If there had been only himself to consider, the old Judge would have remained in the house on River Street. He hated change, but he could see what was happening to the neighborhood. Field, he realized, was growing up, and it wouldn't do to have the boy burdened by what was becoming an undeniable social handicap. They would have to move. That was all there was to it. The knowledge tore a little at his heart and caused him to peer out at the river and not at the youngster who was regarding him so solemnly.

"A lot of memories are stored under this roof," he repeated. Then he smiled. "Maybe, though, son, we can take the best of them with us."

At the peak of the flurried boom Truro experienced with the expansion of the railroad yards, the Judge turned the River Street property over at a nice profit. With the money he built a snug, white, clapboarded house with flagged terraces and graveled walks on Flamingo Road. On the day he and Field moved in, he turned to his son.

"Whatever else happens," he said mildly, "you'll be goin' in the right direction whenever you have to run home."

From the house on Flamingo Road, Field had gone to high school and later to the University at Gainesville.

"If you want to study the law," the Judge said, "you can learn as much there as any place else. They all have to use the same books."

Field thought he would like law. It had come to be much a part of him living alone as he had with his father. He hoped for one of the fancy eastern colleges. Everyone went to the State. He mentioned this to his father.

"There just ain't the money, son," the Judge explained, "an' I never heard of Harvard givin' tuition on a barter basis."

Field had gone to Gainesville reluctantly, feeling he was attending, not so much a college, as a branch of the Truro high school, and then, in his Sophomore year there, the Judge died.

That was three years ago, and Field was twenty-five and alone. Back in Truro he did his best to bring some order out of his father's haphazard affairs. As he wrestled with the Judge's files and account books, sorted bills and the few receipts, he began to realize he had been left little more than the house on Flamingo Road and a few uncollectable fees.

It was while he was trying to decide what his next move must be that Titus Semple waddled up to the front porch one afternoon and, after a careless bang of the heavy brass knocker, pushed the door open and came inside.

"How you, bub?" He gestured at Field with a broad, sweat-covered hand. "Thought I ought to come up an' see if there was a thing or so I could help you along with. Didn't get much of a chance to talk to you at the funeral."

Wheezing uncomfortably the Sheriff swung his enormous body across the room and sank gratefully into the Judge's deep leather-upholstered chair. He overflowed the massive piece of furniture until it was all but hidden beneath him. His great legs were spread out in a fleshy triangle, his belly a high mound of quivering flesh which showed pinkly damp through a sodden shirt of white silk. For a few moments he fanned his beaded face with a rough palm hat and then cautiously settled the headgear on his chest.

"I got careless once," he said in explanation, "an' let my hat fall between my knees. Damned if I didn't have to get me a negrah boy to retrieve it before I could go on."

23

He chuckled reminiscently and fixed mild, blue eyes on Field, who had turned away from the paper-littered desk and was regarding his visitor with ill-concealed impatience.

"Figured you'd be up to your neck in the Judge's papers." Titus nodded sympathetically and allowed the lids to drop half over his eyes as though he were on the point of going to sleep. "I'd guess,". he sighed, "you'll be hard put to find so much as a good dime in all of that."

The relationship between his father and Titus Semple had always been a puzzle to Field. The two of them appeared to have some secret understanding, which included a humorous conception of the world and most of the people in it. In earlier days rarely an evening passed when Titus wasn't a visitor to the house on River Street. There he and the Judge would sit drinking yellow corn whisky, talking, chuckling intimately, exchanging opinions and apparently endless reminiscences. As a youngster Field paid little attention to Titus, but as he grew older the grossness of the Sheriff's mammoth body became offensive. He couldn't understand how his father, a gentleman of the old school in every respect, could tolerate the fat fool.

In his ponderous, elephantine way Titus seemed to cover a great deal of territory in the northern central part of the state. In some manner he always contrived to lay a pudgy hand on most of the things which went on in Truro and the county. He was unaffectedly casual with legislators and governors alike as they came and went. It was whispered he was part of that mysterious "ring" or, even, that he was "the ring," a will-o-the-wisp combination credited with dictating the politics of northern Florida. Strangers, seeing him for the first time, were inclined to laugh and dismiss him as "that fat fellow."

Titus had time for few persons, but one of them was Judge Carlisle, for whom he cherished the deep and abiding affection of a St. Bernard. They understood each other.

Without seeming to mix in politics, Titus wielded a curious power. He seemed to be on speaking terms with half the population of the state. At election times the space around his chair on the Palmer House porch became sort of a forum, a forum where little argument was heard but where Semple drawled sleepy suggestions which somehow were translated as commands. He disappeared frequently from Truro, going no one was quite sure where, but it was rumored he visited the capitol at Tallahassee, spent weeks at a time in the governor's mansion. Of such things he never spoke.

The office of sheriff, to which he was re-elected with monotonous regularity, had long since ceased to have any significance as such. Titus was an anachronism, but his authority was seemingly far-flung. It was as though by sheer bulk he managed to cast his shadow and make it felt.

In a curious moment Field once asked the Judge about Titus.

"Well," his father chortled, "it's sort of like this, son. Things, you see, just don't run. It takes a lot of wheels. The little wheels push bigger wheels, and the bigger wheels push still bigger wheels. Somewhere along the line there has got to be someone who can keep the whole damn thing oiled so it won't squeak an' cause a lot of attention. Somewhere along in there you might find Titus, I reckon."

It was a confusing explanation, Field agreed, but he knew his father well enough to appreciate that the Judge delighted in such obscurities.

After that he regarded Titus with something approaching an uneasy respect. He fed upon the idea that the layers of trembling fat covering the Sheriff's frame were but a disguise and, if they were stripped away, something darkly cold, almost sinister, would be revealed. Older now, he was no longer uncomfortable in the man's presence, and he fancied he could see him as he was, a hogshead of leaf lard, a panting, gross, small-change politician in whom the Judge had found something of a court jester.

Semple's eyes flickered open, and for the space of a few seconds they were shrewdly amused at the sight of Field at the desk.

"Right then," he mused, "you looked a little like your paw when we were all a hell of a sight younger. I seen that expression on his face a many of times, particularly when he ran up against someone or something he didn't like." He chuckled deep within himself, and the sound was that of a contented razorback. Fumbling at a pocket inside his coat, he finally extracted a twisted cheroot, bit half of it off, and chewed stolidly at the piece.

The mildness of the rebuke caught Field off guard, and he suffered a momentary feeling of embarrassment. "Sorry, Sheriff Titus." It was a lame apology. "I didn't mean to look like that. I just got a whole hell of a lot on my mind, an' this clutter the Judge left isn't helpin' me get it off any."

Titus rolled his head sympathetically. "The Judge was a caution." He scratched the back of his neck against the chair

25

and stared at the ceiling. "You got any plans?" he asked after a pause. "Goin' back to the University?"

Field laughed shortly. "No, I guess not. I'd best be lookin' for a job."

"The Judge was sort of set on your bein' a lawyer. Kind of liked the idea yourself there for awhile, didn't you?" Titus was thoughtful.

"I guess so." Field resented the question.

"*Mmmm*." Semple blew out his cheeks, and his eyes all but disappeared. "The expenses, if that's what's worryin' you, could be arranged so's you could go on."

Field shook his head in immediate refusal. With things the way they were, it seemed a little foolish to think of college. He knew the tuition could be fixed. He could even work his way through if he wanted to; plenty of others did.

"I'll swear," he grinned frankly, "I just don't know what I want to do at the minute. Maybe I'll take a job of some kind for the rest of the year until I get things straightened out in my mind."

Semple kept his eyes on the ceiling. "Lawyers," he finally admitted, "is thirteen to a dozen anyhow. Now"—his face was expressionless—"you might get yourself a job down around the yards, firin' an engine or wallowin' in the pits with the hunkies. You might work up some sort of a place behind a soda fountain at Hammer's. You might get yourself a bow tie an' some hair slick an' sell ribbons at Clark's, or you might get yourself a job drivin' one of them buses between here and Apulca. There's a sight of wonderful things a young fella like yourself might find to do here in Truro."

The sarcasm was unmistakable, and Field's jaw tightened as an angry flush crept up his neck. There was too much common sense in what Semple was saying to dismiss it. Truro hadn't much to offer, and in his heart he knew it.

"All right," he agreed helplessly. "You've got something on your mind?"

Semple's eyes were open again, and for what seemed a long and uncomfortable period he kept them fastened on Field's face.

"Yep"—the admission came slowly—"I've got somethin' on my mind. Your paw an' I," he continued speculatively, "used to do considerable talkin' about you when you was a shirt-tailed youngster. He always cottoned to the idea you might grow up to be a big man here in your home state."

He paused, as though expecting Field to make a reply. When the boy didn't speak he continued gravely.

26

"Well, maybe you will. That depends partly upon what you an' a lot of other folks decide. Offhand, I'd say go back to the University. If I was your paw I'd sure say that, but you're alone now an' have got to do the thinkin' an' talkin' for yourself. Since you ain't of a mind for more schoolin' at the moment, then you've got to go to work an' scratch out some feed. If you're goin' to work, then you'd better work along with me so's I can keep an eye on you whether you like it or not."

He crooked a pudgy finger in Field's direction.

"Don't get the idea I'm nosin' into your business because I got nothin' better to do. I just feel that maybe your paw, who was good friend to me, would want me to."

Field wasn't surprised. He had almost been expecting something like this. "What kind of work, Sheriff Titus?"

"Oh"—Field knew Semple was deliberately being vague— "sort of assistant work, I guess we could call it. Yep, that's it. I'll get you fixed up as my deputy. The county ought to be able to lay out a hundred or so a month for a deputy."

There was the guile of an old and wise coon on Semple's face, and Field laughed with uncontrollable mirth. Semple grinned foxily back at him.

"We might even get the county to jack it up to one hundred an' fifty a month. You see there ain't no precedent for the job here in Truro, so we might as well start it right."

Field stopped laughing suddenly. "But," he said, "I don't know anything about being a deputy."

Titus was pleased with himself. "That's where you'd fit in fine. There ain't anythin' to know about it." He scratched contentedly at the hillock which was his belly. "You can make a lot of friends bein' a deputy sheriff. You can make a lot of enemies too. That's the way public life is, no matter how high you go. The only thing you got to watch out for is that you have a few more people who like an' are grateful to you than you have people who hate your guts. An'—this is the most important thing—you got to keep the sharp end of a stick up the butts of your enemies all the time so's they can't turn around an' get at you. Hell, that's all anyone does no matter what kind of an office he holds."

Field rose from the chair and standing beside the desk played absently with the jumbled papers. The idea of his being made a deputy sheriff in this offhand fashion skirted the edge of absurdity. The thought of his being Semple's deputy was funnier still. He dropped the papers and crossed the room to take a chair facing Titus.

"I don't want you to think I don't know what you are doing and that I don't appreciate it, but I just don't understand it."

Semple heaved his shoulders in a movement which passed for a shrug.

"You don't have to for one thing. The other thing is I thought a lot of your paw. I figured you'd be up in the air a little just now an' might like a place to rest your feet. The sheriff's office seemed like a good spot."

In such a fashion Field became a deputy sheriff. What ponderous maneuvers Titus engaged in to make the appointment an actuality he never knew, but he was solemnly sworn in one day, feeling throughout the brief ceremony that he and Semple were playing a ridiculous game of cops and robbers.

His life fell quickly into surprisingly well-ordered channels. He found a tenant for the house on Flamingo Road and took a large front room at Mrs. Stivers's boardinghouse on Oak Street. Thereafter, with only minor interruptions, things went on much the same as before. The duties of a deputy sheriff were, apparently, nonexistent. For the first week or so he waited expectantly around the office in the courthouse for someone to give him something to do. He became the room's only occupant. Semple shunned it as though it were a pesthouse. Finally, out of sheer desperation, Field reverted to old habits. He spent his time as he used to during vacations, fishing on the river or just loafing around town, standing on street corners to talk with old friends or shooting a few games of pool in the afternoons at Martin's. Evenings he went up to Flamingo Road to call on Ann-Evans Weldon or take her to the movies on River Street. He had been doing those things ever since he could remember. The only difference now was that each month he received a check from the county clerk's office for $125.

He took the first of these to Titus. "I feel funny about accepting this, Sheriff Titus. I sure haven't done anything to earn it."

Titus spat at a palmetto bug crawling along the railing of the Palmer House porch where he was seated, missed, and regarded the brown trickle on the woodwork with an injured stare.

"There's a hell of a lot of folks in the state," he said, "who done less an' got more."

Field pocketed the check, and the subject of his salary was never mentioned again, but he couldn't shake off a feeling of guilt every time he deposited the official-appearing piece of paper in the bank.

28

If he had been forced to the truth, Field would have admitted that the job of deputy sheriff suited him far better than he cared to confess. I guess, he thought to himself, I'm real lazy, otherwise I wouldn't coast along like this. In the beginning the job embarrassed him. Old friends, boys of his high-school days, were enviously hilarious over the appointment. Encountering Field on the street, they would pretend to duck away at his approach, yelling: "Sheriff, I'll swear I didn't do it!" His first few appearances in Martin's Billiard Hall were always the signal for someone to shout: "They went that-a-way, Sheriff. I seen them. Buckety-buckety-buck." Fortunately the joke finally wore thin and was eventually dropped. Only Ann-Evans Weldon remained persistently and annoyingly curious.

"For goodness' sake, Field," she exclaimed in exasperation one night, "what do you do? I mean, what is it you do that you should be paid for?"

The Weldons lived on Flamingo Road, a block away from the old Carlisle place. For as long as he could recollect, Ann-Evans had always been part of his background. As a youngster Field found the leggy, pig-tailed girl a persistent shadow. To shake her he had been, by turns, rude, patient, desperate, and long-suffering, but Ann-Evans was not to be denied.

Then one day—he had been eighteen—he glanced across the high-school assembly hall, took a good look at her, and caught his breath. That afternoon he walked home with her in uneasy silence and at a deserted turn of the road kissed her quickly and awkwardly. Ann-Evans hadn't been the least surprised. He remembered this later with something of a shock. It was almost as if she had been content to wait until he made up his mind or accepted the inevitable. Afterward they, Field in particular, discovered love was an exciting and heady wine.

Ann-Evans was Field's girl. She knew it. Field knew it. Everyone in Truro who mattered knew it. Ann-Evans, however, back from school in Tennessee, wasn't satisfied.

"It's all well and good to say you're a deputy sheriff," she continued, "but you've been a deputy for almost three years. It's just a cheap political job, and you know it." She leaned her head against the pillar of the porch on which they were sitting and stared determinedly at the sky. She was angry and wanted Field to know it.

"Well"—Field stretched his legs lazily—"don't make it sound like I'm doing something dishonest."

"It is, in a way." Ann-Evans realized helplessly she was at a disadvantage. It wasn't as though she and Field were actually engaged. If that had been so, she would have felt easier about making demands. As it was, she could only rage inwardly at being taken for granted. Hostesses making up party lists said: "Ann-Evans and Field, of course." That was the way it had always been. At least—and Ann-Evans couldn't help but be conscious of the fact—that was the way it had been until Field dropped college and became a protegé of Titus Semple.

Friends of the Weldons lifted their eyebrows a trifle when told Field was a deputy sheriff. He was set a little apart, and those families new to Flamingo Road were open in their conviction that a deputy sheriff, particularly one who didn't seem to have any county status, didn't belong within the exclusive precincts. There had been general relief when Field rented the Carlisle place.

"Now, honey"—Field was humorously placating—"you don't want to get your pretty head in a worry."

Ann-Evans snorted. She knew she was pretty. She had been told that all of her life, but she was tired of being pretty and sitting on her own front porch of an evening with Field, who didn't seem to care whether he ever moved. Ann-Evans wanted to marry Field. She wanted a home of her own, a blue Packard roadster to fly around Truro in. She wanted membership as Mrs. Fielding Carlisle in the Bellville Country Club and to do her shopping in New York or at least Jacksonville. In the winter she wanted to go to Palm Beach, Miami, or maybe Havana. That was what being pretty meant. It didn't mean movies at the Crystal twice a week with a deputy sheriff or an occasional picnic at Grove's Landing or Shell Springs.

"Damn my pretty head." She was close to tears.

Field slid across the upper step to her side and tried to put an arm around her reluctant shoulders. Damnit, Ann-Evans was right. If he didn't know this he could argue with her. He should have gone on back to Gainesville. By now he would have been on his way to being a lawyer. Titus could have really helped him then after he had passed the bar examinations. Ann-Evans was right up to that point, but there was something else. It was a strange conviction there was something behind all of this.

The idea was as elusive as a summer's breeze, as hard to get hold of as a moonbeam, yet it persisted until it became a certainty that there were strange forces moving which would ultimately pick him up and carry him on. He tried to explain something of this to Ann-Evans.

"Honey"—she yielded a bit to his touch and became soft within the circle of his arm—"you just know I'm not cut out to be a deputy sheriff for good. You've got to know that." He realized his words weren't making much sense but optimistically hoped she might understand.

"No"—Ann-Evans refused to be soothed completely—"I suppose some day you'll be all sheriff, after Titus dies, which ought not to be more than fifteen or twenty years from now, and even then, what's a Sheriff?"

Field shook his head miserably. Ann-Evans should be able to understand.

"Maybe," he said slowly, feeling his way along a faint line of thought, "maybe some day I will be sheriff, but that isn't what I mean. It would be only the beginning." He realized he wasn't making much of a case for himself. "Look," he said suddenly, "did you ever stand before one of those mirrors, you know, the kind that throw and twist you all out of shape? You don't look like yourself but you are, and behind all those tricks of the glass you are yourself. Well, that's how I feel right now about this business of being a deputy to Titus."

"Fielding Carlisle." Ann-Evans straightened and patted the hem of her skirt at her knees. "Fielding Carlisle, you're as crazy as a cooter."

She arose and regarded him patiently for a moment.

"I'm going to bed. Good night."

Doubt took Field in hand. Probably what he had just said did sound crazy. During the months which followed this conversation with Ann-Evans, he asked himself the question many times. If he could only pin something down. If Semple wasn't so damned complacent or indifferent. If he'd say: "Bub, this job was only a prank for you to rest on awhile. Now the ground has dried up a little, you'd best start climbing the hill." If Semple would only say something like that, then he would know where he stood. Instead, Titus rolled along on his way as imperturbable as the great, heavy clouds which piled up in the west every afternoon. Once in awhile he would send his deputy on some small duty, but Field knew he was only being given something to do. The job was a joke. Only, Semple wasn't a joke. Field was sure.

He realized this during those early days of his appointment. Semple had taken him on a deliberate tour; looking back he could be certain of it now. First they had gone to the city hall. There they stopped at the mayor's office. Titus rumbled and wheezed over small talk which seemed to have no meaning to Field. The same thing happened at the police department and in a couple of wide-open speakeasies around the railroad yards. With the same casualness Titus took him in to the office of the railroad's division superintendent.

"Want you to meet my deputy." Titus left this information almost as an afterthought at all of the places, and in each Field sensed a curious change of attitude. This was strange, he thought, since in most cases he had known the men they called upon all of his life. It was as though Titus were establishing a new identity for him.

Once, and that had been a year or so after the appointment, Titus sent for him to come to the Palmer House.

"Got a chore for you, bub."

Patiently wondering what he could do to break Titus of the nauseating habit of referring to him as "bub," Field climbed the steps and took a seat on the porch railing.

"This is sort of a personal matter." Titus was almost diffident. "Ain't got a thing to do with official business or sheriffing." When he spoke in that manner Field was never sure whether Titus was indulging in his idea of a joke or being maliciously sarcastic. "I'd sort of like to have you run up to Jacksonville," Semple continued, "an' see a man for me."

Field snatched at the opportunity. Might be able to kick out a little fun in Jacksonville even if it was for only a few hours.

"What do you want me to do?"

"Just see a man. Name's Dan Curtis. Ever hear of him?" Field shook his head. "Well, he'll be at the Seminole Hotel. Suppose you catch the afternoon train up there. Likely as not he'll have somethin' to send back to me."

"That all?"

Titus nodded as though he wasn't quite sure what Field was talking about. After a moment he leaned back in his chair and shut his eyes. Field waited. You never could be sure when Titus was through talking. Finally he left and drove his car across town to the boardinghouse. It was funny that whatever it was this man Curtis had for Semple couldn't be sent. He thought about this while he changed his clothing and again while he was on the northbound train.

Field always remembered the trip to Jacksonville, principally because it was so damn silly and nothing happened. He took a taxi from the depot up the noisy length of Bay Street and went to the Seminole where he called Curtis from the information desk.

Curtis had been a surprise. Field wasn't quite certain why unless it was the fact that he couldn't imagine him as one of Semple's friends. A tall, grizzled man who smiled only with his eyes when he greeted Field at the door of his room, Curtis nodded his head in recognition of the younger man's name and invited him in. His voice was grave, modulated, cultured, and he spoke so slowly he made the ordinarily trivial exchange of introductions seem important.

He pointed to a bottle and glasses on a low table beside a chair.

"Drink, Mr. Carlisle?"

"Now and then," Field answered.

"Is this one of the nows?"

Field grinned and reached for the bottle, poured himself a good three fingers, and splashed some ice water into the liquor. Curtis drank his straight.

"I think I knew your father," he said. "I met him once, several years ago. I don't get over the state much any more."

"He's been dead for some time now."

Curtis put his glass down. "So I've heard." He studied Field for a moment, apparently unaware or indifferent to the fact that his subject was uncomfortable beneath the scrutiny. "Understand it interrupted your schooling. Planned to go to the law, didn't you?"

Field wondered how he could know, a man he had never heard of before.

"It's too bad you didn't finish," Curtis continued. "Law's a fine background for a young man no matter what he decides to do."

Curtis put a lighted match to the cigar he held and savored its aroma silently. Field, beginning to feel the effects of that first jolt of whisky, was no longer uneasy. He had the feeling he was being taken apart and put together again by Curtis, but it wasn't embarrassing. Without effort the older man led the conversation into personal channels, and Field answered lightly veiled questions frankly. He wasn't sure what it was Curtis wanted, but whatever it was Field wasn't afraid to give it to him. He spoke of his work with Semple, such as it was, and the half-formed determination to return to school.

"Titus is a good teacher," Curtis interrupted. "You'd do well to learn from him." He chuckled openly. "By the mysterious grace of God," he added, "Titus is always underestimated. He makes everyone think he is a fool without trying. That's an enviable accomplishment."

He rose from his chair, crossed to the dressing table, and

brushed his gray hair carefully, cocking his head to see if it was properly in place.

"Good young men," he threw over his shoulder, "who want to make their way and can be trusted are hard to find. They're inclined to be impetuous."

It was a funny thing to say, Field thought, since he had no idea anyone was thinking of him as a good young man.

Later, after a second drink, they had dinner in the hotel's dining room. There was a small broiled pompano and then a fine, thick steak, better food than Field had tasted for years. He was ravenous and glad that Curtis seemed satisfied to concentrate on the dinner and let conversation drop. Over him crept a fine glow of friendliness. Curtis was a great fellow, even if he was a friend of Semple's.

Later—and he was a little surprised at what was obviously a dismissal—Curtis shook hands with him at the elevator.

"It's been nice meeting you, Mr. Carlisle." His hand was firm and cordial, but he cast an impatient eye at the car's floor indicator as though to speed its arrival. "I hope we will have the pleasure of dinner again sometime soon."

Field wasn't quite sure what reply to make. "Sheriff Titus," he spoke finally, "said you would have something to send him."

"Oh," Curtis answered thoughtfully. "Tell the Sheriff," he said slowly, "I said he probably has it." The elevator door slid open. "Well, good night and a pleasant trip home. Give my regards to Titus." He was gone, and Field was left contemplating the grilled-iron door.

He felt he had been made a fool of and on the way back to Truro the following morning sat grimly in the smoking compartment repeating what he was going to say to Titus. He didn't say anything when he saw the Sheriff, however, realizing that getting angry with Titus would be like peppering an elephant with a BB gun. He merely sketched the meeting for Semple when they met.

Titus seemed genuinely pleased. He blew out his cheeks and regarded Field with a bright stare. "Said I already had it, hey? Well, that's fine, suits me fine."

Field never attempted to press Titus for an explanation, and he knew he couldn't very well talk to Ann-Evans about the trip because it didn't make any sense. It made sense to him because it didn't make any sense and seemed to follow logically his association with the Sheriff. He knew what Ann-Evans would say. She'd just wrinkle her nose and tell him he was crazy as a cooter.

During the months which followed, he and Ann-Evans

maintained a wary truce, made no easier by Mrs. Weldon's unsparing criticism of Field's shiftlessness. Field was wasting his time, and Ann-Evans's mother missed no opportunity to make it clear she had no intention of seeing her daughter married to a deputy sheriff.

Most of the time Field silently agreed with her, but he didn't quite know what to do about the situation he had been maneuvered into. Finally he gave up thinking about it and decided to coast along for awhile, waiting for something to happen.

CHAPTER THREE

RIVER STREET SHOOK ITSELF LOOSE FROM THE FEW remaining bonds of what had once been the chief residential district with a bright and noisy thoroughness. Chain-store markets spilled their wares out on the sidewalk in open bins. Barber-shops, candy and soda stands, lunch rooms, and the dime stores shoved against each other and laid the pattern of their lights on the pavement. For all its efforts the town council never succeeded in widening the street sufficiently. The lane of asphalt, studded with concrete traffic posts, was buttressed by rows of automobiles lining the curb while the traffic on it was a paralytic thing of fits and stops. On Saturday nights, when farmers and their families came to town from the outlying settlements, River Street was choked, horns blared, phonographs in the soda parlors screamed, mechanical pianos in the pool halls pounded mercilessly. Only a few hundred yards away from the backs of the buildings, the river moved silently and in primitive grandeur, but River Street was too busy to be interested in scenery and turned away to look upon its own gaudy reflection.

As they moved into the idling crowd Lane dropped her hand from Field's arm. It was almost impossible to walk abreast, and he was constantly forced to fall behind her in single file. Once, as they worked their way through the press before the Crystal Theater, Lane glanced over her shoulder, flashed a brief smile his way, and was promptly jostled into the gutter for her carelessness. He caught up with her in a few steps and cupped her elbow in his hand.

"Need a guide, lady?"

She grimaced with a toothy, burlesque coyness. "I'm trying to find a fella, mister. He's a tall gent with a cowboy hat."

They edged in from the crowd a little and moved close to a drugstore window.

"I know that man you mean, miss. He's usually to be found across the street in the Eagle Café at around this time. Want to have a look?"

Laughing they dodged between the automobiles to the opposite side and halted before a brilliantly lighted doorway. On either side the windows of the building were decorated with what were presumably eagles. From the drooping beaks of the figures ribbons of paint trailed out to carry the announcement: "The Eagle Café for Ladies and Gents."

"Artist who drew those"—Field indicated the windows— "couldn't find an eagle, so he took a buzzard for a model."

"I sure hope the cook isn't so easily satisfied," Lane answered seriously.

The Eagle's dining room had only begun to thin out. Down the center, tables were spaced between a quick-lunch counter and a row of high-backed booths. Most of them were occupied, and Field stood for a moment looking for a vacant place. From the ceiling, puddles of warm air swirled down from the lazy beat of broad-bladed fans.

Lane's nose twitched. There was a familiar smell about the Eagle. It was the damp, steamy odor of food, of soap powder, vinegar, and blue-plate specials accompanied by the sounds of clashing silver, heavy plates, and the senseless hum of conversation.

"There's a booth." Field touched her arm and led her across the room, lifting a hand in greeting to the dozen or so persons who glanced up from their food. Lane was conscious they stared at her with undisguised curiosity.

They took places on opposite sides of the table, and a flurried waitress tossed finger-stained menus before them as she passed.

"Be back in a minute, Field," she called familiarly and dodged between the tables on her way to the serving window.

Lane studied the mimeographed slip clipped to the cardboard and finally dropped it before her. "You order," she invited. "If you come here often enough for the girls to call you by your first name, then you ought to know what and what not to eat."

"First I'll get some cigarettes."

Lane followed his tall, not ungraceful figure with her eyes

36

as he went to the cigarette counter. She noticed most of the persons in the room had a smile or a lifted hand in salute for him. Maybe that was why he was a deputy sheriff, she thought. There ought to be at least one member of the force the people liked.

Seated again at the table Field broke open a fresh package of Luckies, worked one out with his fingers, and passed it over to her. When he lighted it she allowed the smoke to drift up over her face and studied him through the wavering veil.

"You really did mean it, didn't you?" she said after awhile.

"Mean what?" Field looked up wonderingly.

"Getting me something to eat, taking me uptown with you and all. You even remembered the cigarettes." She laughed softly, a throaty bubble, bouncing lightly.

"Sure. Why?"

"I just didn't think you did. I thought it was maybe a different way of going about things."

"What things?"

"Oh"—she settled back on the narrow seat—"things like carnival girls or, maybe, just girls."

The waitress slid the soup plates before them and turned a moist smile upon Field.

"You're late tonight," she commented.

He nodded. Annabelle, he knew, wanted to talk long enough to find out who the girl with him was.

"Rabbit hunting," he said cryptically.

The girl twitched her full hips and winked companionably at Lane.

"Must use quite a snare."

Field chuckled and worked the soup around in his plate with the spoon.

"This is Lane Ballou, Annabelle. Now, how about the rest of the dinner?"

Annabelle ducked her head in Lane's direction. "Just say what you want, Field. If it ain't on the menu, I'll sure get it." She flushed happily and sped away.

"Well!" There was mock surprise in Lane's exclamation. "Now I begin to see."

"What do you see now that isn't in the soup?"

"For one thing, why you don't have to hunt in carnival lots."

Field shook his head. "I guess Annabelle tells that to all the sheriffs. Annabelle is a good girl." He paused as the waitress reappeared with small bowls of relish. "Aren't you, Annabelle?"

"Aren't I what?"

"Aren't you a good girl?"

"Good and ready, Field." She flounced away in delight.

Lane whistled, a muted note of admiration. "Do you go through this every night?"

"Almost. If you don't folks think you are stuck up. Sometimes it gets kind of tiresome, but it's all part of living in a small town."

They finished the meal in comparative silence, and after Annabelle cleared the table Lane hunched herself into the corner and sighed comfortably.

"You're pretty nice, Fielding Carlisle. I'm always going to remember that."

"Courtesy to the tourists. I'll charge it to the county somehow."

Lane shook a cigarette out and rolled it absently between her fingers to loosen the packing.

"Well," she said finally, "aren't you going to ask me?"

"The story of your life?"

She nodded, and his eyes crinkled wonderingly as though he had just discovered something.

"You know," he continued, "I'd almost forgotten I didn't know you. There didn't seem to be anything to be curious about."

Lane's eyes were abruptly grave. "It can happen sometimes." She tapped the cigarette on the table and flicked away the crumbs of tobacco with one finger. "Anyhow, there isn't a lot to tell. Up until I was eighteen, a year and a half ago, I was in an orphanage at Brunswick. Some colored people found me in the back of a wagon. When I turned eighteen I was free to go, only there wasn't any place to go, but I went anyhow. You can get a lot of jobs if you try. I found them all, tossing pots in a hotel at Quitman, kitchen work here and scrubbing there. Then one day Coyne's carnival played Waynsboro, where I was working. A fellow had a doll pitch—that's one of those tents where you try to knock over nigger babies with a baseball—said he could use me, so I went along. When he quit the show Coyne kept me on as a Hawaiian dancer or an Egyptian princess, depending upon the weather. And that"—her lips trembled ever so slightly—"skipping a few details, would bring us right up to 8:30 P.M., October 17, and"—she made a curious sound with her breath—"if you were to ask me why I've told you all of this I'm damned if I could think of an answer."

Field was a little embarrassed. One moment she could sound

38

hard, nasty, the way she did just then. The next time she spoke her voice was timid, almost pleading. It gave him a hell of a funny feeling. He drew meaningless figures on the table-cloth with a toothpick and wondered what he should say. The damnedest notion was in his head. He couldn't shake off the idea it was up to him to do something.

"You know," he admitted honestly, "I've got the notion that somehow I'm responsible for you since I didn't chase you away from that carnival right away. It's like they say about the Chinese when one of them rescues another. Anyhow, that's what I've heard them say."

"No," Her protest was quick, decisive. "There's no reason for you to feel that way. You only acted decent."

Field rubbed the side of his chin with his hand and grinned sheepishly. "I know. The crazy thing about it is that I do and I can't turn it off like a water tap. You're likely to get a Good Samaritan shoved right down your throat."

The rush of the evening meal at the Eagle was over, and the din of supper had subsided to a murmur, punctuated now and then by the staccato clatter of dishes in the kitchen and the tinkle of cutlery against glass. The few remaining patrons, men without families for the most part, leaned back in their chairs, balancing precariously. They picked at their teeth with earnest abstraction and gazed out of the window, wondering what to do with the balance of the night. At the far end of the room three of the serving girls were having their meal. They leaned their heads together and drew away with a rocking motion, gossiping between mouthfuls. Now and then one would rise, walk hurriedly to another table, and gather up the tip before the colored bus boy could reach the station.

The drumming of Field's fingers on the uncovered table in the booth made a soft gallop. Finally he allowed his hand to drop, resting palm down.

"You're sure," he said, "you're going to want to stay in Truro. You can see for yourself it's pretty much like a hundred other towns that have railroad yards. If you went to St. Augustine, Daytona, West Palm Beach, there would probably be a job around this time of year. Truro isn't much of a place for a girl alone."

Lane kept her eyes fixed on a point somewhere above his head.

"When a dog gets tired," she said, "it lies down wherever it is. I guess I feel a little that way now."

Field found himself unaccountably angry. It was all right to talk about lying down, but anyone would know if you didn't get up sooner or later someone would come along and give you a hell of a boot just out of plain cussedness.

"Talking like that doesn't make any sense." He held his voice down. "You've got to eat. You've got to have a place to sleep. You just can't go rooting around a carnival lot like a wild shoat. What can you do? Did they teach you anything at the home where you were?"

Her features were without animation. "Not much I couldn't have learned outside. I sewed, worked in the laundry. We older girls took care of the youngsters. About the most I got out of it was a better schooling than I would have had on the outside." She lowered her head, and a quick smile touched her mouth. "I can do a mighty twitchy hulahula if you think Truro would be interested."

Field snapped a match stick impatiently. Damn it. The more he talked the more he got himself in. The desperate idea struck him that if he could suddenly and miraculously find the girl a job he could brush his hands of his part of the whole thing. The real trouble was, though, she wasn't asking for help from him or anyone. He turned around, and his eyes lighted at the sight of a slim, swarthy man leaning against the cigar case near the cash register.

"Hey," he called. "Hey, Pete. Come over here a minute, will you?"

Peter Ladas was a Greek upon whom had been forced a southern accent, and when he spoke it was as though he were a shade nonplussed at the astonishing combination of consonants and vowels issuing from his larynx. His café had grown from a hole-in-the-wall lunch counter into one of Truro's most important establishments, a fact over which Pete never ceased to marvel since no one knew better than he how indifferent the quality of its food was. He crossed the room now with determined reluctance, his ears sensitive to the degree of heartiness in his customer's voice. At the booth he smiled helplessly and nodded.

"How you, Fiel'?"

"Listen, Pete." Field hoped he was being properly casual. "I just had an idea perhaps you might need another girl to wait table."

Ladas lifted one eyebrow, a sinister-appearing trick, and glanced around the almost empty room, hoping the gesture would answer the suggestion. For good measure he added: "Now?"

Field ignored the sarcasm and indicated Lane with a sway of his head. "This young lady was part of that stranded carnival troupe. She wants a job, and I was hoping maybe you'd need another waitress."

Ladas surveyed Lane without enthusiasm. Someone was always after him for something, jobs, donations, subscriptions to buy uniforms for the school baseball team. He wondered sometimes if his being a Greek had anything to do with it. Without appearing to do so, he ran his eyes over the girl. She was pretty enough. He couldn't blame Field for wanting to keep her in town.

"Evah wait table?" He had to say something.

"Yes." Lane's reply was honest and direct, and Field experienced again that peculiar sensation down the back of his spine at the warm quality of her tone. "I was raised in an orphanage," she explained. "We had to take turns in the dining room."

Ladas took in every detail of her figure, her hands, face, and the sleek brilliance of her head. He wasn't over-optimistic, but you could never tell about such things. It didn't hurt to be practical. His lips pursed thoughtfully.

"I guess I could do it for the Sheriff here." He wavered over the joke. "You could work noon an' suppa for"—he hesitated—"for five dollar a week, your meals, an' tips."

Lane's fingers tightened beneath the table. She hadn't wanted Field to know she was afraid. She hadn't even wanted herself to know. Suddenly she had a foothold, a little, insecure niche. It was food and shelter and a place where she could catch her breath. The knowledge of how grateful she really was made her tremble.

"Five dollars isn't much," Field protested before she could cut him off.

"Oh, no." Lane spoke quickly. "It's fine. With tips I guess it is all right." She lifted her face to Ladas. "When do I start?"

Peter called down the room to where three of his girls sat. "Hey, Annabelle."

Annabelle came forward, wiping her finger tips on the hem of her apron.

"New girl." Pete raised a listless hand in Lane's direction. "She'll be here for noons an' suppas startin' tomorrow." He turned to Field. "See you again, Sheriff."

"Well, now!" Annabelle considered Lane with new interest. "I never would have figured on Peter takin' on more help." She pondered over this minor miracle. "You ever wait table before, sugar."

Lane sensed that the girl was only being curiously friendly, and her nervousness quieted.

41

"Some," she said. "Never in a café before, though."

Annabelle leaned against the partition of the booth. "I guess you can learn," she offered. "All you got to remember is to keep the orders straight, bring 'em in full an' take 'em out empty, an' not drop the tray when someone pinches you in the behind. You get calluses there after a while." The joke amused her. "It ain't really hard work like it looks. Your neck gets tired." She drooped confidingly over the table. "You'd maybe think waiting on a table would get you tired in the feet or arms. With me it's in the neck." She marveled openly at this fact. "Things are funny, you can't say they ain't. Now, I went with a barber once, an' he told me it wasn't his feet or back that got tired when he stood at a chair all day. It was his fingers. What do you know about that?"

She waited for their cries of astonishment. Field and Lane nodded, fastening uniform expressions of surprise on their faces.

"Well"—Annabelle spoke directly to Lane—"you come in about ten in the mornin'. We begin to set up for lunch then." She paused. "Where you livin' now, sugar?"

Lane couldn't help but wonder what Annabelle would say if she told her she had a tent on the carnival lot. "Why, I only got in town today. I'm not settled yet."

Annabelle's eyelids fluttered, and she darted a quick glance at Field and then at Lane.

"Oh!"

Damn the fool, Field thought, did she have to act as if she had caught him in bed with the girl?

"I was going to ask you about that, Annabelle." He smoothed away his irritation with an effort. "I thought there might be a room where you're stopping. It's got to be cheap."

"They're all cheap where I stop." Annabelle was sure now. The girl was Field's pick-up, and her curiosity prompted her to make a suggestion. "I tell you what, sugar. I'm payin' three dollars a week where I am now, but there's a double room to be had for five, two-fifty apiece, if you want to try it with me."

"Say, that would be fine." Field didn't wait for Lane's reply. Better get this thing settled and done with now.

There was a grateful warmth in Lane's voice. "I'd like it a lot, Annabelle. Later, maybe, if you should change your mind I could always move to a smaller place."

Annabelle dismissed the notion with a toss of her head. She was enveloped in the glow of a good deed. "The only things is, you probably couldn't move in tonight, but"—she winked at

Field—"probably you wouldn't want to anyhow." She tucked up her hair with a finger. "Well, as I always say, if you can't be good don't let anybody know about it." Annabelle relished the quip. "I got to run for my date now." She gathered up the check and money in front of Field. "So long you-all, I'll see you in the morning."

Field waited until she was out of earshot and then whistled. "Give Annabelle a minute more, an' she would have had us both undressed." He grinned comfortingly at Lane. "An' me feeling like an old uncle or something. Without so much as moving you're fixed up with a job and a place to stay. I'll swear, I never realized a deputy sheriff could throw so much weight around."

Lane's eyes were suddenly misty. It wasn't always easy to remember that people could be kind, and it did something to you when you did.

"I don't know what to say, honestly I don't."

"Well, don't say anything then."

She dropped her head in a gesture of assent. "All right. I won't. I'll never pass a stray dog any more, though, without stopping to pet it. I know how it feels now."

Field was fumbling in his pocket as she talked, and after a moment his hand slid across the table and into hers.

"There's ten or twelve dollars there, or should be," he whispered unnecessarily. "You take it."

Automatically her lips framed a protest, but it was silenced.

"Damnit"—he was close to being angry—"do like I say. It's bad enough you're so stubborn about sleeping in a tent tonight that I'll probably worry about you. You want me to be sorry I ever let you stay?"

She shook her head quickly.

"All right then. God A'mighty, you got to have enough to help you through the first week. Take it an' pay me back a little at a time. Say." He stopped talking and thought over his words. "Say, I was really getting sore. What do you know about that?"

Without looking at them Lane tucked the bills into a pocket of her skirt. "I know you were. I'm sorry in a way. You were mad because you're uneasy." ·

"That doesn't make much sense."

She smiled wisely. "Oh, yes it does if you're sitting where I am. Well"—there was a lilt to her voice—"shall we go to the carnival, Sheriff?"

Field thought at first she was joking. "You still don't figure on spending the night out there? Why, you got a job. You even got a little money." He looked at her incredulously. "I guess," he added, "you got everything but good sense."

She slid along the bench and wedged herself out from the table to stand beside him.

"I'm starting in Truro from scratch, or at least I did until you came along, but that was starting from scratch too if you look at it the right way."

Field rose and reached for his hat. Anyone fool enough to insist on spending a night in a moldy tent on the circus flat was welcome to it.

"All right, come along."

They were halfway to the door before he saw Titus. The Sheriff was seated at a corner table from where he could look diagonally across the room. The spot had been hidden by the men at the other tables when they first came in, and Field wondered how long Semple had been watching them. Before Titus was half of an apple pie and a large pitcher of milk, and he was staring at the pie with a moody abstraction. Field hoped they would be able to slip out before he raised his eyes. Then Titus lifted his head, and Field realized the Sheriff had been waiting for them.

"Hi, bub." A great hand flapped dismally on the table, and Titus cocked an eye at the ceiling, making of it a beckoning command.

Damn the old fat fool, anyhow. Field knew there wasn't any point in trying to walk out, pretending he hadn't understood.

"Come on"—he spoke helplessly to Lane, who was regarding the scowl on his face with wonder—"old pus-gut wants to know who you are." He took her arm and led her to the table.

"Have some pie, bub." Titus kept his eyes on Lane.

Field shook his head. "Had some. We're just leaving." He knew he couldn't get away with it.

"It's right good pie."

"This is Lane Ballou." Somehow he thought it sounded better than introducing her as Miss Ballou. "Sheriff Semple, Lane."

"Oh"—Lane's eyes were bright—"then this is the man with the flashlight."

Titus tapped at his nose with a knuckle. He never liked to have people say things he couldn't understand. He'd never owned a flashlight in his life, an' what the hell difference would it make to this chit if he had.

"Stranger here, ain't you, Miss Ballou? Knew some Ballous

once around Fernandina." His baby-pink cheeks folded in a smile, but his eyes were steady and inquisitive.

Lane realized she was trembling just a little, somewhere away deep inside. It was like a chill. Funny thing for a fat man like this to do without saying anything.

"I'm from Brunswick." She dropped the statement there to see what he would do with it.

Titus ignored the information. "Sit down an' have some pie."

Lane shook her head. She was damned if she would eat pie just because he told her to. He was telling her to sit down. He was telling Field, also.

"No"—Field put his hand beneath her arm again—"some other time, Sheriff Titus. Lane here's got to get home."

Semple didn't press the invitation. "See you tomorrow then, bub." His eyelids drooped slightly. "'Night, Miss Ballou."

Outside, Field released her arm, and Lane automatically quickened her step to put something behind her.

"That's the boss." Field spoke easily. If he noticed she was trying to hurry he was unconcerned. "Tomorrow he'll want me to tell him who you are, where you came from, how long you're going to stay."

"What will you tell him?" She was breathing easier now.

"Oh, just a rabbit I snared out by the carnival lot this afternoon."

Lane forced a laugh. It was silly to be afraid of a man she had never seen before. Anyhow, she wasn't on the town. She had a job and, after tonight, a room the same as any other girl in Truro. The knowledge of these things made her feel better, and she breathed deeply, gratefully, and her steps lagged. She could walk slowly now. She wasn't running. Not any more, ever, would she run. Looking around her as they moved down River Street, she was aware it appeared different. It wasn't an alien place any longer.

"It's funny"—she was thinking aloud—"what a job will do for you, even a little job like one in the Eagle Café. It makes you feel you belong to something, that something belongs to you. I was scared of Truro when we first came up this way earlier. Now I'm not."

Field grunted, an uncomprehending sound of assent. He was occupied with his own thoughts. After Titus, he conceded, about the only other thing necessary to round out the evening was Ann-Evans. He just needed to run into Ann-Evans and her mother along about now as they came out of the Crystal. That would lay the meringue right on the top. His stride increased perceptibly until they were past the theater's entrance.

Abreast of the Palmer house he turned to Lane.

"Listen," he said, "you better get a room here. The carnival lot is a hell of an out-of-the-way place at night. You get down there alone, and you'll probably be scared to death."

There was an exasperating determination about her as her head shook vigorously. "I'm going to stay there. You see"—she took his arm—"the way I came here, the way I stayed, you finding me and then how things turned out; well, they all add up to something. If I'm going to work in the café in the morning, I'd like to go to it straight from the lot where I started with no way stops in between." She looked at him over her shoulder. "Do you know what I'm talking about?"

Field didn't, and he said so but kept walking.

"Maybe"—Lane's words were almost indistinct—"maybe I don't either, but I'm going to try and find out."

Field fumbled for cigarettes and wondered if she was trying to tell him she wanted him to stay with her in the tent.

He dismissed the idea. It just wouldn't hold water. He had the feeling if this girl wanted to go to bed she'd say so. She'd act like a man about that.

They were back in the section of River Street where the small cottages crouched behind their screens of vines and shrubbery. The porches were vacant now, the chairs shadowed and empty. There was the hush of deep sleep upon the place. At the first of the tracks they had to wait while a passenger train slid past. The Pullmans were dark, but in the last car they had a momentary glimpse of people seated in deep chairs, reading or talking beneath the warm glow of small, shaded lamps. They looked comfortable, secure, self-assured, and, perhaps, a trifle scornful of this junction town through which they rolled so easily. They watched until the two tail lights were bloody pin pricks in the night and then picked their way over the crossing and on to the highway.

The scrub woods at night were a place of brittle sound, for there were few things in it to prey upon each other and small need for caution. Twigs snapped, palmetto fans crackled, and the pine saplings made gentle talk with every passing breeze. There was no menace in the scrub's encirclement of the carnival lot.

Lane felt this as she followed Field into the clearing, and she regarded the scattered, ragged brush with a jaunty air of companionship. Within the clearing itself there was a half-light which, after the eyes had become accustomed to it, made a lamp or lantern unnecessary. The shabby tents crouched like tired old dogs, sagging limply toward the ground. They seemed worn and friendly.

"Don't want to change your mind?" Field touched Lane's shoulder, half-turning her around as they stood before the tents.

"Uh-uh!" she replied quickly, experiencing an exciting sense of possession. For the moment this, the scrub flat, was hers. It was home, haven from a long journey.

He jammed his hands in his pockets and considered the clearing. "I guess," he said finally, "there really isn't anything to be afraid of. It's just the idea. If someone did come around during the night, it would probably only be a negrah who'd run from here to Indian Springs if you let out a holler. If you want to change your mind now, though, I'll take you back to the hotel."

Lane breathed deeply of the scented night air. "No," she whispered. "I'm pretending. I'm pretending my house is here and in a minute I'll walk inside and latch the door. It'll begin to rain then and get cold outside, and none of it can get to me."

"I used to do that when I was a kid." Field laughed self-consciously.

Suddenly he stopped laughing. That seemed strange to both of them, and for a moment they stood close together, the oval of Lane's upturned face a smoky tracing.

"I guess,"—Field's voice caught—"I guess I'm crazy, but I'm going to leave you."

"No." The word was a breath. "No, I don't think so, Field. You can stay if you want to, but you're not crazy if you don't."

He squirmed a little inside. "Anything you want," he asked finally, "matches or the lantern?"

"Cigarettes, mister, please."

Solemnly he handed her the half-filled package of Luckies and with them a tab of matches.

"Nothing else?"

She considered the request gravely. "You might," she said thoughtfully, "let the cat in when you go out."

She waited, sitting on the lower step of the platform until long after the sound of his footsteps in the brush had quieted. With her head thrown back she could see the stars bouncing on the spidery tips of the pines. Night took possession of the flat, and the fire on the end of her half-burned cigarette seemed a red and angry thing. Dropping it to the ground she pressed it out with her foot. After a moment she rose and entered the tent, dropping the soggy flap behind her with a confident gesture.

47

CHAPTER FOUR

"YOU GOT A CUTE FIGURE, SUGAR." ANNABELLE STUDIED Lane appraisingly. "Lots of slim girls don't strip good, but you're kind of like a boy in the places it don't count an' plenty girl in the places that do."

Lane turned from the half-mirror which hung slantingly against the heavily figured wall paper. Talk to Annabelle, she thought, was like breathing. She did it unconsciously. During the past week, sharing the small room at the end of River Street with her, Lane had accustomed herself to the ceaseless patter. Sometimes it was almost cozy, the comfortable drumming of an all-night rain on the roof when you're inside. It had sound without meaning.

"Sometimes I can't help but wonder why you didn't go with the rest of the carnival people. With your figure an' face, you even got manners too." This last was added as a wondering afterthought. "Someone was bound to come along that would do good for you."

Annabelle sat on the edge of the double bed, plucking at the damp feet of her stockings. She lifted the cotton soles from her toes, and they came away with little sucking sounds; the sticky tearing of adhesive tape.

"I liked Truro." Lane's reply was careless. There was no point in attempting to explain things to Annabelle. If she told her she was tired of running, Annabelle would think she was crazy.

"Nobody could like Truro that much. If I had a chance to get out of it I'd go in a minute. Maybe you're a little mixed up. Maybe it was Field Carlisle you liked."

Lane realized with a start she hadn't thought about Field all day. During her first morning at the Eagle she waited for him to come in, managing to keep an eye on the double doors up front while Annabelle was drilling her in the sketchy fundamentals of service the café's patrons half-heartedly demanded. When he failed to appear she carried an empty feeling of disappointment with her which even Annabelle's burbling excitement over moving into the double room couldn't dissipate. When the days shaded into a week, she became curious. It was funny, he hadn't looked in once to see if she was getting along all right. Today she had been too tired to think about anything but the trays of food that kept getting heavier and heavier, enveloping her in a moist cloud, reeking of fried fish, veal, and baked yellow turnips. Through some black magic everything coming out of the Eagle's kitchen carried with it the odor of fish and turnips. Thinking about it now made her want to retch.

She wondered sometimes whether Field had come back that night and finding her tent dark left again. She had expected him. Long after she put up the folding cot and stretched uncomfortably upon it, her senses had been keyed for the first sound of heavy footsteps in the brush. It wasn't reasonable. A man wouldn't just walk away without trying.

"Maybe it was Field, huh?" Annabelle, who went through life like a friendly bitch in heat, sniffed at the idea.

"No-o." Lane's hesitation was genuine. "No, I'd already made up my mind to stay even before he came to the lot."

"Well"—Annabelle planted her feet solidly on the floor and rose from the bed to scratch energetically at her thigh—"that's just as good because even if he is deputy and sort of police Field wouldn't be likely to forget he lived on Flamingo Road. That makes River Street out of bounds."

Lane slipped into a nightgown and sat cross-legged on the bed, her head resting against the not unpleasant roughness of the filigreed iron post.

"If that's what you have to have in Truro," she said casually, "then I'll get a place on Flamingo Road myself one of these days."

Annabelle turned from her splashing at the washstand. Her mouth was half open.

"Goin' to ride right up there on the back of the Eagle?"

"Maybe."

Annabelle patted her face dry. She was undecided whether to laugh or accept the statement seriously. There was something about Lane's face that made her do neither.

"We could have double dated tonight." She rambled off on a safe tangent. "That fellow, the dentist's assistant, whatever his name is, an' Pete from Weaver's Garage were horsin' around in a booth, wantin' to know if you an' me'd take a drive later."

"Where would we have gone?" Lane's voice was sleepy. She wouldn't have bothered with the question if she hadn't known silence would torment Annabelle.

"We could have gone ridin', had a couple of drinks, probably out at George's on the highway, an' jazzed around in the car for awhile."

Lane smiled but didn't open her eyes. Annabelle was as willing as a rabbit. Maybe, she thought, that was why life didn't seem to touch her. Some girls were dirtied by men but not Annabelle. She frisked with sex, skipped with it through fern banks of her own imagining. It left her breathless but unsoiled. Almost nightly, during the week they had roomed together, Annabelle had offered to take her along when she went out after work. Lane's refusals left her puzzled and curious.

"But," she protested one evening, "you got to meet people. You can't live in a town an' not know anybody."

Lane hadn't tried to explain that at the moment she didn't feel the need of knowing any men. She was groping along an unfamiliar passageway. This room, this square, windowed box on River Street, was as close to a real home as she had ever had. She liked to go to it and shut the door.

Annabelle smeared her face with cream from a large jar beside the basin and chattered at her greasy reflection in the mirror.

"In a town like Truro," she persisted, "you got to be friendly. If you're goin' to live here an' have any fun, you can't act like it was one of those carnival stops."

That was it, Lane thought. She didn't want Truro to be a carnival stop. That was why she wanted to walk slowly and alone at first.

"I'll be here for a long time," she said.

"Take a fellow like the dentist's assistant now." Annabelle chased the subject as artlessly as a kitten with a ball of yarn. "He's nice lookin' an' clean. He'd be good for you to know, an' you could probably have a lot of fun together." She smothered the following words in a towel, wiping away the oily cream. "Most fellows don't want double dates, either, so when they ask you to go on one you can be sure they like you."

Lane was drowsy. She wished Annabelle would come to bed. Then they could turn out the lights, and she could push over near the window and listen to the night as it skulked along the river.

"What do you do on your dates," she asked absently. "You can't keep riding all the time, and there isn't any place to go."

"Sure there is." Annabelle was close to indignation. "There's George's on the highway. You have a few drinks an' play the victrola, maybe, dance some. Sometimes we drive to Shell Springs. Sometimes we just jazz around in the car."

Lane pulled her eyelids against the glare of the overhead light. "Suppose you don't feel like—like jazzing around."

Annabelle yelped happily. "Most of the time I do."

Lane's eyes flicked open. "You mean with anybody?"

The denial was quick and emphatic. "Of course not, not in the beginnin' anyhow," Annabelle glanced over the room, noted her things in the proper state of disorder, and then reached for the light cord. "Ready."

Lane nodded and rolled to her side of the bed in the darkness.

"I've got sort of a philosophy." Annabelle wriggled down beneath the light covering and bunched the pillow under her head. "I mean, when you go out with a fellow an' you have a good time, then you ought to do somethin'. In a way it's like splittin' the check. Most of the time"—she was serious—"it's a lot of fun, an' so you're still ahead. Like I always say, you're ahead until you get caught."

Lane could feel her shaking with silent laughter and smiled. She knew if she made no reply to this declaration Annabelle would go to sleep as quickly and as effortlessly as a puppy. Turning on her side she could look out of the windows. The light from a street lamp touched the glossy leaves of the oak tree and made small mirrors of them just beyond the screen. Stretching luxuriously on the cotton sheet, she was again filled with a strange sense of possession.

It was funny, she mused, she should want something of her own. It never mattered before. In the beginning it was even fun with the carnival, the endless succession of small towns and the excitement of the lot. Then, all of a sudden, everything changed. It's like a cat going to have kittens, she thought, looking for a box to crawl into. It would sure be a surprise to Annabelle if she had a kitten in bed some night.

The wind from the river was freshly damp and drifted without sound. This part of Truro went to bed early. Through the branches of the oak she could detect the wavering reflection of lights farther uptown and, if she strained her ears, the subdued hum of movement. It was the whisper which came when one listened to a sea shell, formless and persistent.

Drowsily she tried to imagine what all the little sounds were: the scraping of feet, the *shush* of an automobile tire, a boy's whistle, and someone's laughter. It was funny how they were all funneled together and compressed into one.

Field Carlisle. It was a name to make you think of an early morning wind. Funny he never came around again.

"Sheriff Semple's lookin' for you, Field," Bud Weaver called from a stool at the soda fountain. "Called up the garage 'bout half hour ago. Said if you was to come by for gas to tell you. He's at the courthouse office."

Field paid for the cigarettes at the counter. "You're crazy," he said agreeably. "Titus hasn't been up after ten o'clock in the night since the Palmer House caught fire and the smoke ran him out of bed."

"Well"—Bud was indifferent—"he's up this night or was until half an hour ago."

"Thanks." Field plucked at the foil top of the cigarette pack thoughtfully. He nodded at Weaver and then walked out of the drugstore and across the sidewalk to where he left his Ford. Someone was trying to kid him. Titus wouldn't be caught asleep in his office, certainly not at ten-thirty in the night. Anyhow, if he had wanted him for something he knew he always called on Ann-Evans Saturdays. He could have telephoned the Weldons.

He drove slowly across to Palmetto Street and then down as far as Umatilla Avenue, running his car into the marled parking space before the courthouse.

"Well, I'll be damned."

He stared incredulously at the light fanning out from the windows on the second floor. Save for this one room in the corner of the building, the place was in darkness.

Turning the ignition key he shut off his motor and climbed out. The square was deserted. He strode across it rapidly and up the front steps of the hall. The door was unlocked, and he trotted, not without curiosity, up the stairs to the floor above.

"Hi, bub." Titus was bunched uncomfortably in a swivel chair, his feet resting precariously upon an upturned wastepaper basket. On the desk before him was a half-filled bottle of corn whisky and two glasses. "I must have growed considerable," he said, "since I got this chair ordered for me. It's tight as a rabbit's behind in January."

Field leaned against the door jamb. He still didn't believe what he saw.

"Surprised, hey?" Titus was pleased.

"I wouldn't be more surprised if I saw the minister's wife buck-swimming in the river."

"Well, sit down an' take a drink for yourse'f. It'll ease you from the shock."

52

Field perched himself on a corner of the desk and poured some whisky into one of the glasses. He didn't really want a drink. Ann-Evans had filled him full of lemonade and coconut cake not half an hour ago. He played with the liquor for a minute, swishing it around and around, and then on an impulse tossed it down and felt it snatch its way to his stomach.

"Never was much of a fella for drinkin', were you?"

Field gasped and shook his head. "Not hog dip, anyhow." He forced the words.

Titus beamed and stroked his belly. "I was goin' to wait until eleven for you, an' if you didn't come by that time I was goin' to send out a hound."

"What's on your mind?" Field knew Titus would explain only when he was ready, but he had to ask.

Semple tried to whistle, but no sound came from his fat lips. It looks just like a horse's ass, Field thought.

"How you an' Ann-Evans gettin' along?" Titus apparently wasn't ready to answer his question.

"Same as we have ever since we've been kids." He couldn't understand why he was humoring Titus. It must be that shot of whisky.

"Think about gettin' married, ever?"

"Right now"—Field was laughing—"I'm thinking what the hell you're doing here this time of night telephoning me all over town to meet you."

Semple's face wrinkled into accordionlike folds of pleasure. "You're stubborn," he said happily, "you always were stubborn. Take me for instance. You never did like me even when you were a youngster. You kept right on not likin' me. You sure as hell are stubborn." He sighed contentedly. "Most of the folks in the world never get no place because they ain't stubborn enough. You'd a given up not likin' me long ago if you wasn't so stubborn." He fixed an affectionate glance upon his deputy.

Field moved uncomfortably on the desk beneath Semple's oral pawing and reached for a cigarette. Maybe if he said nothing Titus would get to whatever was on his mind.

Titus squinted at him and then allowed his feet to drop from their resting place. With a heavy roll he rose from the chair and ploughed over to the window, looking out into the darkened court.

"How'd you like to go to Tallahassee, bub?" he spoke without turning his head.

"What for?"

The Sheriff wheeled ponderously. The customary grin of simplicity had vanished from his face.

"For a lot of years, maybe."

This was a different Semple than Field had ever known. He was calculating, flinty. The eyes meeting his were blue chips. Field suddenly realized that a cold wind had swept through the office. He fumbled with the bottle beside him, poured, and drank hurriedly.

"You mean," he asked, "you've got something you want me to do over at the capitol?"

"Not exactly, bub. That ain't it exactly." The words came deliberately, evenly spaced. "How'd you like to go to Tallahassee as a member of the Legislature?"

Field knew his mouth was open, but he lacked the power to close it. Then, he wanted to laugh, only he knew Titus hadn't meant what he said as a joke.

"My God, Sheriff Titus"—he struggled to control the muscles in his face—"I'm no politician. I probably couldn't get a dozen votes right here in Truro, in my own home town. You got to get elected before you can go to Tallahassee."

There was a trace of impatience in Semple's voice. "Nobody asked you how you'd like to get elected. I asked you how you'd like to go."

Field was grateful for that second drink. "You mean you can have me elected?"

"I mean—God Almighty I said you was stubborn—I mean you can go to Tallahassee after the next election if you want to go. I mean I'm gettin' my belly full, an' it's a hell of a big place to fill, with your keepin' askin' how. You take it easy for a minute an' then see then if you can just say yes or no."

He turned again to face the window, his great body blocking out the panes. Field allowed his hand to wander toward the bottle and then drew it back.

"All right, Sheriff Titus," he said, "I'd like to go to Tallahassee."

Semple swung around. His face was bland as a full moon, and his hands rested on the enormous hump of his belly. He chuckled, and once again his eyes rolled and wavered with the uncertain gaze of a baby.

"I figured your paw must have taught you to answer a question right out at one time or another."

He waddled back to the chair, lowered himself into it cautiously.

"Pull up that paper bucket for my feet, will you, bub?"

When he was settled he ducked his head toward the bottle.

54

"We could have us a drink now, together."

He took half a tumblerful straight and poured it into his mouth.

"Aaah!" His lips smacked. "You maybe got somethin' there, bub. Might make good hog dip at that." He grunted contentedly and then sighed.

"I suppose now I got to answer a lot of damn fool questions?"

Field steeled himself to control the elation possessing him. He had been right after all. There was something beyond this business of his being a deputy for Titus. He realized he was grinning fatuously and shook his head.

"Nope."

Semple's eyes widened. "You don't want to know nothin'?"

"Nope."

The Sheriff blinked sleepily. "You just remember that word, nope, an' another one, yep, an' learn when to say them, an', by God, you'll end up in the governor's chair, providin' you say them at the right time to the right folks."

Field had an almost uncontrollable impulse to yell out of sheer excitement. A man going to the Legislature had something to yell about.

"It's got you by the short hair, ain't it?" Semple rumbled.

"Yep." He could yell later when he was alone.

"It'd be a good thing for you to get married." Semple appeared to be drowsy. "A man goin' to the Legislature ought to have a heart of gold an' a wife for the voters to see. I'll take take care of the heart of gold, but you sure got to do the marryin'."

"You mean Ann-Evans?" Field wondered how he could appear so calm with his heart bouncing into his throat with every word.

Titus coughed his answer and made a tentative, swaying motion preparatory to rising from the chair again.

"Ann-Evans would be just about the girl." He was on his feet and reaching for the old Panama hat on the desk. "Yes, sir, bub, Ann-Evans would be the ticket."

He clamped the hat on his head and then pulled a heavy silver watch from his coat pocket and consulted it solemnly.

"We better be goin' now."

"Want me to drive you home?"

"We ain't goin' home." Titus regarded him with surprise. "You didn' think I stayed up this late just to ask you if you wanted to go to Tallahassee. Bub, I could have done that any

55

mornin' from the Palmer House porch. No, we're goin' to take a visit to Lute-Mae Sanders' place."

For the second time that night Field felt his mouth sag open.

"My God, Sheriff Titus! You joking?" He looked for some sign of humor on Semple's face and found none. "I'll swear"—there was no mistaking the bewilderment—"I'll swear if I ever figured I'd go to a sportin' house with you. That's the damnedest way of celebrating I ever heard of."

Titus rebuked him with a slight frown. "We ain't celebratin', bub. If we was, it wouldn't be in no cat house. Just the same we're takin' a run out to Lute-Mae's place."

CHAPTER FIVE

THE HOUSE OF LUTE-MAE SANDERS WAS AS BROADLY proportioned as its owner's magnificent bosom. Built in a flurry of optimism when it seemed the neighborhood might develop into a fine residential district, it stood in splendid isolation now on a street where the other buildings ran to dingy cottages and gaunt, three-storied frame boardinghouses. With its spotless white boarding, long green shutters, and graceful pillars, Lute-Mae's made the exterior of vice, at least, a bright and shining thing.

It was the woman's satisfied boast that she had never been mistaken for other than what she was.

"When I was young I looked like a hooker, an' I was. When I grew some an' filled out I began to look more like a madam, an' I am."

In any town Lute-Mae's would have been remarkable. In Truro it was unique, an institution pointed out by those who lived on the fringes of the district with almost civic pride. If uptown Truro had its new high school, the public auditorium, the courthouse, and Flamingo Road, then downtown Truro had Lute-Mae's.

To be sure, downtown Truro was never privileged to patronize the establishment. Lute-Mae saw to it by scaling her rates far out of reach of those who lived there. The few men who had tried to gain admittance had been sent slinking away, cowed by Lute-Mae's torrent of scorn. This high-handed treatment, instead of driving the frustrated customers to anger and retaliation, had a reverse effect. The district regarded Lute-Mae's formidable person with grudging respect, if not awe, and those who lived in it would point out the house to visiting relatives and new residents with unconcealed admiration.

"The finest sportin' house in the country. You got to be a millionaire or maybe a senator to get on the front porch."

What Lute-Mae considered to be the inspiration of her career were the two brass plates, one affixed to each of the two gleaming columns flanking the steps.

"It come to me like a dream one night." She delighted in telling the story. "It was just like a vision after they took two of my little girls away for goin' at each other's throats with scissors. I decided then an' there the only way to make little girls like I have keep from doin' that way was to make 'em ashamed. That's when I had those plates made, an' I never had a moment's unrest since."

The brass plates, maintained in a high state of polish, bore the startlingly simple legend:

"Academy for Select Young Ladies."

There was a popular story to the effect that one of Lute-Mae's more roguish clients had had duplicate plates made and was in the act of substituting them when Lute-Mae caught him. It was the wag's notion they should read:

"Riding Academy of Select Young Ladies."

Given to outbursts of truly remarkable profanity, Lute-Mae tolerated no such descent from gentility by her girls. In the parlor they behaved with studied decorum. At night they wore evening gowns with not so much as a thread beneath them and twice a week were loaded into Lute-Mae's two big Cadillac limousines and driven around town for a sedate airing. If Lute-Mae was pleased with them, they were taken to Shell Springs where they were allowed to toss pebbles into the water.

Lute-Mae changed her girls every six months, drawing others from sources known only to herself.

"I do this," she would explain to her departing stock in trade, "so's you can see how lucky you bin. It don't never do for little girls like you to get too satisfied with yourselves. A whore that's satisfied don't try, an' a whore that don't try just ain't no good to anybody."

After this tender speech she would wave them tearfully on their way, make each promise to write her a postal card, and then set about implanting discipline and the fear of hell in her new bevy.

Lute-Mae was discreet. Lute-Mae was uncompromisingly honest and forthright.

"You be on the level with people," she philosophized, "an' they'll be on the level with you. If they ain't then you get their hearts cut out."

However alarming this declaration of principles might have sounded, it resulted in Lute-Mae's place becoming known throughout the state. Men—politicians, wealthy farmers, mill owners, merchants, and others on the loose—found in it a perfumed and soft-lighted haven. They stayed for an evening, a night, a week end, or longer, and it was said that for years there hadn't been an election of any political consequence that hadn't been plotted in Lute-Mae's.

Such gossip filled the woman with virtuous satisfaction.

"Anybody can get half a dozen little girls an' start a house," she would remark, "but what I got is more like a gentleman's club. Why, I got important folks who come here just to be away from their families for awhile an' get some quiet. They take things easy, act like the place was theirs. One of my little girls sees they have a cold drink handy all the time an' matches for their cigars. Peace just naturally comes to them. Then, if they got things to talk over with each other, business an' the like, they can do it with nothin' on their minds. They go back home real refreshed."

Stored away beneath the bright yellow hair which Lute-Mae still wore in a Gibson Girl roll was a remarkable collection of data. Her acquaintances and friends were spread across the state, and they included rich man, poor man, beggar man, and thief; bankers and lawyers, pimps and evangelists, prison guards and bootleggers, white and colored. She had intimate knowledge of their strengths and frailties, their appetites and passions.

"I've seen 'em all with their pants down at one time or another."

The expression was one of her favorite and most subtle jokes.

Of the woman's curious position in the state and county, Field Carlisle had an inkling, for Lute-Mae was already a legend when he had been a youngster in knickerbockers. Most of the stories concerning her, however, he discounted as he grew older. Now, sitting beside Titus as the latter unskillfully drove his car down Magnolia Avenue, he was incredulously curious.

"You're not really serious about our going to the Sanders place, are you?"

Semple took aim with the radiator of the machine at a spreading palmetto tree, apparently changed his mind at the last minute, and swerved away from the curb. He sighed with gusty melancholy and grunted.

"I could take you to the City Club," he said, "but you sure would never get to Tallahassee that way."

Field smiled in the darkness and wished mightily he had taken another drink from the bottle back there in the office.

Titus turned sharply off Magnolia and into Cane Street, slowing down only slightly in front of Lute-Mae's before cutting his wheels into a driveway running to a side entrance. There he pulled to a balky halt.

On the small, vine-shrouded porch he reached with one finger, lifted a heavy bronze knocker, and allowed it to fall back with a crash. He whistled a nameless tune and punctuated it by sucking at his teeth.

Field had only time to take in the details of the delicate fluting on each side of the door and the sweeping fanlight above it when the door was swung inward and held there by a bright-colored girl. He couldn't help noticing that there had been nothing furtive about the operation. Men with trouble in their pockets or unsure of their reception, he reflected, evidently didn't knock on Lute-Mae's door. Someone must have taught them better.

"Evenin', Sheriff Semple, suh."

The mulatto bobbed, a little, jerky movement, and ducked her head shyly.

Titus grunted amiably and moved past her. Field brought up the rear.

In a room at the end of the corridor there was a miniature bar, and behind it stood a white-coated Negro. He showed his teeth in welcome but didn't speak.

"If you're thinkin' about another drink, bub"—Semple was almost genial and thumped Field on the back with a bearlike shove—"there probably wouldn't be a better place in Florida to get it at the moment."

While the Negro put out glasses and a decanter of whisky Field tried to adjust himself to his surroundings. He had been in houses before but never, he admitted wonderingly, in anything like this. In the other places there had always been the atmosphere of something dark and unclean, the cloying odor of sweat-dampened talcum, the scent of cheap perfume, the inevitable jangling of a player piano, the burned and scarred furniture with its faded and ragged upholstery. Always there had been the brassy-faced, cow-eyed girls who trailed listlessly downstairs in answer to the call. "Company in the parlor."

Here was the quiet dignity of a well-conducted home. He

turned wonderingly to Semple and found the Sheriff staring indifferently around the room.

"How you, Sam?" he said abruptly, and the voice seemed to come from some distant region in his vast belly.

Only then, Field noticed, did the colored man make a sound. His face lighted, and his head jerked ecstatically.

"Ahm raight fahn, Sheriff Titus, suh, raight fahn, please."

Field controlled an impulse to laugh at this byplay. He downed his whisky quickly, and Semple, who had left his glass untouched, made a rumbling noise in his throat and started for the doorway.

They passed through an antechamber and then into the living room. There were soft table lights here, comfortable chairs, and deep couches. Oil paintings in heavy gilt frames broke the broad expanse of the walls, and a grand piano was dark and richly opulent in one corner. Three girls in evening gowns which clung to their bodies and barely covered their breasts were seated at a collapsible bridge table. They lifted their heads at the entrance of Titus and Field and then demurely lowered their eyes, fingering the playing cards in their hands.

Field had the almost irresistible desire to yell with laughter now. No one would ever believe this if he told it. He didn't quite believe it himself. By damn, but it might be the library at the country club. He wondered what would happen if he began shouting for a drink and a woman. The pictures would probably fall right off the walls. He always suspected that he was saved from finding out by the entrance of Lute-Mae.

The double doors at the end of the room swung gently open, and a second colored maid snapped on a wall switch which sent a cascade of light from a pendant-encrusted chandelier flooding down.

"Titus, you old bag of guts you."

Titus belched appreciatively at the greeting. "How you, Lute-Mae?"

For the first time Field was studying the fabulous Lute-Mae Sanders close at hand. For years he had seen her as she drove through Truro, and now and then they passed on the sidewalk as she was entering one of the stores on River Street. Never before, though, had he been this close to her. She was, he conceded instantly, a handsome woman. Her skin, beneath the soft lighting, appeared fresh and untouched. A large woman, whose curves were deliberately built out in the mode of another day, she moved easily across the floor.

"You old son of a bitch." She spoke to Titus, but her eyes

swept Field discerningly. Her white, sequined gown whispered as she came toward them, and her voice was husky and richly accented. "If you get any fatter you'll have to hire a couple of negrah boys to walk in front an' hold up your belly."

Titus was unperturbed by this prediction. His face wore the happy look of a pleased imbecile, and his eyes were without luster.

"Meet Field Carlisle, Lute-Mae," He waved in a general direction around the room as though to indicate that Field might be found in one of the corners.

"Looks some like his papa"—Lute-Mae considered Field judicially—"an' I always said the Judge was the handsomest man in the state." She turned directly to Field then. "Glad to make you welcome any time, Field."

Titus stared at the ceiling and spoke to a spot somewhere near the center of the chandelier.

"You won't rightly know whether Lute-Mae really takes to you until she gets drunk an' tells you about the Indian bonnet a travelin' salesman once gave her."

He chuckled then, and for a moment his features were animated.

Lute-Mae poked him not too gently in the stomach, and he was immovable. She took Field's arm, and he discovered to his surprise that he liked the touch of her. It must be that last drink, he thought.

"Goldie, Margaret, Dora." Lute-Mae called off the names of the three girls at the table, and they rose, one after the other, in reply. "This here is an old friend, Mr. Carlisle." Lute-Mae was a schoolmistress charging her pupils. "You remember an' forget it at the same time."

"Yes, Miz Lute-Mae." It was the shrill piping of birds on a fence rail. Their faces were brightly intent, eyes upon Field to impress him forever upon their memories.

Field hoped he wasn't looking as foolish as he felt. If this wasn't the damnedest thing, introducing him as though he were a guest at a sorority house.

Lute-Mae turned to Titus. "There's friends of yours upstairs."

Semple nodded and turned his back upon them, deep in a study of one of the pictures.

"Like a drink down here?"

Titus's buttocks quivered in what could be only taken as a negative sign, and he moved slowly and ponderously away from them toward the door.

"Did you ever in your born days"—Lute-Mae's words

61

were filled with admiration—"see such an ass as that?"

Field did laugh then as the incredibility of the past few minutes came tumbling down upon him. He whooped out of sheer delight at the sight of Titus, Lute-Mae, and the three girls at the table. When he finally controlled himself he found Lute-Mae regarding him with approval.

"I was afraid there for awhile," she said seriously, "that there wasn't even a snicker in you, let alone the grace of God to laugh." She placed the palm of her hand against his back and gave him an encouraging pat. "You go on with Titus. You'll get along all right."

He was conscious that she was standing there, watching him, as he followed Semple.

Climbing the stairway behind Titus, Field experienced the same feeling of excitement he used to have as a youngster when he would creep downstairs on Christmas morning for a forbidden peek at the mysteriously bright presents scattered at the base of the tree. At the head of this flight waited something important, important enough to drive Titus to unusual effort. There was a sense of unreality about what had happened this night, and try as he did to dismiss the elation within him he was impressed and silent.

What happened later was so absurdly simple, so out of keeping with the melodramatic picture he had been sketching in his mind, that Field had an acute feeling of disappointment.

In a large front room four shirt-sleeved men were sprawled in easy chairs. A light breeze riffled the curtains in open windows and swirled away the rich smoke of fine Havana tobacco. On a center table were bottles of White Rock, whisky, glasses, and a silver bucket, frosted on the outside from the ice it held. Through a second door Field could glimpse the corner of a bed in the adjoining room. He had to remind himself he was in Lute-Mae Sanders' place and not in some hotel suite.

One of the men he recognized immediately. He was Dan Curtis, the Curtis Titus had sent him to see in Jacksonville. The others were strangers, but when Semple made his muttered introductions something leaped within him at the sound of their names. Undistinguished in appearance, lazily comfortable at the moment, here were the men who were credited with guiding Florida's political machine; the combination of power and acumen which controlled a state.

It was fantastically impossible that they should be sitting this way in Lute-Mae's, lounging in shirt sleeves, drinking whisky and soda. By God, he thought, I wonder what their wives would say if they could see them here.

He shook hands gratefully with Curtis. There was something reassuring in a familiar face. The others, as he met them, were neither cordial nor reserved. It was almost as though they had known him for a long time and his presence was to be taken for granted.

Field was at a helpless disadvantage. He didn't know what was expected of him. Maybe, he thought, in a desperate effort to sum things up, this is the way it is done. Curtis said what he wanted, Titus marked off his part, the others set aside their districts and counties. Then they all got together and helped fry one another's fish. There couldn't be much more to an election than the mechanical counting of votes. Field had heard too much politics from the Judge not to know this was so, and yet, when he was confronted with the system, he found it hard to believe. Somewhere in the back of his mind, as Titus had driven him down from the office, had lingered the notion that he was to be weighed, sounded, and appraised. That seemed foolish now. No one seemed to have any interest in how he felt, what he thought.

"Have a drink, Field." Curtis, as though divining his uncertainty, motioned toward the table and then resumed the drawling conversation, interrupted by the arrival of the Sheriff and Field.

While he mixed himself a drink, Field listened. The men talked in a lazy, indifferent fashion, something about a proposed highway on the east coast. Titus, sprawling in a chair, grunted an assent now and then when a question was put to him. He seemed infinitely wearied by the whole business.

As the whisky crept into his stomach, Field discovered he was becoming irritated, and yet he didn't know what to do about it. Either, he thought, Titus was making a damn fool out of him with this nonsense about Tallahassee and the Legislature, or Curtis and the others didn't think he was of sufficient importance to bother with. He was only something Semple was bringing around in a bag, and they were taking it sight-unseen.

Turning impatiently from the table he found the Sheriff's gaze upon him. He had caught Titus in an unguarded moment, and what he saw shocked him. There was no stupidity in Semple's eyes. They were points of blue-white crystal, calculating, shrewd, and almost thoughtfully evil. Only for an instant, however, did they show that way; then they clouded, and his features relaxed into flabby vacuity.

"I knew your father well, Field." The man Parker, from Lake Wales spoke from the depths of his chair. With a start

Field realized that the quartet had at last given him their attention. "He always said he was going to make a lawyer of you. You were in Gainesville for awhile, weren't you?"

"Two years." Field sat on the edge of a chair, holding the untasted drink between his knees. I'm damned, he reassured himself, if I'll roll over like a puppy just because one of them speaks to me.

Parker waited for a moment, and then, as Field remained silent, a ghost of a smile touched his lips.

"Think maybe we should have some red fire burning an' a parade?"

There was no sarcasm in the question, only a tolerant understanding, and Field thawed beneath it. He grinned.

"I guess," he said honestly, "I was probably expecting something like that."

"It's a natural enough feeling." Parker stretched his long arms above his head and sighed reminiscently. "You take the Governor now. I remember when he first started moving up and saw his picture on a campaign poster. You could hardly hold him. He thought a brass band ought to be around every time he went to the privy. You get used to it, though, an' begin to realize that the only time you can be yourself is when you are alone with friends like this."

There was general laughter of agreement which was interrupted by Curtis.

"I guess the least we could do is to have a drink together. It's as good a thing as I know of to start on the road to Tallahassee with."

Miraculously the tension, as Field had imagined it, was gone. They were talking as old friends, all of them. There was talk of fishing, liquor, and women, of the boom which had struck Miami and spread out over the state. Everyone, apparently, had something to say if for no other reason than to make Field feel at home. Glasses were filled and emptied, and even Titus roused himself sufficiently to take a couple of drinks.

"Anyhow," John Shelton from Volusia complained goodnaturedly, "I didn't come up here to talk politics. My principal aim was to pinch one of Lute-Mae's girls on the behind an', maybe, get Parker into a crap game. I ain't goin' home until Tuesday."

Field realized that Shelton was getting a little drunk, and when the man pressed the bottle upon him he took it reluctantly. An inner caution warned him against drinking too much. God knows if he ever needed an excuse to get himself tight tonight supplied it, but he knew instinctively he shouldn't. It was all right for others to get drunk and bellow at the moon through the window of a brothel, but it wasn't his turn to howl yet.

He noted that Dan Curtis wasn't drinking much either, and there was a nod of approval from the elder man when, after hesitating over the bottle, he filled his glass with soda only. He liked Curtis, had liked him from the moment they had met in the Seminole, and wanted the man to like him. The others were important, but they were more like the men he had known. Curtis was different somehow. Without trying, he stood apart, a great rock of a man whose edges had been worn smooth by the winds of the years.

He leaned against the wall alongside of Field and watched with detached interest while Parker and Shelton prepared to start a dice game on the floor.

"I've a little week-end place out by Lake Surprise." He mentioned the fact casually. "Like to have you come over some time. We ought to get better acquainted." He hesitated, forming a thought. "Don't be fooled," he continued, "by what has happened to you or by tonight here in Lute-Mae's. It isn't all like this, not so easy and simple." He selected a cigar from a box on a low table and bit the end off deliberately. "You've a chance to go far in the state if you want to. You've got a good name, the Judge is well remembered, and a good start with Titus backing you. He's doing that, I guess, partly because of your father and partly because he thinks you'll be popular. Don't ever underestimate Titus, though. He's the only man I know who can make a sow's ear out of a silk purse."

Field nodded soberly. "Thanks, I'll remember."

"Well"—grumblingly Titus worked himself regretfully out of his chair—"I guess we'd better push along, Field. From now on, by the looks of things, it isn't likely you can get into anything around here but trouble."

"Don't run out, Titus," Parker called over his shoulder from the floor. "I'd like to take some of your money back with me."

"Most of the county has been tryin' to do that very thing for years," he grunted complacently. "Come on, Field."

It took Field a minute to realize Titus hadn't called him bub. If nothing else came out of this evening, he reflected, he had progressed that far. He didn't want to leave, though. There was an awful lot of money there on the floor between Parker and Shelton, and he was lucky with the dice. Besides, there was plenty of liquor and Lute-Mae's girls downstairs. He'd like a couple of fast drinks and a chance to become better acquainted. He wondered about the girls. By God, from the way things went on in the parlor, a man'd probably have to call the girl miss when he took her to bed.

Dan Curtis's voice interrupted this pleasantly moody speculation.

"You might figure on running up to Jacksonville, Field," he called, "and see me in a couple of weeks. There may be a few holds I can teach you to practice on when Titus starts wrestling with his constituency."

It was as if he suspected what was in Field's mind and sought to sidetrack him.

In a pleasant, alcoholic haze Field shook hands with Curtis and called his good nights to the crap shooters, who barely lifted their heads but made half-hearted demands that both he and Titus stay.

"I guess I'll run along with the Sheriff." There was genuine regret in the decision.

Titus was already at the door, wriggling his shoulders impatiently. In the hall outside he waited for Field, and they descended the stairs together.

"When you get to the Legislature," he said solemnly, "I want you to see what can be done about havin' all steps go down an' none up. I only enjoy walkin' down."

There were three men in the living room when they entered and with them three girls, not the ones Field had seen earlier in the evening, and he wondered how many "select young ladies" Lute-Mae kept under her roof. Business, he thought, must begin to pick up around this time of night. Then, with a guilty start and a feeling of embarrassment, he realized he not only knew the men but that they also knew him. There was Pritchard, from the Planters' Bank, young Davis, whose father was president of the Merchants' Trust Co., and Langworthy, editor of the *Journal*. They made an oddly assorted trio. He wondered for an instant what they would think of seeing him here and then realized you didn't think or talk about anyone you saw at Lute-Mae's. You couldn't very well, and one hand had to wash the other.

Titus lumbered through the room with the slow determination of a gopher intent upon its hole. Field risked a nod in the direction of Langworthy and received only a blank stare for his trouble.

Well, he'd learned something else. Unless you came in here with a man you didn't recognize him in the parlor. It was a nice arrangement. He wondered, as he followed Titus, how that old bastard Pritchard got away with this late and what his horse-faced wife would say if she knew he was here. He wondered, for that matter, what most of Truro would say if it could glimpse all of them here. Old man Pritchard made a creaky effort to lift the girl beside him to his lap and cackled delightedly as she came with shrill and false protestations of reluctance.

Lute-Mae was standing alone at the bar. It was funny, Field thought, how you could get to like a woman after not saying more than half a dozen words to her.

"Have a drink before you go, Titus?"

The Sheriff shook his head emphatically. "Got a sour stomach now," he protested.

Lute-Mae chuckled. "I'll bet it looks like a vat of green mash then." She beckoned to Field. "I wouldn't feel right if you didn't have a drink with me on your first time here."

He went to the bar promptly. Already the liquor he had taken upstairs was beginning to dull. If a man ever needed a drink he did.

"What'll it be?"

"Bourbon, thanks."

The Negro put out the bottle and a small carafe of ice water. Field poured until the whisky swam around the rim of his glass and then took it fast. When he felt it run its hot course to his stomach, he smiled at Lute-Mae.

"I guess I really wanted that."

"I expected you would."

She walked between them down the corridor, a hand on each of their arms.

"The front door opens too," she told Field. "All you got to do is ring. Most folks, though, like it better to come in this way. You use either entrance any time you like."

She stopped just inside the screen and shook hands with Titus.

"Next time he comes around," she promised, "I'll tell him about the Indian bonnet. That satisfy you?"

Semple blew his cheeks out thoughtfully. "Most folks, I guess, feel that way about him," he almost whispered. "That's how come he'll ride into Tallahassee on a feather."

Field wished that Semple, and even the men he had met upstairs, would be a little less impersonal. He was beginning to feel he was a prize steer to be shown off at the county fair.

Outside Titus worked his way in behind the wheel of his car. For a moment he sat there, staring ahead at the dark bank of oleander and bay trees enclosing the back yard; then he dropped a heavy foot to the starter pedal, and the engine sighed its way into action.

The way uptown led through mean streets where the ugly houses were divided by vacant lots filled with rank weeds. Dim and ragged patches of light dropped to the pitted roads from insect-covered bulbs high on stark poles. It was a furtive and sullen district, drawing its livelihood from the railroad yards. Dingy poolrooms, lunch counters, barber-shops, and cheap clothing stores lined the way, and on the corners knots of men lounged, silent, and resentful.

Titus drove with a maddening disregard for the condition of the roadway, bouncing from one hole to another, his bulk securing him to the seat, while Field had to hang on to the side of the car to keep from being pitched through the top. When they struck the paved surface of Magnolia Avenue Titus sighed happily as though the passage were a major achievement.

"There wasn't," he said thoughtfully, "no real reason for us to go to Lute-Mae's tonight. Things for you been settled a long time. It was just that Parker, Shelton, an' the others were in town, out on a rip for themselves, an' I figured it might be good for you to become acquainted with them this way. They'll be hellin' around the Sanders shop for the next couple of days."

Field allowed a block to slip past before he answered. "It seemed a little funny to see a man like Dan Curtis there."

Titus thrust out his lower lip. "When Dan Curtis's got things to talk about, he'd as soon do it in Lute-Mae's as any place. He probably figured it was a good time to catch Parker there. By tomorrow he'll have them in his vest pocket with his cigars."

Field was silent. That last drink set up an insistent buzzing within his head, and it was good to keep quiet for a moment and allow the cool breeze to brush his face. Anyhow, so much of what had happened this night seemed unreal. It needed thinking about.

It didn't seem possible that men for the Legislature could be fashioned so casually, and yet he had no choice but to believe it had been done that night. He smiled in the darkness and admitted that, maybe, he had listened to too many political speeches. You could get so you believed them after awhile; talk about sterling characters, choice of the people, champions of justice, defenders of the sovereign rights of the electorate. All the time things were probably arranged in someone's office or in a place such as Lute-Mae's.

He opened his eyes and saw they were nearing the court-house.

"Sheriff Titus"—the memory of himself as a youngster playing around the Carlisle yard while Semple and his father sat on the porch made it impossible to call the man simply Titus—"Sheriff Titus, there's something I'd like to know."

Semple kept his eyes on the road, but Field knew he was listening.

"I'd sort of like to know why you are doing this for me." He hesitated and then hurried on. "I'll swear I never liked you much, and I never figured you were fool enough to think I did."

Titus lifted his toe from the accelerator, and the car slowed rapidly until it barely rolled along the shadowed street.

"Why, no, bub," he answered softly, "I never actually did. I kind of felt bad about that in the beginning 'cause your paw an' me were close an' I liked you. You get used to things, though, like maybe you're gettin' used to me. I just got used to your not fancyin' my company."

The car was barely moving and gave a protesting jerk. Semple blandly ignored the bucking.

"I'm goin' to send you to Tallahassee," he continued thoughtfully, "first, because of your paw an' I figure if I don't do somethin' you'll be on the county the way you are now for the rest of your life. That ain't the most important reason, though. I got the feelin' you'll turn out to be a good man, an' I'm tired of tradin' mongrels. When you get somethin' that ain't bred right, you always got the feelin' that in a pinch you can't be sure how it will act. You take a good-bred dog now, as an example like. He may not always like the things he's got to do, but he does them 'cause that's how his blood runs. With you, now, I know the strain. I figure you could be counted on to do the right things."

With difficulty he half turned in the seat and looked at Field, ignoring the progress of the car.

"That's about the way it is, I guess. From now on you got to stop driftin'. I'll see the spadework gets done, but you got to dress things up some. You get out through the county, let people have a look at you, find out what's on their minds. I figure too you'd better settle down an' marry that Ann-Evans Weldon girl. She looks to me like someone that would be good for you. I'll take care of the rest."

At City Hall Square Titus pulled into the curb.

"I guess you'll want your own car from here on." He waited until Field was on the sidewalk. "See you around sometime tomorrow, bub."

Field watched until the red tail light winked around the

corner of Spencer Avenue, and then he walked thoughtfully across the street to where he had parked his car.

CHAPTER SIX

THERE WERE TIMES WHEN, FOR REASONS WHICH HE never quite understood, Titus Semple took himself apart. In a twisted fashion he achieved a savage ecstasy in laying himself bare and writhing beneath the searching hands of his own fury.

The loathing he felt for his grotesque body was constant, and it drove him to degrees of self-abasement, to the scourging of his soul, which left him helpless and exhausted. Inexplicably harried by the black madness, he would plod upstairs to his rooms in the Palmer House and undress before the full-length mirror, unbuttoning his clothing and tossing it to the floor until he stood, a pink and white monstrosity, in front of the glass. His great belly hung tumorlike, rolling down into a pendulous, quivering growth. His legs and thighs, uncertain pillars of glistening fat, shook helplessly with the slightest movement, and his knees were pressed together, splaying out the bulging calves.

Standing in this fashion he forced himself to contemplate every detail of his anatomy until he wanted to vomit. Then, after a few minutes, the torture would leave him to be followed by a curious peace as though the horror had lost its power to be revolting. A crafty, fox-bright fire sprang into his eyes, and he could turn from the mirror without wanting to look back.

Breathing heavily he would go to the highboy of burnished mahogany, and from the heavily scented drawer, in which there were tucked packets of sandalwood, he would select a nightshirt of sheerest silk. This was his vanity, to be able to cover that body with expensive fabric. Slipping into the garment he would walk slowly to the oversized bed, with its special mattresses and his own fine linen sheets, and lower his bulk upon it.

Often he would lie there, staring up at the ceiling, until daybreak moved upon the river and stole over the town. Sometimes he wanted a woman, wanted one so badly that he

70

would twist and roll upon the bed in whimpering agony until he was breathless and the nightdress clung to his perspiring body. He had never taken a woman, not even after he had plenty of money to pay for one. He had tried once, and the recollection of the girl's involuntary expression of amazed disgust at the sight of his nakedness was a searing thing. He had stumbled out of the house that night, half-dressed, clutching at his clothing, and thrashed with terrible insanity through the weeds and scrub in the back yard until he dropped panting to the ground.

Lying on his bed at night he would wonder why things were the way they were and that they had been so from the beginning. People had wasted no time in teaching him that fat boys were supposed to be funny and even grateful of ridicule. A fat boy was supposed to be funny, and so anything done to him was funny. He was to be pushed over backward when another boy crouched behind him. His clothes were to be stolen when he went swimming, and he was to be sent on foolish errands. He was to be ignored at the small social affairs of childhood or treated with contemptuous indifference. He was to be called Gutsy or Fats and laugh because they were comical nicknames. A fat boy was to be uncomplaining and stupid.

At fifteen Titus Semple decided to be stupid. He began being stupid when, one afternoon after school, he was searching for an old blackboard in the basement and caught the principal of the school there with the young and pretty algebra teacher. He walked right up to them instead of running off the way a smart boy should. He was plainly stupid when the algebra teacher burst into hysterical tears and the principal was by turns blustering and craven. That was the term when the principal made him business manager of the baseball team and paid him three dollars a week out of his own pocket for the extra work he was supposed to do. That was the time, also, when he handed in a blank algebra examination paper and saw it marked 100.

At twenty Titus was still stupid. He was so dreamily doltish that he could sit unheeded on the curb before Mayor Osborne's house and watch the city's two trucks hauling black dirt from the bottoms to fill in and make a fine sloping lawn for the Mayor's yard. He could sit there most of the day without anyone paying much attention to him and watch the three Negroes who had been arrested, and were supposed to be in jail, working in the Mayor's yard until sundown when Marshal Pellen came and took them back to jail. That was the summer

Mayor Osborne had him appointed to the police force and gave him a desk to sit behind in a nice cool corner of City Hall.

At thirty Titus was still stupid, although his obvious lack of intelligence had caused any number of persons to wonder how in hell certain things had happened to them. He was so patently harmless no one paid much attention to his ramblings and foolish questions of his thumbing through the open records at the county seat. That was how he discovered Judge Harper and three county commissioners owned the contracting firm that received the award for the brick road running between Truro and Apulca.

That was the year he became sheriff.

Although the need for pretending was long since past, it amused Titus now to continue the farce. It compensated, somehow, for those moments of ruthlessness when he forced himself to stand naked before the mirror in his room. With lowered eyes, the innocent expression of a baby on his face, he liked to rock gently in his favorite chair on the Palmer House porch and watch the surprise struggling helplessly in the eyes of men who were just discovering they were being told to do something and realized they had to do it. It always amused him when he saw they were learning that they were working for him and not he for them. Truro was the pulse of an important and populous county, and without seeming to do so Titus ran Truro and so the county. From the Palmer House porch he had wound a hard and durable political ball. He was pleased to sit there and watch the self-important men playing with it, knowing when he whistled they would bring it to him because they had no other choice.

Truro belonged to Titus from the mayor to the lowly patrolman in Cartown, the railroad district. It belonged to him because he had done stupid things an intelligent man would never have thought of. There was, for instance, the question of a Negro vote. An intelligent man wouldn't have stirred up the colored sections because he knew the white population would ostracize him. Constitutionally the Negroes were entitled to the vote. They didn't go to the polls simply because it was generally understood that the white folks wouldn't like it and cooks, maids, yard boys, laborers, and chauffeurs would likely enough find themselves without jobs if their white employers discovered they were voting.

Titus, being stupid, hadn't thought about that, and he sent colored men he could trust into the Negro district.

There had been furious talk of lynchings, tar and featherings, and a revival of the Ku Klux Klan after the first election day years back when the colored voters appeared at the polls and hesitantly asked to be allowed to cast their votes. Nothing came of it though, and Mayor Packard was swept into City Hall, and Titus Semple rocked a little faster on the Palmer House porch.

After that, during local campaigning, the men who had scorned the Negro vote and affected to assert that they preferred no office at all to being elected through colored ballots were helpless. Furtively at first and then openly, loudly proclaiming their adherence to the democratic theory which entitled all freemen to the ballot, they sought to curry favor in the Negro sections. Still fearful of the social consequences, they made their overtures through an intermediary. Titus was such a fool. He sent his men right down into the districts. There were barbecues and speeches, and if his candidates suffered a loss of social prestige they were elected. The colored districts remained forever Semple's. It was argued with infuriating simplicity, infuriating to his rivals, that Sheriff Semple had given the fun of voting to the colored folks first, with fish fries and Christmas gifts thrown in, and there wasn't any sense in changing over to a man they knew nothing about. If Sheriff Semple told them to do something, it must be right.

In much the same fashion had Titus spread his influence over the county, slowly, craftily, completely. It crept into high places, also, because at first those who sat in the seats couldn't bring themselves to believe he was anything more than a country lout, harmless and burdened down with so much fat that he was bound to be good-natured and easy to get along with. The awakenings had frequently been rude and explosive, but they left Titus comfortable and unmoved in his sagging Palmer House chair.

Now and then he did things which surprised him. Driving homeward after dropping Field at City Hall he thought about this and tried to uncover the reason. Deep within him he suspected such moves to be a form of self-flattery. That he, who had fooled so many, could turn the trick upon himself was a huge joke. This business of Field now, he thought, was sure enough a surprise. At first he had given the son of an old friend a hack job to keep him off the streets. He didn't need a deputy. The boy's obstinacy, his refusal to back down and to be won over, piqued his interest. He couldn't remember now just when he decided to send Field to the Legislature. The idea seemed to have sprung full-flowered overnight. The more he thought about it the better he liked it although the decision still puzzled him at times. It wasn't like him to change horses, and yet here he was preparing to put the toe to John Layton, a faithful enough wheel who expected to be sent back to Tallahassee at the next election.

He sighed. It wasn't as though Field was going to be any too easy to handle, either. Why the hell was he storing up trouble for himself this way?

He drove slowly, his stomach chocked against the steering wheel, holding the car in line.

It was a hell of a note, he conceded, when he got so smart he fooled himself.

At Virginia Avenue he turned into River Street and allowed the car, like a willing nag, to head for the Palmer House.

After Semple's car had vanished around the corner, Field bolted across the road to the parking lot and threw himself into the front seat of his Ford without bothering to open the door. For the past two hours he had been bottled up. Now he wanted to yell and tell the town what had happened to him.

It was a night to get drunk in, he decided. If Titus said he was going to Tallahassee, he was on his way, of that he was positive. The meeting with Curtis, Shelton, and Parker only put a cap on the jug.

Roaring out of the parking space with marl spurting from beneath his spinning wheels he headed toward Flamingo Road. If Ann-Evans was awake he'd make her come out, and they'd get drunk together. He'd rather be with Ann-Evans now than anyone in the world, particularly now when he could make her admit he hadn't been crazy as a cooter by hanging on to that deputy job. He whooped boyishly at the thought of how Ann-Evans and old lady Weldon would look when they heard the news.

Flamingo Road was a gloomy tunnel with the high trees arching overhead to shut out the sky. Field realized disappointedly that it was late. Ann-Evans would be in bed at this hour. He drove slowly past the house and came to a half stop near the curb.

There was a single light in the hall, but he knew Mrs. Weldon always kept one burning since the time they had caught a coon trying to break in. The family was in bed. He looked hopefully up at Ann-Evans's room, wondering if the events of the night wouldn't communicate themselves to her and make her come to the window. After a moment he drew away.

Disappointed, he turned in the middle of the block. He'd go down to Cliff Miner's place and buy a pint. Christ, a man on his way to the Legislature couldn't be alone. Miner would be better than no one to talk with.

On his way back downtown he wondered if he should go out to Lute-Mae's again. There ought, he thought wistfully, to be some fun around there at this time.

Cliff Miner sold his liquor in a back room of the gray shingled cottage in which he lived with Lolly Trevor, whose husband was doing time in Atlanta for bootlegging. Field could see lights in the kitchen as he drove up. A pint of Bourbon, a few drinks, and probably Cliff would ask him how things were going. He could tell him then he was running for the Legislature next year. Someone just had to know about it.

Miner was alone in the rear of the house. He opened the door after first switching on a porch light and peering out.

"Oh, how you, Field?" There was a note of relief in his voice.

I'll bet, Field thought, every time someone steps on the porch Cliff wonders if it is Lolly's husband come to take him apart.

"Got any pints?" Field was casual.

"Only got some rye. It don't pay to bring in pints. These must have got mixed in by mistake." Cliff shut the door behind them. "What the hell you doin' out this time of night?"

He rummaged in the back of a disorderly closet and finally fished out a tin container which held a pint bottle of Chicken Cock.

Field sat on the edge of the table swinging one leg back and forth with slow regularity.

"Donny Allyard"—Cliff was in a conversational humor—"was in a little while ago, that's how come I'm awake. He had a little thing he'd picked up at the bus terminal. Both of them was whoopin' drunk as monkeys."

Miner seemed in no hurry to close up. Field had heard that Lolly got mad at him a couple of times a week and locked him out—she told it herself. This, he reasoned, must be one of the nights.

"How's business?" Field took the package and began working with the little key, unrolling the metal sealing band.

"It stinks. God-damned stills in every back yard have played hell with bootleggin'. Folks don't buy it. They make it." The injustice of this competition and of Lolly's behavior rankled.

"Have a drink with me." Field shook out the bottle and unscrewed its top.

Miner hesitated. "I don't mind if I do," he said finally. He

75

put out a couple of heavy water glasses, and Field measured off two stiff drinks.

"Here's to hell fire."

Cliff nodded and tossed the whisky into his open mouth.

The liquor blew up a warm cloud, enveloping Field, and he smiled companionably at Miner. He'd heard that Cliff had tipped off the federals so's Chet Trevor would get caught. Lolly had moved over the day her husband was taken away. Someone was going to get hurt when they let Chet out.

"I'm goin' to get rid of this damn business." Miner wanted sympathy. "Runnin' in an' out of back doors all the time, drunks wakin' you up in the middle of the night an' wantin' a quart on credit. When you do get a few bucks the police come an' hold you up for your stock, an' you have to buy it back from them or they sell it to some one down the street."

Field was indifferently attentive to the lament and poured two more drinks while Cliff elaborated on the difficulties of conducting a respectable and profitable speakeasy.

"I don't know what a sheriff's office is for"—Miner clutched his glass and glared fiercely at Field—"but I'll swear to God it ought to be able to do somethin' about the police department."

It was a story Field had listened to many times. When the gang at the station house needed a few dollars, they would go out and raid a couple of places and carry off the stock. The next morning the unfortunate owners could come down and make a deal. If they didn't the police sold it to another bootlegger.

"We just have county business, sort of," he explained.

"Well, by God"—Miner was half drunk and indignant—"if this ain't county business, then I don't know what is. Ain't it happening in the county?"

Field crossed over to the sink and drew a tumblerful of water from the tap.

"This is sure enough strong whisky."

Cliff chuckled dourly. "It ought to be. Look at all the good sea air it gets between here an' Bimini."

Field held the bottle to the light and then split what was left between the two glasses.

"You tryin' to get yourself drunk, Field?" Miner regarded him wonderingly.

Field's head was a whirring clock. "I guess," he admitted slowly, "I am a little drunk already."

The half pint of rye poured suddenly on the Bourbon and Scotch he had taken earlier in the evening jolted him suddenly, and then the shock passed away. In its place there crept a delightful feeling of lassitude and indifference. He didn't care any longer whether he told Miner about Tallahassee. Somehow it didn't seem important that anyone know. He just wanted to ride this pink cloud he was straddling.

Cliff finished his drink and walked unsteadily to the closet. He came back with a second can of Chicken Cock and placed it on the table with a bang.

"The other one was on me."

Field pushed the can away from the corner and sat down again. The bare kitchen suddenly seemed homey and cheerful, and Cliff was a wonderful and sympathetic fellow. He felt sorry for him. It was a damn shame if Lolly acted up the way she did and wouldn't let him go to bed with her, particularly after Cliff had seen to it that her husband was sent up to Atlanta so's she could come over and visit. He beamed at Miner, feeling wise and benevolent. Maybe he'd ask Titus if something couldn't be done so's the police would let Cliff alone.

"You're all right, Cliff," he muttered and wondered at his tongue being so heavy.

A rattling on the porch sent the screen door shivering noisily in its frame, and there was impatient stamping of feet on the boards.

"More drunks," Miner said sourly. "You'd think they'd go to bed once in awhile."

He thumbed a wall switch, flooding the stoop with light, and pressed his nose against the wire netting.

"Hell," he said finally and unhooked the door, "don't stand out there. Come on in."

Field saw the two men first and caught a glimpse of a couple of girls behind them. They filed into the room.

"How you, Field?"

"Hi, Johnny, Hi, Tunis." He lifted a hand in greeting and held it statuelike in the air as he recognized the girls.

"Well, for goodness' sake, Fielding Carlisle." It was Annabelle, from the Eagle, and following her was Lane Ballou.

The surprise on Field's face was unmistakable, and Annabelle giggled delightedly.

"We've been to Charlie's. We've been to Charlie's," Annabelle chanted foolishly. Her face was flushed, and she wanted to be kittenish.

Field stared over her shoulder, wondering why the sight of Lane Ballou here with Johnny and Tunis Simms should surprise and, this was funny too, annoy him.

77

"Hello, Sheriff."

He remembered that smile now, how she did it with her eyes and the inflection of her voice rather than with her lips.

"Hello, Lane."

The liquor swept out of his head, rolled away as a patch of ground fog is sometimes snatched up by a breath of wind. It was odd, he thought, he had almost forgotten how she looked, and yet now everything about her was familiar, the way she stood, the sheen of her hair molding an oval face, the dusky coloring of her speech.

"How's the job?" He sat back on the edge of the table. Annabelle, who had been clinging to his arm with determined coyness, released him with a pout.

"Noisy." She smiled as though they shared a secret.

"I want a drink-ee, Field." Annabelle screwed up her face in a childish grimace. "Annabelle wants a drink-ee."

Tunis Simms, a tall gangling youth, stood at the other side of the room dropping nickels into a slot machine with fierce concentration while his brother argued with Miner.

"You know, Johnny"—Miner shook his head vigorously—"that I don't like to serve nothin' on the premises. Why don't you be a good fellow an' take a bottle away with you to some nice quiet place?"

Simms glanced pointedly at the empty bottle and the two glasses on the table.

"That's different." Miner was outraged. "Field an' me were just havin' a sociable drink. That's different than havin' people sit around in the kitchen."

Field picked up the unopened can of Chicken Cock and tossed it into Johnny Simm's surprised hands.

"Go on and let 'em have a drink, Cliff. It's on me, Johnny."

"Ooo! Goody! Drinkin' likker." Annabelle darted at Simms and made a grab for the package. They scuffled with coltish humor during the course of which Annabelle was thoroughly felt and rumpled.

"My God," Miner protested. "You wake Lolly up, an' we'll all get thrown out of here." He hurried to a rack and collected four glasses.

"Mind if I sit down?" Lane slid on to the table at Field's side and tossed her head in Tunis Simms' direction. "He's sore," she whispered.

"Yes?"

"Uh huh. He's real mad, bought me a barbecue and a coke at Charlie's and figures it was money thrown away."

Johnny was splashing whisky into the glasses. "Here's the tiger's milk."

Annabelle screamed delightedly and took her drink. Simms extended one toward Lane, and she shook her head.

"Field?"

"No, thanks. I just had one."

"Tu?" The elder Simms came over to the table, picked up the glass, glared steadily at Lane for a moment, and then walked again to the slot machine and stood there with his back toward them.

"See." Lane was laughing with her eyes again. "He's just not going to be nice until I work out that fifteen cents."

There was the explosive crash of shattered glass as Tunis Simms hurled his drink to the floor. He wheeled, and his face was contorted with anger.

"To hell with it. I'm goin' home."

"Here now"—Miner was alarmed—"that ain't no way to act."

"To hell with you, too." Tunis stalked across the floor and planted himself before Lane. "You comin' with me?"

Field made a half-movement to rise and felt the gentle but firm pressure of Lane's hand on his arm.

"Not tonight."

"This's a hell of a way to act to a fellow that's taken you out." Tunis was looking for an argument.

Lane fumbled in a small change purse and withdrew a dime and a nickel, holding the coins before her.

"Thanks for the loan."

Simms slapped at her finger tips, and the change scattered to the floor. Field lunged forward and was blocked as Lane leaned quickly before him.

"Why, Lane Ballou." Annabelle was indignantly shrill. "Whatever are you doin', breakin' up a nice party." Her eyes filled.

Tunis waited at the screen door. "You comin' with me, Johnny?" he called aggressively to his brother.

Johnny nodded patiently and took Annabelle's arm, pulling her with him toward the back porch.

"How you goin' to get home, Lane?" Annabelle wailed.

Lane waved reassuringly. "The Sheriff'll see that I get back, won't you?"

"Sure." He still thought he ought to take a poke at Tunis. "Sure, I'll run you down."

"You'll be sorry, Lane." Annabelle was maudlin. "Tunis is a nice boy. He didn't mean anythin'. You'll be sorry."

They could hear her protesting above the angry mutterings of the Simms brothers as the trio came around the side of the house.

"Nice company you keep."

Lane cocked an impudent eye at him. His annoyance evaporated, and he reached down, covering her hand, feeling the warmth of her slender fingers as they twisted between his.

"My God, Field." Miner was wistfully hopeful. "Won't you get out of here? If Lolly should wake up now, she probably wouldn't even let me stay in the house tonight."

"Sure, Cliff." He straightened up from the table. "Want a drink before we go, Lane?"

She backed away in simulated terror. "Mister, didn't you see the trouble I was just in over a coke? I wouldn't want to think what would happen if I was to take a drink of real whisky off of a Truro boy."

"All right. Good night, Cliff."

They were barely outside the door before they heard Miner hastily locking it.

"Who's Lolly?" Lane was close at his side as they followed the path around the cottage.

Field laughed shortly. "The wife of a friend."

"Oh."

In the car Field started the motor and then hesitated with his hand on the gear shift. Lane curled up beside him on the seat, tucking one foot beneath her and resting a cheek on the back cushion.

"Want to go home?"

Lane held her face against the cool dampness of the leather. It was strange he should have to ask, that he wouldn't just know and drive away.

He leaned over and brushed her cheek with a kiss, and her mouth softened.

"No," he spoke thoughtfully, "I guess you don't."

Where the city limits ended, the paved surface of the street gave way to a twisting road of rutted dirt running between broad irrigation ditches. White sand was piled in irregular mounds on either side where the dredges had dumped it, and on the hillocks the delicate brown and green shoots of new pine were thrusting upward. Beyond stretched the flat land, clumped scrub and scattered trees, and the air was rich with the scent of earth and grass and pine cooling slowly.

Field drove without haste, dropping his head sideways now and then to glance at Lane. She hadn't moved, but whenever he looked at her he found her eyes upon him.

"Kissin' a carnival kid, Sheriff?"

The words were barely spoken before her hand came up and rested on his shoulder. Fingers touched his coat collar.

"That was dumb," she spoke quickly. "I shouldn't have said it."

Field kept his eyes upon the road and wondered just what the hell he was doing, riding around the country at one o'clock in the morning this way.

"Where we going?" Lane asked without interest.

"Shell Springs, I guess." He was grateful for the question.

"Far?" She snuggled down in the seat.

"Ten miles or so. It's one of the sights," he added. "It's probably the only sulphur-water spring in the state that doesn't claim to have been discovered by Ponce de Leon. From the way the chambers of commerce tell it, old Ponce didn't do anything but leap from one spring to the other. They used to have a sign on the bank which read. 'This Spring Was Positively not the One Ponce de Leon Was Looking For.' Some picnic party finally tore it down, I guess, to build a fire with."

They rode in silence for awhile, the sand in the ruts making a faint musical sound against and beneath the tires.

"What," he asked finally, "were you doing out with the Simms boys?"

Lane threw back her head and laughed happily. "I was afraid for a while," she confessed, "that you weren't going to ask me. I thought, maybe, you didn't care one way or the other."

Damn it, Field thought, I wish I knew myself what I'm trying to do or say. He stepped heavily on the gas, and the car rocketed along the ruts, swaying heavily.

Lane gasped. "I didn't mean to embarrass you into suicide, Sheriff. I'll swear I didn't."

He slowed quickly, took his hands from the wheel, and turned in the seat, allowing the sandy channels to guide the machine.

"I'm not embarrassed." It was suddenly difficult to talk. "I'll be damned, though, if I'm not confused. It isn't as if it were just an ordinary night." He wondered if he should tell her what had happened, what was going to happen to him. "It's just you coming along like this on top of everything else."

He straightened again into a driving position, and the car gathered speed. Talking that way wasn't helping things. It only made them worse, twice as complicated. He hoped he was still a little drunk. That would explain everything. If he wasn't drunk, he thought grimly, he was on the point of making pretty much of a fool of himself.

Shell Springs was cupped deep within an ancient oak grove. It spread in an almost perfect circle of silver, softly polished, taking on a dim radiance from the sky. Here was the mystery of some ageless force deep in the earth sending this clear, cold water sparkling to the surface. There was no sound at night save the unhurried sweep of the overflow into the spillway, a tinkling music of the splash and the heavier drumming as it cascaded over the hyacinth pads and the stumps of rotting cypress.

Field pulled in at the side of the pool and stopped his motor. He searched for cigarettes, lit one for Lane, and held a match to his own. They smoked in silence, for, all of a sudden, there was no longer anything to say. With an almost breathless determination they both refrained from moving, sensing that the slightest shift would bring their shoulders together and dissolve the tense, electric quality of the moment.

"We're going to be in a sure enough fix, Sheriff, if we stay here much longer." The words were no more than a breath, things of fluttering, uncertain wings.

The cigarette ascended in a bright arc and plunged soundlessly into the pool, and Field turned in his seat, feeling Lane move with him until they were close and her head rested lightly in the hollow of his arm.

He held her there, sensitive to her trembling and the sight of something miraculously close to pain in her eyes.

"I never wanted anyone to touch me before, Field. Honestly." Her fingers lightly traced the curve of his jaw, and then the knuckles of her small hand pressed into his mouth. "I wish though"—the complete surrender was shyly given—"I wish that somehow you knew this was going to happen the way I did."

CHAPTER SEVEN

ANN-EVANS, AT FIRST, AND LATER TITUS, UNDERTOOK to teach Field he couldn't tuck a prospective career away in a pocket as he would a baseball, playing with it when the fancy struck him and shoving it out of sight when the game palled.

"You ought to stop sitting around in that Ford of yours at the corner of River and Foster Streets. It doesn't look well, your feet stuck up on one of the doors talking with every colored boy or fish peddler that comes along."

She straightened his tie reprovingly while Field pondered over the fact she had never noticed his habits before.

The hat, of which he was particularly fond, came next.

"For goodness' sake, Fielding Carlisle, stop wearing that outlandish cowboy hat and get something dignified."

Ann-Evans held the unoffending old Stetson between her dainty fingers and dropped it with a shudder on the hatrack seat in the hall.

Once—they were driving home from a dance at the country club—he suggested dropping in at the Palace Lunch for a sandwich and a cold bottle of near beer.

"Why, Field! You don't want to go into such a place."

"Damn it, Ann-Evans," he had exploded, "just because a man's going to run for office, that doesn't mean he can't put the seat of his pants on a lunchroom stool and eat a barbecue with a bottle of Bevo."

Ann-Evans sulked.

In the beginning, on the very day after the meeting at Lute-Mae's, Ann-Evans had taken things in hand.

That afternoon the *Truro Advertiser* had carried the story spread over the front page. Doc Watson, both editor and publisher, didn't care much for Titus Semple. He didn't have to. The *Advertiser* never made any money and probably never would. The best Doc got out of it were printing expenses from a few of the faithful and free meals at the Palace in return for an advertisement. Ads for a barber shop, an independent grocery, and Pigler's meat market were bartered. This, as Watson said, would keep his body together. His soul was his own business, and he wouldn't trade it to Titus Semple.

The news story in the *Advertiser* had been straight reporting, a simple statement of fact that Field's future candidacy for the State Legislature could be taken as a foregone conclusion, considering the source of the report.

On his editorial page, however, Doc really went to work.

The grossness of Titus Semple's shadow prevents our describing it as sinister, since we have always fancied the word to mean something sharp, keen, tempered. We call it evil, though, and in it this day stands Fielding Carlisle, scion of a distinguished Truro pioneer family. Those of us who knew and loved the young man's brilliant father, the late Judge Carlisle, can thank God he is no longer with us to be a party to the shame.

For this newest victim of THE RING, Fielding Carlisle, we have only charity. As a student at the University he might have distinguished himself as he prepared to follow in the footsteps of his father. Instead, he chose to leave the classroom to become the acolyte of a wicked and scoffing charlatan who has made a mockery out of local, county, and state government. Would that on the day young Fielding Carlisle walked into the office of Titus Semple there had been a sign in flaming letters above the door.

"Abandon Hope All Ye Who Enter Here."

As for Semple—we refuse to dignify him with the title of Mr., which he does not deserve, or the badge of sheriff, which he has never earned—his blot is a loathsome thing on the fair state of Florida.

The Editor makes this statement with double confidence. First, in the knowledge that it is true. Secondly, with first-hand information on the assets and financial situation of the paper, we know not even Titus Semple would be such a damn fool as to sue.

Doc Watson liked that final paragraph. For weeks he carried it around, reading from the barber chair to the waiting customers or declaiming from a corner stool in the Palace Lunch.

Ann-Evans hadn't liked it, however.

"Papa says you should sue."

Field had only grinned and patted her leg. His thoughts were not on the Weldon porch this afternoon. He was remembering the still of the night before, the smothering warmth of a girl's mouth, and the dusky coloring of a face.

"Let papa sue him then, sugar," was all he could say.

"Papa thinks it's wonderful for you and that you're as good as elected right now. He said so at lunch when he brought the *Advertiser* home. He thinks, though, we ought to do some entertaining to interest the nice people in you."

"Uh-huh." Absently. He wondered what the nice people would say if they knew about Lute-Mae's.

Ann-Evans held her temper with an effort. She didn't like this fencing. Field was being difficult, difficult and different. He should have come to her excited, bubbling over with wild, foolish plans for the both of them. She pouted prettily; practice before a mirror had taught her this was a particularly appealing gesture.

"I don't think you should have waited to let me hear about

everything through that scandal paper of filthy Doc Watson. Couldn't you have told me, us, about it last night?"

Last night, Field thought. It wasn't only last night, and yet, here he was with a hell of a hangover and the feeling that he had done something shameful, kicked a kitten or maybe slapped a baby. The sensation was still acute, so it must have happened last night.

"Papa said he hoped you would be able to break the lease the Pennemers have on your house and move back to Flamingo Road where you belong."

Ann-Evans bit at her lip. If he doesn't say something now, I'm going to scream.

"I don't know, honey. I guess, maybe, the Pennemers wouldn't be crazy to upset everything and find another place."

"You could ask, couldn't you?"

Field knew she was wondering if the deliberate plural, "we ought to do some entertaining," had escaped him. He knew, also, that it was up to him to say something. The trouble was, he didn't know what to tell her. You couldn't explain to Ann-Evans: "Honey, we'll get married right away, but last night I took a girl, and she was flame and the wind and deep, hot earth." That wouldn't make any sense, and she wouldn't understand. You could say: "Honey, Last night I laid a little waitress from The Eagle Café. I'm sorry about it. I was drunk." Ann-Evans would make a scene: she'd cry, and there'd be weeks of making up, but she'd understand. Only, what you said would be a lie, and, probably, you wouldn't be able to say it after all.

"I guess"—he took the words as they came—"there isn't much sense in worrying about the Pennemers. A house wouldn't be any good to me now, and after the election"—this was the word—"we will most likely be in Tallahassee a lot, during the session, anyhow."

"Oh, Field honey." Ann-Evans was trembling. "I thought"—she was close to tears and knew it—"I thought maybe we had been going together for so long you were too used to me." She was a fool to talk this way and realized it.

Field's arms were around her. "I guess I've always loved you, Ann-Evans; ever since the days I used to chase you home from school."

"And shoot chinaberries at me from that tree on Locust Avenue."

"And take you to the school play every year."

"And kiss me on the top deck of the excursion boat when we came back from the Sunday-school picnic?"

"Uh-huh."

Even as he held her, brushing the soft, fair hair from her eyes and bending to kiss a mouth that quivered, he was thinking: this is the way it had to be. Ann-Evans Weldon would be good for him.

She was laughing now, a quick, nervous sound. "I don't guess"—this a little ruefully—"anyone is going to be much surprised over our engagement, and that's half the fun of getting engaged."

"Surprised? Sugar, people have probably been wondering for years why your old man hasn't taken down his shotgun and come after me."

"Field!"

Ann-Evans had to plan things. The bridesmaids, who they'd invite. Where they'd go. The date, the hour, the church: those things she ticked off rapturously, so engrossed in them she didn't notice that Field was only half listening.

"But, sugar"—the objection was mild—"I'm not near elected yet."

"Poof! Papa says anyone Titus Semple backs is as good as in."

Privately, Field had always considered papa to be a damn fool. He still thought so even though old man Weldon was right about Titus.

"Well, maybe." He was wondering desperately how he could get away before Mr. Weldon came home. "I've got to see Sheriff Titus this evening." He tried to make it sound casual.

"But, Field." She was upset. "This first night. I mean, with everything happening all at once, surely you'll be here for supper?"

"I sure wish I could, but Sheriff Titus said it was important." He wondered how often in the future he was to use the excuse.

"Oh, Field." Ann-Evans wasn't really protesting now. She was thinking. I'll call up Mabel Prettymann first, the little bitch, then Norma Haines, Fern Rodgers, maybe Martha-Jean. This will just about kill Mabel. "You ought to stay, Field. Papa will think it is awfully funny if you don't."

She walked out to the car with him, both arms linked in his, and then stood on the curb while he climbed into the Ford.

"Weedon's have a new blue Packard roadster in their show-room. We'd get to go Tallahassee better in that, Mr. Carlisle."

He winked at her from behind the wheel. "Andrew Jackson did right fine on a mule, Miss Ann-Evans."

For a moment he felt as he always had about her. Slim, lovely, and still flushed with the excitement of the day, she shamed him. He wanted to get out of the car, sit on the running board, hold her hand, and tell her he was, as she had always said, just as crazy as a cooter. A girl walked out of a pine flat one night. That's all there was to it. Instead, he drove away, leaving her to wave after him until he turned the corner.

He was halfway on the road to Apulca before he realized how late it was. If he was going to do the thing he knew he must, he'd have to race like hell back to Truro.

It's funny, he thought, as he walked into the Eagle an hour later, that something like this could begin and end right here in the same place without anyone's knowing what had happened.

He was aware that Pete Ladas was watching from the cash register counter when Lane came to take his order—Pete with the toothpick in his mouth and the melancholy expression of a crocodile on his face. He sensed, also, a difference in the attitude of several men as he passed their tables with a nod of good evening. One or two were elaborately indifferent, but the others seemed anxious to catch his eye and were overly boisterous in their greeting. Truro, he thought, will begin to break down now, and we'll see whose gang is whose. Good or bad, the piece in the *Advertiser* had started things. He wondered where Doc Watson had picked up the story and decided Titus must have circulated it.

Lane placed the menu before him with a mock flourish.

"Good evenin', Guv'nah, suh." Her words rolled with a heavy coating of accent. "Y'all take yo' juelip heah, suh, oh en th' gol' rahm."

He studied the bill of fare seriously. "I'll take a year's subscription to the *Advertiser*, miss."

"We fraish out o' *Advahtaser*, suh, but we got some naice new state senatah."

He looked up at her then, and they both smiled.

"How're you, Sheriff?"

"Not very hungry."

She straightened a fork beside his plate. "That's good, considering where you are."

Lane brought his soup and then a covered plate of hot rolls.

"I feel sort of funny having you wait on me this way."

Her eyes were bright. "I like it. I wondered about it a little, too. I still like it."

"Can I see you later?"

"Ten o'clock every night Mr. Lincoln comes around and frees the slaves."

"I'll meet you then."

They drove out over the Mill Road, past the sagging and confused ruins of the old plant from where, years ago, the stream of yellow, pungent pine boards flowed endlessly to the steamboat landing. The stands of the great brown trees had been bitten into without thought, and now the country was barren, stump-bound, and seared by fires that seemed to spring from the sun itself to ravish the new growth.

As though the way needed explanation, Field said: "It gets better after awhile. This part of the country isn't in the tourist books."

"I was wondering." She leaned back in the corner of the seat, head up, watching the moon as it appeared to slice through ragged pennants of clouds. "Did you know last night you were going to be famous today?"

"Am I?"

"In a nasty sort of a way." She turned a little until, with chin resting on shoulder, she could watch him. "Opinion around the Eagle ever since noon has been divided. One side said you were a smart bastard. The other insisted you were a damn smart bastard. There may have been other descriptions, but I didn't happen to hear them between the blueplate specials on the businessman's lunch."

His mouth crinkled. It hadn't occurred to him that people might think he had connived, planned, and sweetened Titus Semple until the Sheriff did something for him. If they did, it was funny since half the time he hadn't even been civil.

"Do you think you'll be any good at it; the job I mean?"

The obviousness of the question, its simplicity, startled him.

"Why"—he was puzzled—"I never thought about it, Lane." He hadn't and suddenly wondered why. "I'll swear"—it was a sheepish admission—"but it never occurred to me to ask myself. Maybe I just won't be worth a damn to anyone at Tallahassee. Come to think of it. I don't have any special qualification for the Legislature, and that is what runs the state. I never looked at it as a job, only sort of a game. If you won you were elected, and if you lost you weren't." He whistled speculatively. "It's upsetting to think of it any other way."

Off the road the banks ridged high beside the river. Field ran the car through the thin scrub and parked where they could look down upon the stream, moving without sound between tangled banks where moss-burdened trees bent like old men to dip their beards in the water. Here was a silence within silence, primitive and impenetrable.

Lane slid across the narrow seat, thinking as she did of the unfamiliar emotion which this man aroused in her. He was, she mused, neither handsomer nor kinder than other men she had known, and yet she liked to bury her face in the roughness of his coat, feel the strength of his arms, listen to the sound of his voice. There was something in just the man-smell of him which enveloped her, reducing the defenses she had once thought so necessary and making her want to cry his name. Snuggling into the curve of his arm she waited. He stirred restlessly.

"I—I'm going to be married, Lane."

Later she could understand. There hadn't been any other way to say it.

"I thought"—his speech came with agonizing slowness—"somehow I could tell you better this way."

The life which had drained from her fought to return. She was glad he was unable to see what she knew must be in her eyes.

"You knew last night. I mean, you knew you were going to get married."

"Yes, I guess I did. Anyhow, I was pretty certain. Even now"—he turned upon her fiercely—"I'm not sure about anything. I'm doing what I think I ought to do. It's got to be right, it's so God-damned hard."

She smiled a little in the darkness then, and upon this smile came the astonishing realization that she wasn't acting at all the way she should. A carnival kid should snarl of outrage, weep, and, maybe, even curse. Instead, a feeling almost of peace was upon her. The complications, the inescapable involvement which must have followed last night, had miraculously been removed.

"I'm almost glad." She felt him grow tense with surprise. "That sounds funny, doesn't it, Field? It sounds funny to me when I say it. Now we won't have to watch anything die, and that is what we would have had to do. The waitress at the Eagle and Fielding Carlisle. Even the waitress at the Eagle and the Deputy Sheriff couldn't have lasted, could it? Give me a cigarette, will you?"

She smoked heavily, drawing so deeply that the fire hurried down the paper.

"I don't think I'll ever get over you, Field. I don't want to. Maybe I'm a slut at heart. I don't think so, though, because I never felt this way about anyone before."

She carefully dropped the cigarette butt to the floor board and ground it beneath her toe. When she straightened up and turned, her eyes were luminous, her features serene.

"Now," she said, "you can drive me home or take me here. God help me, that's the way I feel about you."

Langworthy's story in the following morning was a masterpiece of effrontery. Reading it, Field grinned. Things were beginning to take shape. Langworthy was Semple's man. The line: "The stimulating effect upon a decaying Legislature of youthful, vigorous blood such as is represented by Fielding Carlisle." That proved it. As the weeks wore on he was to see the pattern form.

There were polite notes from the Johnson Abernathys, the Norton Pritchards, Bakers, and Duvals, inviting him and Ann-Evans to dinner. The public announcement of their engagement had precipitated a shower of small social affairs for them both. These things, the parties and dances, would have naturally followed the betrothal of any local young couple who had lived their lives, gone to school, and grown up in Truro. The invitations from such families as the Abernathys and Pritchards, however, were, Field realized, only a polite movement to get into line. The notion that the prodding came from Titus Semple, rocking in his chair at the Palmer House, cast the design in a fantastic and macabre light.

In contrast to the demands made upon him by Ann-Evans, who was forever turning up with suggestions that they go here or there, do this and that, turn the Pennemers out of the Carlisle home on Flamingo Road, Titus asked little.

"Nice afternoon for a ride out into the country, bub." Titus after summoning him to the Palmer House porch, would squint at the sky and then heave himself out of his chair.

They rode over dusty country roads, stopping at crosspath general stores. Together, in Semple's car, they cut across flat lands to halt at a weather-beaten farm. For everyone, those of the loungers who gathered around the car at the crossroads, the solitary Cracker working a stubbled patch, Titus had a word of news, a bit of information, or casual talk of weather, taxes, the cussedness of a dry season. Now and then he would produce a bottle for a drink. Never, though, was there a word of politics.

"Meet Fielding Carlisle. Friend of mine."

Beyond this brief introduction the Sheriff didn't venture.

"You take a Cracker now, bub." They were driving back from Bancroft. "They're likely to be as skittery as a spring rabbit and as independent as a bull alligator in its den; depends on how you approach them. The way things are, it ain't really necessary for them to do more than to get your name. The time comes for votin', an' they'll say: 'Oh, Fielding Carlisle. That's Sheriff Semple's friend, young fellow we had a drink with or stopped to pass the time of day. He must be all right, or the Sheriff surer than hell wouldn't be ridin' around with him.'"

In such fashion did the two of them cover the district, and Field's brain became a confused jumble of names, faces, and villages, the existence of which he had never known before.

When he protested one day over the roads they were forced to travel, Semple cut him short.

"Be glad you ain't running for office in the North, bub. Up there you got to go around kissin' babies, dirty ones at that. This way your ass get tired but in a different way."

From these excursions and the eternal planning of Ann-Evans, Field slipped away upon occasion to meet Lane Ballou. He had hesitated at first because he couldn't rid himself of the feeling he was taking advantage of her. When they drove it was always to the river ridge. There he knew they both would remember the night he had told her he was going to marry Ann-Evans Weldon.

"You don't want me to forget how things are, do you, Field?"

"I don't know, Lane. Maybe that's it. In the beginning I had the idea of coming here only so you would remember and call it off if you wanted to."

Sometimes they would put the top of the Ford down, crawl into the back seat, and lie there, looking up through the matted trees to where the stars were sprinkled.

"I can't help it, Field." She crept into his arms. "It's just the way things are."

One night—she had met him near her rooming house on River Street after the Eagle had closed, and they had driven to the ridge—they lay in the rear of the car.

"Who's Lute-Mae Sanders?" Lane asked the question idly, and Field sat up so quickly she almost tumbled to the floor.

"What made you ask that?"

"Lord, Governor"—she regarded him with surprise—"you don't have to flang a girl off such a way. I only asked who a woman by the name of Lute-Mae Sanders was."

"Why do you want to know?" He was still startled.

"All right"—Lane shrugged her shoulders—"if that's the way to get a question answered. I was coming out of Sutton's this noon when a big handsome woman with an armful of packages slipped on the sidewalk. I helped her up and sort of let her lean on me to her car. I thought maybe her ankle was twisted and asked her if she wanted me to drive her home. She gave me the funniest look and said. 'Sugar, don't you know I'm Lute-Mae Sanders?' So, I said no." Lane giggled. "This is getting to be one of these 'I said and she said' stories. Then she said, 'Sugar, you sure wouldn't want to be seen driving me home.' I said why not, and she said because if I did I was a God-damned fool and I didn't look like one. Now, who is Lute-Mae Sanders?"

Field roared with laughter. The picture of Lute-Mae flat on the sidewalk in front of Sutton's and Lane Ballou offering to take her home was too much.

"All right." Lane waited until he had quieted. "I still want to know."

He told her then. "You've been in Truro all these months and never heard of Lute-Mae?"

Lane snickered. "We don't have such talk on the table d'hôte." She sobered. "She looked nice, though. Human and, maybe, even kind. I don't know. I only knew that I liked her."

She lay back in his arms, her mouth close to his chin.

"Field?"

"Mmmm?"

"Field, you won't get into any trouble slipping out with me this way?"

"I don't think so, honey. Sometimes, though, I don't care. I've got to have you like this once in awhile. I've got to be able to talk to you; it's like a cool wind off the river on a hot day. It's getting so every time Ann-Evans opens her mouth I expect the words to come out dressed in ruffled organdie."

CHAPTER EIGHT

PETER LADAS DROOPED AGAINST THE EAGLE'S CIGAR counter and rolled his eyes with the expression of an embarrassed hound. There was no heart in him for what he was doing, and the jerky course of a toothpick from one corner of his mouth to the other betrayed his nervousness. He wondered, as he frequently did, why everything seems to happen to the Greeks.

"But I don't understand." Lane was tired. Her feet were

sore from pounding between kitchen and dining room throughout the lunch hour which had just ended. "It doesn't make any sense, Mr. Ladas. You could see for yourself how busy we were. If you let me go you'll only have to get another girl." Lifting a weary hand she pushed a damp tendril of hair from her forehead.

Peter's shoulders raised sympathetically. "It ain't such a good job, Lane." He made a deprecating sound with his lips. "Almost any job wouldn't be worse. The salary ain't good, an' the tips none too big. When you come to the meals you get, well"—his features creased into a companionable grimace—"even I can't stand the food sometimes, and I own the damn place. A girl like you can probably find somethin' better without even half trying."

A helpless desperation clawed at her. Suddenly she was afraid, frightened because these pitiful hours of drudgery were to be taken from her.

"I don't understand why?" Nausea was in her throat at the spectacle of her own pleading.

"It's like I say, Lane. I got to let some of the help go. You bein' the newest, well, you can see how it is."

She shook her head. "No, I don't see how it is, but if you say I'm through, then, I guess I'm through."

Ladas nodded gratefully. "You're all right, Lane. Lots of girls would have cried an' carried on terrible."

"I don't cry, Peter."

"That's good." He fumbled with a crumpled wad of bills, hesitated, and then counted off twenty dollars. "This is sort of for no advance notice."

She took it without eagerness and then grinned. "I'll lay you twenty dollars," she said crisply, "that you won't tell me why I am being fired."

Peter's eyes sparkled. The idea appealed to him. Then he shook his head.

"I'd sure like to take you up on that," he said honestly.

At a table in the back of the room, Annabelle was sopping at a pool of gravy with a piece of bread. She looked up from her plate as Lane sat down.

"What's the matter, sugar? I saw you up there with Peter. Somethin' wrong?"

"I'm fired."

Annabelle's mouth, which was open to receive the dripping bread, stayed that way, and the morsel dropped to the table.

"Why, the old dago stinker," she said finally.

93

"No"—Lane was thoughtful—"I don't think he wanted to do it."

"Didn't want to do it." Annabelle was scornful. "If he didn't want to do it, then why did he?"

"I wish I knew." Lane rose from the chair. "I think I'll take a walk."

"Now, you listen, sugar." Annabelle was at her side. "Don't you worry. We got a room an' a few dollars till you find somethin' else. I can even snitch some food to bring home to you." She brightened. "Tonight I'll begin askin' my regular customers about another job for you. Don't you stew about it. Go on out now an' buy yourself a cold dope an' go to a movie." She patted Lane briskly on the shoulder.

River Street was again alien. Lane felt it as she walked through the front door of the Eagle to the sidewalk. Yesterday, this morning, Truro was a friendly place. When she had gone to work, people had nodded to her or called hello. Now they all seemed to be looking the other way. She knew this was a trick of her imagination, but the illusion persisted. It was as though all of Truro had heard she was out of a job, nearly broke; a carnival kid again about to go on the town. Truro was turning its back for fear she would ask for something.

At the Rexall store she perched on a high stool at the fountain.

"Give me a dope with a little lime, Roy. Lots of ice."

The sallow youth with his thin, blond hair slicked back into a shiny pompadour flipped a glass into the air, caught it expertly, and splashed sirup into the bottom.

"You off early, Lane?"

"Yep." The coke was good and pleasantly tart. She finished it and nibbled pensively on a piece of ice.

"Hot, ain't it?"

"Yep." She was ashamed of herself then. Roy was only trying to be friendly.

"If I had the afternoon off"—the boy was wistful—"I'd take the bus out to Shell Springs an' go for a swim."

"Maybe that's what I'll do." She swung around on the stool. "I'm looking for a job, Roy. Know anybody that wants a girl?"

There was real concern in his quick frown. "Get fired from the Eagle?"

"In a way." It seemed better not to put it into those words. "Ladas is letting some of the help go."

"Well, gee, Lane that's too bad." His forehead rippled with

94

concentration. "I'll swear, right off I don't know of anything, but I'll keep it in mind."

On the sidewalk again she paused, looking up and then down River Street. Before it had always seemed to be a lazy sort of thoroughfare with people moving without haste or much purpose. Now there was a disheartening bustle about the street. Everyone had something to do and wanted to prove it.

Walking slowly toward the south end of town, she caught half a dozen friendly smiles or a shouted, "Hi, Lane." There was a warm, human quality to the greetings, and her mood softened beneath them. She knew a lot of people in Truro. It wouldn't be difficult to find another job once they heard about her being out of work. She was restless, though, filled with the uneasiness of a cat in strange quarters. I guess, she thought, I've forgotten how to be a bum.

With no purpose other than to keep moving, she sauntered the length of River Street to Laurel Avenue and then down to the bank of the brown flood moving so irresistibly through the channel it had been cutting for centuries. A little colored boy, fishing from the shore, ducked his head as she approached and then studied the cork on the end of his line with fierce concentration.

Lane took a seat a few feet away and watched silently as the float bobbed and nodded purposelessly. Finally she picked up a small shell and tossed it. The boy's head jerked quickly at the tiny splash, and he followed the concentric circles with interest.

"Fishing any good?"

The boy smiled sheepishly. "No'm, but hit ain' tiahrin' eithah."

She leaned back on her elbows and gazed at the great white clouds, rolling like loosely packed cotton bales in the sky. The emptiness in the pit of her stomach, the almost unbearable tightness around her chest were being swept away. Here by the river there was a primitive gentleness which made such things as jobs, a place to live, and the ordinary necessities of life seem unimportant. The boy on the bank, she thought, had worked out his own scheme. Even if the fish didn't bite, he wasn't wearing himself out trying for them.

In her handbag she found a crumpled package of cigarettes and beside it the folded bills Ladas had given her. The sight of the money brought a scornful smile to her lips.

You're being a damn fool, she accused herself. You never had twenty dollars at one time in your life before and got along all right. Now, because you're out of a job you want to complain about it to the world.

She lit a cigarette and felt better. She'd get another job. Field. No, she wouldn't ask Field. That was too much like crying to teacher, and, besides, Field had enough to worry about.

She ate that night at the Palace Lunch. For awhile she debated going to the Eagle and then decided against it. The Palace was crowded, mostly by men in grimy overalls or work clothes. They stared at her curiously as she took a stool and then turned again to the food before them or picked their teeth, frowning at their task and spitting particles of food from the corners of their mouths. Lane felt almost cheerful again. This was like the carnival days. She could shut her eyes and see a string of Palace Lunches stretching from Brunswick, Georgia, to Tampa, Florida. Coyne's show had played them all.

River Street looked different at night. She hadn't seen much of it after dark save through the window of the Eagle. Walking slowly, she paused to look in the store windows, examine the alligator handbags and loose skins before Wallace's novelty store, and finally bought a bag of buttered popcorn from the stand outside the Crystal Theater. She popped the swollen kernels into her mouth as she passed along the street and cocked a friendly and impudent eye at those she passed. If I keep this up, she thought, someone will take me for a tourist and try and sell me a lot. Either that or pick me up for a chippy.

Out past Bay Street the way was less cheerful, and she came suddenly upon the yard district with its second hand clothing stores, dimly lighted poolrooms, flyblown candy and drugstores. Once, as she passed a lunchroom, a group of men whistled softly, and she heard the scrape of a foot on the pavement. She hurried a little then and crossed to the other side of the street at the next corner.

It's funny, she thought, that foot scraping. She'd even forgotten now who told her about it, but she knew that was the way a Negro called to a colored girl. He'd just scrape his foot, and if she was in the business she'd turn around or loiter at the curb until he came to pick her up.

The houses and buildings in the district were of a pattern, unpainted and with the gray of neglected age upon them. She knew where she was. This was the cat-house neighborhood. A young mulatto girl, a red print dress clinging to her hips and full breasts, passed her. She wore no stockings, and the absurd high-heeled shoes were over at the side. She looked at Lane and made a mouth of disdain.

"Whaat girl wak on othah side o' th' stree'."

Lane wondered whether she looked as though she was street-walking and then decided the only reason any girl would be out alone here was for a man.

The district didn't frighten her, but she turned around and retraced her steps. The little room shared with Annabelle was a cozy sanctuary, and she wanted, now, to be in it with the door securely shut behind her.

Annabelle was at the eternal creaming of her face when she entered.

"My goodness, I've been wonderin' what happened to you. Have a date?"

Lane tossed her bag on the bed and shook her head. "No, just walking."

Annabelle regarded her with astonishment. "Where is there to walk to?"

"Oh, just here and there. Didn't find out anything about a job for me, did you?"

"No, but I sure told old stink-foot Ladas a thing or two." She turned indignantly. "Do you know what he said? He said if I wasn't so dumb it might have been me. What do you know about that?"

Lane undressed, hanging her clothing carefully over a chair. It might have to last for a long time. She was glad, though, she had bought that new dress at Carver's sale on Saturday. She'd wear it when she went looking for a job tomorrow.

"No one came in tonight? I mean, you didn't happen to see Field?" She tried to express only the most random interest.

"Say"—Annabelle patted her chin briskly with greasy fingers—"I hope you aren't makin' a fool of yourself over Fielding Carlisle. I know he's good-lookin' an' all, but, sugar, the only thing you'll get from him will be a bellyache that'll last nine months. Hey!" Her eyes widened in thought. "You don't suppose that's the reason Ladas fired you?"

Lane paused in the act of dropping a slipper to the floor.

"What in the world are you talking about?"

Annabelle popped her tongue against the roof of her mouth emphatically.

"I'll bet it is. If you been playin' around with him, now that he's gettin' married maybe he figured to have Ladas fire you, an' then if you couldn't get another job you'd most likely go up to Jacksonville or someplace for work. He'd be sure you wouldn't be around to cause any trouble."

Lane placed her shoes carefully beneath the bed. "You're crazy. Field wouldn't do that. Anyhow, there isn't anything between Field and me. He's just been a good friend."

Annabelle sniffed. Plainly she wasn't satisfied.

Lane climbed into bed and turned her face to the window. Annabelle's remark gnawed at her, returning again and again although she dismissed it repeatedly. Field wouldn't do anything like that. He didn't have to. He knew that. She closed her eyes, and the apologetic face of Peter Ladas swam before them. That was the strangest thing of all. If Ladas had merely fired her, she could have understood. To discharge her, though, with such elaborate explanations didn't make any sense.

During the following week the uneasiness within her grew. It wasn't only that she couldn't find work, although she systematically canvassed River Street on both sides from Laurel to Canal; it was the furtive evasiveness she met. Once, at Hardy's Market and again at Marker's candy store she had the feeling both Hardy and Marker were on the point of telling her something and then decided against it.

Field, she read in the *Journal*, was on "a business trip" in Jacksonville. She wanted desperately to talk with him, not to ask for help, but just to talk, to sit quietly and feel him beside her. There was a column, also in the *Journal*, about Ann-Evans Weldon, who had been given a shower in anticipation of the forthcoming wedding. Lane read this carefully. Since that first night Field had never mentioned the wedding. It was almost as though it was something which didn't concern either of them. Now, she was startled to learn the date was set for next month. She put the paper away. I guess, she thought, every girl must make a fool of herself at one time or another. This must be my time.

On Friday she found a job at Carver's.

"You understand," Mr. Carver told her, "this is only temporary. If everything works out all right, maybe we'll be able to keep you on."

On Saturday she was fired.

"Business," Carver smirked helplessly, "isn't so good. You remember I said in the beginning it might only be temporary."

She took six dollars for the two days' work and snapped it in her bag. Hot, stinging tears were in her eyes. I wish I could cry, she thought. God damn it, can't they see they're kicking me and it hurts.

Fighting the temptation to return to her room, she went over to the *Journal* office and paid for a small advertisement in the Situation-Wanted section. Counting her money carefully, she walked down a block to the *Advertiser*. I might just as well, she decided, try everything.

Doc Watson, poring over a freshly pulled galley at the scarred counter, watched her interestedly as she carefully wrote out an ad on one of the yellowed blanks.

"By God," he said admiringly, "I haven't seen anyone do that in this office for years. You really mean you're going to pay for it? Don't want to swap me something?"

Lane smiled wanly. "How much would that be?"

Doc read the penciled lines quickly and then pushed back the green eyeshade he was wearing.

"You know," he said candidly, "you'd be better off spending money with the *Journal*. I don't think it'll do much good in the *Advertiser*." He chuckled happily. "This is the last free press in the county. It's so free I have to give it away."

Lane held a bill out to him.

Doc considered her keenly and then leaned forward. "Say" —he whistled softly—"aren't you the girl from the Eagle?"

Lane stiffened, and the hand holding the money sank slowly to the counter. Why should he say, "the girl from the Eagle"; how should he know who she was anyway?

"Why, yes," she answered slowly, "yes, I used to work at the Eagle."

"So"—Doc clucked faintly—"so you're the girl. Well, what do you know about that?" He pushed at her hand with the dollar in it. "Keep your money, miss. I'll run the ad free for you, even put it in a box on the front page if you'll let me. It won't do you any good, though, I'm thinking."

Lane's amazement mounted. "What are you talking about?"

"Why, miss"—Doc hunched his spare shoulders toward her —"Ballou, that's the name, isn't it? Well, Miss Ballou, I guess right now you're talking to the only person in Truro who'd give you a job, and I haven't got one." He shuffled to the side of the low partition and swung open a sagging gate. "Come on inside here and sit down." He dusted off a chair and when she was seated hopped on the corner of a littered desk. "Now," he continued, his eyes snapping, "what in the world could a little thing like you do to Sheriff Semple?"

"I don't know what you mean, honestly I don't." An apprehensive chill was upon her, though. The same disquieting sensation she had experienced the first time Titus Semple spoke to her.

99

Doc watched her guardedly, and then—it must have been the open bewilderment on her face—he frowned and tapped thoughtfully at his front teeth with a thumbnail.

"Now, what do you know about that? I believe you. I'll swear I really believe you don't know."

"Please"—Lane bent forward—"tell me what you are talking about."

Doc sucked at a frayed copy pencil for a moment. "I don't know myself, Miss Ballou. All I know is if Titus Semple doesn't want a girl like you to work in Truro she isn't going to work. What I'd like to know is why."

"You mean he's sort of passed the word around, and now no one will give me a job. Is that why everyone has acted so funny, almost as if they wanted to tell me something and didn't dare?"

"That's about it."

Amazement and then a slow, smoldering fury possessed her. It was because of Field. She could understand now. By herself she was unimportant to Titus Semple; but somehow he had learned she and Field were seeing each other, and a carnival kid, a waitress from the Eagle, wasn't good for a man who was going to the Legislature.

Doc Watson, watching her, nodded. "You know what it's all about now, don't you?"

"Yes, I guess I do."

"And you're not going to tell me?"

"No."

He sighed unhappily. "What the hell's the good of running a newspaper," he complained, "if people won't tell you anything?" His nostrils twitched. "I'll trade you a year's, make it five years' subscription if you'll tell me."

Lane shook her head. It's curious, she thought, but I'm not afraid any longer. There had been an obscure terror haunting her throughout the week, the helpless feeling that no one was interested whether she lived and worked or dragged down an alley to die like a stray cat. It was grimly humorous to find that too many persons cared.

Doc Watson watched her eagerly, almost as if he hoped to read the answer to his question on her face.

"I'd sure like to know"—he was plaintive—"what a little thing like you could do to rile Titus Semple. He wasn't after you, was he?"

Lane had to laugh then. The notion of Semple in hot pursuit of her was really funny.

"No. It wasn't anything like that. I guess, maybe, he doesn't care for the way I do my hair." She rose. "Thanks for what you told me. It sort of straightens everything out. I guess there wouldn't be much point in putting an ad in your paper the way things are."

Doc waved the idea aside. "I'll run it, anyhow, on the house. If you ever change your mind about telling why Titus is after you, perhaps you'll come to me first."

"I promise." She walked thoughtfully from the moldy office. Things, she decided, needed thinking about.

The warm afternoon sun was a blanket over the Palmer House porch. Titus, deep in his sagging wicker chair, bowed his head and felt the heat flow through him. This was the way he liked to sit, eyes shut, ears attuned to the movement and traffic on River Street. He knew now, without looking, that someone was seated on the railing before him, someone who had walked across the porch. He felt the presence and knew whoever it was was staring at him and that there was both hate and fear in the scrutiny. It amused him to keep his head down and speculate on the visitor's identity.

"I know you're not asleep. You don't have to pretend you are."

The Sheriff's eyes fluttered open, his head raised almost imperceptibly.

"How you, Miss Ballou?" The words were pitched only above a whisper, but there was no drowsiness in Semple's glance. It darted over her with the rapidity of summer heat lighting.

"Did you have me fired from the Eagle?" With an effort Lane kept her body relaxed. She leaned her back against the square pillar, one foot dangled negligently. There was a half-smile of tolerant understanding on her mouth. She would not come to Titus tightly strung and furious. That was the way he would want her. She sensed this.

"Well, now"—Titus played with one of the pearl buttons on his shirt—"there wasn't anything really personal in it, you understand."

"It's personal to me if I don't eat or have a place to sleep."

Titus nodded approvingly. "Yep, I guess you might look at it that way." He sighed windily. "A hell of a lot of people take a mighty personal interest in such things."

"I'm not going to run, Sheriff Semple."

There was a lenient, understanding quality about the expression which pricked at Semple's lips. His head wavered with a suggestion of accord.

"That's what I was afraid of, Miss Ballou."

"I'm not going to run, and I'm not going to cry to Field."

Titus's lips pursed into a rosette. "No," he agreed finally, "I didn't expect you to do either."

Lane battled a desire to raise her voice. She wanted to jolt Semple out of his apathy, though.

"You're a damned fool, Sheriff Semple."

He chuckled agreeably. "You know," he mused, "I was thinkin' the same thing just before you come up here. I was saying to myself, Titus maybe you're workin' yourself right out on a limb. I said, Titus, if Field Carlisle is really gone crazy about a little girl at the Eagle, then tryin' to starve her out of town is about the worst thing you could do. You see"—he squinted at her—"I wasn't sure how bad it was with Field. You comin' here tells me."

"I would have told you if you had asked me. You didn't have to get me fired and then blacklisted, if that's what you call it. I don't mean anything to Field Carlisle, not anything that would ever bother him."

The Sheriff's eyes faded with hypocritical sadness. "That's sure too bad, Miss Ballou. The only thing is, I got the feelin' you could get yourself pretty upset about Field. One of these days trouble would come from that."

He shifted heavily in his chair, swinging it around until the sunlight was behind him and he could look past Lane and up River Street.

"You see, Miss Ballou, Field Carlisle is goin' to the State Senate. One of these days, when he's ready, he's goin' to be governor. Things like that take a lot of watchin'. It's sort of the way you make a good stew. You just can't put a pot on an' let it boil. It needs to be nursed along."

He leaned back in the chair and frowned reminiscently.

"Once," he continued conversationally, "when I was a young fella I had a watchman's job in one of the river warehouses. The place was full of rats, an' once when I went to sleep one of them started to chew on my big toe. After that I went around and stopped up all the rat holes. Long as I kept the holes plugged I never had nothin' to worry about."

Lane was astonished at the violent quality of the rage which swept her like a physical blow. She had asked for so little in Truro: a job, a room, a sense of permanence; some small thing to hold on to.

"This is one that is going to stay out, Sheriff Semple."

Titus appeared not to have heard her. "Sometimes," he added to the story, "sometimes I'd plug up a hole only the rat wouldn't be in it. He'd be scamperin' around the warehouse. There wasn't much for me to do but wait until it come back an' then club it to death."

"I won't be run out of town this way. I haven't done anything." She realized it was a losing fight, talking with a man who was as unemotional as a moccasin, but her anger forced the words.

"Why, Miss Ballou." Titus was pained. "Nobody said anything about you bein' run out of town." He leaned forward, a confidential movement. "You see, Field is in Jacksonville; probably be there for a couple of weeks. Now, you take towns on down farther south, St. Augustine, Daytona, even Miami. There's plenty of jobs for a girl like you. Likely enough you could be packed up by tomorrow mornin' an' catch a train over to the junction."

Lane rose from the railing, brushed lightly at her skirt, and clutched fiercely at her handbag for fear the trembling of her hands would betray her.

"I'm not going to go, Sheriff Semple. I've been booted around for too long. I want to stay in Truro; I've got no place else to go." She tried desperately to batter against Semple's phlegmatic resistance. "I'm not going to go, do you hear?" She was breathless.

Semple's eyes were closed. His chest heaved with a sigh. "I'd sure advise you to, Miss Ballou. I sure enough would."

A formless dread followed her from the Palmer House porch and came pattering behind as she walked up River Street. It was something so real she could feel its presence. In her mouth was the warm, sweet taste of blood as she bit upon her lip to keep from screaming.

CHAPTER NINE

THE COUNTY FARM TRUCK JOUNCED AND CLATTERED through the narrow gateway, and the driver leaned from his cab to yell at an overalled guard.

"Eighteen, Lonnie."

The man studied a slip of paper in his hand and then nodded. "Eighteen, right."

With a protesting roar the vehicle shot across the bare, sun-baked compound and reared to a halt before one of the low, whitewashed buildings encircled by a high fence.

"Home in time for tea, ladies." The beefy, not unpleasant face of the youth was creased in an impish grin as he called over his shoulder to the two rows of girls seated on long benches lining each side of the truck. There were a couple of numbers there, he thought, who would do all right if he could get the chance.

Silently, one by one, the passengers dropped from the tail of the body to the ground and formed into a shambling double line. Their shapeless, maggot-gray dresses hung upon them loosely, and large, sweat-dampened patches showed darkly from underarms to waists. As they moved forward heavy shoes stirred a swirling cloud of dust rising thickly to choke them, but they made no movement to escape it. Their heads were bent in attitudes of infinite weariness, their eyes lusterless, and the dust quickly formed a brown coating on moist faces.

At the side of the building a heavy stream of clear water raced from a standpipe through a V-shaped trough. Here the line broke its indifferent order as the girls relaxed for the first time and grabbed eagerly for the half-dozen cakes of yellow laundry soap spaced along a shelf.

Lane rested her hands, palms down, in the water and allowed it to rush over swollen wrists.

"God, I sure hope I don't get no more lettuce tomorrow." The girl beside her rolled the cotton sleeves of her dress above the elbows and straightened her back with a groan.

Lane smiled faintly. "It sort of ruins you for salad, doesn't it?"

"I'll never eat another piece of lettuce as long as I live." She rubbed the acrid-smelling soap up and down her arms, lathered her hands, and then passed the cake to Lane. "Your bath, Madame." She was a slim blonde with a pert cast to her eyes, and when she smiled the film of dirt on her face cracked. "Maybe I'll get the laundry tomorrow or the kitchen. I sure God can't stand another day of bendin' over those lettuce rows." She transferred the suds from hands to face, working them into a foam the color of the froth on a chocolate soda.

Lane opened the single button at the yoke of her dress and turned the corners inward at the neck. With cupped hands she splashed the soapy water over face and throat and then rinsed from the clear stream. She was lucky to have found a place at the head of the line. The girls at the bottom of the trough had to take the used water as it came to them or wait

104

until those at the top had finished. The water was cool and smelled strongly of sulphur. Lane threw it over her face, spluttering happily and reveling in the feeling of being almost clean again.

"You're out next week, aren't you?" The blonde dried her face on bleached flour sacking and passed the makeshift towel to Lane.

"Uh-huh." She replied absently, thinking: I can have a bath tomorrow night.

"Didja ever think"—the girl was in a chatty humor—"how it is that judges can never say anything but, 'Thirty days'? You'd think it'd get monotonous just sayin' it. Thirty days. Thirty days. Thirty days." She inspected Lane shrewdly. "Goin' back to Truro?"

Lane halted in the act of pressing the rag to her cheeks. The question took her by surprise. Until this moment it had never occurred to her that she could go someplace else. Wonderingly she thought this over. Why, she thought, I'm going to bounce right back like a rubber ball someone batted against a wall. I must like it.

A brief twilight washed the detention farm with a rosy mist, and against it the brown and green of the tall pines scattered around the edge of the stockade were bright splashes of color. In the evening's quiet the scabby white of the buildings and the squat, barred windows in the dormitory seemed less harsh.

Lane breathed deeply of the sharp, cool air, and then the steady clanging of a hammer on an iron hoop caused her to drop the towel hurriedly and take her place in line again. Marching in for the evening meal, she still puzzled over the determination to return to Truro. Thinking about that made her realize she was no longer angry. The fury, the helpless rage which had filled her had subsided leaving her tempered, wiser, and deliberately calculating.

Looking back now, she understood she had given Titus Semple little choice. He had warned her, and she hadn't listened; then he slapped at her as he would an annoying mosquito. It was the sheer brutality of this action which had left her breathless, but its power to goad her to a hysterical passion had been dissipated.

It had been so simple. The Sheriff wasted no time. Two evenings after the encounter on the Palmer House porch she was walking to her rooming house from the movies. She and Annabelle had planned to go together, but Annabelle made a late date, and so she went alone. At the corner of Loomis Avenue a car drew alongside the curb, and one of the two men in it stepped out to take her arm. Surprised and alarmed she had attempted to jerk away, and heavy fingers bit into her flesh.

"You better come on in now." The voice had been toneless. "No sense kickin' up a fuss. You'll have to come anyhow." With his free hand the man pulled a policeman's shield from his pocket and showed it to her. For the first time Lane noticed the letters, P.D., painted on the car's door.

With speechless hatred she heard herself booked at the police station for soliciting on the city's streets. After the first moment of ungovernable temper, when she screamed and protested to an unblinking desk sergeant, she took refuge in cold and bitter contempt. At the hearing next morning she stood slim and defiant to hear herself branded as a prostitute. Heard both police officers solemnly declare that she had approached them while they were seated in a parked car and listened unemotionally as the judge sentenced her to thirty days on the County Farm. He, at least, had had the grace not to add a little moral lecture as he usually did when girls on the town were brought before him.

The ride in the caged truck along with three other girls—flat-faced slatterns, one of which had been picked up around the railroad yards and the other two taken from a Negro crib on the Apulca road—had been a humiliating nightmare. Every nerve in her body had screamed each mile of the way, and she had wanted to beat her fists against the heavy grilling in sheer torment for physical relief.

For the hurt she had suffered, the farm provided an anodyne in long hours of toil and an exhaustion which dropped her, like a helpless clod, to a springless pallet at night, too weary to think. The girls were up at the first gray haze in the morning. Outside, in the biting cool of early day, they washed silently at the trough and then shambled into a low-ceilinged room to eat at bare yellow tables. Thereafter they were parceled off, some to the truck gardens, others to the laundry, kitchen, or lint room. Twleve hours a day, six days a week left scant time for the luxury of self-pity.

After the first shock of her arrest had passed and the horror of finding herself at the County Farm dispelled, Lane found a curious peace settling upon her. It was almost a relief to know she had only to obey orders, observe a few rules, and her life would be diverted into a smooth, dull channel. The farm offered a breathing spell, a brief though unpleasant moment during which she could collect herself and make a personal inventory. The never varying routine of the camp could be followed with numb unconcern, and she didn't even bother to count off the days.

Marching into supper now, she thought again of the question asked by her companion at the washing trough. She had always intended to go back to Truro. The realization of this astonished her. I'll get a damn sight tireder of being tossed into a patrol wagon than Titus will of having me put there, she thought, and wondered at her hopeless resolution. If she had any sense at all, she argued, she'd put many miles between her and Truro. Let Semple and that Ann-Evans girl have Field. I'm getting to be a regular fool for being kicked, she told herself. Then—the discovery caused her to falter in step and jostle the girl behind her—she knew she wasn't going back to Truro because of Field. She was returning for her own sake. She was through running.

That Field hadn't tried to help, write, or even let her know he knew she was in trouble was something that left a dull ache deep within her when she thought about him. It would have been difficult, she admitted, for him to come to the Farm. Too many persons were getting to know him. He might have written a note or sent some message. At first she had worried. Field would hear of her arrest and believe the charge the police had lodged against her. He wouldn't, he couldn't, think she had been streetwalking. Field must know her better, but it was too much to expect that he should see the shadow of Titus Semple along the path she had been forced to walk. There was a certain comfort in the hope that Field hadn't heard of what had happened. The arrest, the sentence, the commitment had been achieved so quickly. There had been no publicity, and Lane understood, also, if Titus wanted to hush the incident, not one word would have seeped from the bare courtroom to the outside.

During the long nights, lying in the fetid air of the farm dormitory where the restless sound of heavy breathing was as constant as the sea's wash, she had had time to wonder at the way of things. There had been time to think of herself and of Field and to marvel at what had happened to her. The caged emotions, of a hundred girls without men were so vital, so apparent, that they almost assumed physical shape. A hundred girls working to the point of prostration, a hundred assorted drabs, petty thieves, and social malcontents, with their heads filled only by the men they would see upon their release or the men they had left and might never meet again. The pressure of their suppressed longings was constant and contagious, and Lane found herself succumbing to it. It frightened her, plucking at her independence, and she realized that to love without hope of return was a terrifying and debilitating experience.

Of the men who had touched her before Field, she had no regrets. They were way stops along the uncertain road she had traveled since childhood. With them she had always managed to remain aloof, and their eager, heedless desire had been spent on something quite apart from herself. She had even been able to feel a certain amused contempt for their noisy writhings and the excitement which left them so helpless and stripped of all dignity. Then, one smoky afternoon a man walked into a deserted clearing. He spoke, and his words were gentle, not cautious or contriving. He touched her hand, and her life welled to the spot. He had taken her and hadn't cared, and because what she had given so eagerly seemed without value to him she was tender, feeling an almost maternal concern. It was odd, she thought, how he could arouse a gentle solicitude and at the same time kindle a fire which consumed her body at the thought of him.

She knew Field Carlisle was not good for her. That she had been sentenced to thirty days on the County Farm because of him was proof enough. The thought aroused no bitterness in her, for she knew she was only an accident—her being where she was counted for so little to Titus Semple. By this time he had probably forgotten her. She had been in his way, or, at least, he thought she was. Now she had been removed, and the page could be turned. It hadn't been a fair fight, and the callous deadliness with which Titus had gouged aroused a mortal fury within her. Tossing restlessly at night she contrived slow and exquisite tortures for Titus, imagined his debasement and obliteration. In the cold light of morning she laughed at these vaporings, yet they returned again and again to fill the gloomy reaches of the dormitory and haunt her for fulfillment.

For the hour allotted the girls between supper and lights out, Lane sought a lonely bench beneath a scraggly pine. Next week she would be released, free to go where she would, and she knew now that meant Truro. It also meant Titus Semple and the prospect of being picked up on some fabricated charge every time she stepped to the street.

I ought to be scared to death, she confessed to herself, instead I'm nosing around like a puppy trying to get at a skunk. The bitter part of the dose she was preparing for herself, she knew, was that Field would be the first to tell her she was

108

crazy. If he only gave a damn, she mused, it would make some sense.

Leaning back against the tree she stared up at the purple sky.

"Thinkin' about your fella?" The blonde, Alice something or other was her name, plumped down on the bench beside her.

"I guess so." Lane half shut her eyes. She had wanted to be alone.

"Me too. I was wonderin' how it would be to go out to South Jacksonville tonight and dance at the pavilion." Alice sighed ecstatically. "You never did say what you were here for." She raised her arms, locking her hands behind her head.

"I was picked up in Truro." Lane was surprised how easily the admission came.

"Oh." Alice tilted her head to look at her. "Wasn't you workin' no place?"

Lane shook her head. She wished Alice would take her curiosity to another part of the yard.

"Well, you're crazy then. Anybody with sense could have told you that hustlin' alone would get you into trouble. That's how the cops keep their record, pickin' up pigeons. If you're in a regular house they leave you alone."

"I guess you're right." Lane was almost amused. She rose heavily. "I'm going to walk around awhile." She strolled aimlessly away, knowing the blonde was following her with contemptuous eyes.

So, she was thinking, I'm a pigeon for the police to knock down whenever they want to be busy. That's what I'm going back to Truro for.

At lights out she crawled between the rough, hot sheets. The packed ticking in the mattress was an unyielding slab, and she tossed upon it restlessly. A single bulb burned at the far end of the corridor, turning the rows of cots into humped grotesques. For the moment the room was quiet, but Lane knew that later it would become a chamber of whimperings, muttered words, unintelligible mouthings as the girls dreamed in heavy fits of slumber. She was always frightened by the sound, for it carried with it the feeling of shifting, tormented animals. Determinedly she shut her eyes and sought sleep before it should begin.

Northbound, racing through the scattered pinelands, the Miamian thundered.

In drawing room A, Field Carlisle stood before the full-

109

length mirror in the door, straining at the knot in his tie. White suspenders dangled around his legs, and his shirt billowed out in back.

From her place on the double seat Ann-Evans Carlisle watched him critically.

"Field, honey"—she made a face of distaste—"did you ever know how sloppy a man looks with his suspenders hanging down that way?"

Field settled the knot into the triangle of his collar and turned with a smile.

"All politicians walk around with their suspenders dragging. Anyhow, they always have their pictures taken at campaign time that way. You know, Senator Fielding Carlisle in the heat of battle." He bent down to kiss her upturned face.

"Besides, you're pretty enough for the both of us."

Ann-Evans rested her feet on the upholstery of the seat opposite her and smiled complacently. Everything had gone the way she had planned. The wedding at the Episcopal Church had been so pretty she almost cried herself, and now she was Mrs. Fielding Carlisle, and Field was going to be an important man. One day they would be taking this very train for Washington, and Field would be a United States senator. Hugging herself she nestled into the corner of the seat and stared out at the fleeting landscape. By turning her head a little she could see Field's reflection in the window. He was the handsomest man in the county, probably in the whole state. More than that, she hadn't married a nobody.

"How long can we stay in New York, honey?"

Field took a pint bottle of Bourbon from one of his bags and examined it critically. "Until my and your old man's money gives out." He twisted the foil from the bottle's neck and worked at the cork. "You have a drink?"

"Straight whisky?" Her nose wrinkled.

"Straight with water."

Ann-Evans shook her head. "I want champagne and cocktails and brandy out of those big glasses I saw in *Vanity Fair*. What will Tallahassee be like?"

"Never been there." He poured two large fingers into a water glass.

"What would happen if a man got drunk on his honeymoon?" Ann-Evans watched critically while he took the drink.

"I guess he'd have a hangover the next morning."

"Poof! You know I don't mean that." She rose and patted at her hair, then came to him, reaching up her arms. "Field, honey, do you really love me? I mean really. I'm not just that Ann-Evans Weldon girl you've always had around?"

He kissed her mouth, and she clung to him. "You know I love you, Ann-Evans. This is the way things were meant to be."

She drew away. "I'll powder my nose, and then we'll go to dinner."

While he was waiting Field poured himself another drink. He had been glad to get away from Truro, for something he couldn't elude had haunted him there. Funny, he pondered, that a girl like Lane would just up and light off without telling anyone where she had gone.

Two days after he returned from visiting Dan Curtis in Jacksonville, he had drifted around to the Eagle Café. When he didn't see her there he thought she must be sick. It was Annabelle who told him Lane had left.

"She just disappeared, left what little clothes she had in the room and went off." Annabelle was worried. "Honestly, Field, I got the feelin' that somethin' happened to her. Don't you think we ought to look for her?"

He hadn't known what to do. Why, sometimes he just had to have Lane to talk with. The more he thought about her the more concerned he became, and even Ann-Evans noticed and commented upon his abstraction.

"My goodness, Field, you needn't get so starry-eyed because we're getting married in two weeks. You act like a bride."

He decided then that Lane had read about the wedding and made up her mind to leave while he was away. It was easier, he guessed, but at the same time they could have talked things over the way they always had.

When he spoke to Peter Ladas, his uncertainty increased. Ladas spread his hands and said that he had let her go.

"But you got another girl in her place?"

Peter shrugged. "Business picked up."

The feeling of guilt followed him, was with him now, riding along on his honeymoon. He poured another drink as Ann-Evans opened the lavatory door.

"I didn't want the information that badly." There was a hint of criticism in her voice.

"What information, sugar?"

"About what would happen if a man got drunk on his honeymoon."

He put the bottle away. "First," he said reaching for his coat, "I'll feed you. Then we'll come back here an' both get drunk. You can tell me in the morning then what happened."

111

CHAPTER TEN

LUTE-MAE SANDERS SAT IN HER FAVORITE CHAIR. IT was a high-backed, flowered-chintz-covered affair occupying the center of a gracious, sun-flooded room she kept as her own at the back of the house. Purple wisteria clambered on either side of double windows facing her, and from the yard the perfume of closely packed oleanders was rich and constant.

This was her retreat. Rarely did the most privileged of her clients enter and then only by invitation when she was in an expansive humor.

"It makes me feel like a grandmother," she confessed. "You know, like a lady."

One of her conceits was to have the maid bring tea and little cakes here in the afternoon, but she invariably left the contents of tray and pot untouched. After admiring the service she eventually mixed herself a couple of stiff drinks from a handy cellarette.

"I sure wish I could drink tea." This was a sincere lament. "The things make the room so cozy an' genteel, but I can't stand the damn stuff. It gives me the gripes."

The maid was always careful to see that the cakes were neatly arranged, but the teapot usually came up empty since the kitchen had long since learned it was never inspected.

Lute-Mae held a tall glass lightly in both hands, resting it upon her knee where the bottom made a damp ring on a magenta taffeta negligée which swirled from a tight waist to a half circle around her feet.

"You're a damn fool," she said thoughtfully.

Lane slid back from the edge of the low chair, leaned against the cushion, and crossed her ankles. She was smiling.

"In the first place"—Lute-Mae put her glass on the table—"you got to be dumb to be like the little girls I got. All hookers are dumb in one way or another, all except the French. French whores are smart, I never figured out why." She meditated on this phenomenon for a moment, admiring it grudgingly.

112

Lane waited. She hadn't come to beg. Lute-Mae could do the talking. Two weeks back in Truro from the County Farm had taught her many things. She learned first that she wasn't going to get a job in town. Respectable work had been effectively closed to her as if she were a tramp. That had been her own fault. The news of her arrest and sentence had never reached the newspapers. Titus evidently felt he had disposed of her and saw no point in pursuing a questionable action. Her reappearance and immediate conduct had forced him to move again.

Walking deliberately up the steps of the Palmer House porch she had crossed to his chair and slapped him savagely in the mouth. Then, without a word, she wheeled about, leaving him there with the red mark of her hand mounting furiously over his lips. Not until she was out of sight of the porch did she start to tremble, and panic was upon her when Annabelle's room was finally reached.

The next day the *Journal* had carried a story of her release from the County Farm. After this she knew she was finished in Truro.

Annabelle, tremulously stanch, usually indifferent to what people said or thought, confirmed this.

"God A'mighty, sugar," she confided, "this here has done it for sure. If you hadn't come back, Titus Semple would probably have let things go, an' nobody would have been the wiser. He just figured to get rid of you." Annabelle had accepted with unquestioning loyalty the story Lane told of the arrest. "Now, don't you see, every man in Truro figures you're a dollar tumble. Why couldn't you have had sense enough to keep away from Semple even if he has done you dirty."

Mrs. Seiver, the landlady, came in then to shriek indignant objections and order Lane from the house. She left without protest, tossing scanty belongings into a suitcase. That afternoon she found a room for three dollars a week on the fringe of the yard district.

Annabelle came to see her when she could, but it was difficult. They both knew the reputation of the neighborhood, and Annabelle was forever in a small terror at the thought of being seen or that while she was there the ramshackle house, covering a multitude of sins, might be raided.

"Sugar," she pleaded, "why don't you go away? I can let you have a few dollars until you're on your feet again." She proffered a folded copy of *Billboard*. "This here is some sort of a theatrical paper I bought at the Rexall stand. Maybe you can find some carnival you know playin' around near here."

Lane sat on the chipped windowsill, staring into the paper-littered street below. A colored boy, knotted in the doorway of a house across the street, was whispering into a mouth organ. "Sometimes I Feel like a Motherless Child"; the notes came faintly as half-forgotten memories.

"I'm not going back to a carnival, Annabelle. If I run now, I'm finished. Don't you see? I haven't done anything. If I let Semple chase me, I'll have to keep running the rest of my life."

"But, sugar"—Annabelle was losing patience— "what's stayin' here goin' to get you? You haven't a job, an' the way things are you're not goin' to get one. My God," her voice shrilled, "if you're still eatin' your heart out over Field Carlisle, you sure are crazy. He's married an' away on his honeymoon. Even if he wasn't he wouldn't touch you with somebody else's broomstick after that piece in the *Journal*."

Annabelle was right. Lane realized how true everything she said was, but her resolve remained unshaken. If she couldn't make a living one way, she could another. The thought no longer startled her. It had happened before with less reason. Now she would be paid for it. Again and again she recalled the cynical comment of the blonde at the County Farm. She had called her a pigeon for the police to knock down when they weren't busy. Other things, also, she had learned at the Farm by listening and remembering. Some of them concerned Lute-Mae Sanders, and she recalled what Field had told her once when they had been parked in his car by the river.

"If Lute-Mae Sanders ever opened her mouth, honey," he said seriously, "this county and most of the state would split open like a dropped watermelon."

It had taken her almost a week to work up the courage to call on Lute-Mae. It's like jumping in a river, she thought, before you really know you can swim.

Lute-Mae hadn't been any too easy to see. The colored maid who answered the door was insolently skeptical.

"Miz Lute-Mae don' nevah see ennyone."

Lane slid her foot into the opening to prevent the girl from closing the door. "Tell her," she said hurriedly, "it's the girl who helped her that day when she fell on River Street. I'll wait here."

The maid left, returning in a few moments. "Miz Lute-Mae don' nevah see anyone, she say, but you kin come up."

Lute-Mae had been bored. Now she was curious, watching Lane carefully as the maid brought her in and finally motioning to a chair.

"Sure," she said, "I remember you now. You in trouble?"

"No," Lane replied, "not in the way you mean, anyhow."

The woman nodded and reached for her highball. "I'd offer you a drink," she said, "only I don't hold with little girls drinkin' in the middle of the afternoon. What's worryin' you?"

"I want to come here and work." It was done. What amazed her was that the words had been so easy to say, the idea so simple to translate into a single statement.

Lute-Mae raised one shoulder, tilted her cheek to it, and eyed Lane quizzically.

"I'm broke." Lane spoke slowly. "I can't find a job. There was a piece about me in the *Journal*, maybe you read it. I had thirty days on the County Farm."

"I never read newspapers." Lute-Mae sipped at her drink. "If I don't know what's goin' on, I can't worry about nothin'."

"Well, anyhow, I've got to do something. Some of the girls at the Farm were always talking about you. I—I remembered that time on River Street, so I came here."

Lute-Mae broke open a fresh package of cigarettes, pushed one out, and then tossed the pack into Lane's lap.

"I wish I knew why you are lyin' to me," she said.

Lane lit her cigarette. "I'm not lying."

Lute-Mae thought this over. "You're either lyin' or you're a damn fool." She brushed her hand lightly over massed yellow hair. "There's lots of different kinds of little girls go into a house. Some of them start as crazy, burnin' hot kids who get pantin' every time they think of a bed. Mostly, though, that kind gets themselves into trouble on the outside. Other little girls are plain, stupid dumb, like a piece of dough. There is still others that just figure, what the hell, it's better than scrubbin' pots an' washin' some man's under-drawers. That's the best kind of a little girl, the one who's already worked everything out in her head. I can't figure you as any one of those. You'd be most likely to break your heart over it an' worry about what you're doin'. I guess, maybe, you're sort of the moody kind." She tamped her cigarette out in the tray; and then, suddenly, her eyes softened, and a slight grin touched her lips. "Come to think of it, though, I was sort of moody myself when I was young. I had a long Indian headdress a travelin' salesman gave me. I used to get drunk an', stark, jay-bird naked, put on those feathers an' sit in the middle of the floor in a house on Laura Street, in Jacksonville, cryin' until I was sittin' in a pool of tears." She stopped abruptly, her mouth half open, staring at Lane. "Christ," she said wonderingly, "what the ever hell am I sayin'?"

Lane almost giggled at the picture. "I'm not so moody," she

115

said simply. "I don't get hungry or want to sleep in the rain."

Lute-Mae contemplated her approvingly. "I think, maybe, you're smart too in addition to bein' pretty." She sighed thoughtfully. "I ain't never had a really smart little girl around me. It might be a novelty." She cocked her head. "You don't happen to be French do you?"

Lane had to laugh then. The conversation was skirting the ridiculous.

"No," she said finally.

"That's sure enough too bad. I always wanted a French little girl around so's I could find out what makes 'em smart. What's your name?"

"Lane, Lane Ballou."

Lute-Mae repeated it. "Lane," she said after awhile, "is a funny name for a girl."

Something caught at her then. Field had said the same thing once. "Lane is a funny name for a girl."

From below a piano sounded. Someone was picking out "Dardanella" with uncertain fingers. Lute-Mae winced at the tune's stumbling progress.

"Sometimes," she sighed, "I wish my little girls wasn't so accomplished."

She dropped fresh ice into her glass and splashed it with whisky. "Here"—she indicated the bottle impatiently—"pour yourself a drink. I'm already doin' somethin' I never expected to do, so you might as well have a drink if you want it."

Lane shook her head. She didn't want to take a drink, not now.

"Suit yourself." Lute-Mae was plainly surprised. "You know"—she appeared to be talking more to satisfy her own curiosity than anything else—"if anyone was to tell me this mornin' I'd be even thinkin' about takin' a strange girl into my house, I'd laughed right in their faces. I don't know a damn thing about you. I don't need another little girl. I think you'll make trouble for me one of these days, an' besides that I got the feelin' you're lyin' to me. If you put all those things together, anybody but a crazy person would say I was foolish to just talk to you."

She left her chair, walking to the window from where she could look down into the neat yard garden. Watching her, Lane couldn't help but think what a beautiful young woman she must have been. Now, as a madam of a sporting house in a junction town, she had an undeniable dignity.

"Look, sugar"—Lute-Mae turned to face her—"I got the damnedest feelin' about you, an' it scares me. I wouldn't tell that to any other woman. I don't much like sayin' it to you, but that's the way I feel. If you're up against it, you can stay here for a couple of days, then I'll let you have a few dollars an' you can get out of Truro."

Lane's eyes were steady. "If I stay I'll work. I'm through trying to pet life and keep it still."

"God damn it but you make me sore." Lute-Mae slapped her hand at the tasseled cord of the window shade. "If I had the sense I was naked born with, I'd get you to hell out of here now. Instead, if you want to stay you can move in. I'm just sucker enough to try to find out why you're lyin' to me." She walked nervously across the room. "Don't think," she continued defensively, "it's goin' to be any different with you than the other little girls. I talked to you here today because I was sick of my own company. After this you'll stay in your own room or down in the parlor. You'll take what comes if they want you, an' don't crawl up here with your nose runnin' if you don't like it. Where's my cigarettes?"

Lane reached out the pack. "I don't want any favors."

"That's good." Lute-Mae drew heavily on a cigarette, brushing impatiently at the smoke. "You sure as hell won't get any." With a snort she put her cigarette down. "Go up to see Doc Morrison; he's in the Apperson Building. Tell him I sent you an' I want a certificate. I sure hope to God somethin' is wrong with you so's I can change my mind."

In the tattered and ravaged jitney which took her across town to Loomis Avenue, from where she could walk to the Apperson Building on River Street, Lane held tightly to herself.

I'm a whore, she thought. A phrase she had read once recalled itself. I'm sin incarnadine. I wonder what it means?

Gropingly she attempted to uncover her emotions and discovered she wasn't feeling anything in particular. There was a lurking sense of excitement, but no regret or, what seemed more important, shame. I ought to be ashamed. That is what they call it in the magazines, a life of shame, yet it hasn't touched Lute-Mae. That, she supposed, was because Lute-Mae hadn't temporized with things as she found them. If I'm smart I'll be the same way. Lute-Mae and Titus Semple, they hadn't given an inch, either of them, ever.

Covertly she watched the half-dozen other passengers in the bus wondering if, perhaps, something of what she had just done could show on her face. They were indifferent to her presence.

Dr. Morrison, seedy, cadaverous, but thorough, grunted unemotionally when she told him Lute-Mae had sent her. A half hour later she was out of his office and on River Street again.

"You're all right as far as I can see. The Wassermann might turn up something, but I don't think so. See that you keep yourself all right."

She had felt shame then, a searing flush of degradation and resentment. Her nostrils burned, and she clamped her teeth together to shut off the trembling in her mouth. The examination had been so icily impersonal. No one had ever looked at her that way before.

On the street she breathed deeply, fighting down the queasy sensation in her stomach.

That was what I wanted, she thought. I don't want to be anything to anyone.

With the shadow of late afternoon upon it, River Street was again foreign but with a subtle difference this time. She walked slowly and in confidence, knowing she no longer belonged on River Street and, also, that it had lost its command to frighten her. For, whatever I am now or will be, I am myself alone. This is my body, and I can give it to a boy in the back seat of a car or it can work for me. I'm through for all time working for it. There was swift release in the idea that she was something apart from that which the men who frequented Lute-Mae's would hereafter pay for. It was as though she had discovered a new and exhilarating power.

Strolling back toward Loomis and the bus stand, she speculated on what life in Lute-Mae's would be like and how she would feel with the first man who took her from the parlor to her room upstairs. Once, when she had been very young, she had tried to imagine what it would be like to be raped. I guess, she thought now, it's something like that. The notion was perversely exciting and remained with her in the bus on the way back to Lute-Mae's.

The same colored girl who had admitted her earlier in the afternoon opened the door for her return.

"Miz Lute-Mae," she said after they were in the hall, "say for you to take the fah r'm upstaih. Mah nahm's Cah'l," she whispered deferentially.

The room was small, neat, and with a single window facing the west side of the big white house. Lane inspected it with a feeling of detachment. It was a place where a girl she knew was going to live.

The maid, Carol, stood in the doorway. "Evrahbody, th' young ladies, eat togethah at seven. Miz Lute-Mate, she say foah you to come see her whin you git back." She ducked away, and Lane was alone.

Across the double bed was spread a powder-blue evening

118

gown of cheap silk and beside it a pair of blue slippers. A twisting, ironic smile tugged at the corners of her mouth as she examined the pitiful finery. Both shoes and the dress had been worn, and Lane wondered by whom and for how long. Hurriedly she switched on the lights at the dressing table and a small table lamp by her bed. The semidarkness had been filled with forebodings, and for a moment she had felt hopelessly alone and frightened—the brave imaginings which accompanied her on River Street had fled.

For a brief time she stood gazing up at the ceiling and then turned and lifted the blue dress from the bed, shaking out its folds and draping it carefully over a chair. Her fingers, inexplicably awkward, fumbled at the snaps of her skirt, loosening it finally to drop listlessly around her feet.

CHAPTER ELEVEN

NOVEMBER'S BRIGHT, CRISP BURR CLUNG TO THE LATE afternoon, and throughout the flat lands the scattered fields lay brown and hard, shot here and there with color from a pomegranate sun.

Over innumerable back-country roads men—afoot, astride work horses, or bundled with their families into mud-spattered cars—straggled homeward. They studied the earth and the sky, hunching a little within their shirts against the season's persistent chill.

The holiday mood with which they had gone to the polls was dissolving. Come good or bad now they had done their part as free men. They had savored spirited argument, drunk with old friends and neighbors, lounged on low-flung porches of crossroad stores while their women and youngsters made unexpected purchases, gossiped, and played. They cast their votes and debated, with mild interest, the inexplicable persistency of the Republican Party's surviving in a district that hadn't voted anything but a Democratic ticket since Reconstruction. Even the Democrats, they agreed, were hard to understand at times. Here the politicians were sending a new young fellow, Fielding Carlisle, to Tallahassee as state senator and letting go a man who had been a good representative for

119

the district. This Carlisle seemed a pleasant enough spoken candidate, but anybody looking for a job was bound to be soft talking.

Anyhow, it was a pleasure to get away from home for a day.

Feeling the evening chill they agreed it was sure enough hog-killing weather. The meat would dress down and cool fine. There didn't seem much point, though, in raising more stuff than a family could eat these days with the market at starvation prices. By God, that's what a legislature was for, to see that the poor man got more than a few coppers. The hell of it was, no matter who the voters put in, nothing ever changed for the better. Things about an election got around, they did that. Here was Carlisle, no one knew good what he stood for, yet his was the name you heard at the polling places. Old Truro family, someone said, up and coming and with smart people behind him so he'd probably turn out right. After all, if a man believed the Democratic Party was best for running things, then he ought to be satisfied to take its word on the fellow it wanted to send to the Legislature. The best way to find out what a man or a mule could do was to give him a field to plow.

In Truro and the district's other urban communities, lights were beginning to ripple down the main streets. Newsboys drawled their wares in a plaintive call. Men, on their way home, stopped in at campaign headquarters for the late returns and took a couple of drinks in the back rooms. This was sort of like the time before Prohibition when you could drop around for a snort with the boys. One of these days they'd get a chance to vote on liquor again, and then all this foolishness would be over. Fielding Carlisle was as good as in, anybody ought to know that since the primaries when Semple and the others chalked up signs on their doorposts. Well, get on home now, or the old lady'll raise hell for having a whisky breath.

On the Palmer House porch Titus Semple belched uneasily over the two helpings of apple dumpling he had eaten for dinner and tuned an attentive ear to the rumblings within his vast stomach. When they struck a certain note he would have to yell for one of the colored boys to bring him some baking soda and water. It was a damn good thing he hadn't gone to Ann-Evans's party. Another belch like that would have blown everyone out of the house.

On Flamingo Road, Ann-Evans dragged a protesting Field to the Weldon's porch for the third time to exclaim over chains of colored electric lights strung from tree to tree on either side of the street. It had been her own idea, for, ordinarily, the property owners only decorated their property for New Year's and Christmas. Ann-Evans pleaded, cajoled, and even threatened until they gave in and Flamingo Road sparkled with festive colors.

On the lip of an irrigation ditch along the Apulca highway, a Negro drained the last drop of 'shine from an unlabeled pint bottle and tumbled happily among the weeds and grass. Bulging between his gums and cheek, where he had placed it for a safe keeping, was a greasy silver dollar. A dollar an' a pint, the white man said, and showed him where to make a mark on the ballot.

In a room at Lute-Mae Sanders's, Dan Curtis sprawled his heavy body the length of a bed, drunk and asleep.

Oil lamps flamed smokily in farm cabins. Crowds were gathering on Truro's River Street. Titus Semple bellowed for baking soda and slumped uncomfortably in his chair. Ann-Evans kissed Field ecstatically and repeated over and over, "Senator Fielding Carlisle." The Negro on the Apulca Road mumbled in misery and choked on his dollar. Dan Curtis's eyes opened slowly, painfully, and he bore in silence the drumming of a thousand insane imps within his head.

On a low, quilted seat before a dressing table, Lane flicked at her nails with an emery board. In the diffused, pink light from the small boudoir lamps, she appeared impossibly young and lovely. A black satin dressing gown hugged her slim body, dropping away in a graceful, pleated fold where her knees crossed, and her skin had a coppery glint. At a movement on the bed she glanced up and smiled sympathetically.

"Feel awful?"

"Worse than awful." Dan Curtis explored his feverish lips with a soggy tongue.

At a small stand Lane filled a tall glass with ice water from a pitcher and handed it to him.

Curtis held the goblet in both hands to keep it from rattling against his teeth. When he had drained it he sighed gratefully and made an attempt to straighten up. He was a shaggy, gray crag of a man, and even with bleary eyes and tousled, silvering hair he bore himself with a certain impressive dignity. The pyjama coat he was wearing had become unbuttoned, and the matted pelt was that of an old fox, but the muscles rippling beneath it and across his shoulders were youthful and elastic. He smiled at Lane as she took a seat on the bed's edge.

"Think I'm a damn fool, don't you?"

"Sometimes, Dan."

"Well, I'm not." He reached for one of the heavy cigars.

121

spread in a row on the side table. "Suppose I could have a drink?"

"Uh-huh." She filled a whisky glass and brought it to him.

"I'm not such a fool as you think." He worried with the idea. "Once a year or so I feel like getting just low-down drunk. That's the time I get away from Jacksonville and come to Lute-Mae's where I can have it over in private. That's really smart."

"It came near not being so private." Lane giggled. "You wanted to take the house apart, board by board, to build a bonfire for a marshmallow roast or something."

"Is that so?" Curtis ruminated on this news.

"Why is it you always want to kindle a blaze? Last year when you came here, the first time I saw you, it was the same thing, only then you wanted to use Lute-Mae and some of the girls for kindling. I think you're a firebug at heart."

Dan grinned embarrassedly. "I don't remember a thing about it." He stretched exploringly and ran the fingers of both hands through his hair. "Election returns all in yet?"

"Just about." Lane picked up her emery board. "I stopped past Lute-Mae's room a little while back. She'd called uptown to find out how things were going. They elected Field Carlisle all right."

"Mmmm." He held out an arm. "Come here."

Lane slid down the bed. He held her gently, without excitement, almost as though he was lonely and wanted to be reassured of her presence.

"Lute-Mae figuring on a big night?" He asked the question apparently without design.

"I guess so." Lane didn't want to move. There was an indefinable comfort in the feeling of that strong arm around her. "Most everyone in Truro will be getting himself drunk on an election-time excuse."

"You're not going downstairs?"

Her eyes closed. "No, Dan, you've paid me."

He shook her then with irate fierceness. "You know damn well I didn't mean that. You did know it, didn't you?"

"Yes, Dan. I don't know what makes me talk that way sometimes." Her voice trembled. The unrelenting perverseness which could strike out unexpectedly at the one man who had been gentle, even kind, sapped her strength.

She had seen Dan Curtis for the first time almost a year ago when he came, as he had now, to consume something within him by a protracted drunk at Lute-Mae's.

"I get a worry wart inside." She wondered then why he

thought an explanation necessary. "Once a year or so I have to burn it away with a drunk like this."

For five days he didn't move outside the room. Food he rarely touched was brought upstairs regularly, and the supply of liquor was endless. He clung to Lane, fretting when she left him for even a few minutes, and talking long and earnestly in his cups. It was not the maudlin spewings of a drunk but rather an argument he had with himself over which Lane acted as a sympathetic referee. She had listened at first in tolerance and then with interest and anxiety, for there were things Dan Curtis spoke of and names he mentioned which were better closeted in his normally shrewd head.

On the fifth day he forced himself into a cold shower and had Lane call the colored maid to clear the room of liquor.

"I don't want to see it when I come out."

Dressed finally and waiting for his car, his eyes were miraculously clear, hand and step steady, and there was the assurance of a man who has himself in check again in his walk.

Smiling at the incredulous look Lane had given him, he patted the side of her face with a big hand.

"It's drastic but effective," he said.

After he had gone Lute-Mae sent for her and passed over an envelope without comment. Inside were five one hundred dollar bills. Lane fingered the money absently and then tossed it to a table.

"Keep it for me, will you?"

Lute-Mae tucked the money in a bag. "Sometimes a man will get you like that," she murmured.

Lane shook her head. "No, it isn't what you think. He didn't do anything more than put his head against me when he slept; that and talk. I just don't have need for so much money right now. Maybe I'll use it up in board and room for awhile if you don't mind."

Lute-Mae leaned back in her flounced chaise longue, twisting reflectively at one of the rings on her fingers. Something puzzling had happened to her during the month Lane had been in the house. For the first time in her life she found herself liking another woman. Time and again she made an excuse to enter Lane's room for no other purpose than to talk with her, idle, comfortable chatter, and, without ever having been told, Lane knew she was the only one of Lute-Mae's girls who could go to the Madame's sitting room when she would. She had asked no favors nor expected any, yet she realized, as did Lute-Mae, that a curious bond had been fashioned between them.

"Why"—Lute-Mae spoke to her hand—"why is Titus Semple interested in you?"

"He thinks I'm cute."

"Well"—Lute-Mae was plainly worried—"he telephoned me last night; said he'd heard I had a new girl. Wanted to know if her name was Ballou by any chance. What do you make of that?"

"He must be rutting."

Lazily Lute-Mae took a cigarette from a silver box, and when it had been lighted she smoked in silence for a moment.

"You know," she said finally, "I'm a persistent crow once I get a notion into my head. I knew when you first came here a few weeks back you were lyin' to me, but I let it go. This is different. With someone like Titus Semple inquirin' about you, I got to know what's goin' on for everyone's sake."

Lane told her then, told her everything from the first time Field Carlisle had come to the empty carnival lot, the nights they had spent by the river, how she had lost her job at the Eagle and the thirty days on the County Farm.

"Well, I'll be damned. All that goin' on, an' me never hearin' a word about it. You sure must have had Titus plenty worried to put him to so much trouble. So it was you an' Field Carlisle?" She studied Lane sleepily. "Crazy about him still?"

"I don't know, Lute-Mae. If I am it's a feeling I've never had before. If he came in here this minute and wanted me I'd go, but there is something else, too. I'd sort of want to mother him, to watch after what he's doing. I get crazy and tender about him all at once. I never wanted anyone's hands on me the way I do his, and yet, all at the same time, I can wonder how he looks when he's asleep. Now that he's going to run for office, I keep worrying whether he'll be a good man and do things he'll be proud of. If you try and add it up, there isn't any answer." She leaned back and stared out the window.

"Well"—Lute-Mae was judiciously skeptical—"you ain't old enough for a change of life, so it surer than hell must be love. Thank God I ain't had to go through either yet."

"What did you tell Semple?"

"I told him yes, an' he like to died laughin' right over the phone. Said he couldn't have figured out anythin' so good himself. Know what he meant?"

Contempt drew at Lane's mouth. "Don't you? I fixed everything for him. One of these days he'll be with Field some place and say: 'Bub, you recall the little piece who once worked for the Eagle? Well, I hear she's on the line now, down to Lute-

124

Mae's.' Then he'll be innocent and pretend he never knew Field had been out with me."

The mimicry of Semple brought a quick chuckle from Lute-Mae. Then she was grave.

"Don't be surprised, sugar, if he shows up here some night, Titus I mean. Field too, for that matter."

Lane rose. "I can wait."

Semple hadn't come. Field, if he knew where she was or what had happened, made no attempt to see her although she half expected him. Dan Curtis had been the surprise.

He had sent her queer things; funny things they were for a man to send to a girl in a house. Once a package had contained an etching of a setter's head. Another time he had mailed her a book about a French woman, a Madame de Maintenon. A third box contained two little porcelain figures. There was never a note with the gifts, but she guessed whom they were from.

Sitting beside him now, knowing he was still angry at the cheap reply she had made to his question, she realized sharply that Dan Curtis was the answer to so much she needed to know. He could tell her, not who, but what Titus Semple was, for she no longer feared him. He had made the mistake of letting her alone.

Through the bedroom's open window the rasping notes of tin horns sounded faintly, and down near Larrimer Street there was the throbbing flush of red fire where someone had set an illumination pot. Distant shouts and automobile sirens punctuated the growing murmur. There'd be broken heads and cuts to mend around the district in the morning.

"Dan?" She touched his temples with her finger tips, and he reached up to hold her hand there.

"Yes?"

"Is Field Carlisle a good man?"

She felt him stir and moved closer in order that he couldn't look up and see her face.

"Why, I guess so, Lane."

"But"—she clung tenaciously to the idea—"if he is a good man wouldn't you know as quickly as if he wasn't?"

She felt him shake a little with silent laughter.

"Not always. You can make a guess at a good man. A bad one you have to find out about." Rolling to one side he turned her half around. "I didn't know politics interested you."

"Oh, I suppose it's just hearing the name so much and about the election. I began thinking if the people outside ever knew what they were voting for."

"Most of the time they don't, and so whatever it is they get it's usually better than they deserve."

Lute-Mae's parlor was becoming noisy. Someone had started the mechanical piano. Lute-Mae had tired of the indifferent talents of her little girls and installed an instrument which played untiringly and on key at the flick of a switch. Its steady beat filtered into the room upstairs, and with it came laughter and sharp, excited cries.

Curtis winced at the sound. There was nothing, he thought, like the sound of a player piano to remind a man where he was. His head throbbed, and the accumulated alcohol of the past three days touched fire to every nerve point in his body. Even the pressure of the light sheet became a rare torture. There was, he realized, something pathetically ridiculous in his presence at Lute-Mae's. Because there was no one he could really trust himself to relax with, he, Daniel Vincent Curtis, had to get drunk in a whore house when the desire was upon him. There was a stupendous irony in this. Here in Lute-Mae's there were no restless hunters. He had made capital for too many years out of the weaknesses of others not to be conscious of vulnerability in himself. There were no ambitions to guard against at Lute-Mae's. He smiled to himself at the notion, wondering idly just what the goal of a whore could be. It wasn't, of this he was certain, to become proficient in the profession. There wouldn't be so many indifferent ones if that were true.

"Would you get me another drink?"

Lane disengaged herself without comment and filled a glass with rye.

Dan gulped greedily at the contents and waited for the quivering inside to quiet. "I think," he said regretfully, "I've had about enough." He rubbed at his bearded face with a sweeping motion of one hand. "That last one seemed to turn on a light down there."

Lane stood beside the bed. She didn't want Dan Curtis to leave now. Once or twice during the time she had been with him, she felt that a rare, sympathetic chord had been in the spinning. She needed Dan Curtis far too desperately to have him go away again, carrying only the vague recollection of a girl who had taken care of him.

"Feeling better?"

Dan waggled his head experimentally. "Yep." —He smiled engagingly. "When I can do that and not see fireworks inside my skull, I'm practically recovered." With a twisting motion he threw his feet over the bed and settled them on the floor.

"You see," he added, "solid, substantial citizen of the Republic; two feet on the ground." He took the dressing gown she brought from the closet.

Sitting on the rim of the bathtub while Curtis shaved, Lane wondered at the stamina which could throw off such a drunk as the man had treated himself to. She had never seen anyone drink the way Curtis did. He wasn't noisy or roving after the first few hours. Although he asked for her when he came to Lute-Mae's this time, she realized it hadn't been for her as a woman. In the beginning he drank steadily. Afterward he slept. From that point on he would sleep and drink, drink and sleep, talking with her in strangely confidential tones during the drinking intervals. As always, though, he kept himself shut away.

Turning his lathered face from the mirror he looked down at her.

"I'm leaving tonight."

She nodded. There was nothing to say. If he had been a man who had taken, or even wanted, her, it might be different. This way she could only wait for him to go.

"Can you drive a car?"

The question startled her. "Why, why yes."

"Good." He turned back to the mirror, talking to his reflection. "I've got a place on the dunes at Pablo Beach. I want to go there now. We won't have a drink. We'll eat dozens of fried eggs, a couple of hams, and keep a coffee pot full all the time. We'll swim in the morning and lie in the sun in the afternoon. Want to come?"

"Yes, Dan." She was afraid to say more.

"That's good. I've a feeling we might turn out to be friends, and I'm curious to know why." He weighed the idea, assaying the notion for its worth while his fingers searched for stray bristles around his chin.

Something of the astonishment she experienced at the invitation must have appeared on her face and reproduced itself in the shaving glass, for Curtis turned away and studied her.

"You're no more surprised than I am, Lane," he assured her. "Better throw some things in a bag."

Leading him down the long, dim hallway, past the closed double doors shutting off the parlor and muting the voices inside, Lane halted in the alcove adjoining the small bar. Lute-Mae was there alone, and her eyebrows lifted at the sight of them.

"I'm taking Lane away with me for a couple of days, Lute-Mae."

Concern, immediate and unmistakable, flashed across in a glance from the woman. "You're sure you're all right, Dan?" She watched him anxiously and seemed relieved at his laugh of assurance.

"Never felt better, Mother Sanders."

Lane, listening to this exchange, felt a truant schoolgirl attempting to slip out after hours.

"Yep"—Lute-Mae was calmly negligent again—"I guess you are at that." She glared at Lane, but there was no anger in her voice. "I'll swear to God I don't know what this business is comin' to. Election night an' a house full of callers an' the little girls runnin' off like they was guests at a late party." She hardened for a second. "There ain't another soul in this place .besides myself I'd trust Dan Curtis to. Don't forget that."

She turned and picked a sheet of paper from the bar, handing it to Curtis.

"I had Luis on the phone for the past hour getting all the returns for you." She smiled confidentially. "You don't have to read it 'less you want to. There ain't nothin' there that'll be a surprise."

Dan stuffed the sheet in his pocket. "Thanks." He turned a quick look of longing at the bottles behind the bar and grinned boyishly. "I almost forgot I don't touch the stuff," he said.

Nervous, unsure, Lane slipped behind the wheel of the black Packard coupé. "I never drove anything but a Ford," she explained.

Once on the Dixie Highway Dan relaxed, lolling comfortably in the corner. "Wake me up when you get outside South Jacksonville."

The night rushed up and over them as Lane drove with mounting sureness. With the coupé's windows closed it was warm and snug inside; the half-lights on the dash gave a hearth-fire touch to the compartment. For almost two years, she was thinking, she hadn't been outside Truro, and not more than a dozen times during the past twelve months had she ventured away from Lute-Mae's. Now she was singing inside of adventure. The headlights laid a fan of gossamer on the road which the car itself never succeeded in touching, crowd though she did upon it.

In the front bedroom of the Weldons' home, Field sat unsteadily on the arm of a chair, his head wagging owlishly at Ann-Evans.

128

"Sugar," he declared solemnly, "you're drunk."

Ann-Evans giggled. She was a little drunk. Even mama and papa were showing their liquor by the time the last friend had left. Champagne, real champagne which papa had ordered from the bootlegger, still tickled the inside of her nose. Not at any of the parties before had there been champagne. Champagne, and she was Mrs. Senator Fielding Carlisle. Everything had come true even to the blue roadster she used to dream about.

"Sugar"—Field cocked his head to one side—"I sure wish I knew if this ringing in my ears is liquor or the echo of people sayin', 'Hello, Senator.'" The thought amused him. "Right now bein' a member of the Legislature don't seem so important, but tomorrow it'll scare the hell out of me."

He rose awkwardly and stumbled toward her, wrapping his arms around her waist and burying his head within the curve of her neck.

"Field!" She twisted impatiently.

"My God"—he was puzzled—"you don't say senators have to give that up." He laughed boisterously at the very funny joke and then was serious. "You're sure this is what we want, Ann-Evans?"

"Don't talk like a loon." She was plucking at the pins in her hair. "You can be governor if you want to. Everyone knows that. But"—she turned around and put her hands against his chest—"we've got to have a place of our own. It was nice living with papa and mama at first, but now you're really somebody, and it won't look well. If you can't get your old home back from those stinking people, then we'll have to buy another place on Flamingo Road. I'm not going to live like we were poor relations."

Suddenly Field was tired. He felt as though he had picked up a handful of dust. There had been no zest in the election, no elation in winning it.

He went to the window and drew aside the curtains. Clusters of the colored lights still bobbled between pockets of darkness where the less enthusiastic neighbors had shut off the current. It was odd, he meditated, how an election could come to mean nothing all of a minute this way and how the face of a girl and the way she spoke should be remembered so well.

"I'll bet," he said to the night, "I'd have made a damn good deputy sheriff at that."

Titus Semple complained to the darkness also at that moment as he heaved his monstrous body on the bed. Repeated doses of baking soda hadn't served to cool the fire within his stomach, and the heat burned to ashes any satisfaction he might have taken in the returns.

"It ain't my guts," he voiced the lament, "no guts a man ever had could hold such torment. Right now I'd trade all nineteen of them new senators for an inch of cool stomach."

Although he brushed the notion away repeatedly, something other than his intestines was troubling him. It made him uneasy, and his eyes kept squinting there in the gloom, trying to pierce the restless fog of apprehension. It's like, he thought, I forgot somethin', somethin' important I shoulda remembered.

CHAPTER TWELVE

ANN-EVANS TURNED A PETULANT FACE FROM THE window. She was sick of Adams Street's noise, disgusted with Tallahassee, bored by the dreary, interminable session of the Legislature which convened in April. In the six months since Field's election she had learned many things.

"I'm going back to Truro." She glared defiantly at her husband, sprawled indolently on the bed, and at Titus Semple, sagging in the hotel room's one comfortable chair. Titus, she thought, was always in a chair and usually where she had to look at him. It was all his fault. He knew that a member of a legislature which met only once every two years couldn't live decently on the few dollars the state doled out for his services. She had imagined a senator's wife as sweeping grandly from one glittering function to another, being greeted with respectful murmurs, fawned upon. She had come with Field to his first session bearing such ideas only to have them smothered by the dowdy wives of her husband's fellow-legislators, blanketed by the knowledge that they were nobodies. The only persons who had bothered to be nice to them were the men after Field for his vote on some pet project. It made her feel cheap and small and, yes, cheated. "I'm going back home, to Truro." She repeated the statement with rising inflection.

Field shaded his eyes, grunted noncommittally, and hoped she would go home or keep quiet. It would be better, he decided, if she went to Truro and took Titus with her. He needed to be alone, particularly at this moment.

"Is Dan Curtis in Tallahassee?"

He asked the question without turning his head, knowing Titus would understand it was meant for him. For a fraction of time the rasping, methodical squeak of the rocker stopped, and when it resumed Field was possessed by the queer notion that it was treading warily.

"Uh." It could have meant yes or no.

He hadn't been mistaken then. The extravagantly improbable had been true, for if Titus hadn't known Dan Curtis was in town he would have said so at once. Dan Curtis and with him Lane. Walking down Monroe Street, from the Capitol, he had seen her standing for a moment beside a car. It was Lane, a different Lane, trim, groomed so expertly that even his un-trained eyes could recognize the perfection. It was a Lane poised, sure, but still with the gypsy life of her head. The in-credible portion of the picture was the man beside her, who must be Dan Curtis but couldn't be. He followed the girl into the car, which drew away while Field stared after them.

"I thought," he continued, dropping a hand over his fore-head, "I saw him this afternoon."

"Shouldn't be surprised, bub." The rocking was freer. "He'd have a lot of business here right now."

Semple drooped his head, shamming mild interest in Field's question and statement. He had known Dan Curtis was here for two days, known it because Dan had sent a note asking him to his hotel. Something had happened to Titus when he walked into Curtis's suite and saw the girl sitting on the windowsill, tapping her heels against the wall and regarding him without recognition.

Dan, with a glass in his hand, had opened the door to his knock.

"Thanks for comin' over, Sheriff."

He had been drinking a little. Titus could tell by the way he dropped the g. Drunk, maybe, and running around with a little chip. Only he wasn't drunk, just feeling rosy, and the girl wasn't a chip any longer.

"Miss Ballou. Sheriff Semple, of Truro."

Dan had been pleasantly cordial. There was no deception behind the introduction.

"How do you do, Sheriff Semple."

You couldn't mistake that voice. Behind his fleshy mask of simplicity, Titus drew the wires of caution tight.

"How you, Miss Ballou?"

"Take a chair, Titus." Dan indicated an ornate, overstuffed piece. "I'll make you a drink." At the small table Dan called over his shoulder. "Lane, Miss Ballou, wanted to see what the Legislature was like in session." He stirred the highball and passed it to Semple.

Every instinct was in play as Titus took the glass. "Ain't you drinkin', Miss Ballou?" He beamed contentedly across the room.

"Yes, thanks. I think I will."

She went to the table with quick assurance, waving away the offer Curtis made to fix a drink for her.

Back at the window Lane tilted her glass in the direction of the two men.

"Health."

Titus experienced a quick admiration and then slowly rising anger. I shoulda, he thought, vomited an' spit her out the first time she lit between my teeth.

For the hour he remained in the room Titus and Curtis talked unconcernedly of the current session and the likelihood of adjournment. There were few things left in the ordinary run of business which were of more than passing interest to either of them. While they spoke Lane sat at the window, her profile clear against the light, apparently indifferent to their words. Through it all, however, Semple had the feeling she was listening, blotting up each sentence as it fell. It made him restless, and he moved in his chair, shifting with almost unthinking discomfort while his mind darted away, following a line of thought and running it to ground. This Ballou girl was either a stupid little whore who had somehow fastened upon Dan Curtis and was satisfied to let old marks stand in exchange for security, or she was a damn sight too smart to be allowed in the open field. He wished he could make up his mind which.

The problem was still with him now as he sat watching Ann-Evans pluck at the curtains, kicking with an impatient toe at an edge of the carpet.

"Know what we ought to do?" Field on the bed was being studiedly casual. "Ought to get up some kind of a party if Curtis is here, have a little fun. My tail is getting tired from resting in a seat, listening to speeches."

"Might." Titus waited. This thing might have to be pulled right to the open. Trouble was if you got your hand on it you'd have to keep yanking no matter how many people the fuss woke up.

"Fielding Carlisle," Ann-Evans was accusing, "you aren't paying even a little bit of attention to me."

"Sure I am, sugar." He wanted to be agreeable.

"Well, you're not. I despise this place, and you don't care." She fixed a moody, recriminating glance upon Semple. "I thought a state senator could have almost anything he wanted. Instead, you'll have to find some sort of a job when we go home just like anyone else."

Titus slanted an eye up at her. "I wouldn't worry none about that if I was you, Ann-Evans. A man knowin' the right tree to sit under can always have somethin' drop in his lap."

Ann-Evans refused to be mollified, and at the moment the Sheriff was content to let her sizzle. He hadn't figured it out quite this way, but it looked as though Ann-Evans was going to be the thing to keep Field in line. A woman who wanted things usually looked first to her own man to put the pressure on. Titus lifted his heels from the floor and dropped them, up and down, down and up, a movement of inward satisfaction. Field had complained he wasn't doing anything. It was a symptom common enough in a new man, but Titus always liked to get it under control. Once—he knew this from previous encounters—an office holder got off on the idea he was a public servant he was likely to be a burr in someone's tail. At this first session Field had introduced a couple of bills of purely local character and then relapsed into the obscurity intended for him. That was common practice. The holdover members of the Senate recognized it as such, and so the new men who came in were allowed a quick fling. Field, though, Titus suspected, was restless, and he didn't want that. It might be a good idea to encourage Ann-Evans in wanting things. An ambitious politician could be handled a sight easier than an indifferent one, providing they only got ambitious about such things as cars, houses, money, and attention.

"I got somethin' in mind for you an' Field, Ann-Evans." He dropped the words smoothly and saw her face clear instantly. "We'll get a move for an adjournment here most any day now. Afterward it'll be time for talkin'."

Ann-Evans was only partly satisfied, but maybe Titus Semple knew what he was saying. After all, he had told Field he was going to Tallahassee and he did. She'd wait and see. Anyhow, in Truro, Field was important, and they'd be back there soon.

Field shifted his head on the pillow. It was hot, and the linen stuck to the back of his neck. Eyes steadfast on the ceiling he replayed the scene on Monroe Street again and again. Dan Curtis and Lane Ballou, the carnival kid, she had called herself. It didn't make sense.

Titus rocked slower, wishing he was on the Palmer House

133

porch. He could think better there. He could think and then, maybe, drive out to see Lute-Mae Sanders, who'd know everything that had happened.

Ann-Evans chafed at the windows, looking down upon Adams Street and seeing nothing, thinking only how stupid a man appeared lying flat on his back and wishing in God's name the hotel would catch on fire so Titus would leave.

In the bedroom of their suite Lane Ballou lay across the counterpane on her stomach, chin propped in both hands, listening to Dan Curtis snort into the basin of cold water where he was rinsing his face after shaving. She smiled with amusement. Dan was filled with outrageous animal sounds. When he bathed he grunted and rumbled like a St. Bernard dog. You could almost see him shake himself. Even washing his hands he made funny, oomping noises as though he were achieving a feat of major exertion. He came to the doorway now, rubbing vigorously at his solid features with a heavy bath towel.

"Had about enough of Tallahassee, Lane?" He twisted his head in a quizzical manner, thinking, as he had so many times during these past months, of her strange attraction.

"I guess so, Dan."

That was the trouble, he pondered into the toweling. He couldn't get close to her. Being with her was like searching out an object through binoculars while the adjusting screw was turning. She'd come into focus sharply one moment and then dissolve into a shadowy unreality. This trip to the Capitol was an example. There were a lot of places a girl might want a man to take her, but the chances were against Tallahassee's being one of them. Then there was her insistence upon living at Lute-Mae's.

They had spent a week in his cottage at Pablo Beach that first time he had taken her away. For him the seven days had been filled with the peace of complete relaxation. They swam, splashing briskly in the sharp ocean water; took long walks along the beach during late afternoon. In the evenings she used to read aloud, sitting by the wicker table within the moon of light thrown by a nickeled oil lamp. Sometimes he would drop off to sleep on the couch and awaken with a start to find her still reading, her voice low but distinct. When he asked for her she would come to him, but in this, as in everything else about her, his hands fastened only upon a wavering duskiness.

He had gone to Jacksonville from the beach, sending her

back to Lute-Mae's, but the deed troubled him until, in a fit of impatient anger, he called Truro on the telephone.

"I'm going to New York for a week or ten days," he said brusquely after she answered. "Tell Lute-Mae I want to take you along."

After he had hung up he went to a mirror on the wall of his office and studied himself there long and carefully.

"I'll be damned," he muttered, and there was unmistakable amazement in the exclamation.

New York was cold, and winter's sharp edge had already slashed autumn from the trees in Central Park. Looking down at it from their hotel room Lane shivered and turned away.

"I'm a Cracker at heart," she confessed to Dan. "Take the sun away, and I begin to shrivel inside."

The surprise Curtis experienced when he decided to bring Lane to New York had increased with the days. Without a perceptible falter she took the city in an unconcerned walk. The hotel, the theaters, and restaurants had, apparently, left her unimpressed. She moved with a sure instinct. So definite had been her touch, so assured and unaffected her poise that he was compelled to comment upon it one night.

"Did you think I might eat with my knife?" Her quick laugh was a thing of lively ripples. "I've been to the movies a lot."

He shook his head. "It isn't that. It's breeding."

Dan had insisted on a coat.

"I've never bought much for a woman before." The admission was made with frank embarrassment. "But I've been to the movies too, and I think the least a girl ought to get out of life is a mink coat."

They had shopped together, for Dan Curtis suddenly discovered he was having a lot of fun. He was never quite sure whether it was Lane's taste or that of the saleswomen, but everything she bought and wore possessed a consummate individuality.

"You know," he told her, for there was no pretense in him, "I'm proud to be seen with you."

Her hand was on his in a quick, spontaneous gesture.

"One of these days, Dan"—he could barely hear the whisper—"you will say something like that, and I'll cry. I don't want to cry, Dan."

When they left New York it had been Lane who insisted she return to Truro and Lute-Mae's.

"I belong there. This"—she allowed her fingers to slide over rich, dark pelts—"this doesn't change that any. This and the clothes and the way you treat me, the way you act before

135

other people, none of those things make me different from what I was before. You've a family in Jacksonville, responsibilities, obligations. A man like you can't have what he wants. That's the funny part of it, Dan. I'm just a carnival kid, so I can tell people to go to hell. They'd expect that of me anyhow."

"But God Almighty"—his protest was sharp—"I can't have you working at Lute-Mae's. I'll get you an apartment in Jacksonville. I'll buy a home for you if that's what you want."

"No." Her head moved ever so slightly. "I'm going to Lute-Mae's. I won't work there. You can believe that. Lute-Mae will let me stay, though. When you want me I'll come."

She left him at Jacksonville.

"I wish," he said, putting her on the southbound local, "you'd tell me what it is you're after. There's something inside of you that won't give. I can't figure it out, and I've always been pretty smart at understanding things. Take me any way you want, talk to me as if I were your father if that's what you need. I'm old enough to be your father by a couple of times at that."

Her tongue flicked maliciously between her teeth. "It's a good thing you aren't. There's a law agin' it, pardner."

After that they had met a couple of times a month. Dan traveled to Truro, or Lane would join him at St. Augustine or Daytona. Once they spent a second week at the Pablo Beach cottage.

In the beginning Lute-Mae was worried, and the first time Curtis came to Truro she took him upstairs to her room.

"In a way this ain't any of my business, Dan. Lookin' at it different it is. You're my friend, an' Lane is—or, by God, was—one of my little girls. I don't know what the hell I'm runnin' here now, a hotel or a sportin' house. All I want to know is if you're sure what you're doin'. A man like you ain't got no business stickin' out his throat an' leavin' a razor handy at the same time. Somebody'll take a swipe at it just for the hell of things."

Dan walked slowly around the room, halted to pour himself a short drink from Lute-Mae's bottle.

"I like her, Lute-Mae. When you like to be with a woman, not only to stay with her, but just because you feel comfortable and quiet when she's around, then you can't very well explain things, not even to yourself. I offered to take her out of here. She wouldn't leave. What do you know about that?"

Lute-Mae didn't know anything about that and said so with

wondering profanity. Later she watched while Curtis and Lane drove off, and there was confused anxiety in her eyes.

The trip which had brought them to Tallahassee had been Lane's suggestion. Dan wanted to drive over to the west coast and then down to Tampa.

"Is it near Tallahassee?" she asked.

"Not unless you're a crow that flies as a crow flies."

"Would you take me to Tallahassee instead?"

He hadn't believed she was serious at first, and, when he realized she was, his wonder increased.

"I'll take you," he said curiously, "if you'll tell me why you want to go."

"I'd like to go, that's all. Anyhow, the Legislature is in session. I read about it in the paper. If politics is your business shouldn't you be there?"

He shook his head. "You don't lie very well, Lane. You don't lie worth a damn. Just the same we'll go to Tallahassee, and, maybe, along the way we'll find out who's the smarter."

Looking at her now, cocked there on the bed, he was ready to confess that for her own purposes, at least, she was the smarter.

"If you're finished with Tallahassee," he continued, "I'd still like to show Tampa to you."

He rubbed at the backs of his hands with the towel and then tossed it carelessly into the bathroom.

"Yes"—she lingered over the words—"I'm through with Tallahassee, but I don't want to see Tampa. Let's go back to Truro."

Sitting beside her on the bed he pulled her head over until a cheek rested on his knee. For a moment he moved strong fingers through her hair with a gentle, thoughtful motion and then rested his palm on the nape of her neck.

"You can go back to Truro if you want to, Lane, but not to Lute-Mae's. We're finished there, you are at least."

"Mmmm. Scratch my head again."

"I'd rather pound some sense into it."

"It's already there, just needs tickling."

Turning until she could look up at him, Lane studied his face for what seemed a long time and then, with a startling change of character, pressed her lips to the lumpy knuckles of his hand.

"What is it you want me to do, Dan?"

"I'll buy a place for you in Truro, if you want to live there. Beyond that I haven't thought much. I'd like you to have a home, security, and some of the things to go with it. Maybe, if

137

you had that, the maggot inside you'd quit gnawing. Do you remember the first night I took you from Lute-Mae's and we drove to Pablo Beach? I told you then I had a feeling we might turn out to be friends and was curious to know why, I'm still curious. So much so that I'm going to put you in a place of your own where I can watch and find out."

He felt her body tighten against him and a convulsive shudder run along it.

"No, Dan." Something almost of desperation was in the cry. "It isn't worth it, Dan, not to you I mean. It makes what I've been after seem so dirty."

For a moment she was quiet, and then her small fist pounded ineffectually against his arm.

"Damn you, Dan Curtis. I told you you'd make me cry one of these days."

CHAPTER THIRTEEN

BECAUSE NONE OF IT WAS REAL ANYHOW—DAN SAID that—32 Flamingo Road had been built as no other house in Truro. Low, shingled with dusty, gray cypress which was relieved by the soft blue of shuttered windows, it half hid itself in a grove of bamboo, picked here and there by crepe myrtle and pepper bushes. Two ancient and weathered oaks held it captive on each side, and from the simple doorway a path of golden coquina slabs wandered carelessly to a picketed gate with its prissy white fence.

Flamingo Road had watched with wonder as the unmistakable touch of magic manifested itself. "The queer house," they called it and made frantic efforts to learn for whom it was being built. The local workmen didn't know. It was a contract from Jacksonville. So the house was fashioned, slowly and with infinite care, and when the carpenters, plumbers, and electricians packed their kits and departed they paused and looked back as though to reassure themselves that this was their work. After them came men to trim the shrubbery, set the sloping lawns, and build a rocky pool in which a bronze turtle performed the prodigious feat of squirting water from its upturned beak. Then, one day, when the yard was velvet a chinaberry tree at the back broke into flower, and the wind was gentle in the silvery green of the bamboo grove, Dan Curtis handed the deed for the property to Lane Ballou.

"It's the sort of a house I might have built for myself if I'd had the nerve," he said.

Lane held her breath as they walked inside. There was a dusky, half-light quality about the hall with its gleaming hand-rubbed paneling that made her afraid to speak. They went through the rooms together and finally to the kitchen where a young colored maid, self-consciously delighted in her new uniform, ducked her head shyly.

"This is Miss Ballou, Sarah. Take care of her."

The girl grinned happily. "Shoh will, suh."

In the living room, with its bright chintzes beneath rough, ax-hewn beams, Dan looked about him with satisfaction.

"This is just about the rightest thing I ever did," he admitted, "and as selfish a one too, for that matter." He took her hand and drew her beside him on the couch. "I don't know whether you'll be happy here, Lane. I'm afraid it's going to be lonely most of the time, lonely and, perhaps, a little unpleasant because there'll be no end to the curiosity about you on Flamingo Road and one of these days someone will find out you've moved up from the other side of the tracks. You'll have to take your chances. Don't open yourself up just so someone can hurt you."

Lane shut her eyes. During all those months while the house was building she had dreaded this moment. There was a finality about it which made turning back later impossible. Lute-Mae had attempted to soothe her.

"Sugar," she had said once as Lane worried around the room, "even a half-witted little girl would know how lucky she was to be in your place—get the nonsense of Field Carlisle out of her head."

Lane was astonished that the woman could be so obtuse.

"I won't be lonely, Dan." She rose hurriedly. "Take me outside and show me around."

They walked about the yard, Lane exclaiming delightedly over its bright perfection. At the back there was a second pool, and around it the broad, green leaves of the elephant-ear plant drew a cool barricade. Purple violets dotted the rim of the pond, and inside it were bright streaks of fire where small fish played.

"I think I like this best of all," Lane breathed. "It's the Never-Never land."

In the double-car garage was a new roadster. Dan pulled back one of the doors to show it to her.

"That," he said, "just about completes the place, Miss Ballou. We hope you'll be satisfied." He pinched his nose and looked down over his hand at her.

For a long moment she gazed into his face. "Do you want me to say anything, Dan?"

He shook his head slowly. "No," he answered gravely, "I was afraid you might. You know"—he touched her chin with his fingers—"you're something special in the way of a woman, Lane. Most girls would have gasped and fluttered and asked, 'Why are you doing this for me?' I'm glad you have better sense."

"But I know why." Her eyes were wide.

He laughed then, the sound subsiding into a deep chuckle. "I guess you do, and when you already know something there isn't much point in asking about it, is there?"

Inside the house again he handed her an envelope. She turned it over.

"Money?"

"Yes." He hesitated. "I suppose I might have thought of someway of opening an account for you, but I didn't."

"I'll be careful."

He smiled. "You don't have to be."

"I didn't mean with the money, Dan." She touched his sleeve. "I meant with you."

Curtis had to leave for Jacksonville early, and they walked together to the gate. Across the street Ellen Parsons, about to get into her car in front of the house, stopped and stared. She was the first of all Flamingo Road to see the people who were going to live in 32, and she experienced a delightful thrill of knowledge. My goodness, she thought, making a pretense of having difficulty in opening a door, do you suppose she's his daughter or wife?

Fiddling with her car she managed to remain where she was until after Curtis had driven away and then darted quick, anxious glances across the street. Lane, turning, saw her. Ellen Parsons nodded tentatively, and Lane, after a second's surprise, bowed slightly and then, turning, walked back to the house.

My goodness, Ellen said to herself, but she's a pretty young thing. Who in the world do you suppose they are? She nearly took a fender off on a handy tree, so absorbed was she in curiosity.

Lane strolled aimlessly through the rooms of her home. It's really mine, she thought. Princess Kalina, the girl from

Lute-Mae's, Lane Ballou, of the Eagle, all of them here on Flamingo Road. My God, what would the neighbors think if they knew? Suddenly she was afraid of being alone. There wasn't anyone she could talk with. The fact startled her at first. Why, she pondered, I don't know anyone in all Truro but Lute-Mae and the girls. Maybe Annabelle, but she didn't know what had happened to Annabelle. There was Field, but that was a long time ago. "I wonder," she said aloud, "how he is?"

In the kitchen the maid watched her new mistress out of the corner of her bright eyes while she wandered about, looking into closets, touching the shiny new taps at the sink, and playing with the icebox catch.

"You live in, Sarah?"

"Yessum, Miz Ballou." Her confidence returned. She never liked the first few hours in a new place. "My room above th' garage." It gave her a sense of importance to be able to explain things.

"That's good." She caught the girl's glance and stepped immediately upon the impudence growing there. "You can take the rest of the afternoon off. I'm going out." She was incensed with herself at being angry. She should have known, or asked Dan, about such details.

At the garage she sat behind the wheel of the roadster for a little while, smoking a cigarette with her head tilted back against the seat. I don't know what to do with myself. The silent confession worried her. Never before that she could remember had her life seemed so uncertain. Briskly she flicked the ignition switch, stepped on the starter, and backed carefully down the driveway.

In the street she halted, looking at 32. It's mine. It's mine, and yet the oftener I say it the less real it becomes. With her fingers she pinched at her bag and felt the deeds and envelope Dan had handed her. Even this failed to reassure her. I believe, she wondered, I'm afraid to go away for fear that when I come back it won't be here.

Driving slowly she counted the numbers along Flamingo Road. The Carlisle place was 110. Field had pointed it out to her late one night on their way back from Shell Springs.

"Ol' Cahlisle plantation, ma'am." He whistled a bar of Dixie. "Carpetbaggers came an' took hit away from de young massa." For all his flippancy Lane sensed it had hurt him to have to rent the place.

She took in each detail of the house, wondering if Field,

by now, had moved back to it. There was no one in sight, and the garage was empty with its doors open.

Truro was almost strange to her as she drove down Myrtle Street and into River, and she regarded it with new interest. There was the same lively air about the main thoroughfare, and the traffic was heavier if anything. Risking a glance from the road she took a quick look at the Eagle Café, and farther down the street her fingers gripped dead white on the wheel as she came abreast of the Palmer House. She didn't dare look up then.

Out on the Apulca road she drew off to one side and leaving the car walked across and down to the circus lot. It was unfamiliar. For some reason she couldn't explain she had hoped to recognize something here. It was just a barren clearing, stump-cluttered and weed-choked.

She almost ran to the car and once in it turned around and drove quickly back uptown.

I've just got to talk to someone, she thought. I ought to be gloating, satisfied. Instead I'm scared to death. Without conscious thought she swung into Loomis Avenue and down through the district to Lute-Mae's.

In his office at the Ponce Title and Mortgage Co., on River Street, Field cocked his feet on the desk and grinned waveringly at Titus. He was a little drunk, knew it and liked it. Old pus-gut didn't, though. He could see that.

"Drink, Sheriff?"

Titus stretched his legs. "Why, yes, bub," he said pleasantly, "I'll chew on a little piece of likker for a minute with you."

The geniality didn't ring true. Field sensed that as he reached into a half-open drawer of the desk and withdrew a bottle and two glasses. Titus measured his drink, squinted at it, and then drank slowly.

Field watched him cautiously. For the past two days he had been drunk, and he knew Titus knew it. It's funny, he thought, listening to the Sheriff grunt over his last swallow, I never cared much about drinking before. Now it seems I almost have to have it every now and then. He looked at the bottle and decided against sampling it again now.

"You an' Ann-Evans gettin' along all right?" Titus thrust out one cheek with his slab of a tongue.

"Why"—Field was startled at the question—"why, sure. Sure, what makes you think we aren't?"

"Nothin'. Nothin'. I was just wonderin' why she's out to that country club by herself most of the days an' why, maybe, you aren't there too. Looks like some fresh air might do you good, an', besides, it never hurt a man in your position none to be seen with his wife."

Field laughed. It was an uncertain sound. "I don't play golf." He tried to pass it off as a joke.

"Well, learn." There was a whip to the command, and the Sheriff's temperateness fled beneath it.

Field almost jumped in his seat.

"Now," the Sheriff continued, "look at things this way, bub. I'm a reasonable man, ain't I?"

Field fumbled with a package of cigarettes and finally succeeded in extracting one.

"Why," he said, "I never thought about it. Come to think about it, though, I don't suppose you are. No, by God, I don't."

"I wisht"—Semple eyed him—"I wisht I knew for sure whether it was you or the likker talkin'. If it's you I'll take it better."

Field's feet came off the desk deliberately. "It's me all right, Sheriff."

"That's good," Titus almost beamed. "I told you once I was tired of tradin' in mongrels. If you'da tucked your tail between your legs right then, I'da tossed you back into the scrub just like I would a dead cat."

Field poured himself a drink, poured it carefully, steadily and waited.

"Field"—Semple's eyes were closed—"I'm goin' to make you governor of this state. Not today nor tomorrow I ain't. Not maybe for six years or so. Another term in the Legislature after this one expires ought to season you. Come next, an' you can begin to raise your voice some and, by God, I'm goin' to send you to the Mansion. I ain't never had me a governor." His eyes snapped open. "Right now I ain't so sure if I get you I'll have one, but it's a chance I got to take. I'm goin' to have me a man in Tallahassee, but I got to skin a hell of a big bear to do it."

Field's eyes were on the desk clock before him. A long second hand moved silently. Its relentless pursuit of time was hypnotic, and he couldn't tear his gaze away. He wasn't surprised at what Titus was saying, only amazed at his calm acceptance of the declaration. "I ain't never had me a governor." In that one statement was revealed the festering lust which had rotted these years within the man.

"Now," Titus continued meditatively, "a man to the Legislature is one thing. He can stand on the street corner, chew a piece of twist, an' spit in the road. He can walk around with one gallus down an' patch in the seat of his pants if he wants to. That makes him one of the people. A governor is another thing. It's time you begin hoein' in the right row. That means Ann-Evans, the country club crowd. You got your home back. You got the money an' the position to do it. There ain't anythin' you need, is there?"

Field shook his head. He was sober now, thinking well if slowly. Titus didn't talk nonsense. Everything he had done since the day he had made him a deputy proved that. The Ponce Title and Mortgage Co. was an example.

"I can't have you sittin' on the curb whittlin' at a piece of white pine." Semple had been off-hand about the matter. "From now on you're vice-president of the Ponce Co. I'da made you president only the fella runnin' it's pretty good an', besides, a vice-president don't have to do nothin' but draw a salary. I'll see it's more than enough for you an' Ann-Evans to do what you want."

It had never occurred to him before, but Titus Semple must be a wealthy man. He'd have to be. Field could see that now, and he began to wonder at the multitude of trickles from over the county which must find their way into his well.

"I ain't never figured you for a damn fool, bub." Titus drummed on his belly. "Only a damn fool would turn down what I'm offerin'."

Field rose from his seat at the desk, walked down the room and back. The words, "I ain't never had me a governor," dogged his footsteps. What the hell. He already was Semple's man. He knew that; Titus, Ann-Evans, the Weldons, Clarks, and others, they all knew it too. What difference would it make if he sat a little higher?

"No," he said unemotionally, "I'm not a damn fool, Sheriff."

"That's what I figured." Titus heaved himself up. "Stop this drinkin' by yourself. Do it with the right people. You were born to most of them. You take care of that, an' I'll begin thinkin' about the bear I got to skin for us. We got plenty of time."

With an effort he pulled himself from the confining narrowness of the chair.

"Oh"—this was an afterthought—"you got a new neighbor on Flamingo Road. Know about it?"

Field shook his head absently.

"Yep. Dan Curtis."

Field was genuinely surprised. "You mean Dan Curtis has moved to Truro, on Flamingo Road?"

144

"Well"—Semple's bulbous nose waggled—"sort of by proxy, you might say. He built the new place, 32 it is."

Field understood what Titus was telling him, but a desperation, born of a bastard fancy, forced him to hear it all.

"Who's living there?"

"Oh"—Titus pretended to think—"little girl Dan's got. You know her, that circus girl, used to work at the Eagle. She's been on the line to Lute-Mae's for the past two years, about."

"You're crazy." Even as he shouted the denial Field realized that Titus wasn't making an idle statement. "You're crazy as hell."

"Shhh. I never figured you'd get so upset." Titus was pained and shocked.

"Why, you're insane, man. Lane—she, well, Christ, a girl just couldn't disappear into Lute-Mae Sanders's for two years without me, without anyone, knowing about it."

"Shuh, I don't know why not." Titus settled his hat. "Lute-Mae's girls don't get themselves out much, an' so unless a man was to go there lookin' for one he wouldn't be likely to hear about her."

Even after Titus left, Field still didn't believe what he had been told. He sat at his desk, staring at the clock until the silent sweep of the spidery indicator enraged him to the point of slamming the timepiece face down. Lane in Lute-Mae's. That was where she had gone. It had to be true. There was no other way to account for her being with Dan Curtis in Tallahassee back in April.

He took another drink and then rammed the cork into the bottle, hammering it with the heel of his fist. The raw whisky clawed at his throat, but when the shock subsided he felt better.

"Lane Ballou, the carnival kid," he said aloud. "From the Eagle to Flamingo Road by way of Lute-Mae's." His laugh was brittle.

For a long time he regarded a calendar on his desk, peering at it until the figures ran together. Honesty was beginning to assert itself. It was a hell of a fine time for him to feel anything about Lane Ballou. If she had gone to Lute-Mae's, then he was certain it had been because she wanted to. No one could have driven her. What was it she had said? Something about running. That was it. "I'm tired of running." Well, she wouldn't have to, not with Dan Curtis beside her.

That was the damnedest part of the whole business. Dan would know you couldn't set a girl up and keep her on a street like Flamingo Road without everyone there learning about it sooner or later.

He smiled at the idea of Lane Ballou on Flamingo Road. By God, she'd ram it down their throats if she wanted to, and if Dan Curtis was of a mind to he'd help. It ought to liven the street up like a rabbit with a thorn in its tail.

Unexpectedly he felt better. I didn't know where she was, he thought, and if I had I probably wouldn't have done anything about it except go out there to see her when I had the chance. If you're that sort of a born bastard, then it's simpler to admit it.

At a washstand behind a screen in a corner of the office he splashed cold water over his face, combed his hair carefully, and set his tie in place.

I'll swear, he was thinking without amusement, if I can take a girl out of the circus lot and start her going so she ends up on Flamingo Road in four years, I ought to be able to make a better deal for myself than I am. It was a deal he was making with Titus Semple. There was no mistake about that. If it could be swung he'd have the governor's chair a few years from now, and Titus would have the governor. It didn't sound so good.

Before a small shaving mirror he pulled at his cheeks, flattening out the lines with his fingers. I'm getting flabby, he admitted, inside, too, where it can't be seen.

His car was at the curb where he had left it, parked in defiance of a neat police sign which unmistakably asserted such a thing was against the law. He couldn't see that being a member of the Legislature had made much difference. He used to leave his car there when he was a deputy sheriff. He snickered sourly over this. Of course, he hadn't been vice-president of the Ponce Title and Mortgage Co., then. One of these days—he mulled the notion over—I'm going to find out what a title and mortgage company is and what a vice-president of one does.

Once off River Street he drove slowly, thinking of what Titus had said in the office. I got to skin a hell of a big bear to do it. Those had been the words. He hadn't paid much attention to them at the time. Now they reoccurred. There was only one hell of a big bear Titus Semple would have to skin, and it was Dan Curtis. He realized that now and wondered if the first step in the skinning could be Lane Ballou. He whistled quietly at the thought. Titus had seemed too well pleased with the knowledge of Lane's being on Flamingo Road, kept by Dan Curtis.

The fancy plagued him all the way home, and he dismissed it with difficulty as he turned into his driveway. Ann-Evans's car was there, the roadster she had always talked about, which old man Weldon had given her as a wedding present. She invariably left it in the driveway, a habit he found increasingly annoying. A lot of things about Ann-Evans, he realized, were picking at him. Underneath her light-headed chatter, childish enthusiasms, and juvenile emotions, Ann-Evans was as calculating as her old man, almost as ruthless as Titus Semple. She just went about securing her ends in a different manner.

She came out on the side porch as he stepped from the car, and he could tell she was in a flurry about something. He was sure of it when she ran down to meet him.

"Field, honey," she bubbled, "I know the most exciting thing. What do you think?"

Bending he kissed her, but she drew away, eager to unburden herself.

"Ellen Parsons came to the bridge at Norma's this afternoon, and what do you know? The people who built that cute place up where the Pointers' lot used to be have moved in." She backed off, waiting for his expression of amazement.

"That so?" He took her arm and turned toward the house.

Ann-Evans was disappointed but not deflated. "Yes, and Ellen says she's the prettiest thing you ever saw and he's a great big man with gray hair. She doesn't know whether he is her husband or her father."

"Why didn't she ask them?"

"Fielding Carlisle, don't be silly. How could she?"

Inside the house he wanted a drink, and Ann-Evans pursed her mouth with a disapproving gesture.

"You've already had a drink, a couple, maybe."

"Well, by God, I want a couple more, maybe." He was angry.

Ann-Evans gave a little squeal. "You needn't yell at me."

He patted her cheek then. "I'm sorry, sugar." He was. Ann-Evans couldn't be blamed if he was upset. "Tell Delia to bring me a drink, will you?"

"I will if you'll listen about the new people at 32. Who do you suppose they are?"

Ann-Evans perched on the arm of the couch while he sipped at a highball.

"Ellen said the girl had the most stunning suit on, tailored and so smart. Nothing you could get in Jacksonville she was sure."

147

"I'll bet the man wore pants too." Field was beginning to enjoy himself.

"You are a silly." She was mollified now that he was paying attention. "Sugar"—he could sense her eagerness—"do you think I ought to stop by there, you know, make a call or leave a card? Ellen said she was sure they were important just by the way they walked and looked, the man in particular."

Field's roar of delight almost unseated Ann-Evans. Something wonderful was about to happen on Flamingo Road. He wasn't sure just what it was, but he could see it coming. Ann-Evans, Ellen Parsons, the Rodgers, and the Bissels, and somewhere among them would be Lane Ballou. The picture took on a macabre quality. Maybe it was the liquor he had drunk, but it became a thing of unearthly shapes and struggle. Titus and Dan Curtis, Ann-Evans and Lane. Christ yes, throw in Lute-Mae for good measure, and don't forget the Governor. He was aware that Ann-Evans had moved away from the couch and was watching his laughter with something close to horror in her eyes.

"Stop it, Field!" She was frightened and uncertain. "Stop it this minute, do you hear?"

The mirth died as quickly as it had been born leaving him empty, nauseated.

"I'm sorry, sugar," he mumbled.

"Field"—Ann-Evans was worried—"are you drunk; I mean have you got those D.T.s or whatever it is they call them?"

He shook his head. "No, I'm all right. Something struck me funny, I guess." He drained the glass and lit a cigarette. The smoke was without taste. "What was it you were saying, sugar?"

She was uncertain. "Maybe you ought to lie down for awhile."

"I'm all right. Go on. You said something about paying a call at 32."

"Well"—this fearfully—"I only asked if you thought I should stop in." Her hands made vague gestures.

The demon was tickling at his insides again, but he kept a straight face.

"Why, sugar, I guess it would only be a neighborly thing to do. We might even ask them to dinner. Why not?"

"Oh." Ann-Evans was reassured. "I think we should too, only you've been so funny lately, not wanting to see anyone or go places. It would be perfectly thrilling to meet some really distinguished and important people. After all"—she dabbed at the hair behind her ears—"it isn't as though we didn't have something to offer in return."

"Sugar"—he was solemn—"you go right on and make friends if you want to. I wouldn't be surprised if the new people up at 32 turned out to be the most important folks on Flamingo Road."

CHAPTER FOURTEEN

FROM THE BEGINNING, ON THE DAY WHEN DAN CURTIS told her he had bought the Pointer lot for her home, Lane knew she couldn't expect to live on Flamingo Road and be overlooked by Truro. The district was too closely knit, the city too small. At the time she hadn't cared, for it had seemed an ironic jest; yet, as the weeks wore on and the establishment settled, she was frightened.

"Sugar, I'd spit right in their eyes an' make 'em think it's soda pop." Lute-Mae, who considered the residence of one of her little girls on the Heights in the light of a personal venture, offered the counsel without hesitation.

Lane shook her head dispiritedly. That wasn't what she wanted. With Dan away—he rarely came to Truro more than twice a month—she fled to Lute-Mae for company.

"It isn't that. People are too nice to me. Don't you see, I don't want to make fools of them." Nervously she crushed out a cigarette just lighted. "If they'd only let me alone I wouldn't have to worry all the time. The trouble is they try to be friendly."

"Put it down to the general curiosity of one bitch about another, an' you'll be closer to the truth. Women just aren't naturally companionable. I wouldn't worry none about what happens to 'em. If you sniff around long enough, you're bound to run into a bad smell sooner or later." Lute-Mae kicked off red and gold sandals and wriggled her toes complacently.

Lane wasn't satisfied. Lute-Mae wouldn't or, maybe, just couldn't understand. There was the woman across the street, for instance. Sarah, the maid, told her the family's name was Parsons. Ellen Parsons was doing her best to live up to a neighborly tradition. Twice she had waved a cheery greeting as she was driving off, and once, on the first day, she had made a timid attempt to speak. Then there was that nice-looking elderly man who lived a block or so away and evidently walked downtown every morning. Seeing Lane by the pool in the front yard he lifted his hat and paused to compliment her on the lawn. These and others would be friendly, take her into their homes and come to hers if she gave them a chance. For this they would draw nothing but mortification. It was bound to happen.

"But I don't hate people." There was something of despair in the cry. "There is only one thing I want. One thing I'm going to do."

"Titus Semple?"

Lute-Mae lifted her foot, twisting it around while she gave critical examination to her big toe.

"I'd get rid of that idea if I was you. It's likely to turn into mighty bad poison." The words were dispassionate, but there was no mistaking their sincerity.

Lane rose abruptly. Once everything had been so clearly defined in her mind. Now she was becoming confused and uncertain. It was hard to nurse a hatred for so long. There were times when she even forced the memory of Titus Semple, reminding herself she had wanted so little: a job at the Eagle, a room with Annabelle, some tiny measure of security, and Field to come for her when he felt like it. Titus Semple wouldn't let her have that. He ran her for the chase.

"Sometimes," she admitted, "I think Flamingo Road must be softening me up."

"It'd be God's own blessing."

"I don't know." Lane picked up her gloves. "I used to think I did." She looked at the bag in her hands and then at Lute-Mae. "I don't know where I'm going right this minute. Except to come to you I haven't been in downtown Truro since I moved into 32. I read the books Dan filled shelves with, tell Sarah what I want for lunch and supper, telephone the market, and then take the car and drive out to Shell Springs."

Lute-Mae sighed. "You'da made a wonderful little girl for me, Lane, if it wasn't for the bee you got in your pants. I don't know as I ever took to anyone like I did you. I was about to sit up here, bein' respectable the whole damn day, an' let you run things when Dan Curtis come along." She regarded her sitting room dourly. "Now, since you left, I don't take no joy in my little girls no more, an' the house is goin' to hell."

Driving homeward later, taking the roundabout back road she usually used, Lane impulsively turned off into Magnolia Avenue and followed it down to River Street. I might as well, she thought, get it over with. If I'm going to stay in Truro, I can't spend the rest of my life skulking up and down alleys or hiding behind the door.

In her purse was the envelope Dan Curtis left with her on the day they moved into Flamingo Road. From it she had taken what was needed for the market, grocery, and other household bills, paying them and Sarah's salary as they came due. There had been five thousand dollars to begin with, and most of it was intact.

The first move in the direction of respectability, she assured herself, is a bank account, and I'd better open one now before I lose my nerve.

In front of the Merchant's Trust Co., of Truro, she parked her car. After a moment she stepped to the sidewalk and walked briskly inside.

Harley Davis glanced up from behind his desk. The sight of her brought a baffled expression of half-recognition to his face. It was as if he were seeing someone he should remember but couldn't quite place.

"I'd like to open an account." Lane pinched the edge of her lip between her teeth. No wonder he is looking silly, she thought. He'd be even more puzzled if he could remember where it was he saw me. Young Davis was one of Lute-Mae's clients. He came often for a young Cuban girl called Mincie until Lute-Mae let her go.

Davis rose hastily and pulled a chair forward. "Certainly." He darted a perplexed look at her, and his mouth dropped open slightly as though he were about to say something else. "You, you'll want a checking account?"

"Yes, please." Lane placed the envelope on the desk. "There's about forty-six or -seven hundred dollars there, I'm not sure."

He counted through the money rapidly. "Forty-seven, twenty." His pen was poised above a card. "And your name?"

"Lane Ballou." She spelled it for him, knowing it would mean nothing. "The address is 32 Flamingo Road."

Davis wrote in a neat, precise hand. "We"—he was a little embarrassed—"we usually like a reference, Miss Ballou. You understand"—he paused—"it's sort of a protection for everyone."

She nodded. "Sheriff Titus Semple."

If he looked at her now, she knew she would scream with laughter. He didn't, although a slight frown wrinkled his brow for a second.

"If you'll just give us your signature there." He indicated a

151

line, and Lane wrote above it. Davis blotted the card carefully Plainly he wanted to say something.

"I'd like a large checkbook for household use." Lane had to speak. She was afraid of what might happen if she didn't.

Davis put the checks and account book into an envelope. "Thank you for your business, Miss Ballou." He handed the package to her. "You know," he said self-consciously, "I'm sure I've met you before someplace." He smiled invitingly.

Lane nodded. "Why, yes," she said distinctly. "I used to see you often at Lute-Mae Sanders's house."

There was something so pathetically astounded about his face, an expression of consternation, fear, and furtive panic that Lane wanted to call back the words. She hadn't meant to be malicious. In the split second before she spoke, she had the fancy she was being forthright, imagining the time had come for honesty. Some day, sometime, someone would point her out. It was simpler to have it done and over with by her own lips. Now, though, seeing the shock on Davis's features she wasn't sure.

"Ahh . . ." The man made a pitiful attempt to say something, but speech was not in him.

"Thank you." She couldn't bear to stand there longer. In her car again she was ashamed. Something, she reflected, is rotten deep inside me. It didn't used to be there. Walking from the bank she had felt Davis's eyes upon her. He was worried, that was the odd part of it all, he was worried because she knew. The anxiety, if there was to be any at all, should have been on her part. Instead she was feeling a freedom of release. Maybe, she mused, as the starter took hold, maybe Lute-Mae was right. Spit in their eyes and make them think it's soda pop. She realized, however, she would find no satisfaction in such an attitude.

"I wish to hell"—she spoke aloud—"I wish to hell I was back at Lute-Mae's."

Long distance was trying to get her when she reached home. Dan had been calling from Jacksonville. Waiting for his voice, Lane realized how much she had missed him. There was something so substantial in his presence. He was solid, sure, knew about everything.

"I'd like to borrow your house tomorrow evening, Miss Ballou." He was in high good humor over something.

"With or without me?" She could almost see him smiling.

"Oh, with you, I guess, if you'll wash your face and wear shoes."

"Do I have to do that?"

"Uh-huh." Curtis's laugh crackled over the wire, and then his mood changed. "I've got business to talk over with some of the boys. Thought, maybe, we could have a little poker game at the same time. Never can tell but what I might pick up enough for the rent."

"What time will you be down?"

There was a momentary hesitation. "I'll get in on the five o'clock train. Meet me?"

"Of course, Dan. Anything you want me to do?"

He was evidently thinking. "Well, might have Sarah fix some things to eat, bake a ham or something. There's plenty of whisky or should be unless you've taken to solitary drinking."

"I have it on my corn flakes in the morning."

He chuckled. "Beer might go good. Know where to get some?"

"No, but I'll find out."

"Say"—there was a certain touch of wonder in his voice—"this sounds domestic as hell, doesn't it?"

It did, and the realization of it was doing something to her. Her nose was stinging, and she blinked rapidly.

Giving her orders to Sarah later, Lane was conscious of an unfamiliar flush of excitement. She had something to do, someone to plan for. I'm acting like a bride with her first dinner. The idea amused her. Next thing you know I'll be joining a garden club.

Cliff Miner had beer. "It's Canadian ale," he explained over the telephone. "Hardly nobody wants to pay for it, but I got stuck with some."

She ordered the four cases he had and stood over Sarah while the girl stocked the icebox. "It shouldn't be too cold, Sarah." She'd read that somewhere. Critically she rechecked the list. Baked ham, potato salad, pickles, olives, a pot of home-baked beans, bread, White Rock, ginger ale, extra ice. It was all there.

Something of her concern transmitted itself to the maid. "Don' worrit none, Miz Ballou. Ah'll git everythin' fixed fahn."

Sarah began to feel at ease in the household when there was something to do for men. In the beginning she hadn't quite understood the establishment. The Mr. Curtis had hired her, but he'd only been back two or three times since. At first she had expected other men, but when her mistress continued to live alone, going out rarely and never seeing anyone, she wasn't sure what to think. This fuss now over men coming to the place was more in the normal way of things, and her eyes grew bright and her movements quicker.

153

The following afternoon, a full hour before train arrival, Lane was dressed and restless. She had never felt this way about Dan before. Maybe it was because he had asked her to do something for him. It made a difference. When she could stand the house no longer, she took the car and drove out on the Duval highway; anything to kill time until five o'clock.

There was no mistaking him as he stepped from the Coast Line express. Towering above the other men on the platform, he looked around and, catching sight of Lane, waved.

Waiting for Dan to come through the gates she tried to understand what she was feeling. There was something of gratitude, excitement, a sense of security, and a sudden slackening of the nervous tension which bound her.

With Curtis beside her, his bag in back, she slewed through the gravel driveway and out into Lake Avenue. Dan regarded her from the corner of his eyes.

"In a hurry?" He asked the question mildly but with interest.

She relaxed then. "No." Her voice shook a little. "I only wanted to get away from the depot before you changed your mind and got on another train." She waited for a moment and then continued. "I've never"—this with painful honesty—"felt that way about you before, Dan."

At the house Sarah had ice, whisky, and soda waiting on a table, and she took Dan's bag, carrying it without instructions to Lane's room. White people, she thought, did an awful lot of inching around about nothing.

Over a drink Curtis eyed Lane speculatively. Perched on the arm of a chair, glass in hand, she was radiant, alive.

"You look different somehow," he said.

"I am different, today at least."

"Happy here?"

"No." She held her glass tightly, fingers laced around it. "No, most of the time I'm not happy at all."

She told him of the small things which had happened: Ellen Parsons, the man down the road, Davis in the bank.

"I go to bed at night wondering what I'll do when the time comes, worrying for fear I'm going to hurt someone, specially you. It's been a long time since I gave a damn what happened to other people's feelings, and I can't get used to it."

"Is that why you told Davis who you were or, at least, where you had come from?"

She wasn't sure whether he was angry or curious.

"No. I guess at the time I thought it would be better to get things over with."

154

He laughed then. "You don't imagine young Davis is going to tell anyone and be asked how he knows?"

That hadn't occurred to her. It made sense though. She marveled at her stupidity. Then she remembered Titus, only she didn't want to tell Dan about him. Hurriedly she finished her drink.

"Who's coming tonight?"

Dan stretched out on the couch, his feet dangling over one end. He sighed contentedly.

"Oh, some of the boys. There were some things to talk over. I had the notion we might do it here."

"Is"—it was strange how the words came, almost as if someone else was doing the talking—"is that why you built the house? Sort of Lute-Mae Sanders's without the girls?"

There was something so bleak in the eyes he turned upon her that she shivered.

"Why, yes, Lane. If you want to put it that way. Only"— he seemed undecided—"only I had hoped you wouldn't."

The glass fell to the floor. There was no strength in her hands to hold it.

"Damn me." She cried. "God damn me to hell." She crossed and knelt by the couch. "Why do I talk that way, Dan? What's there inside to make me say such things?"

His mouth softened, and he lifted her chin with his finger tips. For a long time he studied her drawn features and then pinched her cheek lightly, understandingly.

"I guess, maybe, you're the only one to answer such a question, Lane." He paused. "Make me another drink, will you?"

She accepted the diversion gratefully, thankful for his tolerance and wondering at the obsession which harried her so unexpectedly. Dan, watching her, felt both pity and curiosity. He had long ago ceased to speculate on why he had done the things which resulted in this house on Flamingo Road.

"You were going to tell me who is coming." Lane, drink in hand, turned from the table.

"Oh, yes." He propped his head against a cushion. "I don't think the names will mean anything to you. Earnest Parker, from over at DeSoto, John Shelton, from Volusia, a couple of the boys from Marion, Jackson Ulee from Dade, and Titus Semple, you met him at Tallahassee last year."

He hadn't purposely left Semple's name until the last. She was sure of that. Always she wondered if Curtis knew about Semple. There was the chance he did, for Lute-Mae might have told him. Titus himself, if it would have served a purpose, would not have hesitated even after seeing them together at

Tallahassee. Dan's features, however, were innocent of any deception.

"Can you play poker and talk business at the same time?" Lane asked the question in all sincerity. Somehow the two didn't seem to go together.

Dan smiled. "The winners can always talk and usually do. The losers say, deal the cards." He chuckled over this. "It's an old Texas saying."

"Is Titus, Sheriff Semple, important to you, Dan?"

He humored her. "As important as the county, the district."

Lane toyed with a button on her dress, afraid to be transparent, wanting to ask more questions.

"Is, is he more important to you than you are to him?"

Dan glanced up then, a peculiar expression of concern on his face. He studied her carefully.

"What is it you want to know, Lane?"

She shook her head. "Nothing, just trying to fit people together." She rose from her chair. "Will you have something to eat before they come?"

"No." He watched her thoughtfully. "No, but I'd sure God like to know what it is you want." There was only frank interest in the statement. He wasn't annoyed.

She laughed because there was no answer. "I think I'd better change now." She halted abruptly. "Oh, I almost forgot. Do you want me to come down? I mean, should I?"

Dan swung into an upright position. "Of course. It's your home, isn't it?"

"I've got writin' on a piece of paper sayin' it is, mister."

"Well"—he stood beside her—"then why shouldn't you be here?"

Lane dressed carefully, wondering at the strange trick that was bringing Titus Semple to this house. Dan was downstairs, prowling through the kitchen, picking, she knew, at the buffet, talking with Sarah, whose high-pitched laughter she could hear now and then. The knowledge gave her a peculiar sensation of peace, of strength and confidence. The house needed a man. Every house did.

Lane was still in her room, purposely lingering over dressing when the doorbell sounded faintly. It startled her to realize that this was the first time anyone had rung at her door. Unexpectedly tense, she waited, listening for voices, wondering if she would recognize Titus Semple's. There was only a confused murmur and above it, now and then, the hearty tones of Dan's welcome. She didn't want to go down until they were

156

all there, particularly Titus. Somehow, she felt it would give him an advantage to find her waiting.

When the suspense became intolerable she gave a final quick glance in the mirror. There was no excuse for delaying longer, but if she could have reached Dan she would have begged off.

The living room was already cloudy with cigar and cigarette smoke. Dan, seeing her as she crossed from the staircase, rose, and the men, after a surprised glance across their shoulders, followed.

"Miss Ballou, gentlemen." Dan waited for her and then carefully introduced them singly.

Titus struggled to get out of his chair, pretending he was having difficulty in leaving it, but Lane realized he deliberately deferred the gesture of courtesy. There was an apologetic smirk on his face, but behind it his eyes were frosty.

"How you, Miss Ballou?" He stretched out a moist hand, practically forcing her to take it, and the sensation was that of holding a cold slice of liver.

Lane made an instinctive movement to press a handkerchief against her palm. The man frightened her, even now when she was in her own home, secure and with Dan Curtis at her side. Although he did nothing more than stand there, staring at her with the empty intensity of a halfwit, she had the feeling of relentless pursuit.

"Nice comfortable place you got, Miss Ballou." Titus stood until she was seated on the couch between Shelton and Jackson Ulee and then took a chair directly opposite where she would have to face him. "Ain't a house in all of Truro like it."

Lane ran the hem of a black lace handkerchief through her fingers. Dan was leaving her on her own. She sensed this and wondered if he had offered any explanation, who she was or why they had been invited here. There was, she knew, a frank, even friendly curiosity on the part of the men about her. They waited, not rudely, but with interest.

"Lived in Truro long, Miss Ballou?" John Shelton tried to help.

"Miss Ballou's one of our old residents." Semple nodded happily.

Lane took the highball Dan brought, flashing an uncertain smile up at him as she did.

"Is it true"—she fought the nervousness threatening to envelop the words—"what Dan says about poker games in Texas, that the winners whistle and tell stories and the losers say, deal the cards?"

It must be a good joke, she thought, for the men laughed

heartily, and the tension evaporated. She drew a long breath of relief.

"I God, Miss Ballou," Jackson Ulee drawled with an appreciative grin, "I ain't never been ahead often enough with these bandits to know for sure about the winners. Sure God, though, the losers want the cards dealt so's they can lose more."

"That doesn't sound very sensible." Her confidence was returning, and there was a certain mockery in the glance which met Semple's.

"Ordinarily speakin', Miss Ballou"—Titus's eyes were heavy—"most folks ain't sensible at all. You'd think they would be, but they ain't. They just sure ain't, an' that's a pity, too."

The words might have formed a trite generality, only they didn't. Lane rose.

"There are a lot of stubborn people in the world, I guess, Sheriff Semple." She touched her fingertips to John Shelton's shoulders as he started to get up. "No, stay where you are. I want to see the maid, and then I'll get out of your way."

In the kitchen she leaned against the icebox, shaking with fury. God damn his insolence, she thought, to threaten me here. Sarah rolled her eyes, watching her mistress apprehensively.

"You ain' feelin' a-raight, Miz Ballou?"

"I'm all right." She snapped the words and was sorry.

"Yes'm."

"I'd just put everything out there on the small table, Sarah"—she had control of herself again—"and let them help themselves. I guess they'd rather have it that way."

"You ain' goin' t' eat nothin', Miz Ballou?"

"I'm not hungry." She smiled. "Things look nice, Sarah."

The girl ducked her head delightedly, grinning with pleasure.

From the dining room came the scraping of chairs, and then Dan entered the kitchen. He snatched at a sliver of ham as Sarah carried it past, and there was an inquisitive quirk at his mouth.

"I didn't know," he remarked, as Sarah left the room, "that you and Titus Semple knew each other, before Tallahassee I mean."

"Do you think we did?"

"Uh-huh." He chewed contentedly on the ham, watching her with his head cocked to one side like an expectant puppy. "You see," he said, swallowing the morsel, "I know Titus even if I don't understand you so well sometimes. He reserves that

158

particular form of obscure speech for persons whose hides he's after."

"I'm out of season."

Dan nodded. "All right, Lane." He was quietly puzzled but not worried. "You'll get around to telling me about it one of these days."

She reached out and squeezed his hand. "Probably." She steered him toward the door. "Go on to your poker game now. I won't interrupt, maybe only to say good night later."

After Dan had gone she walked out the back door and into the garden. Against the heavy darkness of the yard, light from the windows made a broad checkerboard. The night was quiet, and in it the trickle of water as it splashed into the elephant-ear pool had a metallic tinkle. Suddenly she was afraid of the shadows, and she hurried around to the front of the house, letting herself in there, and slipped unnoticed upstairs to her room.

CHAPTER FIFTEEN

IT HAD HAPPENED AS SHE ALWAYS KNEW IT WOULD, quietly, without warning or design.

A fouled sparkplug, a loose connection, she never learned which, set the car to bucking on River Street, and because Weaver's Garage was handy she drove in and asked one of the boys to look at it.

"Lane's a funny name for a girl."

The voice drifted over her shoulder from behind as she sat waiting while the mechanic dove beneath the hood. Imperceptibly, gloved fingers closed about the edge of the wheel, and her eyes shut.

"Field's a funny name for a man." The words were a breath. "Hello, Sheriff."

When she turned he was standing beside her, leaning on arms crossed over the door's edge. He was smiling, but there was no strength in the expression. Gone, also, was the ready impudence once worn as a bright feather in his hat. It was all she could do to smother a gasp of surprise.

"Remember me?" Field drew himself erect.

"Sort of." There was a quick stab in the realization of the

159

truth. He was a man she only sort of remembered. Maybe that wasn't it at all. Maybe he just reminded her of someone she knew.

"I'm the fellow who chases girls out of carnival lots."

He was making such a desperate effort to recapture a mood they once had shared. There was something so pathetic in the attempt. Lane wanted to cover his mouth with her hand and spare him further humiliation. He must have seen what was written on her face, for his laughter trailed off weakly.

The mechanic closed the car's hood with a clatter. "Try her now, Miss."

Lane stepped on the starter, and the motor slipped into action, running smoothly.

"How much?" she called.

The man shook his head, wiping greasy hands on a piece of waste.

"That's all right, miss. We'll catch you the next time." He walked away.

For a moment she stared straight ahead and then spoke impulsively.

"Can you come for a ride with me, Field?"

There was a flash of the old cockiness. "If you promise I won't have to walk back."

It was a foolhardy thing to do. She realized this while backing out of the garage, yet there hadn't been much choice. To have driven away, leaving him to stand there, would have been impossible. Without conscious thought she skirted the town and turned off into the old mill road. The car, she reflected later, seemed to have guided itself. Not until they were in the section which paralleled the river did Field speak.

"It seems funny for you to be driving me along here." He searched his pockets for a match.

She wanted to cry out: "Field, what have you done to yourself?" Instead, she pretended absorption in a difficult stretch of road.

"You can run off here to the river," he directed. "The trail we used to take."

That was it, Lane thought. It was the flaccid, self-conscious attempt to reach a familiar footing by reminding her, with every word and gesture, he remembered. There was something almost servile in the maneuver. She risked a look at his face. My God—the fancy shocked her—Field even looked a little like Titus Semple. There was a craftiness clouding the features and with it an artificial air of buoyancy and the cheap shallowness of a professional backslapper.

At the river's edge she stopped the car, shutting off the motor. Field lit a cigarette and handed it to her.

"It's been a long time since I've done that."

"Don't, Field." She laid a hand on his arm. "Please don't keep talking that way. There's something, something almost dirty about it. Maybe I can't explain, but, well, you don't have to. I remember everything, better than you do I guess. When you spoke to me in Weaver's, before I could even see your face, everything you had done or said, the way you used to smile and how you felt . . . it was all there. It hurt so I couldn't breathe for a second. Then, when I looked at you, it hurt worse. Oh, Field. What are you doin? Where have you gone?"

He twisted the cigarette between his fingers. "I asked myself the same question about you once."

Lane shook her head. "No you didn't, Field. Not seriously anyhow." She covered his hand with hers. "You were always so honest with me, Field, I think I liked that best of all. You never pretended. Don't start now."

He shifted restlessly. "But I didn't know what had happened to you. I didn't hear until Semple told me a couple of months back, after you had moved to Flamingo Road."

"Would it have made any difference, Field?" She patted his hand understandingly. "You know it wouldn't. You're just trying to feel sorry for yourself, the way people work themselves into a crying jag. I think you've got the idea you ought to comfort the fallen woman, be charitable to the outcast; something of the sort."

"But"—he was sincerely baffled—"I don't understand what made you do it."

"Because I'm that kind of a girl, I guess." She leaned back against the cushion. "Believe me, a place like Lute-Mae's can make a hell of a case against virtue."

"Now there's Dan Curtis."

She was angry, furious in a way a mother can be at an unreasonably sulky child.

"Now there's Dan Curtis." She mimicked him. "Dan has been good to me. Anyhow, he hasn't done to me what Titus Semple has done to you." It was out, and there was no calling the words back.

Field's mouth drew into an angry line. "You don't understand about such things."

Her laugh was a thorned whiplash. "What makes you think I don't understand? Have you any idea who the men are Dan brings to the house, men who have become friends of mine. whose talk I can't help hearing? Do you know what they call

161

you?" Her breath came rapidly. "They call you the Sheriff's pratt boy. God Almighty, Field. I'd rather see you digging ditches and going home at night to a cabin than to be Semple's man."

She thought for a minute he was going to slap her as an almost insane fury contorted his features, and she shrank a little into the corner.

Then he seemed to wilt, an actual physical deflation. His face was haggard and drained of all color.

"I don't believe it," he muttered illogically.

Lane experienced both exasperation and tenderness. Speaking to him that way had been like sending a little boy home from a party because his nose was dirty or, worse, because he hadn't been invited.

"Field"—he had to believe her—"think things over, look back. Who are the men Dan Curtis invites to the house? John Shelton, Jackson Ulee, Link Niles, Parker: they are all there every couple of weeks or so. They do more than play poker, they are friends. They drink and they gamble and they talk, and whatever it is they decide they are friendly about it. Titus Semple has been over a couple of times, but he is always asked, I know that. Now, you're the senator from this district, and Dan has never once invited you, and it isn't because he has any idea you and I knew each other. Can't you see what it adds up to? They just take it for granted you are Semple's man and not worth bothering about."

He smiled half-heartedly. "You don't make it sound very pretty."

There was something so weary in the admission. Lane felt ashamed.

"I'm sorry, Field."

"No." The words came reluctantly. "I guess you should have told me. If I had any sense I might have figured it out for myself. Things have been so easy, riding on the little red wagon while someone else pulled. I never thought much how it looked from the sidewalk."

Even as he spoke Field realized he was lying. He did know, had known, and despite this knew he would continue to ride. There wasn't anything else he could do. The things he had taken from Titus. . . . It cost money, a hell of a lot of money, to live as he and Ann-Evans had been living these past months. Bills from the country club, bootleggers, caterers, grocery stores, and markets: they piled up, and he would go to Semple for the money. At first he had been reluctant to accept the help.

"You can't elect a governor with marbles, bub. If I ain't worried, why should you be? Long's you spend it on the right people there won't ever be a complaint from me."

If he quit Titus Semple he wouldn't have anything, not even a job. The place on Flamingo Road would be up for rent again, and he and Ann-Evans would likely enough be living with the Weldons. There would be one more session of the Legislature, and then on the following November he would be up for re-election. Hell, he just had to run again. It wasn't much of a job, he could see that now. Legislators were elected principally on local issues, piddling stuff as compared to the state itself; but a man did get known in his own district, and with the right backing he could go a long way.

"I don't know anything about politics," Lane frowned, "but I can't help hearing a lot of things with Dan around." She smiled hopefully at him. "I should think a man could be on his own after awhile. I know you can't get elected by standing on a soap box on the corner, but it does seem as though a man, once he was in, could make a name for himself, show the people he wanted to work for them. Then, maybe, he could be the voters' man and not Semple's." She studied him carefully. "You have an anxious look about you, Field. It wasn't there before. That's what Titus Semple has done for you. He's made you want something you can't get by yourself."

It wasn't the simple truth which hurt as much as the realization that the years which seemed to have compressed him into an ordinary mold had given Lane stature. This didn't make sense. He was a state senator; it counted for something. She was a girl who had been on the line at Lute-Mae Sanders's. Now she was being kept by a man on Flamingo Road. Yet with it all, there was something bright and fearless about her while he was uncertain, irresolute.

"You know"—he tried to divert the conversation into easier channels—"you're the object of considerable curiosity on Flamingo Road."

"I suppose so." She was disappointed. There had been so much to say.

"Yep, it's all I can do to keep Ann-Evans from running up to borrow a cup of sugar just to have a look at you."

"No, Field." She turned quickly. "Please don't let her come."

"I don't know why not." He was serious. "I told her once it wouldn't surprise me if you turned out to be the most important person on the Heights. I thought then I was joking. Now I'm not sure."

163

Despite herself Lane giggled. "You know what Dan calls me? He says I'm a backwoods Madame de Maintenon. I had to read a book he sent me about her to find out what he meant."

"Are you"—he found the question difficult to phrase—"happy? I mean, is everything all right?"

"I guess so, Field."

She was happy, now, this minute; she realized that. Truro no longer frightened her. Flamingo Road hadn't intruded to spoil the life being built for her. It was almost as though she had always lived there.

As for the town itself, she rarely gave it thought. Her first ventures into River Street had been timidly apprehensive, and then she discovered she was practically unknown. Now and then she would see a familiar face, someone she had known at the Eagle, and would wait for the surprised recognition. It never came. Frequently she found people looking at her, sure she was someone they knew. At such times she tossed a nod or a brief hello and went on, leaving them to wonder who she was. Once or twice, in the markets or drugstore she encountered people who spoke her name.

"How you, Lane? Been away?"

Never more than that. If they had once read the item which appeared in the *Journal* after she had been released from the Farm, it seemed to have been forgotten. Truro was booming, and in its restlessness there was either tolerance or indifference. It even began to be fun, going downtown in the mornings, shopping for things she didn't need, knowing women turned to look after her as she passed, enviously admiring her clothes and figure.

Dan had been right. Such men as Davis at the bank and others who occasionally went to Lute-Mae's and who might have remembered said nothing. They couldn't very well.

Doc Watson, of the *Advertiser*, spotted her, but she hadn't minded. One morning, coming out of Carver's, she bumped into his spare, shambling figure. Watson tipped his hat, started to mumble an apology, and then his keen blue eyes twinkled. He surveyed her carefully and whistled.

"My God, Miss Ballou, you're a wonderful testimonial to the efficacy of the *Advertiser's* Help Wanted columns. You are," he added with a shade of doubt, "the Ballou girl, aren't you?"

"Yes"—her smile was warm—"and I never did thank you for that ad."

"You never told me about you an' Titus Semple, either."
He walked beside her to the car. "There's also a little item
dealing with the County Farm I'd like to get cleared up some
day. You see," he said, holding open the door, "I know something about young girls, raised four myself, consequently I
never believed the County Farm story. Maybe"—he hesitated—"it isn't really diplomatic to bring a thing like that up,
but I'm a reporter at heart. Can't get over the habit of sticking
my nose in other people's business."

It was strange, but the reference hadn't hurt. The incident
itself was without meaning.

"Can I drop you someplace?" She motioned to the seat
beside her.

"No-oo. I'll walk. It's good for what's left of my liver." He
closed the door gently. "I hear lots of things," he ruminated.
"One of them is you're living on the Heights." He grinned.
"Now, if you'll tell me it's none of my business and to go to
hell, I'll be on my way."

"Everything is a reporter's business, I guess." There was
something so compellingly friendly about the man she couldn't
be angry. "It's a right nice house. Why don't you stop in some
time?"

"You know"—his voice was soft—"I'm going to do that very
thing." He lifted his hat, and a lock of gray hair fell across
his face, lending a rakish touch to his appearance. "Thank
you for the invitation, Miss Ballou."

She told Dan about the meeting, and he seemed pleased.
"He's a good friend to have, a little helpless maybe but good.
He got in Titus Semple's way once and never recovered, a
common failing of those the Sheriff skins." He touched her
chin with the back of his hand. "They may get their hides
back, but somehow they never quite fit again."

She turned now to Field. "That wasn't quite the truth then,
when I said I guessed so. I am happy, only it's hard to explain.
It's not something you're glad to have but a thing you want
to keep, take care of."

"Is he, Curtis, going to marry you?"

"I don't think so. Can you think of any good reason why
he should?"

He frowned. "Well, only because it might make it easier for
you."

"Did you want to marry me?"

He flushed. "We, it wasn't the same thing."

"No." Her lips were parted, lingering over the sound. "It
wasn't the same thing. It was pretty wonderful, though, for

165

me. It never happened before, not that way." She pressed the back of her head against the seat. "Kiss me now, Field. Like this while I have my eyes shut." She waited for his mouth.

He was awkward, rebelliously self-conscious, and finally, when he raised his face, their eyes met and suddenly smiled.

"It's gone." He spoke with wonder. "What do you know about that? It just isn't there any more."

Lane's breath was deep, filled with gratitude. "I had to know, Field. I've been carrying something around with me for so long. I had to know if it was real." She reached up to touch his face tenderly. "It's good to be sure I don't have to be afraid." She straightened, placing her arms across the wheel. "Will you come and see me, Field?"

"If you want me to."

She nodded. "Always. Now"—she reached slowly down and touched the ignition switch—"now I think I'd like to go home right away."

Flamingo Road was powdered with the blue dusting of late afternoon when she drove up the graveled run to the garage. Sarah had set early lights in the living room, and their glow, washing through partly drawn blinds, made the house seem warm and welcoming from the outside. For the first time Lane experienced a fierce possessiveness. This was home. It belonged to her and she to it, and there was a lilting confidence in the snatch of song she hummed after putting the car away.

Sinking into a deep chair, waiting for Sarah to bring tea, she marveled at the stubbornness with which she had harbored a ghost. For four years she had clung to the shadow of Field Carlisle with the persistency of a schoolgirl jealous of a first love. And, she could wonder when it had happened, on what day it had ceased to exist, it just wasn't there when she tried to touch it again. Even Field had known when he kissed her and was strangely relieved.

Curled in the chair Lane looked around the room, seeing it anew and through different eyes, and in that moment she wanted Dan Curtis to be there, quizzical, half-amused, comfortable, and—she knew this to be true—a bit puzzled. She could think of Field and feel sorry for him. It wasn't pleasant to see the spiritual erosion of a man whose hands and body had once borne the power to create such bitter-sweet agony. She could even meditate on Titus Semple, feeling fury no longer but only a revulsion of spirit. Of the other things, the County Farm, Lute-Mae's, the cheap, snarling little man who had taken her in Coyne's carnival: they were disconnected parts of a dream someone else might have had. They formed an unpleasant story once read.

Sarah arranged tea on a small table beside her. "You lookin' good this aftahn'n, Miz Lane. Mus' be happy 'bout somethin'." She smiled confidentially and patted the hot water jug with her fingers to test its warmth.

"I am, Sarah. Something wonderful happened this afternoon." She locked hands behind her head and stared at the ceiling. A man lost in the woods and suddenly coming upon a paved and well-marked road would feel this gratitude, this relief.

"Will you have suppah heah latah, en a tray, o' inside, Miz Lane?"

"I don't know, Sarah, I'm not sure I'll ever be hungry or want anything again."

There was something, though, she wanted. Abruptly she left the chair and went to the telephone. She had never called Dan before. He had given her his office number. "Just in case," he said. She asked the operator for it now and waited while the request sped and spanned the distance to Jacksonville.

"I—I don't know what to say." She made the confession after the call was completed.

"Anything wrong?" Dan at the other end was concerned.

"No. I just wanted to"—she laughed embarrassedly—"I only wanted to hear your voice."

She could almost see him thinking this over, searching for a motive.

"I've been out all afternoon. When I came back I realized I was home, and, well, I guess I wanted to thank you or something. I never have."

"Oh." He seemed relieved. "You're sure that's all?"

"Yes, Dan."

"Well"—she knew he was smiling—"this is sort of a new role for you. I think I'll come down for the week end and enjoy it."

"Will you really?"

"Saturday afternoon."

"I'll be at the station Friday night, waiting. Good-by, Dan."

For a long time after he had replaced the receiver and pushed the telephone to one side of his desk, Dan sat staring at the instrument, his fingers tapping soundlessly. It was late, and the offices of the Curtis Construction and Development Co. were quiet and deserted. He had remained in his office, high above Hogan Street, because he wanted to think. Without effort on his part the loose threads of his life were being gathered together, and he was fascinated by the inexorable process, working outside and independent of him. The unexpected call from Lane was only another manifestation of the relentless execution of forces beyond his control. It was a disturbing notion, and he pondered over it, half annoyed, half analytically curious. A few moments before he had been on the point of telephoning Truro, and then the decision was taken from his hands.

Leaning back in his chair, his eyes roamed around the office walls. In severe black frames there was the record of Daniel Vincent Curtis. Set down in black and white photographs were the mills he had built, phosphate plants constructed; there were pictures of giant dredges biting away at drainage canals, photographs of turpentine camps, railroads. Scattered among them were flashlight accounts of banquets, testimonial dinners, inaugurations.

In the beginning his excursion into state's politics had been in the nature of a defensive foray. He had invaded to frustrate the invasion of others. He built, but as he went from one project to another it became plain that his work had to be protected, and so, little by little, he moved upon the state, helping to elect here, planning a defeat there. Money, time, and boundless energy had been poured into the campaigns, and then one day he awoke to find himself the hub of a complex machine.

He hadn't consciously sought the position. There were disadvantages in being both lever and fulcrum. For his native state, however, he had an abiding faith and affection. From the dune-scattered coastal areas, through the mysteriously beautiful pine stands, to the lake and ridge section farther inland, Florida frequently spoke to him of greatness, unrecognized and neglected. If the men elected to govern it were, for the most part, his men, then they were as worthy as those offered by his opponents. If there was graft, chicanery, and furtive manipulations in the high places, then such things had to be expected. They formed the irritating fuzz on democracy's peach.

As the years consolidated the power of Dan Curtis, he felt the obligation of guarding it against the predatory instincts of the men who shared some measure of it with him. There was no denying the Semples of the world, but their eternal questing could be confined. He fenced the range through which they could prowl, eternally vigilant, understanding but firm.

At fifty-seven, Dan Curtis had seen his life as simply ordered. He was wealthy by any standards, and if all of the money which flowed into his hands was not as clean as it might have been he felt no qualms about its condition. What he took came from other men: from the stupidly conniving, the avaricious, the combinations which insisted they were smarter than he, but not from his state. If tax assessments favored his enterprises, franchises and contracts came his way, then he built good roads, operated efficient utilities, and, now and then, cut a small slice of pie for his investors. It was more than they would have received from the Semples.

His children were grown and married. His wife, a pallid creature, delighted in her garden clubs, her civic charities, her orphans and poor, asked nothing more of him than to be allowed to pursue her way.

The chart of the devious but well-marked channel he was following had been before him. There seemed little to do but trace it to the end, and then—he clung to the analogy—unsuspected shoals developed. Someone changed the lights while he was in midstream, and he found their appearance both exciting and vitalizing.

At first it used to amuse him to shut his eyes and try to imagine the sort of girl or woman he might have taken if the choice had been deliberate. Always she emerged as Lane Ballou, but never, through the most fantastic workings of his mind could he conceive of her coming from a bawdy house. That was the supreme jest. There were times when he separated this sequence of his life, scattering the pieces as parts of a puzzle, and then coldly and with an unflinching eye to the facts tried to put them together again. This, he would say, is Dan Curtis. This is a little whore from Lute-Mae Sanders's house in Truro. Then he would become impatient and sweep the picture away. It was only partly true. He was Dan Curtis, but Lane was never anything but Lane Ballou. Life had made no more impression upon her than a wind in the scrub does upon a high-flung cloud. She moved serenely and untouched above surface turmoil.

So sure of this had he been that the home he built for her on Flamingo Road had come as a spontaneous gesture. It was as though the place was a right she had somehow been denied. She hadn't belonged in Lute-Mae's any more, well, any more than he had. That they had come away together was proof enough of this.

It surprised him a little to realize he hadn't been amazed at the confidence with which she accepted the house and the responsibility it implied. He, in turn, had felt no doubt in inviting his friends and associates there. So sure, apparently, was

Lane of herself that she communicated this confidence to him.

He smiled thoughtfully. So certain had been her hands, so completely possessed her movements, that such men as Jackson Ulee, Shelton, and the others admitted her presence as mistress of the place on Flamingo Road with open admiration. Ulee, lean, hard-bitten, and infected with the native suspicion of a Cracker, was her frank and outspoken admirer. Never, in speech or deportment, was there the suggestion that a mis-alliance had been contracted. Their attitude toward Lane Ballou was touched with the deference they might have displayed toward the wife of a friend. If anything they were more careful.

The fortnightly gatherings, all-night poker sessions on Flamingo Road, became events at which old suspicions were banished, new bonds wrought. For the first time they found themselves sitting around a table, friendly, open, and unmindful of sectional jealousies and individual greeds. Open covenants, Dan mused, openly arrived at.

To the house on Flamingo Road there came crates of select fruit from Jackson's groves along the Indian River. Walter Haines was forever sending Lane some small curiosity from Tampa. Parker and Shelton never failed to remember her with something, a note, flowers, and once John had sent a cocker spaniel puppy from a prize litter. She was, Dan thought, all things to all men.

Only Titus Semple remained curiously remote, almost scornfully, vindictively aloof. This puzzled Dan, and time and time again he had been on the point of asking Lane about it. They shared some dark and bitter brew, an unhealthy potion. Of this he was sure. Sooner or later one would force it to the other's lips, and the knowledge, the conviction, of impending disaster was strong within him. He thought about it now, sitting alone in his office, and was half-determined to force an answer to the mystery.

CHAPTER SIXTEEN

DEEP IN A WICKER CHAIR ON THE PALMER HOUSE porch, Titus Semple rested. His head was bowed, chin sunk until the pinkish jowls puffed upward into rolls, robbing his features of all line. His eyes closed as he steeped himself in a toxic broth of slow bubbling fury. Viciously he was turning upon himself, but the vile stench of his rage penetrated into innumerable dark corners throughout the county. It seeped into the great prison at Raiford, across the striped gangs of convict labor hired by the state to private contractors. It crept through drawn windows in Truro's cribs and brothels and drifted into the police department and mayor's office alike. With it went the whisper: "The Sheriff's loose."

Convicts who had been subsisting on about twenty cents a day out of the allotment of sixty-five cents set aside for the sheriff's office tightened their belts and looked for the deluge of stinking sowbelly and wormy grits they knew was coming. Pinched-faced drabs along the line in the railroad district waited anxiously for "the man" to tell them what his collections were to be from now on, and word went out from the police to bootleggers and 'shine runners in the flats alike that hell was cooking. "The Sheriff's loose." Turpentine men who had made deals to take convict labor at sixty cents a day instead of the prescribed dollar, none of which ever reached the state's treasury, wondered resignedly what the push would be and waited for word from Truro.

The Sheriff was going to need money, a lot of it, and none knew better than those to whom the news was sent where it was to come from.

Immobile, outwardly drowsing, Titus stirred his bile. He had made a mistake, and Titus Semple didn't like people who made mistakes. He was a man who had pricked his finger, ignored the accident, and awakened to discover he was dying of blood poisoning. The pin prick, he realized, was a waitress at the Eagle Café, a little chit from Lute-Mae's.

He wondered now why he hadn't instinctively recognized the menace when she returned to Truro after the prison farm. An ordinary woman would have been frightened, timid, and anxious to keep out of sight. Instead, this one ended up on Flamingo Road, out of reach but in a position where, deliberately or otherwise, she could cut him slowly to pieces.

The house at 32 Flamingo Road was too important. More, it threatened to become a citadel impossible to assault. For years Titus had thrived on the petty dissensions, sectional greed of district and county leaders. He had fattened on them, waiting, suggesting, watching, and eventually forcing his own ambitions through the broken ranks. When men couldn't agree Titus invariably had counter moves to propose, compromises which ultimately worked to his own advantage. Now, the establishment on Flamingo Road challenged the deadly simplicity of this procedure, for where men met in harmony, played cards, and settled their differences in amiable discussion there were few chinks to be pried at. There had been a time when Parker and Shelton would stop off at Truro to see him. Now when they came they went to Flamingo Road to be made welcome by a hot-eyed slut who had had the impudence, a week ago, to whistle shrilly at him as she went flying past the Palmer House in the roadster Dan Curtis bought her.

He admitted there was no point in sniping at 32 from a hotel porch. He had tried, and the memory caused him to stir uncomfortably. It had been a futile, childishly enraged gesture to begin with, and the girl made a fool out of him.

Lane had been awakened, not by the ringing of the bell, but by heavy pounding on her door, drunken yells, and cat-calls from the yard.

"Company. Company in the parlor." The derisive screams were piped in high falsetto. "Open the door, sugar. Lute-Mae sent us."

From her window Lane could see shadowy figures on the lawn. There was no doubt in her mind where they had come from or who sent them. Swaggering toughs from the district's pool halls and speakeasies, they whistled and tramped through the flower beds, pausing to look up at darkened windows.

"Company, Lane. Company in the parlor, sugar."

She saw a light go on in the Parsons' house across the street. That was what they wanted, the entire neighborhood to hear their obscenities.

Trembling, consumed by murderous ferocity, she went to the bureau in Dan's room where he had left a pistol. "You're alone," he suggested, "can't tell but what it might come in handy."

Holding the pistol—she had never fired one—Lane ran downstairs, trying to shut out the hideous sounds beating against her ears. With a sweep she flung the door open and stood silhouetted in the frame. The man before her gazed stupidly, his eyes traveling to the gun. Then, slowly he began backing away.

"I'm going to start shooting." Lane kept her voice level.

The confusion evaporated.

"I'll give you one minute to get out of my yard." Her words were sharp and distinct.

The man standing at the door mumbled protestingly, but his eyes never left the pistol as he sidled to the steps and down them. He licked nervously at his mouth, and then feeling the

172

walk with one foot he turned and broke, running toward the open gate. Silently, with backward glances, his companions joined him. With a yell of cheap bravado, they scattered and disappeared down the street.

Nausea gripped at Lane's throat as she closed the door. With a little whimper she dropped to her knees behind it, sobbing with dry, rasping sounds.

There was no need to wonder who had inspired the scene. She knew, was as certain as if she had seen Titus Semple with the filthy mob. After the hysterical rage passed she could feel an exultant contempt. Without trying she had reduced Titus Semple to this shoddy gesture.

Lane never told Dan of the incident. He wouldn't have believed Semple could have had anything to do with it. Not unless the entire story was spread before him could he understand, and Lane hadn't wanted him to know. She locked the secret away in a chest of unpleasant memories. Some day it could be taken out.

His heavily burdened chair squeaked complainingly as Titus moved in it now. He was ashamed of himself, ashamed, not for the deed itself, but at the puerile imagination which inspired it. He should be above such tricks. It seemed as though he couldn't think straight any more. A senseless and unreasoning resentment was robbing him of all cunning. If he had thought he would have known a stunt like that couldn't do any good. If anything he was pushed into defending himself against the girl's unspoken scorn.

Once, later, he met Curtis at the house by invitation, but the cool indifference in the eyes of the girl who stood at Dan's side robbed him of confidence. He fumbled with words and ideas, displaying an uncertainty which caused Curtis to look at him in surprise.

Important and far-reaching legislation was due at the forthcoming session. Dan, for one thing, wanted an amendment to cut away some of the underbrush through which the state's representatives had to struggle. Because of legislative charters many of the municipalities' problems, presented in the form of local bills, had to be thrashed out at Tallahassee. These consumed time and energy at the expense of the state.

"You might," Dan suggested, "have your young Carlisle introduce it. Give him something to do."

Titus wasn't thinking about legislative sessions. Behind his cloudy eyes he was weighing Titus Semple against Dan Curtis. To hell with him and his legislation. The time had come to start bear skinning. He wanted to get away and whet his knife in secret.

That evening he called Field. "You come down an' see me, bub," he suggested. "We got work to do."

Into Field's incredulous ears he dropped fragments of an idea.

"We ain't goin' to wait no more, bub. You're goin' to enter the primaries for governor next year."

"You're joking."

"I ain't made a joke in a hell of a long time now, bub. It ain't likely I'd start now." Titus sucked at his lower lip. He was obsessed by the feeling he was being forced into something, and he didn't like it.

"Will they run me?" Field watched Titus. He didn't understand any of this.

"They'll run you all right when the time comes. Right now, though, nobody but you an' me knows what's goin' to happen. It's time you got movin' around the state some. This is goin' to be a sight different from sendin' you to the Legislature."

Even as he spoke Titus realized he was hurrying into unnecessary trouble. A few more years, handling Field right, and he could walk into the Mansion with Carlisle on his arm. He was mad now. It seemed he was mad all the time, and anger warped his judgment, twisting things out of proportion. He knew former Governor Watterson, from Orange County, had already been picked to succeed the incumbent, whose term was expiring. This was decided long ago, and he had been party to it.

"I've heard talk of Watterson." Field was cautious.

Titus blew out his mouth. "They ain't goin' to support Watterson, bub. They'll carry you into Tallahassee, smack through the primaries and general election, or I'll blow the whole damned outfit out of the state an' into jail."

"I thought you were going to wait a few years." Field imagined Titus looked like an angry puff-toad.

"We ain't goin' to wait." He leaned back in his chair. "I'm fixin' a speakin' tour up for you, only it ain't supposed to be nothin' more than a little campaignin' for your re-election to the Legislature. Bear down on things like helpin' the poor Cracker, takin' from the rich an' givin' to the poor. Talk about lowerin' taxes on farm lands an' raisin' them on utilities. You'll be surprised as hell to find out how many contradictin' statements you can make an' still get believed by everybody. Make speeches on prison reform; almost everybody's got a relative in jail or on the way. It goes good when they think things are goin' to be better for them."

The Sheriff's face twisted into a complacent smile. He was feeling better already for the conniving. By God, let 'em sit on their behinds up on Flamingo Road. They'd have Fielding Carlisle for the next governor, or he'd take 'em apart, piece by piece. He knew where the joints were. With Field in the Mansion he'd run Dan Curtis and his little black-headed bitch right across the flats until they were ragged.

"You go on home now, bub." Titus absently indicated the door with a jerk of his head. "Don't try none to figure things out."

Hot resentment flooded Field. The fat son of a bitch, he thought, chasing me out as though I were a bellboy. For a moment he was tempted to tell Titus to go to hell, and then he sagged inside. What, he kept asking himself, would there be left if he did? He knew the answer: swift and certain oblivion, with a querulous Ann-Evans to explain to and old man Weldon for a never satisfied employer.

After Field had gone, Titus sat in his room thinking. He was going to need money, that and all his guile. Well, he had one, and the other wouldn't be hard to raise; a little squeeze here, a pinch there. None of this would have happened, though, if he'd clubbed that girl down in the beginning, but who in the name of sweet God would think she'd tie on to Dan Curtis and make him like it.

Sitting in a warm corner of the Palmer House porch now he raged over his carelessness. In a way he could lay a lot of the blame on Lute-Mae's doorstep. If she hadn't taken the girl in! By God, if he hadn't stopped before she was run out of the county, then Lute-Mae would never have had the chance to take her. Just the same it would serve Lute-Mae right if he had the roof torn off her place. He was further incensed by the knowledge that Curtis had come down to Truro that afternoon and this minute was probably at the house on Flamingo Road fondling a little slut whose eyes could set a man on fire.

At the moment only one thing pleased him. Field was getting attention on this tour. The fellow hired to write his speeches knew his business because the stuff was getting in the newspapers. It sounded fine even if none of it meant anything. It sure sounded good; Titus admitted this admiringly. Field was talking about things most people understood: old-age pensions, homes for the needy, public health service, lower taxes, kicking out the politicians, good roads, and rural bounties. There was a little something there for everyone.

There wasn't any question but what Field made a great appearance on a platform. He looked sometimes, Titus imagined, like the Judge, and that was good. Most office holders had a hungry look. Field spoke and acted as though he believed what he was saying. It had been a fine idea to have Ann-Evans go along with him. She might not be any too bright, but she was pretty enough for the men and dumb enough to suit the women. Women were suspicious of a smart female.

Titus watched carefully to see if any of the newspaper reports or brief editorial comments suggested, perhaps, Senator Carlisle might be practicing for the gubernatorial race. He was chasing pretty wide for a state senator without ambitions. A man who went outside his own district usually had something on his mind. It was too early for the political observers to begin analyzing motives, and this suited Titus. When the time came for talking he'd do it and into the right ears.

At the moment he wanted only to sit where he was, suckling at a poisonous teat. Maybe Dan Curtis would telephone him. If he didn't, then it would only be further evidence of the Ballou girl at work. By God, if he could only break her down into saying something. This way he could never be sure how much she had told Curtis, and a Curtis angry would be harder to cut down than a Curtis surprised.

In the room he and Ann-Evans shared at the DeSoto Hotel, at Tampa, Field ranged up and across the dull red carpet, walking in an effort to rid himself of a restlessness which tugged at him ceaselessly. If it weren't for the fact he had a speech to make before the Daughters of Something or Other in the evening, he'd get roaring drunk.

"For goodness' sake, Field," Ann-Evans complained over a piece of knitting, "what in the world is the matter with you? I get the fits just seeing you go back and forth."

Ann-Evans was enjoying herself. In the receptions, the crowded halls so carefully arranged by Titus Semple, she saw an enthusiastic recognition of Field as a statesman. If she didn't understand what he was talking about, then she accepted the fault as hers and additional proof of her husband's cleverness. It was exciting to travel around this way, and Field seemed to have a lot of money to spend. Probably the state was paying for everything. The notion pleased her. It was about time.

Looking at her Field wondered why, how, he had married

176

a girl he couldn't talk with. If, at this moment, he should say: "Ann-Evans, I don't like any part of what is happening to me. For the first time, I think Titus is stretching himself too far. I'd a hell of a lot rather quit the whole damn business and find a job," she would call him a crazy cooter or insist he had been drinking.

It wasn't, he thought, that he minded taking orders. No one was ever completely his own man. It was the feeling he was being led around by the nose. A remark Dan Curtis made at Lute-Mae's popped into his head. "Titus," Dan said, "is the only man I know who can make a sow's ear out of a silk purse." He couldn't help wondering if this had happened to him.

"I'm going to have a drink." He snapped the statement at Ann-Evans as though she had been arguing with him.

"For goodness' sake"—Ann-Evans was startled—"you'd think I'd taken the bottle and hidden it. Go on and have a drink. If you'll order some ginger ale I'll have one with you."

This was what Ann-Evans thought of as being a "good sport," an understanding wife. She didn't like whisky, never had, but if a woman wouldn't drink with her husband now and then he could always find someone who would. She left her chair, crossing to the bureau mirror while Field telephoned for room service.

Powdering her nose she examined herself critically. I'm really awfully pretty, she thought. Tilting her head from one side to the other, she smiled happily. Marriage, if anything, had made her more attractive than ever. Men looked at her in a different way, too: sleepy glances which gave her a funny tingling sensation. It probably wasn't nice, but it was exciting.

"How much longer are we going to be away from home, Field?"

"Couple of weeks." He sat on the bed, watching her primping. "There's a date for Titusville, one at Daytona, and another in St. Augustine. After that I guess Titus will let us come home." He added this with grim humor.

A colored boy brought ice and ginger ale. Field mixed Ann-Evans a drink and poured out a straight slug for himself.

"You know, Field"—Ann-Evans sipped pensively at her highball—"you're getting a little fat, kind of jowly. They say liquor will do that to a person."

It wasn't whisky. He was fat inside. He felt fat, stuffed, pusy.

"I'll wear it off bending down to kiss all the behinds on the way between Truro and Tallahassee."

The shocked expression on Ann-Evans's face made him feel better.

"Fielding Carlisle, you ought to be ashamed!"

He wasn't. The whisky warmed his stomach, brightened his eyes.

"I'll only kiss the pretty ones, sugar."

On the table was the speech he was to deliver in the evening. Flipping through it he paused to re-read certain paragraphs. It was all good common sense. Delafield, a little professor of economics and political science Titus had dug up, knew what he was talking about. The trouble was, Field thought, the words were Delafield's and the voice of Carlisle was the voice of Semple. It would be a hell of a shock to Titus if a man was to take the speeches he had been making to Tallahassee and follow them the way he would a map. The politicians would probably lynch him in self-defense. Such things, simple, every-day truths, never elected anyone. Issues sent a candidate to office. There were issues over this or that, but they usually boiled down to an assertion that the opponent was a half-witted bastard who beat his mother and papered his walls with fraudulent stocks and money grafted from the voters. At the moment Field realized he didn't have an issue. It was too early. There must be times, he pondered, when his audiences wondered why he was talking. A man might just as well come out on a platform naked as without an issue.

This thought also occurred to Walter Haines, for he had said as much to Field yesterday in the hotel dining room over lunch.

"You be sure an' see Walter Haines in Tampa," Titus admonished him before he left. "Walter sort of carries Hillsborough County around in a pocket to sharpen his teeth on. I'll fix it so he'll be expectin' you."

Haines turned out to be a grizzled, tobacco-chewing man who appeared to find something humorous in Field's tour.

"Pretty far off the range, aren't you, Senator?" He poked suspiciously at the dish of shrimp creole before him. "What hell's broth is Titus Semple cookin' this month?"

Field hadn't known the answer, and so he smiled in what he hoped was an enigmatic fashion.

"Must be somethin' new," Haines continued drawlingly, "campaignin' for your district down here in Hillsborough." He grinned suddenly "Glad to have you, anyhow, Senator."

Glancing at his prepared speech now, Field thought this tour must be something of a mystery to several other persons, Dan Curtis among them. Often he wondered what had gone wrong between him and Curtis. In the beginning, from the day he went to Jacksonville, he felt Dan Curtis wanted to be his friend. He said as much, invited him to Lake Surprise, offered the benefit of his experience. Something happened, though. The interest sloughed off. Perhaps—he recalled the galling words Lane had spoken—they, Curtis and the others, recognized him for Semple's man.

"Is being a senator at Washington better than a senator in Tallahassee?" Ann-Evans rested her glass on the arm of the chair.

"Huh?" Field looked up from the manuscript.

"I was only wondering if, maybe, you couldn't have Sheriff Semple arrange for you to go to Washington. They say it's lots prettier than Tallahassee and more interesting, too. Of course, it wouldn't be anywhere as close to home, but it might be fun for awhile."

"Why sure, sugar. Only the other day he said, 'Bub, how would you like to be president?'"

"You're joking, Field." Ann-Evans wavered. She wasn't sure.

"It won't be a joke if this limb the Sheriff and I are sitting on is sawed off, landing us both in your old man's lumber yard."

Ann-Evans was airily unconcerned over such a dire prediction. Titus Semple worked miracles. He said Field would go to the Legislature, and he had. He promised her the home on Flamingo Road back, and she got it. He told them Field would be taken care of, and so he was a vice-president of something or other to do with mortgages.

"I'll bet when the limb is sawed, if there is one, Sheriff Semple won't be on it, and if you're smart you'll be with him."

Ann-Evans disposed of all problems for all time. Maybe, Field thought, she's right.

"I think I'll go down on Franklin Street and buy a hat or something." Ann-Evans was bored.

"All right, sugar." Field considered the pint bottle on the table. He'd like another drink, but Ann-Evans always made him think she had caught him smoking an opium pipe whenever he took one. "You run along. I've got some work to do on this speech."

"Be sure it's on the speech and not that bottle."

There were times, Field reflected, when he found considerable pleasure in the possibility of Ann-Evans's just going off somewhere and dying. He wouldn't want her to be hurt, no accident, no pain; just a nice, quiet death. All men, wives too

179

for that matter, he imagined, must feel the same now and then.

"I'll have the bellboy come up and sit on it while you're gone."

"You're a silly." Ann-Evans was feeling the one drink. "I'll bet he wouldn't do it."

Field stretched out, resting his feet on the footboard, crushing a pillow beneath his head.

"How would you like to come to bed with me," he asked casually, "instead of buying a hat?"

Ann-Evans giggled. "You say the nastiest things, Field Carlisle."

He almost yawned but caught himself in time. "I suppose so. Anyhow, I guess we'd have to ask Sheriff Titus about it first."

Ann-Evans had the feeling she should get angry over this. Sometimes Field was hard to understand. She busied herself at the dressing table, dawdling, wondering if the subject was to be pursued.

My God, Field was thinking, she isn't really any good at that. It's like taking a picture of September Morn up in a hayloft.

"Well"—Ann-Evans was reluctant to leave—"I'm going out now." She waited.

Field did yawn then. "All right, sugar. Maybe, tonight after the meeting we'll go some place, the Tampa Bay Casino or to a crib in Ybor City."

"You do talk nasty." Ann-Evans was mad.

"Uh-huh." Through half-closed eyes Field was watching a fly on the ceiling. Long after Ann-Evans left, slamming the door emphatically behind her, he followed the insect's aimless progress around a light bulb. Finally he slept.

CHAPTER SEVENTEEN

PERCHED ON THE TOP OF A PACKING BOX IN THE basement, Lane watched a shirt-sleeved and unfamiliar Dan Curtis tinker with a small, power-driven jig saw bolted to a bench. He worked like a boy, struggling with apprehensive concentration. Finally he stepped back and regarded the result critically.

"What's in here, Santa Claus?" Lane tapped with her foot on the case beneath her.

"Huh? Oh." Dan grinned. "There's a lathe in there."

"What's a lathe?"

"It's a thing you turn wood on."

"Is that so?" She forced her eyes wide. "Well, what do you know?"

He laughed then, dusting specks of sawdust from his trousers.

"Think I'm crazy, don't you?"

Lane shook her head. "No," she said tenderly, "I think it's wonderful."

Diffidently, almost with embarrassment, Dan had come to her with the idea.

"Would you mind," he asked hesitantly, "if I put up sort of a workshop in your basement?"

She hadn't believed he was serious.

"It's just an idea of mine." He hurried the words. "You see, I'm a tinkerer at heart. I like to do things with my hands." He held them out as though to verify their existence. "Once, when I was a youngster, I had a corner in the barn, tool chest, saw horses, and everything. Then the barn burned down, and my father couldn't afford to buy me even a chisel. Ever since then I've wanted a shop of my own. The kids at home, in Jacksonville, used the basement for a playroom at first; later a bar was put in it."

"So you never got your workshop?" Lane pouted, trying to make a joke of the story, but she didn't feel it was funny. It gave a tug at her heart.

"No," Dan continued reminiscently, "I never had my shop." He bit the end from a cigar. "So, I thought if you wouldn't mind I'd like to fix up one downstairs. Sometimes when I have to think I can do it better planing at a piece of straight pine."

The notion of Dan Curtis's being denied a workbench and a saw or two should have been comical, but it wasn't somehow. He was so serious.

"But"—she didn't know quite what to say—"but couldn't you have, well, I mean there must have been other places besides the basement; the garage or something?"

Dan shook his head. "It isn't the same. When a man likes to tinker he likes to do it in his home, not outside."

It was the first time he had admitted to a common ownership of the Flamingo Road house. Lane hesitated to breathe for fear he was going to qualify the words. He didn't, though.

181

Leaning back in his chair, the cigar smoke forming a wavering streamer above his head, he coddled the idea.

"I looked around down there the last time I was here," he continued. "It would be fine, plenty of ventilation."

She went to him then, seated herself on the chair's arm, touching his head with hers.

"Dan, you can put a steam derrick in the living room if you want to. You know that."

In this moment it seemed to her everything she had ever wanted, the dreams of a child, the romantic imaginings of adolescence, the simple realities of an adult had resolved themselves into this corner of a room on Flamingo Road. There were tears in her eyes, and she pressed her cheek close into his wiry, gray hair for fear he should see them.

"Well." A robust note of pleasure was in the exclamation. "That's great."

Lane sniffled quickly and laughed to cover the sound. "During the week," she offered, "Sarah and I'll go round breaking legs off chairs just so you can fix them when you come down."

He had been as delighted as a kid with a new pocket knife when he found the equipment he ordered safely delivered to the basement.

Sarah brought beer and sandwiches to them, and Lane watched while he unpacked and bolted down the first of the treasures. With the jig saw in place now he beamed enthusiastically.

"In a minute I'll plug in the motor, and we'll see."

Lane cocked her head skeptically. "Is that the sort of a saw the villain always feeds Nellie, the beautiful cloak model, to?"

"No. They use a buzz saw for that."

"Mmm. I was thinking. Nellie would have to be a midget."

Dan screwed a connection into a socket, flipped a switch, and the jagged, vertical band flashed wickedly up and down.

"What do you think of it?" God at the close of the sixth day couldn't have been any more pleased.

"When you're not here I'll come down and have it scratch my back."

He turned off the power. "Let's let the rest of the stuff go until tomorrow."

Hand in hand they went up the inside steps, through the kitchen, and into the living room.

"Want a drink?"

"I don't know, maybe." He was in the chair which by mutual understanding was his. "You know," he said, "I don't care much about drinking any more. It's a damn funny thing, come to think of it."

Seated cross-legged on the couch, Lane watched him gravely. Sometimes, this was one of them, she wanted a lot of words; strained to say the things she felt.

"Are you happy here, Lane?" He asked the question as though it was one he had been considering for a long time.

She nodded. It must be apparent in every move she made; each time she spoke her happiness should have cried aloud for him to hear.

"I think about it a lot." Dan stretched long legs before him. "I wonder if it wouldn't be better for you to make friends here on the Heights, have other people to talk with. A woman needs that more than a man. You could join the country club if you wanted to, get out with people of your own age. I wouldn't be afraid. Nothing can happen to you now."

"I never learned to play golf in the carnival." She smiled. If he only knew how small was her need of anything outside of the little world he had built here.

"But"—he was plainly puzzled—"don't you miss having someone?"

"But I've never had anyone, Dan." She kept her eyes on her hands. "Maybe you won't believe it, but Lute-Mae Sanders was the only woman I ever thought of as a friend." Her laughter was short. "Most of the time I was too busy running to make friends."

"Now that you've stopped running . . . ?"

Her face lifted. "Now I've stopped running I'm out of breath. It'll take a little while to get it back."

Dan grunted and rose, walking to the front door and opening it. The afternoon air was fresh and crisp, charged as though by a giant atomizer with the heavy odors of oleanders and honeysuckle. He breathed of it deeply.

"Let's go someplace," he called over his shoulder, "take the car and drive, maybe, over to St. Augustine, have dinner there, and sit on the sea wall in the moonlight."

Lane was out of her chair at the suggestion. "It would be wonderful." Her eyes were shining. She wanted Dan to come to Flamingo Road, wanted him there always, but now and then small fears clutched at her. The house meant too much to have it become a cheap rendezvous where they sat behind bolted doors. That must not happen to it.

At the garage Dan considered the sky judicially. "Let's take your car. We can let the top down."

Lane kept her face straight. It was a funny habit of his,

183

looking aloft and then making plans, daring God to let it rain or become cloudy after he decided the day was to be fair. I'll bet, she thought, he'd have a law passed at Tallahassee against it.

Once on the broad highway, leading cross-country to the east coast, the car seemed to skim through a deep channel cut in the pines.

"It's a good road," Dan remarked with satisfaction. "I built it."

Only through such scattered bits of information did Lane ever glimpse the Dan Curtis away from the Heights in Truro. "A road I built, a mill we put up, the spur line I laid out." He mentioned these things, not as achievements to impress someone, but as jobs done he was proud of. She could drive as fast as she cared to on this highway. It was a good road because he had built it.

Now and then Lane would flash a quick, sidelong glance his way. Always she found him looking at her, not staring but quietly considering her profile and the movements of her wrists on the wheel. When their eyes met in this fashion something warm and completely understood passed between them. Once, she could tell he was laughing deep inside over something.

"What's funny?"

He settled himself, half turning toward her. "Well, first I started thinking about you and me, how we seem to get a lot of fun out of things most persons take for granted. After that I began adding up our combined ages and dividing by two. The way it came out we're both only middle-aged. Then it occurred to me I only felt about thirty-five, and after that I decided all men my age with a young girl must say the same thing to themselves. The idea of succumbing to a universal fallacy, weakness if you prefer, tickled me."

"But I never think about it." The protest was born of sincerity.

"No, I can tell you don't. There are a lot of things you are smart enough not to think about."

Lane slowed down, loafing through the main street of the little town of Moultrie. Not until they were out of the limits did she speak.

"It isn't that I haven't thought about them: the other things; Flamingo Road, Lute-Mae's, Truro, you. I just don't talk about them. There's a difference."

"Sounds mighty complicated." Dan was amusedly indulgent.

"No." The denial was emphatic. "They all mean the same

184

thing. I worry, sometimes, because of what might happen to you through me."

Dan threw back his head and laughed. "You'll be looking underneath your bed at night for Titus Semple."

Lane was so startled she almost pulled from the road. "How, how did you know about Semple?"

Dan smoothed a cigar, caressing the wrapper with long fingers. "I don't know about Semple, Lane. I've had the feeling for a long time that you hate the Sheriff, and he's uncomfortable in the house on Flamingo Road when you are there. You know," he continued slowly, "if I really wanted to learn what's between you two I could ask Lute-Mae."

"It's a short story."

"Well"—he bit at the cigar's end—"let's leave it this way. If the time comes when you think I ought to hear it, you tell me. Don't wait for someone else."

"Do you remember my asking you once"—Lane was driving slowly, thinking—"whether Sheriff Semple was more important to you than you to him?"

Dan nodded, smoking calmly.

"Well, I had the idea he might transfer something of what he felt for me to you, so I wanted to know if because of me he could harm you."

They were in the outskirts of St. Augustine, still west of the narrow San Sebastian River. The car crept through the Negro district.

"No." Dan was smiling no longer. "But he's up to something. I'd like to know what. One of the reasons I suggested driving over here this evening was to try and find out."

"Not only the sea wall by moonlight?" She stuck the tip of her tongue out at him.

"Oh, I counted that in too, but"—he squinted down at his cigar—"young Fielding Carlisle, Semple's protegé for the moment, is speaking in St. Augustine. He's been talking all over the state for the past two months. It isn't like Semple to run down blind alleys for exercise. I thought, maybe, if I could listen to Carlisle, perhaps even talk with him later, I might get some sort of an idea what Titus is after. Carlisle's a neighbor of yours. Know him?"

"Yes, Dan." She couldn't let Curtis make a fool of himself before Field. "I know Field. When I first came to Truro, he helped me. We—" With her eyes she beseeched him to understand, to save her further explanation.

"Oh." Comprehension was apparent in the tone. "That's how you knew Titus?"

185

"Yes."

"Well." He considered this for a moment. "So that's why you wanted to go to Tallahassee for the first session after the election."

"Yes, Dan." Desperately she hoped he would understand. "But it's all over. It was finished the day, the first time I telephoned you at your office in Jacksonville. I guess that's why I wanted to talk to you so badly. I was grateful and happy."

She kept her eyes on the road, threading through the traffic and across the short bridge. The car rattled over railroad tracks and on to the rough brick surface of King Street.

"I'll tell you what." Dan spoke as though they had been discussing plans for the evening. "Let's drive up Bay Street and around to the fort."

Lane dropped her head in assent. "Nothing more you want to know, Dan?" Her voice was small.

"No." He winked companionably at her "I'm glad you told me, though, before I introduced you to Carlisle. That sort of thing happens in the movies, and someone always looks pretty silly while it's going on."

She couldn't trust her voice at the moment. It was all absurdly simple now, but it was simple only because Dan made it seem so. Not until they were on the street running parallel with Matanzas Bay did she dare venture a question.

"Are we going to see him, Field, I mean, tonight?"

Dan considered the question. "No, I guess not if you don't want to."

She was being foolish and knew it. Either it was over or it wasn't. If it was finished, then seeing Field couldn't make any difference. Parking the car near a twisted and wind-beaten cedar, she shut off the engine.

"Why don't we try and find out where he is staying and ask him to eat with us? Wouldn't that be better than listening to his speech?"

They walked slowly up a small knoll toward the ancient Spanish fort, gray with the centuries upon it. Always there was a hush here; visitors unconsciously lowered their voices, and even the city noises of St. Augustine itself seemed muted.

"I don't know why not." Dan was turning her question over in his mind. "It'll be a damn sight easier on my digestion than listening to Semple's wind in the rafters; Semple by the courtesy of Senator Fielding Carlisle and the Democratic Party."

Once across the narrow drawbridge spanning a grass-grown moat, Lane again was captured by the spirit of this stout

186

coquina bastion which had defied assault and the years. She and Dan came here frequently; always when they were in or passing through St. Augustine they halted to revisit the spot. Save for an attendant the fort was deserted at this hour, filled with the mocking whispers of the men whose bones crumbled beneath dungeon floors and the open court. Standing on the parapet, looking across the bay to the sand spit of Anastasia Island, Lane liked to close her eyes and imagine she could see Spain's heavy galleons attempting to beat their way through the inlet far below. Sometimes, if she listened hard, she could hear bright, clear bugles, the steady tramp of booted feet as the guard was changed, and the deep-throated roar of a sunset gun calling the town behind doors.

"Old places never really get old, do they, Dan?"

A fresh wind from the sea was in their faces as they leaned against a shoulder-high rampart from where some soldier, long forgotten, had sighted down his heavy piece.

"The ghosts haunting them never do." He smiled. "Maybe that's the reason." He spread his hands on the rough surface of the wall. "Ghosts are always dancing a rigadoon or something of the sort, so they can't let their arteries harden."

They walked back down the narrow flight of stone steps, through the court, and past the gate keeper, who nodded a relieved good night. At the car Dan looked at his watch.

"Let's pick up a newspaper. There ought to be some sort of an advertisement of where Carlisle's to speak. I'll telephone there and find out where he is staying. Then we can ask him to dinner."

Parked before a drugstore on King Street, Lane waited while Dan went in to buy a paper. No matter how she considered it, the night's prospects were awkward, and she wondered now why she had suggested dinner. Probably, she thought, to prove something which didn't need proving.

Dan returned, a newspaper rolled in his hand. "He's at the Alcazar. I telephoned and asked him, them rather, to meet us at Papa Pellecier's."

"Them?" Lane looked curiously at him.

"Yes, his wife's with him."

"Oh, Dan. You shouldn't." She was sincerely concerned. "They're neighbors in a way. So far I've managed to keep a jump ahead of Flamingo Road. This is liable to start a lot of unpleasant things."

"Be good for you, likely enough." He slid in beside her and patted her knee comfortingly. "Time you made some friends on the Heights."

She shook her head, driving away from the curb. He either refused to understand or couldn't see what he was doing.

Tucked away in a sagging frame building on Hypolita Street was a dingy little restaurant where Papa Pellecier, lean and shrunken and possessing a great contempt for most of his patrons, worked unbelievable magic among his pots and pans. Dan had taken her here the first time she came from Truro to meet him in St. Augustine. Badly lighted, beset by innumerable odors, its tables uncertain and cloths spotted, Papa Pellecier's was not in the guide books, but from its smoky kitchen came unforgettable shrimp and crab gumbo and chicken pilau. They came if Papa Pellecier wanted to take the trouble to prepare them, which wasn't usually the case. Most of the clientele suffered meat balls and ragouts, hash or fried fish and watery grits. It was Pellecier's way of getting even with the world.

The earth's surface, according to Papa, was fairly crawling with "damn bastards," and if some of them insisted upon inflicting themselves upon him, then such fare was better than they deserved.

For Dan Curtis and the little girl who always came with him he cherished a deep and lasting affection. For them he would consent to cook, setting out his triumphs on a clean tablecloth, whisked with a flourish from the depths of an old sea chest in the corner of the room.

Seeing them enter, his wizened face tortured itself into what the uninitiated might have taken for a snarl but what was really Papa's special smile of welcome for those he considered not to be bastards. Mr. Curtis and the little girl were not bastards because they never said, fix us this or cook us that. They waited patiently for what his mood of the moment would produce.

"Ay, ay, ay," he cackled delightedly, snatching at the dirty cloth. "It is time something good happened to me." He beamed at them. "All day I have sat here stinking." The notion gave him a gloomy satisfaction.

"The world is filled with bastards." Dan intoned his part of the ritual solemnly.

Papa was overcome by this evidence of sagacity. He nodded unhappily. "Black and white, Mr. Curtis. Black and white, yellow and brown."

Lane tried to hide her mouth with a compact. The routine never varied. In a moment more Pellecier would scuttle toward the back room, shifting with the hasty movements of the big blue crabs he popped into caldrons of boiling water. For awhile there would be silence, and then the old man would return bearing two bottles, one filled with a dry scuppernong wine, the other holding a powerful grapefruit brandy, both of his own making.

He set the bottles before them now. For his part Prohibition was nonsense promulgated by the bastards, who were free to enjoy it if they wanted to.

"There'll be four tonight, Papa." Dan ventured the suggestion.

The little man pursed his lips doubtfully. He wasn't quite sure but what Mr. Curtis was overreaching himself. Finally he nodded.

"For you, Mr. Curtis, yes." He slithered toward the kitchen from which, almost immediately, there arose furious shouts, muttered curses, and the banging of pans on the old cast-iron wood stove. Papa was conceiving.

Dan poured brandy for both of them. It had a delicate chartreuse color and clung to the glass.

"Mad?" He smiled across the table.

"No." The brandy was green fire.

"You see"—Dan leaned back in his chair—"I sort of feel responsible for young Carlisle. Titus Semple sent him to me in the beginning. We talked, and I thought the boy would turn out to be a good man, good for the state not just for Titus. Well, you know what happened. He was elected to the Legislature. Since then I haven't seen much of him. It's Titus's district, after all, and he's been running it well for a good many years. Now, though, the Sheriff is busy about something outside his own back yard. In a way that concerns me a lot. I wouldn't like to see Field sent up a creek without a paddle to satisfy something in Titus." He poured himself a second brandy.

"Me, too." Lane held her glass out.

"So," Dan continued speculatively, "I thought, maybe, if we all sat around and talked as friends, I might be able to save Carlisle a lot of trouble."

"Did you"—Lane absently fingered her glass—"did you tell him, them, I was with you?"

"Of course, why not?"

Facing the door she had been the first to see Field and Ann-Evans as they entered. They stood, looking around uncertainly, not quite sure they were in the right place. She noticed Ann-Evans wrinkled her nose distastefully.

"They're here now," Lane whispered, her eyes on Field.

Dan turned in his chair, lifted a hand in greeting, and Field nodded quickly, touching his wife's arm, turning her attention to the table.

Field made the introductions hurriedly. He seemed nervous and unsure of himself.

Ann-Evans was bubbling. She noted every detail of what Lane was wearing in a rapid glance. Indefinite rumors, scandal-tinged, had begun to blow the length of Flamingo Road about the girl who lived at 32. No one was quite positive there was anything wrong, and this made the speculation all the more fascinating. It seemed that men were always coming and going and that Daniel Curtis was a too frequent visitor, and then Ellen Parsons reported excitedly on the terrible commotion in the yard one night. In a way Ann-Evans was disappointed. An adventuress, if this Miss Ballou was one, should be mysteriously slinky with wickedness stamped upon her something like a scarlet letter.

"Gracious"—she spoke as though she were out of breath— "I've been wanting to meet you for the longest time. I even"— she made the confession in a whispered note—"stopped in one afternoon, but there was nobody home."

"Come again, won't you?" Lane smiled encouragingly.

Dan was busy with the brandy. "This," he explained it, "sort of fortifies you for Papa's heavy hand with the pepper."

Field drank his in a gulp, lifting the glass in a wordless toast that bordered on ungraciousness. He's worried, Lane thought with surprise, worried and ill at ease.

Ann-Evans sampled her liquor with the tip of her tongue, squealing at its bite.

"My goodness," she exclaimed, "I shouldn't think you'd be able to taste anything after a couple of these."

Even under the stimulus of Papa's brandy and wine, the dinner was a dismal failure. Tactfully and with understanding interest Dan attempted to talk with Field about the speaking tour he was concluding, but Field volunteered nothing, replying only to direct questions and, in a surly manner, allowing the burden of conversation to fall upon the elder man. He appeared to be unreasonably irritated by Ann-Evans's inconsequential interruptions and once ventured a weary, "Oh, my God," at a remark she made about his speech at Titusville. There was almost something of guilt in his studied avoidance of Dan's effort to be friendly.

This was a new Field, and Lane felt amazement mounting as she watched him. Somewhere along the road he had lost the charm of frankness, the slightly quizzical attitude toward the world which colored his speech and gestures. She tried to

190

reconcile what she was seeing with the memory of the man who had walked from the circus clearing and into Truro with her one night. There was hypocrisy, evasiveness, and sly confidence about him now, and, she thought with horror, the mark of Titus Semple in every move he made, each word spoken.

Dan finally gave up. His keen eyes were on Field, and a hard line traced itself about his jaw.

Ann-Evans, oblivious to the tension, chattered across the table to Lane. They were going to see a lot of each other from now on. She was just dying to see the inside of the house at 32. It was the most interesting thing to have a new neighbor on the Heights.

Dan looked at his watch. "Don't want to hold you up, Field," he said. "I know you probably want to get to the hall a little early." There was no mistaking the dismissal.

Field ignored the implication, and in his complacent acceptance of Curtis's suggestion there was something of a shoulder shrug. He finished his coffee leisurely, neither hurrying nor delaying departure. In his own mind he had justified his attitude. Dan Curtis was curious. All right then, why the hell didn't he come right out and ask what he wanted to know? He wasn't a kid to be fed a lollypop and then questioned. If Titus hadn't told Dan anything, then it was because he wasn't ready to talk, and it looked as if he was on Semple's team from now on. Political balances had been upset before. Maybe Titus was going to do it again.

They finally left with Ann-Evans volubly earnest that she and Lane, all of them for that matter, would get together the very next day. Lane was both sorry and envious. She was such a pretty girl, and Field had behaved like a sullen brat.

After they had gone Dan laid his hands on the table and then suddenly laughed.

"Well," he said, "what do you know about that?"

He wasn't annoyed. The situation had become increasingly clear as he talked and Field forced replies. Titus was going to bolt, how or from what corner he didn't know, but he realized the Sheriff was impatient.

"I'm ashamed of him." Lane was.

"No," Dan reflected, "I wouldn't feel that way. I'm sorry for him. When the Semple virus gets into the spine it's likely not to leave much of a man." He finished his brandy. "Should we go?"

"Are you going to hear what he has to say?"

Dan shook his head. "I don't think so. Sitting on the sea wall in the moonlight would be a better way to pass an hour."

Papa Pellecier followed them to the door. He much preferred for Mr. Curtis and the little girl to come alone; then
he could sit with them at the table and drink brandy.

"Ay," he croaked, "the world is full of bastards, Mr. Curtis."

Dan laughed with honest enjoyment. "You know," he said,
"wouldn't be surprised but what you're right, Papa."

CHAPTER EIGHTEEN

THE JAWS OF THE MAN STANDING BESIDE SEMPLE'S
car worked nervously.

"Good God, Sheriff," he muttered, "you know what'll happen to me." He turned and spat at the ground. "I been over-
seein' Mr. Curtis's plantation here in Walton County for
fifteen years. Jesus, you can't ask me to do nothin' like this."

"I ain't askin' nothin'. I'm tellin' you what I want done."

In the darkness the huge body of the Sheriff seemed to be
without form. It loomed, an indistinct blob, from behind the
wheel. A hundred yards away light from the windows of a
neat frame house dropped in squares on the pine-needle-
covered yard. Titus had parked his car in the shadows, blowing
upon the horn until the man, Lassen, came outside.

"I'll swear, Sheriff"—Lassen twisted his lean body desperately as though he were trying to shake off something which
clung to him—"I just sure enough can't do it."

Titus clicked his tongue commiseratingly. "You'd hate to see
that boy of yours go to Raiford on a second-degree murder
charge, wouldn't you now?"

"It warn't no murder. Del did what he did in self-defense."

"That's what Del says." Titus emitted a little whistle.

"Yeah, but we got witness." Lassen made a pitiful stand.

Titus smiled in the darkness. "Maybe you got a witness,
maybe you ain't. If I was you I wouldn't take no chances on
my boy being sent up like he surer than hell is goin' to be."

"I'll swear"—Lassen shook his head, but there was no protest
left in him—"I'll just swear I can't do it."

Titus snapped on the car's lights and stepped upon the
starter.

"You'll do it, Burr, just like I told you." The words were
flat and cold. "I'm goin' to send you them four negrahs. You

put 'em to work here like I say. Maybe I ain't goin' to do nothin' with 'em. If so, all right. If I do need 'em, you do like I say, an' I'll have that boy, Del, of yours out an' home. Either way I'll take care of him, an' you don't need to worry none. But, by God, if you cross me on this I'll send him up for the rest of his life, an' you know I ain't foolin'.'"

The car swung slowly around in the flat open space and then bumped into a rutted road. Burr Lassen watched until it turned from the lane into the main highway, and then, with head bowed, he shuffled back to the house.

Titus was pleased with himself; even the prospect of spending the night away from his own bed in the Palmer House couldn't dim his satisfaction. During the two weeks he had been absent from Truro he had woven an evil rope, strands for which had been gathered in dark and strange places. Now he was satisfied. I'll hang 'em all to the same limb, he chortled, just like play toys on a Christmas tree.

Looking for trouble Titus found it with the sure instinct of a destructive raccoon. Driving across the corrugated road leading into Bradford, where he would have to spend the night, he polished and fitted together his pieces of mischief. He chortled at their number and the malefic pattern they formed. Their number and quality delighted him. One piece in particular, a segment chanced upon, was almost too good to be genuine.

"By God," he spoke aloud over the noise of his engine, "who would have thought Watterson would have got himself tangled up with such as Julio Garcia? Why, that Garcia's been in trouble since they sewed his belly button."

Evidence of corruption hadn't surprised him. He hunted for it, knowing where to look. If a man sat by a hole long enough, something usually came out. Not only had he found the holes, but he poked down them and up popped Deveris Watterson. Watterson and Julio Garcia, a slick little mobster who figured he was smarter than the United States government.

Constitutional provision which prevented a governor from immediately succeeding himself had kept Watterson out of politics these past four years. Now he was ready to run again, backed by Curtis, Ulee Shelton, Parker, and the others.

Titus made sucking sounds of delight with his lips. By God, when he dropped what he had heard, particularly the Garcia business, they'd wish they had a rattlesnake in their laps instead of Watterson.

Careening recklessly down Bradford's main street he parked before the frame hotel. He was tired but not too tired to enjoy his secret. Curtis would take Field now and wheel him into the Mansion, or he'd turn all hell loose in the state.

Registering in the smeared book on the desk he asked about something to eat.

"Only ham and eggs, Sheriff," the owner apologized.

"Ham an' eggs, a pitcher of milk, an' a hunk of pie if you got it."

"Yes, sir." The landlord was impressed with his visitor, and as he gave the order to one of the colored boys he wondered what brought the Sheriff from Truro to an out-of-the-way place like Bradford.

Titus eased himself into an uncomfortable chair, regarding the smelly living-room lobby with distaste. He never liked to spend time away from home. Right now, however, there wasn't any help for it.

"Quite a piece out of your county, ain't you, Sheriff?" The proprietor was curious.

Titus nodded without comment. On any other night he might have exchanged gossip with the man. It never hurt to make friends. Right now, though, he wanted to think. Carefully he went back over the past two weeks. Save for this little business with Lassen on the Curtis plantation, an extra precaution, everything else had been made to order for him. He sighed gratefully. It was good to know he was still capable of a trick or two. For awhile there, something had been eating away at his confidence. It started with that black-headed trollop Dan Curtis set up on Flamingo Road. Funny—he meditated on this—how a little thing like that could upset a fellow, twist things around so he couldn't think straight.

"Got supper ready for you now, Sheriff," the landlord called from the dining room.

Titus rose heavily. Every time he thought of the Ballou girl it did something to him. Well, he'd get rid of her along with the others. There persisted within him, however, a reluctant respect for Lane Ballou. Once he even ventured to speculate on the combination she would have made with him and Field. Ann-Evans was all right but too much milk toast for a man with stomach.

Titus ate carefully, sopping at the yolk of the eggs with slabs of bread and methodically working his way through most of an apple pie. He liked to eat while he was thinking. The two seemed to go together.

Tomorrow he'd be back in Truro where he could rest on the Palmer House porch and tie things together. Right now it looked foolproof, but everything had worked out too well to get careless. He'd been soft and slipshod with the Ballou girl and look what happened. This time there wouldn't be any mistake.

Leaning back, pushing the table away from his belly, he sucked at a tooth and thought raptly of Dan Curtis. Dan was going to gag some before he gave up Watterson, but he'd disgorge the old coot and be glad to get Field by the time things were over. Titus couldn't remember when he'd been lying on a softer spot. He luxuriated in it, mentally rolling the way a cat does in a bed of catnip.

For the hundredth time he went over what he intended doing. Step by step he traced the moves. He'd get Dan and the rest of them right in the house on Flamingo Road and then push the red-hot poker up their behinds. God A'mighty, he mused, but there's goin' to be some yellin' on the Heights. If Curtis wants to be reasonable, he thought, I'll forget about the rest although Watterson may get himself in a tangle without my doin' anything. If Dan was stubborn he'd let 'em all have it an' get himself a governor to boot.

He flipped a half dollar to the surprised colored waiter.

"You around all night, boy?"

"Yessuh!"

"Well, give me a call early in the mornin', about six-thirty, an' see you got a hot breakfast waitin'."

He stopped for a few minutes at the desk, talking with the hotel owner. Now that he had something in his gut, he could afford to be pleasant.

The man was delighted. Stories of Truro's sheriff had percolated through the state. He was, reports insisted, a man of fabulous guile. Looking at him now the landlord experienced a shade of disappointment. He was only a fat fella after all who looked as though he wasn't any too bright.

"Supper all right, Sheriff?"

Titus nodded, his vacant blue eyes roaming casually around the lobby.

"Eggs were fresh, anyhow," he admitted shortly. From a glass cup he gathered a small handful of toothpicks. "Get me a handy room with a good bed?"

"Yes, sir, right on the next floor. Used to be the bridal room. Best bed in the hotel." He winked portentously over the joke.

Titus grunted skeptically. "Nothin' here on the ground floor? I sure hate to climb steps."

"No sir. Ain't a room down here but those me an' my wife an' my daughter an' son-in-law use. The steps ain't bad, though."

Titus considered the short flight and thought wistfully of his oversize bed at the Palmer House.

"All steps are bad," he argued. "Come on, then, let's get 'em over with."

At the end of the hall the landlord threw open a door and stepped aside proudly.

"Genuine brass bed. Don't see many of those any more these days, Sheriff."

Talkative old fool, Titus thought. "I told the dining-room boy," he said aloud, "to wake me at six-thirty. Don't let him sleep on me."

"No, sir, I sure won't." He was disappointed over the guest's lack of enthusiasm. "Good night."

Titus belched and shut the door.

He undressed slowly, whistling tonelessly, and then cautiously lowered himself to the bed. It creaked alarmingly and sagged in defeat as the great weight was put upon it. Finally Titus was settled, and then he realized he had forgotten to put out the single electric light. With a sigh he turned over and burrowed beneath the covers, shading his eyes with one of the pillows. To hell with the light.

In the morning he wasted no time getting out of Bradford, and once his car was on the main highway he allowed it to rocket along, indifferent to the patches of traffic which seemed to spring from nowhere. The road was broad and smooth, and he could divide his attention between it and his thoughts. He savored the latter; they seemed fresher and better this morning.

Once across the line he regarded his own county with a patronizing inspection. A county was going to be pretty small stuff after the next election. He'd have a state to range in then with Field in the governor's mansion. Field was all right. He hadn't made a mistake there. The boy was a little balky at times, inclined to buck when the whip touched his flank, but some leeway had to be allowed for any man. He'd been all right on that speaking trip, too; sticking to what was written for him and keeping his mouth decently shut otherwise.

In Truro's outskirts he decided against going to the Palmer House and turned up toward the Heights and Flamingo Road, eventually pulling into and up the driveway of the Carlisle home.

Field, sitting in the breakfast alcove, called to Ann-Evans. "Put the hens to laying, sugar, here comes old pus-gut." He watched critically as Semple bowled across the lawn.

Breathing heavily Titus rumbled through the house to

196

where Field sat at the table. It would have been better, he conceded now, to have sent for Field. Didn't do to have him get the notion he was being catered to. He smiled weakly at Ann-Evans, who was fussing prettily over his appearance.

"I'll have something for you in a minute." She patted at the flowered cloth and indicated a seat.

"Had breakfast, Miss Ann-Evans." Titus considered the narrow, high-backed bench with horror. "Might take a little coffee in the bottom of a cup if you can get me a chair I can sit in." He consented to recognize Field's presence. "How you, bub?"

He looks, Field thought, as happy as though he had just cut his crippled grandmother's throat while she wasn't looking. Titus in a good humor was apt to be up to a lot of trouble for someone.

"Mornin', Sheriff Titus."

Field turned to the breakfast before him, waiting while the maid brought in a chair for Semple and the Sheriff settled himself.

"Drove in from Bradford this mornin'." Titus clasped hands across his belly, fingering the flesh beneath his shirt with sensual pleasure.

"I heard you were away." Field chased a piece of bacon across his plate. "We got back last week, came right over from St. Augustine the same night after the meeting there."

"You done all right, Field." Titus nodded approval. "You done fine. Set a lot of people to wonderin' what the hell you was up to an' then left 'em still figurin'."

"Met Dan Curtis in St. Augustine. He invited Ann-Evans and me to dinner." Field pushed his cup to one side. Titus, he knew, hadn't come over just to find out what he ate for breakfast.

Ann-Evans brought the Sheriff's coffee herself and then tiptoed elaborately from the room. She wanted him to understand she knew a woman's place when men were talking.

"I figured Dan'd be around to see where the smoke was comin' from an' why." He closed his eyes dreamily.

"I think he got sore at me."

"Bub, if you make a man wear a pair of shoes that pinch him some, then he's bound to take a dislike to you." The Sheriff's eyes flew open, and he winked rapidly.

Field couldn't help wondering if it ever occurred to Titus to question his loyalty. How, he thought, can he be so sure I'm going to keep at heel once all this contriving has brought down his birds.

197

"Why, bub"—there was a silky whisper in the Sheriff's voice—"I figure to make you the biggest man in the state. There ain't much else you could be worryin' about. Is there?"

Field realized he was staring at the almost invisible pupils in Semple's eyes and that a chill of apprehension was enveloping him. Good God, he thought, the man isn't human. How could he know what I was thinking? In his nervousness he dropped a cigarette and fumbled for it on the floor, grateful for the opportunity to avoid Titus's bland questioning for a moment.

Titus rocked his body gently on the chair. He liked to trip Field in those moments when what was running through the younger man's brain was written so plainly on his face and in his eyes. It wasn't much of a trick. Greed and awkward cunning always showed in a man. All anyone had to do was watch for it. It shone plain as a lantern on a roof. He knew it frightened Field when he was caught, and it was always a good idea to keep a man a little scared.

"No"—Field drew heavily upon the cigarette—"no, I suppose not."

Titus bowed his head in agreement, then looked around the room.

"You know," he said, "this is the first time I've been in this home since your daddy died an' I came up here to offer you a deputyship. You're a lot smarter today than you were then, bub."

Field smiled sarcastically. He hoped the Sheriff was right. Sometimes, particularly right now, he felt he needed someone to wipe his nose. Until this moment he had been wavering, wondering if Titus Semple could really be cleverer than the combination Dan Curtis held. Looking at the Sheriff now, he understood. The man was possessed of a reptilian treachery and the persistence of a beaver. He'd do what he had set himself to do.

"Sometimes I wonder, Sheriff Titus." He made the admission dispiritedly.

"Shuh." Titus blew between his teeth. "A young fella is naturally skittish, same as a colt. A touch of the bit does him good. Gets his mind off himself an' lets him do some thinkin' about the race to be run."

"You've been out of town some time, haven't you?" Field wanted the subject changed.

"Two weeks." Titus fingered the brim of his straw hat. "My behind never will be the same from all the strange beds I laid it in. You know"—his tone shifted to one of a shocked sur-

198

prise—"you'd be surprised the things I run into on my travels around the state. Why, bub, there's been pardon-sellin', peonage, thievin' right an' left from the treasury, roads paid for by the commission an' the members holdin' stock in the contractin' firms. Why"—he shook his head dejectedly—"even former Governor Watterson is about in a fix."

Field worked desperately to keep his features straight. So that was what the old bullfrog had been doing. He might have guessed.

"Is that so?" He injected startled wonder into the exclamation. "What do you know?"

Titus pursed his lips. "You'd certainly be surprised, bub. It's hard to believe. Why"—there was regret in the words—"if I was to tell you what Deveris Watterson has been up to, you wouldn't believe it. No, sir, you just sure wouldn't."

Field played along. "Why," he added the shocking speculation, "I'll bet it would even surprise Dan Curtis, maybe, John Shelton and some others, too."

Titus, apparently, was overcome by the suggestion. His lids dropped, and he sighed in audible pain over the world's iniquities. When he raised his head again to look at Field, his blue eyes were swimming.

"It'd sure be a shame, bub, to have to tell 'em. I don't know as I'd have the heart unless I was really pressed. It's a bad thing to destroy folks' confidence in their fellow-men."

"Maybe"—Field tamped the fire on the end of his cigarette into the coffee saucer—"maybe you won't have to say anything."

Titus shook his head doubtfully. "I don't know, bub. I'd sure like to think I wouldn't. If things got made public it might send a lot of people to jail. I'd hate to see anythin' like that happen."

Field slid out from behind the table. No wonder, he thought, Titus had seemed so pleased with himself. He knew there was no point in asking for details. The bear-skinning department was Semple's.

"I've got to get downtown. Coming?"

Semple settled the broad hat on his head with a gesture of resignation. It was almost as if he had said he could no longer face Truro, so ashamed was he at having discovered the world fretted with dishonesty in its public servants. Field knew he was enjoying himself. He oozed satisfaction.

"I suppose I might as well." Titus ambled toward the living room. "If you don't see me for a week or more, you'll know I got in my bed an' can't get out."

Ann-Evans waited impatiently in the front room. She had a feeling that the Sheriff's visit was a portent of things to come. Titus Semple didn't make social calls, she knew this, but looking from him to Field in an effort to catch some hint of what they had been talking about she found only blankness.

"We, Field and I," she ventured, "wish you would find time to come up on the Heights oftener."

Titus figuratively patted the bright top of her head. "If I ever go visitin', Miss Ann-Evans, I'll start with you. I sure enough will."

He waited while Field shook himself into a coat and kissed Ann-Evans good-by. Then, together they walked out to where he left his car.

"Want me to drive you down?"

"No." Field preferred to be alone for the moment. "I'll take my own. If vice-presidenting gets too bothersome I can always leave when I want to."

Behind the wheel Titus pretended intense absorption in the horn button. He worked at it with his fingers while the mechanism bleeped dolefully.

"I don't suppose," he said, looking up abruptly, "I should ought to tell you not to say nothin' about what we've been talkin' over."

Field clicked the door shut. "No. There wouldn't be any reason to."

The starter whirled beneath the Sheriff's foot. When the engine started he smiled delightedly.

"No," he suggested, "talk about such things might upset public confidence. We surer than hell wouldn't want anything like that to happen."

He backed rapidly down the driveway and skidded into a turn which raised a shrill scream from the long-suffering tires. Field waited until he passed out of sight down Flamingo Road's avenue of trees and then went to the garage for his own car.

Come good or bad now, he realized, he had taken hold of the Sheriff's stirrup and there was no letting go.

CHAPTER NINETEEN

ON THE PARTLY CONCEALED SIDE PORCH OF LUTE-Mae's, Lane hesitated a moment before putting her finger to the bell. She had never entered this way before, always using the front door with a gesture of stubborn defiance. Today she deliberately avoided the broad, unsheltered steps, running her car into the driveway and parking it at the back of the house out of sight.

Inside, a deep-throated chime sounded in response to the bell. Lane smiled at this evidence of delicate progress. The signal, once a rasping buzzer, had always made her jump.

Months had passed since she had seen Lute-Mae. Although Dan never said anything, she realized he didn't like to have her come down here. The side entrance she thought with twisted humor, was either a concession to him, or she had been cleansed in the blood of Flamingo Road. She wasn't sure which.

Lute-Mae had called her on the telephone. "Slip away down here an' see me, sugar. I got a real feelin' I'd like to talk with you again."

The request had been colored with uncertainty. Lane was worried.

"Anything wrong?"

Lute-Mae's denial hadn't reassured her.

"Would somethin' have to be wrong for me to want to see you again?" The counter-question was an evasion.

Driving across town, through the ragged fringes of the district, past the grimy reaches of the yards, Lane reflected on life's singular trick, snatching her from the neighborhood into which she now entered. A man, drunk and with the fever of liquor upon him, had come to Lute-Mae's and found in her whatever it was he was seeking: peace, comfort, or the cool touch of a hand. When he left she went with him. It was as ordinary, as miraculously simple, as that.

Twisting through the mean streets, Lane found she could regard the district as a curiosity, an odd corner of the world which might be flashed upon a movie screen as part of a travelogue from an unfamiliar section of the globe. Drab neglect and poverty were scrawled across the dreary fronts of the houses as unmistakably as if they were the dirty words chalked on every vacant wall by the children. They never had a chance, those youngsters. Uptown Truro was afraid to give them one. They were so many. The district festered, feeding upon itself, drawing breath from its own putrid stench. Little girls gave themselves for a penny, a stick of candy, the promise of an ice-cream cone to slack-faced youths in their teens. They grew older and wiser, raising their demands to a quarter, and finally ended in one of the dollar cribs if disease hadn't done for them. The boys haunted pool rooms and pressing clubs, working only when forced to and roving in eager, savage gangs preying upon the women and the helpless. When the fights, the stabbings, the quick murders and the ceaseless turmoil of chattering insanity raised too loud a voice, then uptown Truro would send its squads of police to club the offenders into sullen order.

Many times Lane thought of what would have happened to her if it hadn't been for Dan Curtis, and always she found no answer.

Lute-Mae's wasn't the district. The impressive white house was scornful of its surroundings, but Lane knew the district could be, and probably was, the cesspool for Lute-Mae's. If not the line in Truro, then one like it in some other town. There was no escape, and yet, for her, there had been. Thinking of this she was certain, though, she never looked upon Dan Curtis or Flamingo Road as a refuge. Actually, Lute-Mae's had not been repugnant. She went into the house because she wanted to, intent upon making it serve her instead of she it. Perhaps that was why nothing seemed to have touched her, not even Dan at first.

Only now was she beginning to realize what Dan Curtis, the bright doll's house on the Heights, represented. Yet, even these things, by accepted standards, were on the shady side of respectability. The idea of Dan Curtis's being anything but respectable tickled her fancy. Even in Lute-Mae's, closeted in a room, bleary-eyed and tormented, he kept something. Both of them had, and perhaps that was why they had come away together.

Waiting for the maid to answer the bell, she wondered if the change she felt so completely was apparent to everyone else. It wasn't only the way she could dress, the freedom of movement and action, the knowledge of security. Something inside was different. Her emotions were saner. and she could look at life with a certain detachment. That was it. She wasn't mad at the world any longer. It was a give-and-take business. She understood now.

Carol, the little colored girl, opened the door. Her face was expressionless for a moment, then she grinned delightedly and made a half curtsy.

"Miz Lane, y'u shuah look good. Ah couldn' raightly recognis' y'u at firs'."

Anyhow, Lane thought, Carol thinks I'm different.

The maid led her down the long, quiet hall. At the end the double doors to the living room were open, and Lane glanced in. A pretty girl in yellow and purple silk pyjamas was stretched out on a sofa. She lowered the magazine she was reading, glanced curiously at the visitor, and then went back to her story.

Lute-Mae, Lane decided, must have relaxed her discipline. It was something new to find one of the girls in the parlor unless she had been sent for.

The house was without sound, so quiet it might have been deserted. Lane planned her visiting time to find it this way, but even so she couldn't be sure. She had never recovered from her astonishment in discovering that men came to a house during the afternoons, even at midday. During her first weeks here she found herself regarding such visitors as an unusual species. The deed seemed appropriate only to the night.

Carol took her upstairs, ceremoniously guiding her to the rear of the house as though she didn't know the way.

"Miz Lute-Mae suah lookin' foahwar' to seein' you agin, Miz Lane." She whispered the confidence. "Bin lacin' up an' down th' house ahal mawnin, wondahin' whin y'u comin'."

She tiptoed to Lute-Mae's door and rapped softly, opening it finally and stepping aside to allow Lane to enter, and then closed it gently.

Carol, Lane saw, still had the fear of Lute-Mae, if not God, in her.

"Well, sugar." Lute-Mae was reclining. There was no other word for the position. Lace and ribbons cascaded from her costume and spread in a tangled sheen on both sides of the chaise longue. "I'm that glad to see you I'd almost get up."

Smilingly the two regarded one another with something close to affection. Seeing her, Lane couldn't help but wonder to what Lute-Mae would have turned if the life she led hadn't been opened to her. Physically, temperamentally she was the perfect madam.

"How're you, Lute-Mae?" Lane dropped comfortably in a

chair at her side and considered the room approvingly. "Those new yellow drapes make the place brighter."

"Mix yourself a drink, sugar." She motioned toward the small table. "I don't know when I've had someone I like to talk with."

Lane passed over the invitation. "You're looking fine, Lute-Mae."

The woman turned up her nose. "I'm like an old pot we used to keep under the bed. It looked fine, too, until someone kicked it over and broke it." She sniggered. "Made a hell of a mess then."

There was the hearty vigor of a dung pile about Lute-Mae, vital but unsuited to sensitive nostrils. Lane laughed inwardly. The words fell harshly upon ears which had been tuned to the accents of Flamingo Road.

"You know"—Lute-Mae studied her guest—"sometimes I guess I should be sore as hell at you. Things ain't never been the same around here since you left. One of my little girls even got herself knocked up. Can you imagine something like that happenin' in this house?"

"You don't think I did it?" Lane's eyes were innocently wide.

Lute-Mae's throaty laugh of pleasure boomed around the room. "I'll swear but it's the only thing I don't blame you for. Go on"—she flicked a hand toward the decanter—"have a drink, even if you are a lady these days."

Lane made a drink for herself, not because she wanted it, but to allow Lute-Mae to keep talking without interruption. For all the woman's joviality, there was an undercurrent playing beneath her words.

"Not only did you go away yourself, the only little girl I was ever friends with, but some of my best trade went with you." She waved an imaginary protest aside. "I don't say they do the same things at your place on Flamingo Road they did here when they'd have a get-together, Johnny Shelton an' the others, but they don't come around like they used to. All I got left is an ordinary cat house, high priced but ordinary. It once was more important than the City Club."

"Why, Lute-Mae"—Lane was sincerely worried—"I never thought about it that way."

Lute-Mae rose in a smother of silken foam, dropping a half-finished cigarette into her empty glass.

"Don't pay any attention to me, sugar." She walked across the room. "I'm only talkin' because I don't know what to

204

say." She returned and sat opposite Lane. "You seen Dan Curtis lately?"

"Why, yes. He comes down every week end."

Lute-Mae nodded; tiny threads of concern pulled at her mouth. "Listen, sugar. I hear lots of things. Hardly a day passes but what someone comes in here with a piece of news of one kind or the other. I got where I am by knowin' people, rememberin' 'em, doin' a little somethin' here an' there when it was needed. There ain't a corner of this state, from a pimp's hangout in Ybor City to the garden back of the governor's mansion where I don't know someone. Now an' then, when they think I ought to should hear somethin', they see I do."

Lane placed her glass on the floor. This was what she had come to hear, the reason Lute-Mae sent for her.

"Titus Semple is stewin' up hell's own soup for someone, an' from where I sit it looks as though, maybe, he was goin' to spoon it out to Dan Curtis an', likely enough, if there's any left, to some others."

Lane for a moment was caught in an unreasoning panic. It was the same formless terror she had experienced on that day, years back, when she walked away from the Palmer House porch leaving Titus rocking deliberately in his chair.

"If you ask me why I'm tellin' you this about Titus, who's been friend to me for longer than I can remember, then all I can say is I never really got over bein' crazy about Dan Curtis."

Lute-Mae glared defiantly at the younger woman as though expecting argument.

"But I don't understand." Lane was puzzled.

Lute-Mae tossed up her hands. "I don't understand either. All I know is what I hear. Titus has been in a lot of places, travelin' farther an' faster than he ordinarily does. There's people he's talked with an' to, questions he's asked. In the beginnin' I thought maybe he was still after you, figurin' on throwin' you off the Heights. Now I ain't sure. He's diggin' a hole for somebody a lot bigger. Maybe there's room in it for you. I'll swear I don't know. If I did I'd go to Dan Curtis myself. This way, though, Dan'd only laugh at me. That's how come I asked you over here. A man'll usually listen to a woman in bed."

"But why should Titus Semple want to break with Dan?" Lane looked helplessly at Lute-Mae.

The woman tapped a cigarette against her knee. "Maybe Dan would know?"

Automatically Lane took the cigarette Lute-Mae extended

and then laughed suddenly as the ridiculousness of the situation appealed to her.

"The worms are chewin' on many a poor son of a bitch right this minute who laughed at Titus Semple." Lute-Mae would not be denied.

The smile vanished from Lane's face. "I wasn't laughing at Sheriff Semple," she said slowly, "it just struck me as funny that Dan should need advice or information from me."

"Maybe he don't." Lute-Mae seemed relieved at the suggestion. "If he don't need it, then no harm can come from tellin' him what I said. If he does need it, then he'll need it bad. You tell him what I said. Dan Curtis knows I don't scream at mice."

It was late when she left Lute-Mae's, and Lane drove hurriedly home. It was Wednesday. Dan might call. He did, sometimes, telling her what train he would take Friday. On the way cross town she tried to imagine how she could tell him the things Lute-Mae wanted him to hear. He would laugh at her. She was sure of it.

Dan had laughed. He came to Truro on the Friday morning train, taking a taxi from the depot and surprising her at breakfast in her room.

Sitting on the edge of the bed while she finished her coffee, Dan listened solemnly. Even Lane was forced to admit what Lute-Mae had told her sounded fantastic and cheaply melodramatic when repeated in the light of day.

"Lute-Mae ought to take something for those hot flashes," he assured her and then tossed back his head and laughed until tears chased each other down his cheeks.

"But, Dan." Lane was not convinced. "Suppose she's right?"

"Why"—Dan's answer surprised her—"she probably is right. I wouldn't doubt for a minute Titus is up to something. He always is. It's in his blood right along with the red and white corpuscles. Elections are coming. Sheriff Semple—and he has plenty of company—would like to ride next to the rail. If he could chase me out, he would. I'd do the same thing to him if it was necessary."

He leaned over, lifted the tray from her lap, and placed it on the floor. Lane smiled wanly. The memory of Lute-Mae's convictions was still fresh.

"But"—she wondered if he would be angry—"suppose Titus wanted to do more than ride you away. Suppose he wanted the track all to himself. Could he . . . well, could he do anything to you? I'd feel better if you told me."

Dan regarded her gravely. "If you put it that way, I suppose a lot of unpleasant things could be stirred up. Even if your hands aren't really dirty, they may look so if someone turns a floodlight on them."

He rose from the bed, leaned over her for a moment, and then bent down to kiss the top of her head. She reached up with one hand to hold him there.

"I get scared, sometimes," she whispered. "I'm afraid something will happen to, to us."

He drew away and took her hand. "There isn't anything in the world you should be frightened of, Lane." He grinned. "Not unless a hungry man can scare you. If one can, then you'd better start screaming because you're looking at him this minute." He gave her a gentle tug. "Get out of bed, woman, and feed a man before he starts beating on you."

"Yes, sir." She was humble.

To all appearances Dan was completely absorbed in his breakfast, but watching him from the other end of the table in the sun-speckled dining room Lane had a feeling he was flavoring, not Sarah's waffles and coffee, but Lute-Mae's chanting of evil. Once or twice he caught her grave glances and smiled good-humoredly only to be lost in abstraction a moment later.

After breakfast he went into the small library and busied himself at the telephone. Dressing upstairs Lane could hear him putting through several long-distance calls and then talking steadily after the connections were made. When she came down again he was lounging in an easy chair by the open casement window, smoking with enjoyment and, apparently, high good humor. He brightened at the sight of her.

"There's something about a woman in a blue linen suit," he complimented, "that fills my eye. I suppose now I'll have to take you someplace instead of playing in the basement workroom."

She sat on the arm of his chair. "We could ride out to Shell Springs. Take a picnic lunch, maybe?"

"Mmmm."

"I'll do all the driving and chase the ants off your plate while you eat."

"Mmmm." He was contented.

"And we won't have chicken salad or dill pickles, either!"

"Fried chicken?"

"Yep."

He picked her up as he rose, carrying her toward the kitchen while her face buried in his coat. Lane didn't want to cling in this fashion, but she was overcome by a desire not to let him go.

From her corner of the kitchen the colored girl giggled

delightedly as Dan strode in bearing his burden. The antics of white folks were a secret joy.

"Fried chicken, Sarah," Dan ordered, "lots of soft, fresh bread, and some cold beer in a hamper. We're going on a picnic."

"But"—Lane wriggled down—"we have to order the chicken from the market first and then cook it."

"You mean it isn't ready?" he demanded. "I thought this house came complete with everything."

"No hot and cold running chicken, though, Mr. Curtis." Lane was almost giddily happy in finding he considered what Lute-Mae said of such little importance that he could forget it immediately.

"I'll have the matter taken care of in the morning." He cracked her smartly on the rear. "Go ahead and get things ready if you want to. I'm going to the basement and potter around. That's what old men are always doing, isn't it? Pottering or puttering, I forget which. I'll try both."

While she superintended the basket packing and waited for a market downtown to rush up the broilers so hurriedly ordered, Lane could hear indistinct humming from the basement as Dan experimented with a variety of motors and mechanical saws. He was at his "whittling," and the sound of it filled the house with peace. Moments such as these were becoming increasingly frequent. It seemed to Lane that without trying they had achieved a rare companionship of understanding. Dan's week ends were stretched into four or five-day periods, and when he did return to Jacksonville it was with undisguised regret.

"This is really home now," he admitted thoughtfully to her one evening. "I don't quite know how it happened, but it is."

In the beginning Lane couldn't help wondering about Dan's family. Did they, or at least his wife, miss him? Was someone, a woman she had never seen, being hurt? Only once did she mention her curiosity, admitting honestly to herself it was nothing more than that. She felt no guilt, no sense of robbing. Dan's life away from her was something remote, mysteriously detached.

Dan smiled, a flash of something close to wistful sheepishness, at her question.

"You know," he said, "I don't think I'm even missed. At first I didn't like the idea. Now I'm used to it. Anyhow, there is nothing we have put together which they could ever have had; nothing you and I share that was ever a part of me open to them." Lane knew he always spoke of Mrs. Curtis as they or them. It was a peculiar trick of conscience, this use of the plural.

When the lunch was finally ready and packed into her car, she called to Dan, and he came from the basement, smelling of freshly sawed pine and with eyes bright beneath tousled hair.

Not until they passed through Truro and were on the road to Shell Springs did he mention what had been occupying his mind while his hands were occupied in the workshop with tools.

"I started a little smudge this afternoon"—he spoke slowly— "just on the chance there was more to what Lute-Mae told you than I wanted to believe." He chuckled. "Maybe a smudge won't smoke out Titus. Maybe it'll have to be a real fire."

Lane was uncertain. She didn't know what reply to make. There was so little she understood in Lute-Mae's conversation or in Dan's words earlier in the morning.

"What are you going to do? I mean, what can you do?" She tossed a helpless smile his way. "I don't even know what you are talking about, Dan," she confessed. "I only asked because I thought you wanted me to."

Dan nodded approvingly. "I did. You see"—he dropped an arm across the seat, touching her shoulders—"if Lute-Mae heard anything worth listening to at all, then it could mean a great many things. So I did some telephoning, invited half a dozen people to the house for next Saturday. Maybe Titus won't want to come, but he'll almost have to and"—he chewed for a moment on his cigar—"he can't lie to everybody at once and get away with it. He might fool me. He might fool all of us separately, but I don't think he is smart enough to handle everything at once if it is tossed in his lap. About next Saturday I'm going to begin dropping things right there."

Lane was reassured. Dan made everything sound as harmless as a game of checkers. She leaned confidently against his arm.

"I'll bet you're the smartest, anyhow." She winked and wrinkled her nose at him.

They rode in silent pleasure through the level country, barely touched by an early spring which had done little more than dampen the soil and lend a musky odor to the air. Most persons, seeing this portion of Florida for the first time professed disappointment in not finding the lush, tropical picturesqueness they had been led to expect. There was beauty in the flat lands, however. Lane knew this now although they had once appeared ugly and severe. The country had character unsoftened by feathery palms or tangled, flowering vines.

"Do you think this is pretty?" She asked the question suddenly.

Dan nodded as though he were aware of what prompted the question. "There are two kinds of Florida," he answered, "one part is for the Crackers and the tourists. The other, this section, just for the Crackers. I'm a Cracker. I guess you have to be to understand it."

They were almost to the turn-off for Shell Springs before he spoke again.

"There are some things I'm getting straightened out," he said. "I intended talking to you about it anyhow, so don't think this business of Lute-Mae's word of Titus has anything to do with it. I'm having my bank fix up a transfer of enough to take care of you if anything should happen to me."

"Oh, Dan!" Lane shook her head vigorously. "I wouldn't want that."

"That's what the girl said about a baby," he laughed and then was serious. "I don't know how I could ever forgive myself if I just let you drift this way. It's got to be so I know you'll not want anything ever again. This is a better way, arranging it now; then there won't ever be a smell as there would be if you were a party to a will. I want you to have the place on Flamingo Road, and I want you to have it so nothing can ever touch you there. Anyhow"—he patted her shoulder—"I'll probably outlive you by twenty years. If you look at it that way, then you're really not getting anything, see?"

Silently Lane parked the car at one side of the pool. It had never occurred to her that Dan wouldn't be there, that a day could come when the home on Flamingo Road would be only another house. She shook her head quickly.

"If you're not with me, Dan, I won't want anything. You don't have to worry."

CHAPTER TWENTY

Titus Semple toiled heavily down the broad steps of the Palmer House and stood for a moment on the sidewalk. With a tongue which felt at the corners of his mouth

210

he tasted the evening's damp and breathed deeply of the soft air. It was his air, his night, his town and county, and, in a couple of hours from now, his state.

The Sheriff was on his way to 32 Flamingo Road, and he tarried deliberately. Perhaps never again would he walk from the Palmer House porch charged with the triumph which now warmed his insides like rare old whisky. He wanted to cling to the sensation for awhile. Later he would have to share it, but here on the pavement he could enjoy it alone for just a little longer. He made a compellingly grotesque figure. Legs spraddled apart, braced against his bulk, his face, a mellow, hairless expanse, he stood looking benignly down upon Truro.

For a week he had been preparing for this night, ever since Dan Curtis telephoned.

"Having some of the boys in next Saturday, Titus." Dan's voice betrayed no emotion. "Like to have you stop in. Bring young Carlisle with you."

"Why, sure, Dan." Titus squeezed with a damp hand at his fat breast out of uncontrollable ecstasy. "Be glad to come. I'll have to find out about the Senator, though." Deliberately he accented Field's title.

Dan grunted noncommittally, and after he hung up Titus sat grinning impishly into the mouthpiece for all the world like a schoolboy who had smeared the inside of teacher's desk with tar and was waiting for her to open it.

He didn't ask Field to go with him. "Dan Curtis is havin' a meetin' Saturday to that little slut's place on Flamingo Road. There's likely to be considerable fireworks. If you sit tight to home you may be able to hear 'em."

"Trouble?" Field asked with interest.

"A sockful, bub, an' they're gettin' nervous 'cause they can't figure whose foot it's goin' on."

Titus dressed carefully for this evening, and the gleaming, cream-colored Shantung suit he wore fluttered in the breeze seeping down River Street. He liked silk next to and on him, and the suit was one of a dozen made up for the summer months to come. It was a trifle light for the season, but he was immune to temperature tonight.

Mechanically he lifted his hat in response to the greetings of the men and women who passed him. Some of them he didn't recognize, but they all knew him. Everyone knew Titus Semple. He was Truro's fat boy. His features were expressionless as he chuckled silently.

Finally—he had wrung what he could from the moment— he crossed the pavement and entered his car. The street lights

211

were snapping on. He was late already. It might be a good idea to drive around town for half an hour more. He wanted to be damn sure they were all there when he arrived.

Pulling away from the curb he cut into Planchette Alley. Never could stand River Street at night with the traffic on it. This way would take longer anyhow.

As Titus drove in the general direction of the Heights three things were happening in different parts of the state, events which moved as chessmen pushed by an invisible hand.

Four Negro boys sat on the ground before a whitewashed cabin on the edge of a plantation in Walton County.

In a broad, high-ceilinged room in the Cortez Hotel, at Miami, a slender finely featured man lay on his bed in his underwear. A fresh wind floated in from Biscayne Bay, tugging at flowing curtains. At a bureau, clad in a sheer slip of black crepe, a pretty blonde girl poured ginger ale into glasses half filled with cracked ice and rye whisky. Her eyes were on Julio Garcia, on the bed.

In a cell at the Walkerville prison Del Lassen sat on his bunk, fingering a letter many times read.

Scattered as were these persons, the whispers of their speech and movement rode with Titus Semple along Flamingo Road.

One of the quartet of Negro boys on the Walton County plantation dug his broad toes into the damp loam and laughed.

"Boy," he said, "y' ain' mekin' no sense. Ef dey wuh fixin' t' shoot y' dey suah ain' goin' t' al dis heah trouble, sendin' y' t wuk en a fahm." The words were thickly accented with a deep river sound.

A second Negro nodded in agreement and gave a playful push at the bent and sullen back of a third buck.

"Deevah," he said, "Jo-John's raight. Ef th' jail wan' t' git rid of y'u, ahl one of th' guard do is say, nigger fatch me 'at buckit en a run. Y' run fuh it an' th' guard up wid 'is gun an', Wahmm! Dead nigger! Tryin' to escape th' guard say."

Deever bent a trifle lower and shook his head doggedly.

"Ain' no min' whut y'u say," he repeated. "Nigger don' git tuk frahm jail an' give jobs en a fahm like dis widout reason."

He raised his eyes and stared into the sky.

The fourth Negro sprawled against the worn flight of steps leading to the cabin, whistling softly.

"Ain' no job"—he cut his melancholy music short with the assertion—"ain' no job a'tall whin y'u ain' drawin' no wagis, come Sattidy."

They all laughed then, even the boy whose yellow face

212

was creased with doubt, and the sound clouded up with the richness of heat from a bog.

They lolled in the gathering darkness, indolently and with the unconscious ease of cats. Their work clothes were worn and stained and their bodies carried a sharp, sweet scent of which they were unaware.

The yellow boy traced his knuckles into the dirt.

"Man say," he whispered, "we wuk heah frahm now on. It ain' seem raight."

The Negro, Jo-John, laughed delightedly. "Boy y'u suah was en Raifor' frahm now on so wuts duh dif-rance. Y'u wuk theah en y'u wuk heah. Dif-rance heah is Mistuh Lassen say ef evrathin' behave us can go off th' place now en thin, come Sattidy."

They rested in silence. In the distance they could see the spotted lights of Burr Lassen's house, and from somewhere in the distance a dog barked sharply three times. Across the broad, stubbled fields the night air rolled, gathering warmth and body from the earth as it came. Deep on the horizon was the darkness within darkness of the great pine stand, and above it now the early moon, like a slice of ripe grapefruit, slid into the sky.

The Negroes burrowed to themselves, humming spontaneously, a gentle minor wail which took form as they played until it throbbed with an aching loneliness and bewilderment.

At the moment, Titus was driving the length of Flamingo Road, past 32 where two cars were parked before the house and a third was tucked deep within the gloom of the driveway. There were lights in all the windows, and as his car rolled slowly past he caught a glimpse of Dan Curtis. Well, they'd wait.

In the Cortez Hotel, glasses in both hands the pretty blonde girl turned away from the bureau.

"You goin' to take this drink lyin' down, Julio?"

The man wriggled into a half-sitting position, his handsome mouth smiling provocatively. Even, white teeth set against dark skin flashed.

"I'll take it in an enema bag, baby, if you'll give it to me."

The girl came toward him, walking on the balls of her feet. Through the transparent slip her body was pinkly warm. Her breasts, small pears, lifted gently. The man raised a hand lazily and touched one of them while the girl caught her breath with a sharp, almost purring sound.

"You're pretty, Julie." She caressed him with the words. "You're pretty, even lying around in your underwear this way, but you scare the hell out of me."

Julio Garcia marched his finger tips down the girl's thigh and then twitched at the slip, coaxing her closer.

"Come sit down, baby. I been lookin' at you from across the room long enough."

She settled herself beside him, and he lifted one leg, bracing the knee to give a support to her back. Like a child she sipped her drink, experimenting, not quite sure she liked it. Julio swallowed, and the highball gurgled noisily in his throat.

"I'm scared all the time, Julie." She wasn't complaining. "I'm just so scared I don't know what to do."

Julio slid a sensitive hand exploringly over the faint roundness of her belly. Jesus! He'd never had a girl like this one before. Picked her up at a juke joint where she was waiting on table. "Want to go with me, baby?" He held her fingers to the table when she brought the check. She just looked at him and, releasing her hand, began to untie the wisp of an apron she wore. He felt the easy slope of her pelvis. God Almighty! A man could go grazy over something like this, and the funny part of it was she could look in a way that made you think she had pigtails with little ribbon bows on them hanging down her back.

"I won't get you into any trouble, Lee."

She licked at the rim of her glass, and her eyes were pensive.

"I near died today," she said, "when I went into Burdine's an' bought things, givin' them those bad twenty-dollar bills. I near died I was so scared."

Julio Garcia leaned heavily against the pillow and laughed happily while his fingers dug spasmodically into her leg.

"Those bills were all right, baby." He patted her in appreciation of the joke. "If that money wasn't good, then there ain't a bill comin' out of the government mint what is. I only wanted to find out how you'd act."

She rested the glass on her knee and looked at him. "Why you bastard," she remarked without fervor, "why, you bastard!"

Julio's eyes sparkled. He pulled her over on top of him, feeling her writhe, twisting one shoulder up, pressing close within the curve of his arm.

Her lips were parted, and the tip of her tongue lay flat against the lower lip.

"I won't get you into any trouble, Lee." He nipped at her ear, his teeth making first white and then red marks. She moaned at the touch. "We ain't bothering with hot money retail. What you had was part of the five grand I got from the old boy. Five for one I deal him. He sent five grand of cold for twenty-five grand of the hot. That's the way we'll always work. Let the suckers take chances passing tens and twenties. We'll only wholesale it. What I give you to spend will always be good."

Her body was coming to life in his arms; she rippled along him with the involuntary movements of a snake in the sun.

"You're so smart, Julie." She breathed against his eyelids.

Julio slid downward from the pillow. "You'd think I was smarter still if I told you who the old boy is, baby. Jesus, what a stink it'd make." He sucked at his tongue with pleasure. "An' next year, baby, we'll make a million dollars right here in the state an' be as safe as if we were playin' tiddlywinks."

She snuggled against him, her fingers tugging at the jersey silk of his undershirt until the fabric gave suddenly and ripped from shoulder to navel. Her gasp was a thing of pain, and she buried her face into the hollow of his neck while her fingers worked convulsively over his chest.

"You beautiful bastard, Julie." Her words were muffled. "I don't care much what happens to me. You dirty, beautiful bastard."

Julio Garcia dropped the drink he had been holding, and it fell to the floor, shattering with the crisp tinkle of glass and ice. Then he reached up and pulled at the short length of chain connected with the switch of the bed lamp.

The girl was whimpering like a lonely puppy.

Titus retraced Flamingo Road, swinging into the curb at 32 behind the other cars. With stubby fingers he groped at the ignition key, and after the motor was stilled he turned off the lights and sat in the darkness.

Delmer Lassen, on his bunk in the jail at Walkersville, reread the letter from his father for the fourth time in as many days.

Dear Del, [The words were badly formed, scrawled on blue-lined tablet paper] this is just a note to tell you we are all well and that Josie, your setter bitch, littered yesterday for five pups. Your mother sends her love and joins me in wishing you were home.

Del Lassen raised his eyes and glanced around the narrow

215

cell. It was filled with damp, the creeping wet of walls covered with many coatings of whitewash which held the moisture. Hung on the outside of a barred door an oil lantern smoked and dripped a feeble light into the cell and across the letter in his hand. Since that nigger went crazy and tried to burn down the jail they kept lanterns outside.

You know [his father wrote laboriously] your trial is on the calendar for next month, and although we know you done what you had to do there ain't no sense in pretending we ain't worried, as feeling over the killing has been high. I'm writing you now to say the worrying is over. Last week I had a visit from Sheriff Titus Semple of Truro. The Sheriff don't do nothing for nothing as maybe you know, but he wanted a favor and I done it for him. I guess you understand what this means.

Del rubbed at his face with the heel of one hand. He sighed with relief as he had done each time these words met his eyes.

The whole thing won't likely take over one day, the way I figure things, and then you'll be free, and you shouldn't worry none that folks will hold anything against you. A man released after a regular jury trial has got a right to raise his head up again. So, we just wanted to let you know Sheriff Semple is interested and everything will be all right.

I will close now because your mother is waiting for me to drive her into town where she wants to buy some new preserve jars and other things for the house. She sends her love to you again as do I.

Del tucked the letter into the pocket of his shirt and, pulling off his shoes, stretched out on the corn-shuck mattress. It crackled pleasantly, rustling like wind in dry leaves. He hoped to God the old man wasn't gettin' himself into a fix with Truro's Sheriff. Titus Semple, he'd heard, never really let a man go once he had him good.

Damn Ronnie Johnson's soul to hell, gettin' drunk on shine that way an' startin' a fight when he knew they were all liquored up. Ronnie had pulled a gun. He'd seen it although the police swore there wasn't no gun any place around later. He'd never figured he'd kill a man with that clasp knife Burr gave him for Christmas, an' he wouldn't have if Ronnie hadn't gone for a gun. Now, by God, he'd been rottin' in this Walkersville jail for five months.

He patted the letter in his pocket. If Titus Semple told Burr things were going to be all right, then they were. He was through worryin' about what could happen. The letter in his pocket wouldn't have made him feel any better if it had been a pardon from the governor.

A guard came along the hall, removing lanterns from the occupied cells and carrying them in a jangling cluster.

"Sleep good, Del," he mocked.

Delmer Lassen grunted and rolled over, nudging a saucer into the shuck-filled pillow for his cheek.

Titus slid out from behind the wheel and walked up past the cars parked ahead. There was amused contempt on his face as he noted their sheen, their heavy expensiveness. The boys might be happy to have a bicycle pretty soon. By the time he and Field got through the next four years, they'd be as hungry as sparrows in a snow storm.

At the gate of the sugar-icing picket fence he halted, both hands resting on the uprights, and studied Lane's house as a malevolent gust swept him. Never could he remember feeling this way about anyone. This girl, a guttersnipe from a broken carnival, represented all the derision and indignities which had been heaped on him as a boy. By her presence here on Flamingo Road she challenged everything he had so cunningly contrived. She was the spirit of defiance, hooting at him, and the sight of her made him feel ugly and ponderously impotent. Sometimes he would dream of taking her to bed, fouling and debasing her there until she was reduced to quivering humiliating agony.

She would go, and so would the house. This he would save until later. It was to form no part of the demands he would make tonight. In his own way, slowly and with infinite care so that each moment should yield the utmost satisfaction, he would take her and the house apart and scatter the pieces in Truro's sewers.

So consuming was the fury holding him that he could barely restrain himself from kicking and crushing at the neat flower beds lining the crazily bright walk from gate to door. He wanted to range through the yard, tearing, uprooting, despoiling all evidence of the beauty planned for her.

He could feel the sweat creeping out all over his body. It was mean sweat, the kind you could smell. He was familiar with the odor. There was no one to see, and so he halted in the middle of the path, waiting until the spell left him. He didn't want to walk into the house accompanied by this insensate rage.

The moon tossed a wispy scarf over the miniature gardens and trailed its silver through the rock pool. Dwarf firs and shrubs crouched like little men who waited to resume some fantastic game once this intruding stranger left. There was a deep, expectant hush in the night.

Titus breathed easier. The fever left him, and he trudged up the coquina slabs. If he was careful here, careful but unyielding, everything he wanted would be placed in his hand. Things would be better that way. The men awaiting him formed a solid wall. If necessary he would crack it, but only if he had to. The smart thing to do would be to keep it intact, a wall for him and Field to sit on. It would stand forever, patched here and there when the time came. But by God, if they forced him he'd smash it right now, before their very eyes.

At the simple door he waited a few seconds and then slowly put his finger to the bell button.

CHAPTER TWENTY-ONE

FEAR AND INDECISION SAT AROUND THE TABLE AT 32 Flamingo Road. The emotions, so closely akin, were the companions of all save Titus Semple and Dan Curtis. These two held themselves apart from the timid: the men of little resolution who fiddled with glasses, tapped nervously at the edges of ash trays with cigars and cigarettes, or gazed vacantly up at the wavering canopy of smoke drawn above their heads.

For the second time Dan repeated his challenge. "I'm not going to let you get away with it, Titus."

At the sound of Curtis's voice the half-dozen men in the room looked hopefully toward the end of the table, but as they realized the words only further threatened their security they lapsed again into apprehensive silence.

Titus, deep in a heavy chair, stared musingly down at the monstrous expanse of his belly: an evil and unsmiling Buddha contemplating his navel.

"Why, Dan," he mumbled, "ain't that, maybe, the wrong way to look at things? I'm just offerin' you a good man."

The assertion brought a quick smile to Dan's lips. He shook his head.

218

"You're offering us Carlisle for governor, if you want to put it that way, but what we'd get would be Titus Semple."

The Sheriff's eyes flickered, a brief tribute to the humor in the charge. For the others he spared not so much as a glance. He was done with them.

One by one, with the sure but heavy touch of a master butcher, he had laid them open, tagging the exhibits exposed with records, photostatic copies of checks, bank statements, and incomes. He told them where they had rooted and when and spread the black register of illegal contracts, title transfers, pardons, bootleg connections, and land condemnations. This he did while talking in a sleepy voice, the bored tone of a teacher lecturing to indifferent students. He started with Des Wingate, from Orange, and a sewer contract for which the taxpayers had several miles of unjoined pipe, tossed hastily into a shallow ditch and covered with sand. He ended on the opposite side of the table with Shelton's franchises in St. Lucie.

Segment by segment he formed a mosaic of petty thievery, corruption, criminal connection, bribery, and maladministration, and when he finished each man recognized which part was his.

Des Wingate, unable to stand the monologue any longer, had risen to his feet and shouted.

"Why, you bastard. You can't scare me. You know you won't say anything because if you do you'll go to jail along with the rest of us."

Titus nodded in happy agreement. "Why, yes, Des. A few little irregularities might be tied to my tail, but"—his voice was the whisper of tearing silk—"you see, the difference is I'll have a governor to get me out. You, why you an' the others just won't have a God-damned thing."

With a gesture of being wearied of the game he swept the notes and papers carelessly toward the center of the table and turned to Dan Curtis.

"I got 'em in triplicate," he explained and grinned without malice.

"Nothing for me?" Dan cut the end from a cigar with a small-bladed penknife.

"Why, yes, Dan." Titus was genially reassuring. "I got somethin' for you too, only I'm hopin' maybe there ain't goin' to be a reason for givin' it to you."

"I'm disappointed." Dan held a match to his cigar carefully, watching Titus across the flame.

Semple shook his head. "Oh, you shouldn't be, Dan. I went

to considerable trouble an' thought on yours. It's a dandy, a sure enough jim-dandy."

Titus patted lovingly at the sheer silk of his shirt. There wasn't any point in talking to the others. They were as scared as treed 'possum. They'd blow with the wind now. Titus was delighted with himself. He had taken the men by their necks without warning. They were waiting as he expected when he came in the house. A couple already had taken one drink too many. The others were mellow, unsuspicious, and greeted him with good-natured gibes. Only Dan seemed to know why he had come, and Dan waited until they were settled around the table in the dining room. The others must have thought they were going to have a poker game.

"Been pretty busy lately, haven't you, Sheriff?" Curtis asked the question offhandedly.

Titus always admired this quality in Dan. Open fighting was a method he respected even if he rarely resorted to it himself.

"Yep," he said dreamily, "I been measurin' the governor's chair for Senator Carlisle."

By God! That stopped them. Eyes wide, Titus gazed around the table with the pleased expression of a child holding a new toy.

Parker, Shelton, Niles, Wingate, and the others thought he was indulging in an obscure joke. They laughed, a sound which was deridingly hilarious at first but petered out to an uncertain cough or humorless chuckle.

"Your memory's getting bad, Titus." Dan's remark was gently chiding. "The name's Watterson. The chair already fits. He sat in it before."

Titus didn't change his expression. "Maybe you pronounce it that way, Dan, but it's sure spelled C-A-R-L-I-S-L-E."

That had done it. No one was laughing now. They turned to stare at him, and then there was the crackle of surprised indignation as each man tried to say something at once, raising voices to lift them above the confusion.

"What the hell are you trying to do, Titus?"

"For Christ's sake, Semple, you know good as anyone Watterson is goin' back."

"Every man in Volusia is goin' to vote for Watterson."

"You can't shove no wet-behind-the-ears kid down my throat without my pukin' him all over you."

The words rattled like shot in an empty gourd or sang with the angry sound of hornets. The Sheriff lowered his eyes as though the noise offended him. Only Dan Curtis refrained from adding a voice. He waited until the sudden fury had worn itself to muttered sarcasms, abrupt slappings at the table.

"There's nothing against young Fielding Carlisle, Titus." Curtis's opinion was calculatingly soothing. "He's just not ready."

Titus fingered an ear. "Maybe not, Dan," he agreed. "But I am."

"You're bein' a fool, Semple." Link Niles pushed his chair away from the table in disgust. "Marion won't take anyone but Watterson. I won't an' that means my county won't."

"Why, Niles"—Titus was patiently reproving—"I figured to have you in jail by the time the primaries came around. If it was necessary, I even thought about havin' Senator Carlisle introduce a resolution at the next session askin' for an investigation of the Highway Commission."

He saw the fear unmistakably stamped on the man's face, and because such panic, springing from uneasy consciences, is contagious he let them all have it. He didn't accuse. He told them what they had stolen, how and when, and to each charge he tossed something of substantiation: copies of their correspondence, records of closed bidding for public contracts, photostats, bank deposits outrageously out of proportion to incomes. He slapped their mouths with fraud and deceit.

"The public," he admonished, "is likely hardened to a little rootin' at the trough, but it's possible it might get pretty sore at discoverin' you boys et the trough too."

There was nothing to be gained by their tossing Truro in the Sheriff's face. Wingate tried it.

"Why, sure, Des," Titus agreed without rancor. "I plucked a goose here an' there. It costs money to run an organization in a county as important as Truro. All I'm sayin' is I'll forget your geese if you'll forget mine. After that we'll all forget about Watterson and throw the weight behind Senator Carlisle."

He scratched at a spread leg, and his nails made sissing noises against the silk. His eyes as he studied the faces of the men around him were no longer vacant.

"You see," he continued, "if you ain't willin' to do this, then sure as a bull has horns, I'll send you to jail. At least I'll get the indictments. That'll keep you so busy runnin' that I can take Senator Carlisle through the primaries myself."

"You'll split the party wide open. It'd take fifty years to put things together again." Parker was whining. The note was unmistakable.

"It surer than hell looks that way." Titus was properly sympathetic.

"What makes you think you could carry Carlisle as an independent?"

They were all stalling for time now, waiting for either Curtis or Semple to make up their minds for them.

"I wasn't figurin' on him as an independent. He'll go to the primaries as the regular candidate."

"And Watterson?" Dan was mildly inquisitive.

Titus beamed upon him as he would on a particularly bright pupil. He'd been waiting for this.

"Why, Dan," he said, " Watterson is goin' to be in a federal prison." He clucked his tongue, disturbed at the prospect. "I ain't said nothin' about Watterson because you'd sure enough think I was talkin' through last year's straw hat. In a way I'm doin' you a favor by offerin' Carlisle in his place. Watterson has got himself in about the damnedest jam you could imagine. They'll get him sooner or later, even if I don't say nothin', an' all of us would be in a fix tryin' to explain how come the party was supportin' him. All I figured on doin', just in case we can't agree here tonight, was to speed up things a little. The only thing worryin' me this minute is they'll get him before I'm ready an' the stink will cloud up things for any party candidate. Then I'd have to run Field independent."

He knew they didn't believe him. Well, he hadn't believed it himself at first. Prissy old Watterson, full of hymns and hallelujahs. The backwoods bible belter with a bear by the tail.

Dan Curtis studied the fine white ash on the tip of his cigar.

"I don't suppose," he suggested, "you would want to tell us about Watterson."

The sound Titus emitted was almost a giggle. "Why, no, Dan. It'd sort of spoil things, don't you see? Even if the boys here was to promise me somethin', I ain't sure I could believe it. So the best way for me to let you know what Watterson has been up to would be for Senator Carlisle to do it at Tallahassee. It'll make him quite a figure, sort of one of them crusaders, you might say."

There was no need for Dan to glance at the faces of the other men in the room. Titus had beaten them down, one by one, until they were ready to crawl into his pocket. He couldn't blame them. The Sheriff had dropped some nasty packages in their laps. Even he, calloused to the spectacle of graft and indifference to the public, had been astounded at the number of dead cats Titus tossed on the table. It was unreasonable to expect small men could resist the temptation to fatten in positions of trust. God just didn't fashion them that way. It was easy enough to blame the system, but Dan Curtis knew it was the best system yet devised. It couldn't be treated lightly, though. The good in it must be eternally balanced against the bad by unceasing vigilance. It was too easy to shrug and admit the imperfections. The Titus Semples were waiting for that.

He had no patience for the men at the table. They were greedily stupid; their fears and willingness to capitulate rose, not from any sense of shame or stirrings of conscience, but only because they had been caught. For a moment Dan felt a great weariness. He was half tempted to throw them to Titus, but even as he toyed with the idea he knew he couldn't do it.

This was a great and pleasant state, and he didn't want to see it turned over to Titus Semple for looting. If Carlisle was older, wiser, yes, stronger, it might be worth the chance and save a lot of heads. But Field Carlisle had become both ambitious and vacillating, vain and impatient. It frightened him to think what Titus could make of such a combination.

As surely as the Sheriff had prepared the noose for the men in the room, including, he speculated wryly, Daniel Vincent Curtis, so just as certainly was he telling the truth about former Governor Watterson. Titus wouldn't talk simply out of appreciation for the sound of his own voice. Somewhere, somehow he had turned over a log and found Watterson there with the grubs.

Dan passed a hand over his face, pulling it out at the chin in a beard-stroking motion. He knew Titus was waiting. In its way this was a compliment, for the Sheriff was too wise not to know he had the others dangling at the end of a string, the cord looped through their gills and knotted. They were gasping and pleading to be dropped back into any water, even Semple's puddle. He was sure if he turned Titus down they would go crawling and flapping with the Sheriff.

It wasn't only the single term of a governorship which made him hesitate. Titus might be judiciously checked during the first four years. Once in, however, he would find himself another Carlisle and alternate them in the Mansion, corrupting, demoralizing, feeding small greeds, until the decent people of the state found themselves divided, without the will to resist. He knew that with the power which laid at his hands these years he had failed, been tolerant where he should have been severe, indulgent when the circumstances called loudly for denial. Now he was face to face with unhealthy fruit of his own nursery. He sighed inwardly. It would be so easy to toss up his gloves and tell Titus to take what he wanted.

"I'm not going to let you get away with it, Titus." He repeated himself for the third time.

Des Wingate emitted a little strangling noise in his throat. He rose unsteadily and went to the sideboard and poured himself a straight drink of whisky. There was an uneasy rustling of movement from the others at the table. If Titus Semple and Dan were going to fight it out, then they were going to be trampled. No longer was it a question of who was right or wrong, what was good or bad. They had lost interest in such ethical abstractions. What leered in their faces was the spectacle of indictments, possibly jail. They saw themselves stripped and ludicrously naked.

"Now, Dan." Shelton coughed, his features set in a forced, conciliatory smile. "Maybe Titus's ideas are worth listening to. Young Carlisle might come along all right. If what Titus says about Watterson is true, then oughtn't we go easy until we find out?" He fumbled with a cigar, dropping it to the table twice before he could get it to his mouth.

Shelton gave them hope. They began arguing, talking at once, falling over themselves to line up on the bright side of justice and cast out Watterson, who, according to the Sheriff, was unfit for public trust. So enthusiastically did they cling to this song of purity that Dan found himself being maneuvered into the position of a party bolter. No longer was the Sheriff the renegade, holding them up, threatening a schism. Dan Curtis was the apostate. They frowned and snorted at him, thumped the table and waved fingers. When the excitement subsided they had convinced themselves that this was what they had wanted all the while. Only Dan Curtis prevailed against them.

Throughout the comedy Titus sat with bowed head, fingering the buttons on his shirt. Once he raised his eyes, gazed mockingly at Dan, and then dropped them drowsily.

Dan was forced to remind himself that these men, now openly accusing him of wanting to destroy them to prove his stubbornness, were, or had been, his friends for years. In younger days they had roved and roistered, snatched at this prodigal state out of sheer exuberance of being alive and vital. They had run things because they were men built to call the measures. They profited, grew strong and powerful in their own communities first, later in their counties, and finally in the state itself. For all their depredations, early minor derelictions, they had helped build a state. They sent good men to Washington, gave lip service to God and their energy to the party. They stole some, but then so would other men. It was part of the price of democracy and cheap at that. What hurt now was the knowledge that the years had robbed them of the will to fight back or to take a licking, still clawing.

The Titus Semples of the world, he thought, must be equipped with an acute sense of smell which enabled them to scent decay while it was still below the surface and take advantage of the hidden cancer. Their timing was always perfect. It couldn't be chance.

Once, he reflected, these men, bullied and threatened as they had been this night, would have told Titus to chase a flying goose. They would have ferreted out every bit of offal, every old bone the Sheriff had ever buried and hauled the stinking pieces to his doorstep. They would have rubbed Semple's nose in his own dirt and kept him so busy wiping it off he wouldn't have time or strength to pursue them.

Now they cringed, frantically trying to bolster up their false fronts of respectability. They were frightened, grown soft as slugs in rotten meat. They were ready to crawl after Semple, eager for his droppings.

Dan felt nausea in his throat.

"No." Dan bit the word.

Titus's eyes were milky. A button he was playing with on his shirt front snapped with a brittle sound. He moved slightly in the chair.

"Why, Dan"—one thick lip folded over the other until his mouth had the appearance of a soggy pocketbook roll— "I'm sure sorry to hear you talk that way."

Both of Curtis's hands were on the table. He straightened his body, and the light struck full on the fine silvering of his hair and threw shadows of angular strength across his face.

"I'm not going to let you get away with it. Titus. If Watterson is bad, lay it out here on the table. Then we'll all decide what's best, but you're not going to run it your way."

There was a sharp sound of several breaths being drawn at once. It raced around the table.

"No, Dan. The way you want it just wouldn't suit me. It's got to be Carlisle. I always figured you for smart, Dan. Me, now, I ain't half so smart, but I know what I want, an' I'm aimin' to get it with or without you."

"Threatening me?"

The reply was long in coming. "Why, yes, Dan." Titus fondled the words as if they surprised him. "Come to think of it, I'm doin' just that."

Dan rose without haste, walked quietly to the buffet, and mixed himself a highball, dropping in small chunks of ice until

225

the liquid threatened to overflow. He drank deliberately, and when the glass was emptied carefully replaced it on a tray.

"It shouldn't be hard to figure from now on." He made a sweeping motion with his head which included all the men at the table. "You've got to make up your minds whose back yard you want to dig in."

He was too wise in the ways of those who confronted him not to know the answer. He knew every man there was repeating a remark Titus made earlier in the evening. They were taking what comfort they could from it. Titus had said: "I'll have a governor to get me out." Each man caught at the scant assurance. If Titus and Dan locked, there would be trouble. If they played with Semple, why—Dan could see the relief flooding their faces—there wouldn't be any trouble at all, would there?

Link Niles cleared his throat, started to say something, and then sank into embarrassed silence. One by one the eyes dropped beneath Dan's steady inquisitiveness.

Dan smiled, but there was no humor at his lips. "Well, boys, it's nice you dropped in."

There was no ignoring the dismissal. They rose from the table, affecting casualness. They yawned, stretched, and attempted a jovial weariness, breaking into ripples of small talk which was sound without significance.

Titus hoisted himself to a standing position, eying Dan reproachfully.

"I sure hate to see you so stubborn, Dan. If you want to take a kind of vacation for awhile, why, there wouldn't be any point in a lot of trouble to get things in an uproar."

Curtis shook his head. "I'll see you in a good, hot hell first, Titus."

The Sheriff nodded regretfully. "I was afraid you'd be that way, Dan." He clucked. "I'll swear but I hope you untie yourself from Watterson. He's goin' to smell. Matter of fact"—Titus considered the point—"it might save a lot of confusion if I got him on the telephone an' told him he wasn't goin' to enter the primaries an' why. I wouldn't do that if I didn't like you real well, Dan."

Dan saw them from the house, watching from an open doorway while they strolled with too elaborate deliberation to their cars. A wintry smile of regret frosted his eyes as they drove away. Fifteen minutes, half an hour at the most, he thought, and the telephone in Titus Semple's room would begin to ring. One by one, as individuals, for they were still a little

226

too ashamed to make public confession, they would drop their pretenses and creep for shelter within the Sheriff's fold.

Aside from a determination that Titus must not boost Fielding Carlisle into the seat of nominee for governor, Dan was a little confused about his emotions. He felt both regret and contempt, but he wasn't angry. I ought to be raving sore, he mused, and wondered that he was only tired. He shut the door gently and snapped off the outside lights.

For a moment he stood alone in the middle of the living room, once glancing up at the ceiling. Lane hadn't come down all evening.

"I think I'll stay in my room tonight, Dan." She hadn't wanted to confess that even the knowledge of Semple's presence in the house frightened her. "Sarah has plenty in the icebox if you want to eat. She knows what to do. I'll wait for you."

Wandering without purpose around the house now, turning out a light here and there, snatching at a thin slice of ham from a platter on the buffet, Dan tried to unsnarl Semple's tangled references to former Governor Watterson.

"What the hell"—he spoke to an empty chair—"do you suppose he's been up to?"

The chair, as he expected, had no answer to the question, and finally he gave up. Whatever it was he would have to find out. With Watterson's prestige he might be able to make a fight even without the combination's support.

Lane was sitting up in bed reading when he came into the room.

She smiled impertinently. "Well, I see you've still got your hair. The Sheriff didn't scalp you after all."

"No, but he let out a couple of preliminary war whoops." Just the sight of her made him feel better. "He's bound and determined to run young Carlisle for governor and he came loaded down with prods to keep everyone in line."

"Dan!" There was quick concern in the exclamation. "You aren't in trouble?"

He leaned over and patted her hand, tempted for a moment to drop his head in the soft hollow of her shoulder and rest there. This, he thought, is all I really want. What in God's name makes me so stubborn? What the hell do I care if the Semples take over the state?

"No," he chuckled dryly, "but Titus made me a promise after I told him I wouldn't go along with Carlisle."

"God damn him."

The vicious lash in her voice caused him to lift his eyebrows.

Lane laughed uncertainly. "Don't be surprised when the carnival brat comes out in me." She reached up and pulled his head down. "I only try to be a lady for you. I mind my business on Flamingo Road, stay away from Lute-Mae's, wear the kind of clothes I think you'll like, read books I don't understand, and watch my grammar. Underneath, though, I'm still Lane, the kid from a carnival pitch. When I say God damn him, I mean it in spades."

Dan whistled softly and then threw back his head and roared with laughter.

"I could tell you something about Semple," she said mildly, "that you wouldn't think was so funny. I didn't."

The laughter died as quickly as it had been born. Dan's gray eyes were serious, probing.

"I've always wondered about you and Titus. Ready to tell me now?"

For what seemed a long time, Lane fingered the pages of the book she held, riffling through them abstractedly. Finally she shook her head.

"No," she said. "I would if I thought it would do any good. You'd only get mad, and when you're fighting Titus you can't afford to get mad."

She dropped the book and reaching up quickly put her arms around his neck, locking her fingers and pulling herself against him. For minutes she clung there saying nothing, but her body trembled. Suddenly she was crying wildly and without restraint.

"Carnival kids don't cry." He spoke tenderly.

Her grip tightened. "Dan, Dan. Don't let anything happen to us. I don't know what I'd do. Once, I wanted to be on my own. I didn't care for anyone. Now, you've broken me down. If anything happened I wouldn't want to live. That's how it is, Dan."

He tried to soothe her but knew he was being clumsy. She pressed her mouth to his ear, holding it there.

"Pick me up and take me into your bed tonight, Dan. I'm scared to be alone."

CHAPTER TWENTY-TWO

IN A ROOM IN THE CORTEZ HOTEL, LITTLE LEE Brunner, her eyes filled with the stars of excitement, was about to make Titus Semple's telephone call to Deveris Watterson unnecessary.

She awoke as she had every morning since she went away with Julio Garcia: excited and filled with wonder over what had happened to her. Always she was afraid to open her eyes, fearing they would find only an empty bed and Julie gone. Beautiful, wonderful Julie, who had taken her from a roadside juke joint and dressed her in perfumed silks, sheer stockings, and fragile, spindly shoes. Now she raised her eyelids a trifle and through the slits saw the tangled outline of Julie's head against the pillow. She felt him with her slim legs, touched his shoulder with her finger tips. Reassured, her eyes flew wide, and she sighed blissfully. He was still here. It wasn't a dream.

Cautiously she slid from her side of the bed, careful not to disturb him. Julio didn't like to get up in the morning. "Only dopes and roosters wake up early," he told her. Just the same she couldn't stay in bed. Getting up early made the wonderful days so much longer.

Naked she stood before the full-length mirror of the bathroom door and surveyed herself with a giggle. Julio didn't mind how many expensive nightgowns she bought. He thought it was cute, but he wouldn't let her wear them.

She stretched on her tiptoes and pirouetted before the glass, halted with hand at mouth, and peeked over her shoulder at the bed. Julio would get sore as hell if she woke him. It was too bad he didn't like the mornings. If he did, then she could call room service and have a breakfast table set up by the window where they could see the bay. As it was she had to go to the dining room, but that wasn't so bad—flowers on the table, everything crisp, silvery, and white with the waiters saying: "Yes, Miz Garcia, No, Miz Garcia, Th' melon alraight, Miz Garcia."

She dressed quickly and snickered again. The only time she got to wear clothes was when Julio was asleep. Today, today

229

after breakfast she would go shopping again. Burdine's was wonderful, Burdine's had everything, and Julie didn't care how much money she spent. He'd just toss his wallet and say: "Take whatever you want, baby." That's the way Julio was.

Ready to go downstairs she looked through the pockets of Julio's trousers and found only a few crumpled bills. There was more, part of the five thousand he got last week. He must keep in one of the bags. She searched quietly, not because Julio would mind her taking the money. Whatever you want, baby. He sure hated like hell to be wakened in the mornings, though.

She found the money in a brown envelope. She had never seen so much before. Fifty-, one-hundred, ten- and twenty-dollar bills. She stripped off a dozen, indifferent to the denominations, and stuffed them in her purse. Julie would laugh when he saw the stuff she bought. He'd laugh and make her come back to bed with him again. Oh, he was a wonderful, beautiful bastard, Julio was.

Flagler Street, newly washed, sparkled in the sun. Miamians swore the fire department scrubbed it every morning for the tourists. Lee walked down and then over to Burdine's.

At first Lee thought it was some sort of a courtesy, Burdine's way of showing how they appreciated a good customer. The young lady, looking a little flustered, hurried back with her change, and then a man asked her if she wouldn't come to the manager's office.

When the manager started talking, she didn't understand. He was soft-spoken, seemed to like her, but Lee realized he was purposely detaining her. Then the other two men came in and began asking questions: What was her name? Where did she live? How long had she been in Miami? Where did she get the bills she spent in the store that morning? She knew what had happened. Julio was a son of a bitch. He lied to her when he said the money was good. He was a lying son of a bitch. He stayed in bed in the morning, letting her go out to change bad money, the kind he sold for good money. The men—they said they were federal officers—didn't give her time to catch her breath. They just kept asking questions, hard and fast, and Lee began to cry. She told them about Julio, where he was, what he said about making a million dollars. She cried at the thought of all the beautiful things she bought and couldn't have, and then she got mad.

Julio awoke slowly. He kept his eyes shut because he knew someone was in the room. Lee was there, he could tell by the perfume she used, but someone else was with her. He could feel them standing by the bed.

"All right, Garcia."

Julio got out of bed slowly, and when he was on his feet he slapped Lee across the mouth half a dozen times before the men could grab him.

"You stupid little fool" His spittle trickled down her cheek.

Street noises were only half heard in Dan's office, high in the Curtis Building, but he caught the unmistakably raucous note of the newsboys with an extra. Curious, he sent one of the girls down for a paper.

With the *Times-Union* spread on his desk he stared unbelievingly at the eight-column head.

WATTERSON NAMED IN COUNTERFEITING RING

He read the Associated Press story, with a Miami dateline, carefully.

Deveris Watterson, former governor of Florida, today faced arrest on charges of aiding and abetting an alleged million-dollar counterfeiting ring.

Two federal indictments linking the former Governor with financing a counterfeiting conspiracy were returned here today. Others named in the indictments were Julio Garcia, Lee Brunner, described as Garcia's companion, Mateo Valdez, and John Enfant. With the return of the indictments a bond of $35,000 was set for Garcia, alleged head of the syndicate, and $15,000 for each of the others.

Watterson is alleged to have furnished $20,000 to the ring to finance the purchase of printing presses and equipment with the understanding that he was to receive $50,000 in counterfeit money as his part in the investment, the indictments charge.

Dan whistled incredulously. He couldn't believe what he was reading, and yet it was there, bold and black in type.

Garcia [he continued down the column] was arrested in Miami after the Brunner girl attempted to pass two $50 notes in a department store. The woman led federal operatives to Garcia's hotel where he was arrested.

Watterson could not be located at his home, but a capias for his arrest was expected to be served today.

There was more to the story, interesting but unessential details, and a history of Watterson's career. Dan read no farther.

His hand slammed over the paper in anger. So Titus wasn't bluffing. He might have known he wouldn't. He warned him Watterson was going to stink. Well, by God, he was right.

A reluctant admiration filled him. The Sheriff was thorough. The more he thought of the scandal, however, the surer he was that the exposé of the former governor's underworld connections was not Semple's doing. The timing was bad. Titus would have waited until he had him and Watterson out on a limb and disposed of them both at the same time. No matter how ignorant Dan might have been of Watterson's part in the affair, he would have been linked with him once he openly supported the man in the primaries. No, the gun went off a little too soon. It caught Watterson but missed him.

"He'll start sniping in earnest now." Dan spoke to his reflection in the glass-topped desk. "I better get ready to shoot back."

Until this moment he hadn't envisioned anything more than a particularly rough and tumble political fracas. The Watterson story shaped things in a different mold. He'd either have to get out and leave things to Semple or hunt some bullets to load a gun of his own with. If Titus had been able to ferret out Watterson's connection with a counterfeiting ring, where even the federal men failed, then it was a cinch he hadn't overlooked anything from the birth of Daniel Vincent Curtis to this hour and minute. What he can't find, Dan mused, he'll invent. He didn't like the idea.

The Watterson scandal slashed across the state with the bright fury of a scrub fire and sent men scurrying to cover in the unreasoning panic of animals.

Jubilant, Field sought out Titus. He found the Sheriff at the Palmer House, hat dropped over his eyes, feet propped on a cane-bottom stool.

"We got 'em on the run, Sheriff," he crowed. "We sure enough got 'em by the short hair."

Titus lifted his head and stared morosely at the younger man as he balanced uneasily on the porch railing. Field, he decided, was getting to be pretty much of a damn fool. He was drinking again, too, and his features were beginning to show signs of a permanent bloat. The years weren't being any too kind to Carlisle.

"Go 'way, bub," he grunted wearily, "I'm thinkin'." He saw anger crimsoning Field's face and relented. "It's all right, bub"—he softened a little—"I got a gut ache caused by Deveris Watterson."

Field was puzzled. "My God," he said, "I thought you'd be tickled."

Titus shook his head. "This ain't goin' to do us any good, Field. One bad fish makes the whole box smell. This business of Watterson, breakin' over our heads before I was ready, is likely to be blamed on the whole party. God A'mighty, it might even start a reform wave. There ain't nothin' worse than a reform wave. The damnedest people get into office, an' it takes years to get 'em out. You see, I sort of figured to have you give Watterson a push into the jug. It'da made you a defender of the public an' such. This way nobody gets credit but the federal officers, an' they ain't running for office. It's a cryin' pity not to be able to capitalize on it. The whole hell of it is I couldn't catch Dan Curtis in Watterson's bed."

"You don't think Dan Curtis is mixed up in it, do you?"

Titas spat between his legs and wheezed mirthlessly. "Bub, I sometimes wonder if I ain't made a mistake about you. Course the hell Dan didn't know anything about it, but if it could have been held off until Watterson had his backin' you can see the fix it would put him in. This way we just got a dead rabbit we can't eat."

"Well"—Field was cheerful—"it cleans up the track a little. Watterson would have been a strong man to beat. This way there isn't going to be much to run against."

Titus wanted to tell Field to get the hell off the porch and let him alone. Instead he fixed his one-time deputy with a sour eye.

"You'll be surprised what's goin' to come creepin' out from behind the moldin'. Candidates are goin' to be as thick as peanut hulls as a baseball game. There ain't a bible slapper in the state but what is gettin' his tail warmed up for the governor's chair. There'll be more talk of professional corruption and sin than you'd hear in a year of evangelist meetin's."

One thing alone served to cheer Titus. Watterson insisted on crying his innocence. He was yelling frame-up, blaming his opponents. Titus was wise enough to know he was making a fool of himself. The more Watterson screamed about persecution, the more personal the scandal became. It served to distract attention from the party itself. Some people might even believe it.

Field was deflated. He had expected to find a triumphant Titus. Instead, the Sheriff was in a skeptical humor which mad the governor's mansion seem farther away than ever.

From the beginning the possibility of his ever reaching it seemed part of a fantastically wild dream. At the moment he was without confidence in the Sheriff to achieve the miracle.

So gradually had Semple absorbed him, so completely was he now possessed that he seemed without identity of his own. Instead of being able to think for himself, he was waiting to be told what he must do and how he should do it. Once the humiliation might have cut him. Now he felt nothing but anxiety. Long ago Lane had searched out the trouble. She had told him he looked hungry. He was starving. His ego was in the final stages of malnutrition. That was why he sat so often in the office assigned to him at the Ponce Title and Mortgage Co., drinking steadily. When at noon he went to the City Club for lunch the Negro doorman hailed him delightedly as Senator and the waiters rolled the word on their tongues as though it held a magic to transport them from this world. He realized that in a vague way the City Club was proud to have a state senator on its rolls. It lent a certain prestige to its membership. But as an individual, as Fielding Carlisle, he was without significance. There were times when he suspected that his being a representative to the Legislature was without meaning. He carried the colors of Titus Semple. This had been hinted at one day over the luncheon table when Walters Hanscom, who had large mill and timber interests in the county, was discussing a drainage project which would affect his holdings. In the middle of the conversation Hanscom said: "I guess I better speak to Titus." The affront hadn't been deliberate. It was unconscious, which only made the true situation more apparent.

Titus's gloomy forecast of things to come, even though Watterson had been removed from the list, filled him with apprehension. God, if he didn't get this he wouldn't be anything. He no longer cared that Semple would have him sent to the Mansion to serve his own ends. It was important only that he get there. Titus was welcome to the profit. Field wanted the distinction. He was in desperate need of it.

For all his apparent indifference to Field's presence, Titus was watching the younger man carefully. There was a fine distinction, he knew, between softening a man up and breaking him down completely. A man had to give, but it didn't do to let him get so he wouldn't hold shape. In many ways Field was something of a disappointment. In the beginning it had been different. There was a stubborn spirit coupled with an eager willingness to get ahead, to be somebody. One counterbalanced the other. Now, though, most of the spirit was gone, and in its place was a sullen aura of defeat which alternately made him almost cringingly eager or silently patient.

Titus had scant respect for the voters. They were fools for the most part. Organization was a fetish. They joined parties and clung to them blindly, marking their symbols with docile triumph, electing, year after year, the men their party selected without regard for ability or integrity. A small proportion retained their independence, scorning to be led. They switched from party to party, but they didn't elect. The great unthinking mass did the electing.

Now and again, however, even the sheep rebelled. The insurrections were short-lived, but they occasioned considerable damage. In the face of the Watterson scandal their temper was likely to be uncertain. It might take a strong man, someone to capture the imagination, to hold them in line.

Slowly the pinprick of doubt began to fester. It mightn't do at all to enter Field in the primaries. Maybe it would be a whole hell of a lot better to pick someone from downstate, far removed from the stench set up by Watterson.

The Sheriff's rocking slowed and finally ceased altogether. He wasn't bound to anything. Field could go back to Tallahassee for the next session to finish out the last half of his term. Later there would be time to think of allowing him to run for senator again.

The bright gleam of intrigue fired the Sheriff's eyes, and in this moment the political career of Fielding Carlisle ended with brutal finality. Titus felt no strainings at his conscience over what, in his mind at least, was an accomplished fact. Neither did the confusion of those men who a week ago had pledged their support to his candidate disturb him. They'd take what he gave them. As for Field, he'd find something else.

Already he was running down a mental list of possible candidates who might be counted on to conduct a term as governor with the proper appreciation for the power behind the election. Stimulated by the tonic of his deceit. Titus expanded. He thrived on surprise, and the knowledge that standing before him was one who would experience the shock of it made him feel kindly, tolerant toward the victim. A moment ago Field had irritated him. Now he was humorously amused by his presence, and the thought of Ann-Evans's wails of chagrin over Field's abandonment brought a quick snicker.

Tomorrow or the next day, he was thinking with the intent. single purpose of a rooting hog, he'd take a run downstate and have a talk with some people at Miami. The section could use the publicity of a governor. There'd be plenty of people there willing to talk business.

Field, indecisive, disturbed, sat on the porch railing and stared unseeingly down River Street. It seemed such a hell of a long time ago that he was his own man, feet cocked on the dashboard of his Ford, parked at a corner in the sun while folks he knew passed and called good-naturedly to him.

Titus, wearied of looking at him, dropped both feet to the porch.

"I got to think, bub," he said shortly. "An' when I think I got to be alone. See you tomorrow."

Bitterness and something dangerously close to hatred infected Field at the moment. His eyes were flat and uncolored as they met those of the Sheriff's. I'll get him, Field was thinking, I'll get him if it's the last thing I do. More than ever now he wanted the nomination Titus could hand him. It was a club with which he would beat Semple into a screaming pulp. This thought alone checked the rage which sprang to his lips. He nodded indifferently.

"I'll be seeing you."

From the porch Titus watched while Field crossed to the sidewalk, entered his car, and drove away. Then he hunched around in the chair until the sagging wicker fitted him comfortably and stared raptly at his feet. Field was becomin' a nuisance, anyhow, runnin' into debt, gettin' himself drunk. Hardly a month passed but what he needed money for something Ann-Evans wanted. Well, he'd be all right in the Legislature, an' if he behaved himself he could go back, maybe.

Smiling slyly Titus thought of Dan Curtis. This Watterson business must have kicked the seat right from beneath him. Looking at things that way, now that he was no longer concerned with Field, the premature disclosure of Watterson's activities didn't make much difference. What was needed between now and primary day was a rip-snorting, cracker-box speaker who would rant at the corruption as represented by Watterson and deal from the bottom to Titus Semple while he was doing it. There was going to be a hell of a lot of noise made in this campaign, and Titus didn't intend to be out-shouted. He'd get down the state and pick a man. Later would be time enough to tell the boys about him. He'd make a deal, and they'd have to come in. The Watterson indictment would have them all so scared by now they'd be afraid to go to sleep at night without having all the lights on. Maybe they hadn't believed him at first. Now they wouldn't whistle without asking him if it was all right. He sighed happily.

At the moment the only thing disturbing him was the knowledge that Dan Curtis would have to be taken care of before he could move freely. Dan was smart and he was determined. It was just too damn bad he couldn't see things his way.

Titus closed his eyes against the street's glare. Thinking of what was going to happen to Curtis filled him with a warm and comfortable feeling. With an effort he roused himself. Right now was as good a day as he would get to start the fire to burning. It was a hell of a lot of trouble, having to move around and leave the sunshine, but Dan wouldn't wait and neither could he.

On the way up the easy, sloping flight of steps leading from the lobby to the second floor, Titus heaved himself awkwardly. This was the hell of having to do something in private. He had to walk for it.

At the hallway he paused, catching his breath, while his mind darted away. He didn't think he could make the indictment against Dan stick, but he could get it, and the publicity would fix him until long after primary day. Once he got Dan against the wall, he'd go after the little bitch on Flamingo Road.

No matter how he viewed things, Titus could see only the prospect of an unrestricted romp. It had been a hell of a long time ago since he had so much fun. He even loosened a trickle of gratitude on behalf of Dan Curtis for making it possible.

In his room he settled into an old Morris chair. His breath was short, both from exertion and excitement. When he found he could talk again he reached for the telephone and put in a call for Jacksonville.

CHAPTER TWENTY-THREE

LANE TWISTED UNEASILY BENEATH THE GENTLE BUT persistent tugging at her shoulder and then snatched eagerly at returning consciouness. The night had been filled with dark torment and nightmares from which there seemed no escape.

To awaken in her own room with the placid face of Sarah bending over her brought the quick gratitude of relief.

"Telephone, Miz Ballou. Lady say it importan' an foah me to wek you even ef you is asleep."

Struggling into a sitting position Lane shook off sleep and took the extension phone Sarah held out to her. Calls were a novelty. During the year and a half she lived on the Heights, save when Dan rang, the telephone hadn't sounded more than a dozen times. Short panic gripped her as she thought something must have happened to him. Her voice was husky and clouded with worry when she spoke.

"Sugar?" At Lute-Mae's familiar accents she relaxed. "Sugar, where's Dan Curtis?"

The brusqueness of the question revived her fears. "I, well, I don't know, Lute-Mae. He hasn't been in Truro for more than two weeks."

"Well, I got to talk to him. You got to talk to him. What the hell kind of a man is he, goin' off an' not lettin' you know where to reach him?"

Lane tried to laugh, but it was a feeble effort without conviction. She sensed dismay rather than anger in Lute-Mae's question.

"I don't know, Lute-Mae. I mean I don't know where he is. He telephoned yesterday evening from Tampa. That's the last I heard. He didn't say how long he would be gone or where he was staying."

"Well, we got to find him. By God, it takes a big man to be stubborn. That's why I always liked to pick me a runt. They ain't so sure they know it all. He wouldn't listen to what you told him for me once. Now trouble is goin' to pop like firecrackers on Christmas Day."

Lane held the telephone tightly to her as though to smother the ominous words. For a moment she was half convinced it was still a dream. This was only a continuation of the terror which had haunted her throughout the night.

"What is it, Lute-Mae?" She forced the words.

"I don't know for sure, sugar. All I do know is you'd better try an' get Dan in Tampa, or wherever he is, an' tell him to find out what the hell is goin' on over to his plantation in Walton County. Whatever it is Titus has got both hands in it. The word was brought me last night by a friend I got over that way. He didn't know much more than I'm tellin' you, but Dan ought to understand. At least he can snoop around some."

"Oh!" For an inexplicable reason Lane was relieved.

"Don't say oh, like somebody goosed you. God A'mighty,

didn't you see what happened to old Watterson? You think it was just an accident?"

Sitting up in her cheerful, sun-splashed bedroom Lane felt hopelessly ineffectual.

"Well"—she was doubtful—"I don't think Dan would like me interfering. He, well, you know what happened the last time. He laughed at me."

Lute-Mae's reply was rasping. "Watterson ain't laughin', sugar. You can bet he ain't."

Lane rested the telephone in her lap. She didn't want to offend the woman. Lute-Mae had been too good a friend. She was fond of Dan, too. Whatever she did or said would be because she liked them both. It seemed unnecessarily harsh to shut her off.

"I'll think it over, Lute-Mae." She compromised. "Maybe I can locate Dan in Tampa."

There was a moment of silence at the other end of the wire. "All right, sugar. I suppose you know best." She switched the subject abruptly. "How you been?"

"Oh, I'm fine. You?"

"All right, I guess. I just can't work up much of a fever for anything these days. About the only excitement I get is tryin' to keep up with old droopy-gut Titus. Ain't he a wonderful skunk, though?"

"Maybe"—Lane thought of the day stretching ahead—"I might come over and see you this afternoon."

"I'd sure like that." Lute-Mae was sincere. "Just the same I think you ought to try an' reach Dan. Tell him I said there is somethin' funny goin' on over to his place in Walton. If I knew more I'd tell him."

With the receiver back in place, Lane hunched herself in the middle of the bed, the instrument in her hand. For the moment she idled with the notion of calling Tampa and asking the operator there to try and locate Dan Curtis at any of the hotels. If he was in town the telephone company could probably find him.

Somehow, though, Lute-Mae's dire prediction of what Titus Semple was up to didn't disturb her this time. Dan was old enough and wise enough to take care of himself. It seemed silly for her to keep running to him with some tale of Lute-Mae's, no matter how well intentioned it was.

She had read of the arrest of former Governor Watterson, and the same evening Dan called from Jacksonville.

"I'm going to be away for two, maybe three weeks," he told

239

her. "I'll be moving fast, so I can't tell you where I'll be. Need anything?"

"Only you."

"You're easier to satisfy than I am. I need a governor. Read about Watterson?"

"Yes. Is it, I mean did Titus do it?"

She could almost see him as he pulled at his ear with a familiar gesture, trying to frame an answer.

"No-o. I don't think so. He sure as hell knew about it, though, and," he chuckled, "I don't like to have anyone smarter than I am. Well"—he was suddenly crisp and business-like—"I've got a train to catch. Take care of yourself. I'll call you."

He had telephoned almost every night. Once he was in St. Augustine. She half hoped he would ask her to come over and meet him, but he didn't. Again he was at De Land, another evening at Miami, and two days ago the call came from Tampa. He might still be there or on his way to Jacksonville, possibly even Truro.

Putting the phone back on the table beside her bed Lane rolled out from beneath the fluffy coverlet. If he called tonight she would tell him what Lute-Mae had said. Otherwise she wouldn't bother him. Dan made out all right for a good many years before Lane Ballou came along. He could probably be trusted by himself now.

Sarah brought her breakfast, placing a small table by the open casement windows where she could catch the freshness of the spring morning. She liked to eat here, alone, one story above the tangled greenery of Flamingo Road. It gave her the odd sensation of being perched high in some tree, out of reach of everyone.

Lane and the Heights had arrived at a tacit understanding. If her neighbors knew who she was or where she came from they kept the information within their own tight little circle. Sometimes she thought they must know, but her studied aloofness was her protection. Once, it was shortly after the time she and Dan met Field and his wife in St. Augustine, Ann-Evans Carlisle made a timidly excited telephone call. Her inquisitive friendliness was shunted aside, Lane making a vague promise to stop by some afternoon. She never had, though, and Ann-Evans's call was not repeated. Field, she thought, must have spoken to her.

It was strange—the notion reoccurred frequently to Lane—she was never conscious of being alone, without friends. This tight, bright house and Dan when he could get away were all she really wanted. In the back yard, beside the garage, she had a small flower garden of her own which was the despair of the colored man who cared for the lawn and shrubbery. In it a little of everything was planted, growing with vigorous confusion. She tended the plot carefully, leaving the front and side yard to Amos, who regarded her and her garden suspiciously. The mornings she spent back there. Sometimes she drove downtown but not often. When she did she was always in a hurry to return. There was nothing on the other side of her neat picket fence she was jealous of.

Left to herself in the evenings she read. The built-in bookcases which covered one side of Dan's study wall were filled with volumes: history, biography, fiction, poetry.

In the beginning she approached the formidable shelves with self-conscious timidity, afraid of her own ignorance. As she read the hesitation vanished. She knew most of the words. This alone astonished her at first. The men and women who could write wrote simply. She began to understand herself a little better. Most of the books had something to contribute, a bit here, a point of view there. After awhile she began to see the general outline of a pattern, a design which must be almost universal. She and Dan, Field, Lute-Mae, Annabelle, old Coyne, Titus: everyone she had ever known had his or her counterpart in those books. Believing this it was possible to look at life from a vantage point of detachment much as she was contemplating Flamingo Road through her bedroom window. Everything that had happened to her had happened before and would occur again. The phrase, variations on a theme, she had read somewhere dropped into her thoughts.

The slewing of tires on the graveled driveway interrupted her meditation. Looking down she could see only the top of the car which jerked to a halt below. She waited for the driver to step out. It couldn't be Dan. He would have continued around to the garage. Whoever it was still sat behind the wheel, and after awhile Lane began to feel that the car must have driven itself, a phantom automobile without chauffeur or direction coming to rest in her yard. She was about to call Sarah when the door opened and the bent figure of a man half stumbled from the front seat. He clung to the swinging door for a moment, swaying lightly, and as he turned she had a glimpse of a drawn, unshaven face. It was Field. Field, tousled and drunk.

He slammed the door shut, leaning against it, and then with visible effort straightened up and, teetering on unsteady feet, disappeared beneath the overhanging roof. She could hear the heavy clumping of his step on the porch and then the distant sound of a bell as he rang at the front door.

She didn't want to see Field, certainly didn't want him in the house as drunk as he appeared to be: Sarah could send him away with the excuse that she wasn't in. Field, though, would probably go to sleep waiting for her return, and then there would be trouble getting him up and out.

He was in the living room, slouched deep in a chair, elbows propped on spread knees, face in hands.

"Well, Field?" Lane was angry. He had no right to come into her house in this condition.

He lifted his head, peering up at her through outspread fingers. His smile was flabby, confused.

"I'm sick, Lane," The confession was lifeless, taking her by surprise. "I feel like hell."

She had expected some maudlin attempt at humor; heavy familiarity; the usual approach of drunks who are uncertain of their reception. Instead, Field was spiritless. She felt sudden pity. His clothing was rumpled, looking as though he had slept in it, and his face unshaven.

"What in the world has happened to you?" She stood looking down, trying to decide what to do.

Field shook his head wearily. "I guess I got in a bottle an' couldn't get out." He winced at the knives hacking his skull.

Lane knew she ought to send him home. It was the sensible thing. He should be there. In the face of his apparent helplessness she softened. It was difficult not to remember so many things which would be better forgotten.

"Think some black coffee would stay down?"

Field tried to smile. "Maybe, but I need a drink to lace it there."

"That's sure, slow death, and you know it." She felt easier. He wasn't going to be difficult.

Field rose painfully, a man haunting himself. He staggered a little, clutched at the back of a chair for support, and ventured a weak laugh.

"I wish I could be sure. I sure God do."

Lane only stared at him, wondering if this could be the Field she once had known. It wasn't only the hangover. That was an affliction to make sad jokes about or endure in silence. Something inside of Field had collapsed. If he only wouldn't stand there, weaving slightly with a foolish smirk of shallow bravado on his mouth. Watching him she could wonder that she ever flamed at the touch of his hand, waited eagerly for him to take her. There was something almost repulsive in the recollection. Pity wasn't akin to love no matter who said it was. Pity was love's dirty ashes blowing in your eyes.

"Go upstairs to the bathroom, Field." She took him by the arm, leading the way. "Shave and clean up. There's a razor in the cabinet. I'll have Sarah fix you some breakfast. You'll feel better." On second thought she went up with him, guiding him through to Dan's bathroom and taking out shaving soap and safety razor. "Don't go to sleep now," she warned.

Sarah made fresh coffee, and Lane poured a single but large drink of Bourbon and put it beside his cup. If Field had any idea he was going to get drunk all over again, he was mistaken. She glanced up at the sound of his slow, careful tread on the staircase.

The shave improved his appearance a little, but it was more than surface cleaning he needed. He took the drink standing at the table, and the glass clattered against his teeth.

"My mouth dodges." He was embarrassed.

"Drink some coffee. It'll do you good."

"I'll try." He leaned over the table, pulling a chair beneath him.

Lane waited while he made a noisy attempt at swallowing.

"Will you eat something, scrambled eggs, bacon?"

He shook his head. "Could I . . . would you give me another drink?" He was pleading without dignity.

Lane sighed. "If you'll promise to go home." She poured a drink and handed it to him. "Where have you been?"

"In the gutter. I've got a nice section staked out in front of the Palmer House."

"You ought to be ashamed of yourself."

"What for?" The liquor revived a flicker of character. "I got a boot in the tail that landed me in the street. That's where I belong, I guess."

"You do if you stay there." She was impatient. "What happened?"

Field pried at a crumpled package of cigarettes, finally spreading it on the table and picking one out with shaking fingers.

"The Sheriff's got himself another boy." His mouth twitched. "Bub"—it was a grotesque imitation of Semple's accent—"maybe I got to hold off on you a little longer. You go on back to Tallahassee for the rest of your term. Probably we'll figure somethin' out later." He tried to laugh, and there was a croaking sound in his throat. "I've been a damn fool to believe him all this time. Now there isn't anything." His eyes were watering, and the corners of his mouth jerked nervously.

243

Lane suspected that he was on the verge of a crying drunk, and the thought repelled her.

"You're acting like a child." Even as she spoke Lane was thinking Dan ought to know that Titus's plans were changed. For one reason or another the Sheriff had decided Field wasn't strong enough to carry a campaign. "Truro's your home, people like you. Titus isn't everything."

"He is when you're in my shoes."

"Well, then, you've been wearing them too long." She was incensed at the whining note in his voice. Remembering how he once had been, confident, eager, unafraid, she almost shuddered. "What's happened to you, Field? Where have you gone?"

She realized immediately this was a mistake. He wanted to be sorry for himself, openly with abused explanation. His body sagged helplessly.

"He kicked me out like I was a stray dog. After all I've done."

Lane couldn't control her feelings. "You haven't done anything. For years Titus Semple has been carrying you around. You've let him make you soft, fat, and frightened. Tell him to go to hell, find something to do if you don't want to stay in politics. This is your town as much as his. Fight him for a piece of it."

There was an indefinite sneer around his lips. "Sure, it's easy enough for you to say." He glanced around the room. "You've done all right, haven't you? From Lute-Mae's to Flamingo Road on your behind." He laughed slobberingly.

For an instant Lane thought she would kill him, but rage consumed her strength. She could only sit and shake as though with a chill. It was hard to believe she had heard aright. He couldn't have said that to her, not Field.

Slowly, she was afraid to trust her legs, she rose from the table.

"Get out, Field. Get out of the house now."

The defiance left him. "I didn't . . ." He attempted to mumble an explanation.

"Get out. Hurry." She could feel her eyes burning. In a moment more she would scream.

With incoherent mutterings he shuffled through the house. From the dining room Lane could hear the front door slam and a moment later the grinding of the car's starter.

Oh, my God, she was thinking. I can't cry. I can't ever cry at what he said. I mustn't even remember it.

Again at the table, hands clenched before her, she tried to

244

remember he was drunk, disappointed, and hurt. She thought hard of her first night in Truro. He had been gentle, kind. He found her a job and helped her find a place to live. That was Field Carlisle. The man who had just left the house was something fashioned by Titus Semple. He was a stranger, this man, speaking words put in his mouth by Titus.

Gradually the bitterness ebbed. Her fingers unfolded and opened before her on the table. She was no longer quivering. Emotion left her limp, and she didn't want to move.

Finally, forcing herself from the chair, she walked from the room, through the kitchen, and out into the back yard. At the moment the house was stifling. She needed to breathe. With half a dozen ruthless words, Field made her remember everything she had succeeded in forgetting. Those were the words whispered along Flamingo Road, in Truro, everywhere she went. Only, it wasn't that way. She and Dan knew. They understood. Why couldn't the others?

For the balance of the morning she found things to do around the yard and even in the house. An astonished Sarah saw her mistress washing a few dishes at the sink, shaking out cushions, dusting bookshelves. If she kept busy it was easier not to think.

Try as she did to keep occupied, the hours dragged with an agonizing deliberateness. Finally Sarah called her for lunch, and she went in to pick indifferently at food without flavor. It was no good. She'd have to get out of the house for awhile.

She bathed and dressed with more than usual care. It seemed important that everything about her person be as dainty and flawless as possible. She had made up her mind to go downtown where she would see people and be seen by them. Inside she was crying to be hidden and left alone.

Wandering into Dan's bathroom, seeking to find something of him, she swept to the floor the towels Field had left draped across the washstand. The razor lay dismembered on the shelf above the basin, and she wondered idly where he had put the used blade. In revolt against the things he had handled, she left the room for Sarah to clean out and went downstairs.

There was nothing she needed in Truro, but she drove downtown, went to the bank, and drew some money. The teller was pleasantly respectful, his eyes showing admiration. They chatted for a moment. On River Street she stopped in at several stores, making small purchases. It was a queer form of defiance but in a way served to erase Field's words. These people didn't believe what he had said. They were friendly. A little of her confidence returned, and by the time she finished her aimless tour she was almost cheerful again. It was silly to take the filthy words of a drunken man so seriously.

In her car again she remembered Lute-Mae's telephone call and her half promise to come over during the afternoon. Well, she'd do that also. Perhaps Lute-Mae had gone on her own and tried to reach Dan at Tampa.

She drove rapidly crosstown, over the yard's tracks, and through the district, pulling in at the white house's side entrance.

Lute-Mae was in what she described as "a state." Lane suspected this from the nervous worry with which the little colored maid, Carol, greeted her. The suspicion was confirmed by the sight of Lute-Mae pacing determinedly up and down her room.

A grunt acknowledged Lane's presence. Lute-Mae was in a mighty wrestle with something.

"Did you locate Dan Curtis?" The woman snapped the question in her stride.

"No." Without waiting to be asked Lane sat down and began drawing at her gloves. Lute-Mae would cool off in a minute. She always did.

"Then you're gettin' as butt-headed as he is." She stopped walking suddenly and sank into her favorite chair. "Christ, I don't know why I should get my bowels in an uproar over the rest of the world. Got enough trouble of my own as it is." She smiled quickly. "Glad to see you, sugar. Let's have a drink."

Lane nodded. She needed one. These visits to Lute-Mae's were becoming increasingly rare, and each time she came to the big house Lane was struck by something slightly comical in the call. The sweet girl graduate back to visit the hallowed halls. Little Red Riding Hood, over the hills to grandmother's. Some trace of the amusement she was feeling must have shown itself, for Lute-Mae eyed her suspiciously.

"I was always a hell of a one for laughin', too, when I was your age."

Lane was contrite. "I wasn't laughing, Lute-Mae. It just struck me funny, my coming to see you this way and then the two of us sitting around, gossiping, and drinking whisky like a couple of old rips on a back-room tear."

"Come to think of it, you're right. Don't know as I ever passed more than a dozen words with any other little girl." She drained her glass and refilled it, nodding toward the bottle for Lane's benefit.

"Help yourself when you're ready." She held the glass in

246

both hands, staring down into the liquor. "I'm about to get myself drunk."

"I don't believe it."

"Yes I am, sugar, an' it's a hell of a sight, let me tell you." She drank heavily and made a mouth of disgust. "The worst part of it is I hate the stuff."

Lane leaned forward, reaching for a cigarette. "What was it you wanted to tell Dan?"

Lute-Mae whistled scornfully. "This is a fine time to be askin' me. Whatever is goin' on over to Walton is probably done by now. I didn't know much anyhow. It was just somethin' a fella told me. Seems there's some sort of funny business on a plantation Dan owns over there. After Watterson I got worried. From what I hear, old Titus is in a throat-slittin' mood. Anybody who sticks his neck out at this time ain't short of bein' a damn fool. I only figured to have Dan pull his in if it was out so much as an inch."

Lane frowned. "He's never said anything about a plantation, but I guess that wouldn't mean anything."

Lute-Mae tilted her glass back and forth, rocking the ice within it. "Friend of yours down the hall," she said abruptly. Lane was startled. "What are you talking about?"

"Carlisle." Lute-Mae bit at the name. "Come here drunk early this afternoon. I sure would have sent him away, only I was afraid he'd wind up in some crib along the line. He was that bad off anything might have happened. Make a hell of a smell if a senator was found stuck up one of them alleys. Ordinarily I don't let drunks come into my house. They're always lookin' for trouble an' usually find it. Field, though, is sort of different."

Lane drew a sharp breath. She wanted to get out and away. "I think I'd better run along." Her hands fumbled nervously. "I . . . it's late."

Lute-Mae watched her closely. "Why, sugar," she marveled, "you ain't still got it for him, have you?"

There was something almost nauseating in the thought, and Lane's denial was fast. She wouldn't, though, tell Lute-Mae what had happened this morning.

"No! Oh, no! Lute-Mae. You don't understand."

"Well"—the woman was soothing—"sit still then. He ain't goin' to see you. He's up there in the front room like a hog on ice this minute. I told little Gracie to look in on him every now an' then to see when he start's pukin' on the floor. Other than that he ain't goin' to bother nobody for hours."

247

Lane wasn't satisfied. She knew she ought to leave. Field was breeding trouble.

"I better go."

Lute-Mae pretended not to hear. "I'll swear," she said, "but there is somethin' disgustin' about a cryin' man. He drunk most a quart of whisky since he come here. Wanted in my room at first, but I wouldn't have it. Then he started to blubber about how Titus done him. He ain't got nothin' to live for. He's been messed on by Titus. All I could get out of it was that Titus ain't goin' to let him set up for governor. Hell, that ain't nothin' to cry about, like it was a sugar tit." She cocked an eye at the bottle beside her and then grunted impatiently. "When I see what whisky does for people I'm tempted to go round with a hammer an' smash bottles like old Carrie, whatever her name was."

"Dan told Titus he couldn't run Field." Lane was thoughtful. "They broke over it, so that can't be the reason."

"I wisht he'd go home, whatever it was that started him on this souse. A wife's the only person who ought to have to stand him now." She shook her head. "It's funny thing, too. When I first saw him a few years back, just before you come to me, he was a fine smart fella. Titus was as proud of him as if he was his own bastard. I be damned if I can figure how a man can go to pieces in such a short time."

The first scream was of shrilling terror and brought both Lane and Lute-Mae to their feet. The sounds which followed were short, staccato cries of hysteria.

"God A'mighty." Lute-Mae was at the door, wrenching it open.

Lane could see the girl, eyes wide, dressing gown open and trailing behind her naked body. One hand was stuffed to her mouth and over it poured choking gasps of panic.

Lute-Mae grasped her roughly by the arm. "What the hell is the matter with you, Gracie?"

The girl could only nod dumbly and point up the hall toward the front of the house. Lute-Mae pushed her aside and hurried away.

Gracie dropped to her knees; her head hung down swaying back and forth with a crazy circular motion. She moaned, and then, as Lane watched in fascinated horror, she was sick and her long hair trailed in the vomit.

Lane backed away, unable to take her eyes from the spectacle. From a distance she half heard Lute-Mae call to someone. Gracie was groveling, sobbing horribly and slobbering with sticky, burbling sound.

Then Lute-Mae was back. She stepped over the prostrate girl and slammed the door behind her.

"My God"—Lute-Mae was breathing heavily, but her words were measured, wonderingly calm—"he done it. He sure enough done it."

Lane didn't need to ask what had happened. It seemed as though she must have known from the beginning when the girl's scream ripped through the house.

"You never seen anythin' like it, an' I hope I don't again." Lute-Mae took the bottle with a miraculously steady hand and poured herself a straight drink. "He just took an old safety-razor blade an' drew a line acrost his throat. You ain't never seen such a mess."

Lane had to sit down. It was impossible to stand longer. He had been thinking about it while he shaved. That was why the blade was missing from the razor. She felt a horrified pity. Maybe, maybe, if she had been kinder this morning? She should have talked to him, been sympathetic. Poor, foolish Field. She shut her eyes, trying to block out the recollection of him as he sat at the table.

"You better get out, sugar." Lute-Mae was being practical. "I've got to call for the police. You wouldn't want to be found here. Folks wouldn't understand."

Lane nodded. She couldn't speak. Lute-Mae thrust a drink into her hand, and she drank it. There was no taste to the whisky.

"I'll go in a minute." She could hear a scraping movement outside the door. Gracie was trying to crawl away. The sound of her retching was clear.

"I knew he was bad"—Lute-Mae was blaming herself—"but I never figured for him to do a thing like this. I'da stayed by him or let him in here."

"You're sure. I mean, there isn't any chance of doing something for him."

Lute-Mae's anger was only a shield. "Don't be a damn fool. When they get cut that way they stay cut. Don't you suppose I know?"

Lane nodded. She walked toward the door but could not bring herself to open it. Turning helplessly she looked appealingly at Lute-Mae.

"Is the door, you know, the one up front . . . is it?"

Lute-Mae took her shoulder gently. "It's closed, sugar. Get on away now an' pray to God nobody you know sees you leavin'. I'll fix Carol so's she'll be too scared to remember you was here. Don't worry none about the police. There'll be one hell of a sweat over this."

She opened the door. Down the corridor, leaning against the wall, Gracie cowered, sobbing with dry, grating rasps.

"Get the hell in your room, Gracie," Lute-Mae shouted, "before I come an' kick you in."

Clinging to the wall the girl sidled along until she came to an open doorway. They heard the door slam and a key snap in its lock. The house was again without sound.

Lute-Mae patted Lane hurriedly on the back. "Go on now, sugar. I can't wait much longer." She blew puffingly between her lips. "Titus," she said, "is sure enough havin' himself a season, ain't he?"

CHAPTER TWENTY-FOUR

THE PITIFULLY DRAB SUICIDE OF FIELDING CARLISLE in a Truro bawdy house smothered the Watterson scandal and glutted a state with sensation. The story rocketed through the peninsula, gathering weight and color as it sped. Here was something close to the affections of the man in the street. It confirmed his suspicions that all politicians were cunning swine at the public trough. They roistered, wenched, pocketed dirty money, and honor was not in them.

From a hundred pulpits the story, embroidered in scarlet, was shaken before avid parishioners, who roared with bull-like excitement. Of what had sent Field Carlisle to a bloody bed nothing was said, for little was known. It was enough that he had been found with his throat cut on a whore's scented couch.

Truro gorged on the tragedy, and because it occurred where it had a dozen of the ramshackle cat houses in the district were raided and their women hustled off to jail. The authorities cut a swath of indignation around Lute-Mae's but avoided touching so much as a blade of grass in her yard.

Ann-Evans, in hysterics, was taken to her parent's home and closeted behind drawn blinds against the vindictively curious and the friendly malicious. The house on Flamingo Road was locked and shuttered. Truro reluctantly took up the steady beat of its existence, and Titus Semple rocked in his chair on the Palmer House porch.

Try though she did Lane was unable to unseat the ugly suspicion which rode her. Field had asked for so little that morning. He came to tell his troubles and be reassured. He wanted to pour out all the bitterness which had secreted itself within him during the past few years. Instead of sympathy, something so readily at hand, he found only the cheap scorn of the secure for the uncertain. It was too easy to be smug, and that was what she had been. No wonder he flared in anger.

Sitting alone in her home on the Heights, she had only to look about to be reminded that everything led back to Field and a bewildered and defiant girl in a gloomy carnival lot. Save for him she might have trailed along an uneven road, ending God knew where. She hadn't been complacent then. She clung to him, and he took care of her. In return she had been scornful of his weakness.

Beyond expressing a conventional regret Dan seemed uninterested in Field's suicide. He was busy elsewhere, and upon those rare occasions when he could get to Flamingo Road he was preoccupied and, Lane suspected, worried. Things weren't going any too well, evidently.

Once—he was sitting on the edge of her bed—he mentioned Field.

"You know"—there was something of regret in his voice— "I told Field, Titus made sow's ears out of silk purses. I forgot to tell him he sometimes kills the sow, too."

Lane discovered that she had to force herself to go into Truro. Every store front, each street corner reminded her of Field. She had met him here. He had waited there. They drank a dope at this soda counter. It was funny, but she thought of him oftener now that he was dead than she had before. Maybe, she mused, a woman never really gets over a man who has made love to her. She shuts him out, and they go on, sometimes never seeing each other again. But, once in awhile, a snatch of laughter, a whistled tune, a familiar scene would come along, and she would think: Why, he sounded like that. He laughed once right here at something I said. It wasn't that she still wanted the man, but the touch of him couldn't be entirely erased.

Driving down River Street one morning she passed Titus as he waddled out of the Eagle Café, sucking on a toothpick and contemplating Truro with the happy air of proprietorship. Her car was halted only for a few seconds by the traffic light, but it was long enough for her to experience a sickening revulsion at the sight of the man.

They had killed Field Carlisle. Together they did for him. Titus started the murder, and she through her thoughtlessness sped it on to its shoddy ending.

Perhaps, though, Field had been dying for years. She tried to find a grain of comfort in the thought. He was marked out from the first day Titus offered his aid and a deputyship. What happened would have happened anyhow.

In many ways the death of Field affected her relationship with Dan. Because of it she found herself thinking about the life she was leading and wondering how strong she had become. If the props Dan supplied were swept away, could she stand alone? The house on Flamingo Road was home only because he came to it. Her life, stripped of friends, barren of companionship, was pleasant, even exciting, because Dan supplied everything she needed. It was impossible to feel alone knowing he was usually within telephoning distance and would come if she called. What frightened her was the realization that he might not always be there.

Their life together was an easy mixture of mutual respect and companionship. Never had she pretended to be inflamed. Dan would have sensed the lie. Their physical relationship was gratifying to her only because she found an intense satisfaction in simply being near him.

"I'm a pretty cold fire for you to warm your hands by." He made the admission half jokingly, part seriously.

"I'll keep them in your pockets then."

Never again was the subject referred to, and on this understanding they built their life. It was a good life, too, only she was becoming afraid of it. No longer was it possible to imagine herself alone. She tried, but where Dan ended so did the story. There was nothing after him. The knowledge robbed her of confidence. She worried when he didn't call, was sensitive to his moods. At times when he was in Truro she had to force herself not to follow him about the house, trailing like an uncertain puppy.

Dan couldn't help noticing the change. "What's the matter with you?" he asked one evening. "You're as worried as a cat with a litter of kittens that won't stay in the box."

She sat on the floor at his feet, her head resting against his knee.

"I'm not sure. Growing pains, maybe. They'll wear off." She turned the subject away.

It was a week after the Carlisle affair, and Dan was only

spending the night. In scattered moments he told her what he was trying to do. As best he could he was lining up an opposition to the forces created out of his own organization by Titus.

"I'm doing a hell of a lot of fence repairing," he said, "but what I have to use for rails won't stand much battering." He sighed wearily. "I'll do what I can. If it isn't good enough the people of the state will have to look out for themselves."

Lane mentioned what Lute-Mae had told her about Walton, but she shrugged it off.

"Some old wives' tale. Titus wouldn't waste any time out there on my plantation. As a matter of fact"—the admission was grim—"I don't think he's particularly worried about me. I wouldn't be if I was in his place. Right now the only thing that would beat a machine candidate would be an insurrection at the polls, and that's just a dream the independents take to bed with them to keep their feet warm. It doesn't happen."

She drove him to the station on the following morning.

"I wish," she suggested, "you'd try and find out what Lute-Mae was talking about. She was worried."

Dan tapped a finger beneath her chin. "I've a better idea. You go down to the Palmer House, catch Titus asleep, and put a bell on him. Then we can keep track of his movements by the tinkle."

The more Titus thought about Field Carlisle, and he was forced to drag him into his scheme of things at least once a day, the angrier he became.

Not only had the damn fool slit his throat, raising a hell of an uproar, but he did it in a place like Lute-Mae's. By God, that was gratitude. Here he was on the eve of a primary campaign with all politicians stinking under the noses of the voters. Nobody could tell now what they might do. The thought of a strong independent running away at the general elections just because the voters were mad over such things as Watterson and Carlisle gave him a case of indigestion a cart load of bicarbonate couldn't cool.

Field's suicide also routed him from his porch chair just when the weather was getting pleasant. He had to sit up in his room these days. Every time he went to the porch some crying gut would come along and tell him it was too bad about Field Carlisle. Hell, he knew it was bad, but he couldn't stream at the eyes half a dozen times a day just because people expected him to. It was like some damn Punch and Judy show out there on the porch whenever he tried to sit for a minute. Sure as he did he'd have a congregation of mourners.

The Sheriff was happily unconscious of having any part in the tragedy. Of course, he'd had to tell Field about the plans for running Burns instead of him, but men didn't cut their throats over such things. Field was a weak sister. He might even have picked himself up a dose from one of Lute-Mae's girls, if he was in the habit of goin' there, an' was scared to take it home to Ann-Evans. That, likely, was the explanation. A man would have to be pretty well set up, though to take a razor blade to his gullet.

Sitting in his room before the window, which was as close as he could get to River Street with comfort these days, Titus pondered over this and other things.

Dan Curtis, he reflected was chasin' in circles. Before this business of Field interfered, their trails had cut each other a couple of times; but now, with Burns, he had the east coast sewed up, and Dan didn't know it. Burns had been an inspiration. They'd run him on a businessman-for-a-job-of-business platform. This always tickled the voters. Made them think they knew what they were doing.

It wouldn't be smart just the same to discount Dan. Once the son of a gun got mad he'd be apt to do anything, might even run himself out of spite. That was why, earlier in the week, he had sent for Burr Lassen.

Dan's overseer from Walton waited until dark before he would come to the Palmer House, and then he slipped up the stairs to Semple's room like a boy through a cane patch. Once again the man protested weakly over what the Sheriff was forcing him to do, but in the end he broke down and gave in.

"Mind you, Burr"—Titus coddled the notion—"I ain't really thinkin' it will stand up in court, so you actually can't do no real harm. All I'm lookin' to do is get Curtis out of the way for awhile, keep him busy until after the primaries."

"You sure won't be forgettin' about my boy, now would you, Sheriff?"

Titus reassured him. He didn't tell the man, however, that young Lassen's trial had been moved back again and again in order that he might keep a club over the father's shoulders.

"You do like I say, Burr, an' there ain't nothin' in this world to worry you."

Reluctant, dispirited, Lassen agreed and left. As long as there were Burr Lassens in the world, little, irresolute men who got themselves into trouble, things would be secure for the Semples. Titus comforted himself with the knowledge.

That Burr and a few others might go to prison for perjury, conspiracy, or an assortment of minor crimes, once what he had prepared for Dan Curtis was uncorked, was of little importance. As long as Dan was loose he was a threat, and it wasn't Titus's habit to encourage such dangers.

Right now there wasn't anything for him to do but wait. All the strings were out. It wasn't even necessary for him to touch them. Any morning now Dan would wake up and find a loop around his big toe. He'd holler like hell, but it would take some time to undo the knots. He'd get out all right, but the noise he made would scare a lot of people.

For all that he was confined to quarters, the certainty of Dan's trouble made him almost cheerful. In a way, he pondered, it was a shame he an' Dan couldn't see together. The way he looked at it, a state was to be run. Either you ran it yourself or left the job to a lot of damn-fool amateurs. Dan, on the other hand, wanted to mix things up.

From the window he could look down on River Street. By God, he could remember tearin' barefoot through the sand right along here as a youngster. He was always runnin', it seemed, while a lot of skinny kids chased him. He remembered them all. Some moved away to other parts of the state. Those who remained had reason to remember with him. He'd put a burr in their blankets many a time when the chance came along. The others, out of his reach in Truro, would have an opportunity to do some recollecting once he had Burns in Tallahassee.

Turning away he settled himself in the Morris chair. With time on his hands, nothing to do but wait, he was restless. He thought about Lute-Mae. That girl of Dan's had been in the house the day Field killed himself. Lute-Mae should have told him. As it was he didn't find out until after the inquest. Then it was too late to pull her into the stink.

It would have been a choice piece of meat to drag along Flamingo Road. The more he thought of this, the angrier he became at Lute-Mae. If she was trying to string along with this little bitch and Dan Curtis, then he'd have her hide with the others.

With a grunt he was out of his chair again. He couldn't stand the room any longer. How the hell could he keep track of things sitting up here away from the street? He'd go down to the porch, and if anyone came along, wanting to talk about Field Carlisle, he'd pretend he was asleep.

The ancient staircase of the Palmer House creaked beneath his weight. It had been complaining for years, he thought, every time he stepped on it. In a way the stairs were sort of like Truro. They sweated and they groaned, but they carried him.

With a happy sigh of gratitude he sank deep within the limp wicker of his chair on the porch. This was a whole hell of a lot better. A man got out of touch with things shut up in a room.

Hat over his face he feigned sleep, but his ears were acute. Without looking he could tell what was going on. After these years he could tell just by the sound what time it was.

Without wanting to, he found himself thinking again of Field Carlisle. A fellow he'd almost raised ought to have been a little more thoughtful. Field should have known the trouble his killing himself that way would cause. The bad thing about Field, he realized now, was that he never had been what you could call really smart. He was stubborn, and after he took to drinking he was mean. Titus had respect for these qualities, but a man should be smart with them.

Well, he'd done his best for him. Even the old Judge, if he was alive, would have had to admit that. He'd done his best, but Field couldn't carry the weight. A man who would cut his throat in a cat house just because he was disappointed was only a fool.

He was drowsy. Thinking this way always made him sleepy. His body twitched slightly, and the wicker crackled with the sound of breaking reeds. If no one came to bother him, he could take a nap before supper time.

Suddenly he chuckled. He'd figured a way to get rid of the pests who wanted to talk about Field. Tomorrow he'd stop in a drugstore and buy himself a package of safety-razor blades. Then, every time someone came up to him mewling about poor Field, he'd just hand him a blade. By God, that'd stop the nonsense.

CHAPTER TWENTY-FIVE

IN HIS HOTEL ROOM AT TAMPA, DAN CURTIS drew the latticed blinds against the afternoon sun's thrust. An electric fan in one corner whined helplessly at the unseasonal heat which wrapped the city in a sticky blanket and turned the bay into a steaming saucer the color of oiled pewter. High as was the room no wisp of breeze reached it.

Loosening collar and tie he peeled a damp shirt away and tossed the sodden garment to a chair. Whatever the hinges of hell were, he thought, they couldn't be any hotter than Tampa this day.

Pouring whisky into a glass piled high with rapidly melting ice cubes, he drank slowly, nuzzling the coolness. Liquor, he knew, was a damn poor substitute for a fresh wind, but it was the best he could think of at the moment.

He undressed slowly, each movement characterized by weariness, and when he was stripped and naked stretched out on the bed. He was tired. So tired that at the moment he no longer cared what Titus and his freebooters accomplished. He was grimly conscious of the unpalatable truth that it didn't make much difference how he felt or what he did. Titus was moving in. An organization to stand him off couldn't be whipped together in a few weeks. He had tried, meeting only with vague promises, half-hearted encouragement, or downright refusals of allegiance. He was being chased into a corner by the very combination of forces he had created.

With closed eyes and the pleasantly hypnotic drone of the fan in his ears, he wondered again, as he had many times during the past two weeks, why he should care if Titus pilloried a state. His own affairs were secure and out of the Sheriff's vindictive reach. The better part of his life had been spent in politics, and over this period he had seen both good and bad administrations. Florida survived them. There was a native greatness in her which was impregnable against the petty blights, the political termites, and moral damp rot. It would be simple good sense now to let Titus have his day.

The conviction plagued him, though, that the state was in for a brutal rape, an attack so vicious and stealthy as to leave it torn and helpless. Titus was no buccaneer to plunder and swagger away. He would fasten a grip on the state and its people that might never be loosened save through internecine conflict. For a matter of twenty-five years he had watched and studied Titus Semple and his methods. Born of a strange bitterness the Sheriff's ambitions spread slowly but with sureness of running tar. He absorbed Truro at first, then the county. Now he was out to smother a state. Dan knew that this was no extravagant fancy prompted by his own defeat. A democratic people reared to the notion that all politicians were liars and thieves were inclined to accept them as the evils inherent in the system. One was as bad as the other, so the argument ran. What point then in becoming excited?

That was the attitude he had encountered on his swing through the strategic districts. Save in the cases of old friends he was regarded as a man ousted, trying to scramble back to the table.

A man carrying a torch, he decided, usually gets nothing more for his pains than a shower of hot sparks down his neck.

In his heart, however, he wasn't satisfied. Florida had never been ridden by a Semple whose rowels would cut sure and deep.

Well, he wouldn't quit. He'd see things through the primaries and the November elections. Then, win or lose—there couldn't be a draw—he'd cut out. There was much of the world to see and, it occurred to him now, so little time to see it in. He and Lane would go off some place, knock around Europe, and maybe China, Japan, and Hawaii. There was nothing to hold him.

The fan reboiled the same heavy air, pushing it over him in pallid gusts. He drowsed uneasily. It was too hot to sleep.

On the writing table the telephone whirred with a tinny sound. Dan regarded it with loathing. He didn't want to talk with anyone. There was nothing more to be said. He ignored the call, but the hotel's operator was persistent. Finally, with visible effort, he hauled himself from the bed. The next time he'd look around before he took a room and see that the telephone was handier.

His eyes flickered with surprise at the voice coming over the wire. Hall Jamieson, of the Curtis Co.'s law firm in Jacksonville was at the other end.

"I've been trying to locate you all over the state." There was no mistaking the concern. "Why didn't you let us know where you were?"

With his free hand Dan poured some whisky into a glass and drank it while Jamieson talked.

"What's the matter, Jamie?" Dan was good-humouredly attentive. Jamieson awoke in the morning worrying about what was going to worry him during the day.

"Why, not much, Dan." Jamieson was heavily sarcastic. "Not a hell of a lot. I only called to find out how you were. Oh, yes. I almost forgot. You were indicted by a Federal Grand Jury here today on a peonage charge. Seems you're working your plantation over in Walton County with convict labor and not paying for it."

Dan slowly replaced the glass. "Are you drunk, Jamie?"

"No, by God, but I'm going to be." The words crackled. "What the hell you been up to?"

Dan whipped the fog from his brain. At the moment he couldn't make any sense out of what Jamieson was telling him. Peonage. The word had a nasty sound. Enforced labor to work out a debt. In the woodpile, somewhere, was Titus Semple. That was what Lute-Mae wanted him to know, what Lane tried to tell him about the Walton County plantation.

Anger shook him, rousing all of his faculties. "Why, the jury must be crazy, Hall. The only niggers I have on the place at Walton have been with me for years. A Grand Jury wouldn't indict without evidence."

Jamieson's impatient snort rolled into his ear. "There was evidence. Four niggers—wait a minute, I'll read their names to you." There was a brief silence, and then Jamieson was at the telephone again. "Here they are. Jo-John Walker, David Minas, Deever Stepson, and Arthur Bates gave testimony. Your overseer, Burrell Lassen, also appeared."

"Why"—Dan was thinking rapidly—"you know damn well I never heard of those boys. As for Burr, I don't believe it."

Jamieson's laugh was without humor. "You don't suppose I've spent all afternoon trying to reach you because I felt funny and in the mood for a joke. I'm telling you that the Grand Jury indicted you today and there's a warrant out this minute. You better send for the newspapers and read it for yourself."

"All right." Dan's voice was even. "I'll do that."

"You don't seem worried?" Jamieson was curious.

"Why the hell should I be? Your know it won't stand up."

"Anyhow"—Jamieson seemed relieved—"you better get here. Can you leave tonight?"

Dan couldn't halt a smile. By God, Jamie believed it at first. "Sure," he said. "I'll take a sleeper out. Call you first thing in the morning."

He waited until Jamieson had hung up and then signaled the hotel operator, asking for an afternoon paper. Then he poured himself a double Bourbon.

The story was smeared over the front page. He read it with mounting amazement.

Marshal Thomas Miller today holds a warrant for the arrest of Daniel Vincent Curtis, prominent political leader and Jacksonville contractor. Curtis faces indictments for peonage, and his whereabouts are unknown.

Appearing before a Grand Jury here were four Negroes, laborers on a plantation operated and owned by

Curtis in Walton County, and the overseer of the farm, Burrell Lassen.

Charges in the indictment are that Curtis, through influence, secured the pardon of David Minas, Deever Stepson, Arthur Bates, and Jo-John Walker and that contracts were then drawn up for the Negroes to work out some debt which it was represented had been incurred in obtaining their pardons. The Negroes testified that they were threatened with return to prison if they didn't work.

Burrell Lassen, under questioning, submitted that the Negroes had been sent to him after an alleged telephone call from Curtis and that subsequently he received the contracts, which he forced the men to sign.

Dan didn't bother to read more. He tossed the paper into the air and laughed until he was gasping. That bastard Titus cooking up a thing like this, knowing it wouldn't stand but satisfied to keep him hopping and the object of a scandal. The son of a gun!

Despite the fact that he realized Titus had tied him up, temporarily at least, Dan was unable to escape the humor of the situation. The Sheriff was a genius. There was no other word for him. He hunted and he rooted, and what he couldn't find he manufactured. Dan Curtis had been as effectively shunted from the political picture for the moment as if he didn't exist.

One thing alone worried him. He couldn't understand how Semple reached Burr. Lassen had been with him for years. He grew up on the Walton property. He wouldn't have done this unless the Sheriff had him by the throat. The hell of it was that Burr would probably go to jail for perjury once the thing was cleaned up; Burr and maybe some of the Prison Board. Semple, though, was in the clear. Of this Dan was certain. The State and government could investigate their heads off, and they probably wouldn't find anything unless Burr talked, and Burr, apparently, was so far out on a limb he didn't dare. The idiot would probably take a prison sentence before he opened his mouth.

Telephoning to the porter's desk for sleeper reservations out on the Seabord, Dan considered the many facets of the indictments. The immediate sensation, of course, served the Sheriff's purpose. He was without opposition. With a grin Dan admitted he'd cut a sorry figure attempting to promote honest government with an indictment hanging over his head. The hell of the whole thing was that it was so absurdly simple. There was the sincere appreciation for a good trick in the admission. Titus was probably laughing his head off this very minute.

With his reservations made, Dan took a shower, dressed without haste, and had a couple of drinks in between. Tomorrow, not that he cared much any longer, he'd start a little fire himself. Titus better have himself well covered, or he'd sure get smoked out. The courts wouldn't find much humor in the trick.

Dan couldn't resist an appreciative chuckle. The indictment didn't really disturb him. He saw in it only an example of fine old undercutting by the master bushwhacker, Titus Semple. In his best days he had never so effectively disposed of an opponent as had the Sheriff. It was a damn pretty piece of maneuvering no matter how he looked at it.

Secure in the knowledge of his innocence, confident that the charge would dissolve in open court, Dan failed utterly to understand how seriously it might be viewed by others. Jamieson's concern should have warned him, but it didn't. From where he stood Titus had just outdrawn him. There wasn't much more to it than that.

Not until he was ready to leave the room did it occur to him to telephone Lane. He glanced quickly at his watch, decided he wouldn't have time, and promised himself to call first thing in the morning from Jacksonville. The crazy kid might worry at that. Most persons didn't know the difference between an indictment and a conviction.

On the northbound train he enjoyed his dinner, finished a cigar out on the observation platform, and went back to his drawing room. He always slept well on trains, and for the first time in hours he was comfortably cool.

The express pounded through the night, and Dan snored in the deep unconsciousness of a man with an untroubled conscience.

A cold and unfamiliar panic clutched at Lane Ballou as she read the story, which was an afternoon sensation in Truro. The words peonage and indictment meant little. She had to hunt them in the dictionary to find out what they implied. All she was sure of was that Dan was in trouble, the trouble which had been inching upon him ever since the night Titus Semple tossed his defiance on the dining-room table in the house on Flamingo Road.

It was the trouble brewed once on a fall evening in an empty carnival lot and steeped to bitter nightshade over the years she lived in Truro. Because of her, the illusion persisted, Field

Carlisle had tasted it. Now it was being pressed upon Dan Curtis. She and Titus Semple scattered a slow and deadly blight.

Throughout the afternoon she sat by the telephone hoping Dan would call. She needed the sound of his voice to be reassured, for there was nothing but empty fear within her. For the first time she realized what it meant to be alone. In all Truro there was no one to whom she could turn.

The story of Dan's indictment, as she read it, was only half understood. Of grand juries, peonage, and processes of the law she knew but little. She was helpless to think in the face of them. Of only one thing was she certain. Titus had struck Dan down, hitting with the same venomous accuracy he once loosed upon her. Worry and ignorance magnified the Sheriff in her mind until he became a baleful creature of such power that no one could stand against him.

The hours dragged, and the telephone stood mute. Dan must know she would be frantic with worry by this time. The only reason, then, he hadn't called was because he couldn't. He might even be in prison.

Loneliness and suspense built themselves into the silent walls until the house itself became hateful. She had to get out. Suddenly—and she caught her breath in a gasp of relief—she thought of Doc Watson. He would explain what the newspaper story meant. She could talk to him. The knowledge gave her quick courage. Watson would know. Packed away in his grizzled head was the wisdom of the world; at least she was ready to believe this at the moment. He was Dan's friend, also. Dan once said as much. The comforting thought tagged with her as she went to the garage for her car.

At the sound of a step Doc Watson swung about in the creaking swivel chair, ducking his head to see against the light. Then he smiled.

"Why, hello, Miss Ballou." He rose and pushed wide the counter gate.

Lane stood for a moment. Now that she was here she didn't know what to say. It seemed foolish to come running to a man she hardly knew expecting him to understand her lonely fright.

Watson blew ineffectually at the dust-coated chair beside his desk and smiled apologetically. The gesture sent a warm flood of relief rushing over Lane. He was wise, kindly, and he liked her. She had been right in coming.

"You know"—Doc waited until she was seated—"I had a funny feeling I might hear from you." He scratched the side of his head with a puzzled grin. "Sounds queer, doesn't it?"

He tapped at the front page of the *Journal*. "I guess this story must have started me thinking about you."

Lane leaned forward. She felt quieter inside, hearing him talk.

"That's why I came." She paused. "I . . . well, I don't know anyone in Truro. I had to find out what it meant. I was nearly going crazy sitting alone. Then I thought of you. Maybe I shouldn't bother you but," she smiled wearily, "but here I am."

"Dan Curtis hasn't called you?" There was surprise in Doc's question.

"No." Lane looked around the musty office. "May I, will it be all right if I smoke?"

"Sure." He leaned back peering over his finger tips while she lighted a cigarette. "I've got a little cool corn here in a bottle if you'd like a drink."

"Later, maybe." Her smile was grateful. "Now all I want to know is what the story in the paper means."

Doc's eyes brightened. "Seems like one or the other of us is always after information, Miss Ballou. Just what don't you understand?"

"Nothing. I only know Dan is in trouble. Does the story mean he is in prison, that thing about a warrant for his arrest and all?"

"No, Miss Ballou." Doc scouted the idea. "I wouldn't worry about Dan Curtis being in jail. Likely enough he's on his way to Jacksonville from wherever he was. The indictment simply means that certain evidence was presented to the Grand Jury, evidence of peonage on Curtis's Walton plantation. The Grand Jury handed up an indictment. Dan will then be arraigned, that means brought before a judge." He spoke slowly, tracing the steps as simply as he could. "Bail will then be set, and eventually Curtis may have to stand trial. I don't believe it will go as far as that."

"But"—Lane was confused—"it doesn't make sense. Why should Dan be in trouble over four Negroes?"

"Why, Miss Ballou?" Doc's eyebrows lifted in mock surprise. "You sure know the answer to that. You don't mean to tell me you haven't already figured out Titus Semple in the picture."

Again Lane experienced the sharp lash of fear. She had been hoping, trying to assure herself, that Titus had had nothing to do with the trouble. There was real terror in the admission that he was actually after Dan. She hadn't wanted to make it, even to herself.

"Yes, I suppose so." The words were dragged from her.

"Maybe"—Doc slid out a drawer—"we ought to have a touch of corn after all?"

The raw whisky scorched and gagged her, but she took it, reaching hastily for the water.

"Oooo!" Tears gathered in her eyes.

"You just let it set there for awhile in your stomach. Pretty soon you won't be worrying about anything." Watson patted the bottle affectionately. "It's a specific for man and beast, but usually the beasts got too much sense to take it."

Lane had to laugh. She was feeling better. It hadn't been a mistake to come.

"What I can't understand"—Doc laced and unlaced his fingers—"is how Titus cooked up this stew without burning his own fingers. There's a lot of trouble simmering for someone."

"Dan, you mean?"

"No-o." He was reassuring. "I don't expect the indictment will stick. Even Titus wouldn't be optimistic enough to think it could."

"It'll hurt Dan, though, won't it?"

"Well"—Doc searched her face with gentle eyes—"an indictment isn't exactly a citation of honor. It's got Dan where he won't be able to lift much of a finger for the elections. That's about all Titus wanted."

Lane rose. Her mind was easier, but within her the familiar hatred for Titus and everything he represented was being fanned into a bright heat.

"You think Dan is all right then. I mean"—she risked a weak smile—"he couldn't be in prison?"

"Shuh, no. You go on home, Miss Ballou, and sit by the telephone. It ought to be sounding off pretty soon unless Dan Curtis is on a train where he can't call or doesn't think the thing is important enough to worry about."

Driving through downtown Truro on her way to the Heights, Lane was beset by the strangest of all fears: that she was once again in an alien and hostile encirclement through which she must move with stealth and caution. The familiar pattern of the town was as foreign as River Street had been on the first night she walked along it with Field Carlisle. The illusion clung with the tenuous horror of a spider's damp and sticky web.

To escape she hurried with a reckless disregard for traffic, streaking through the business district and Flamingo Road.

Not until she was inside the house with the door shut behind her did the fancy evaporate.

There had been no call from Dan. Of this Sarah was sure. She hadn't been out of the kitchen all afternoon. Lane tried to remember every reassuring word Doc Watson had spoken. Dan must be all right. Something would have told her if he wasn't.

She ate a lonely and tasteless dinner in the living room from a tray placed next to a chair within reaching distance of the telephone. If Dan called she wanted to have the receiver off at the first sound of the bell.

Throughout the evening she nodded in fitful starts, curled deep within Dan's chair, one hand outstretched with finger tips resting at the telephone's base. Such moments of sleep as came to her were crowded with the bloated shape of Titus Semple. In her dreams he seemed to disintegrate, oozing off into jellylike masses and then reforming. The process was like a rhythmical pulse beat, and she awoke from it each time with an increasing dread and the feeling that the Sheriff was creeping in and upon her, crawling through invisible cracks around the doors and windows and filling the room with a suffocating stench.

Her hand clutched at the telephone, gripping it tightly as a weapon.

Titus waited impatiently while the colored man arranged a table in his room at the Palmer House. He was eating alone tonight, shut away from Truro. Ordinarily he liked to sit in the Eagle Café watching folks, wondering what they were thinking about. The place was his private anthill, and from the Eagle Café he could keep an eye on it after it was too dark to see any longer from the hotel porch. Around his feet were scattered afternoon papers: Jacksonville, Tampa, Miami dailies which had come in on the late train. It would have been more fun reading them, he admitted, if the stories had all been differently worded, but they weren't. In the absence of other information they contented themselves with the press association report. It was still good reading, but by now he knew the dispatch by heart.

It had been a good trick. Just thinking about it made him glow. There was old Dan, caught like a bug on flypaper. It wouldn't hurt him, and he'd probably get away, but he was in one hell of a mess.

Titus beamed upon the Negro waiter, an expression at once bland and foxy, and the boy was so startled he almost dropped a dish. Mistuh Titus don' usual smile thataway, he thought apprehensively, and ducked out of the room, hurrying to the pantry to share the news with the help. It was common knowledge in the Palmer House that when the Sheriff was too agreeable someone was due for a thorn under his tail.

Titus would have been happier if he had someone to share the meaty bone of triumph with. The funny part of it was that there wasn't a damn soul he knew who'd really appreciate such a joke. Dan Curtis, now, well, Dan would have made a fine companion. The trouble was, with the joke on him, he probably couldn't understand it. If it had been another fellow, then he and Dan could enjoy it together.

With the belly noises of a hog in a sweet-potato patch he ambled around the table, picking at the celery, olives, inspecting the linen and silver perfection of the single service.

He had ordered everything for tonight which ordinarily gave him indigestion: rare roast beef, a thick crab gumbo to start with, baked acorn squash, mashed potatoes, caramel ice cream. The way he felt his stomach could take ground glass and never quiver.

In a way it was too bad, he thought, that he had arranged to toss a skunk into Flamingo Road tomorrow. Coming, as it would, so close on having Dan tripped up, this joke was going to lose some of its flavor, but there was no help for it. By tomorrow night he'd have Dan's little strumpet on the run back to the gutter where she came from. He'd get her fixed so she'd never want to show her face on the Heights or, maybe, even in Truro again.

Hunting happily along the table he felt the excitement of the chase pound within him. For awhile back there he'd had the uncomfortable feeling that Truro was wriggling out from between his fingers. When one thing went wrong, like the case of that little bitch, then everything worked loose. By tomorrow, though, he'd have all the worms in a can again.

CHAPTER TWENTY-SIX

SLENDER, SHIMMERING BLADES OF SUNLIGHT, KNIFING their way between drawn blinds, awoke Lane. She twisted uncomfortably in the chair and then suddenly realized that the telephone was ringing. Innumerable times throughout the night she had fought out of sleep, convinced that the bell was sounding. Each time she answered it, however, the instrument was a lifeless piece of metal and plastic until an operator's bored and impersonal voice cut in to ask her number. Now, afraid to trust her senses, she waited until the bell sounded for a third time. It wasn't a trick of overwrought nerves. The phone actually rang.

"Jacksonville calling." The long-distance operator spoke. "One moment please."

It seemed longer than a moment. A little lifetime elapsed before Dan's familiar voice reached her.

"Oh, Dan." Her tones were shaky, and the receiver against her ear trembled.

"Why"—she could tell he was surprised—"what are you doing up?" He laughed. "I figured to have a few minutes in private with Sarah."

"Dan, I've been so worried." She wanted to tell him it was more than worry, that dread and terror sat with her during the long and silent night. "I waited for your call."

"All night?"

If he laughed now she would scream.

"Yes, Dan."

"Oh." The wire was silent for a second or so; then Curtis's grave and measured tones marched along it. "I'm sorry, honey. I suppose I should have known the story would sound worse to you than it really is. I might have wired from the train or called from Tampa. You see," he was trying to explain, "it sort of took me by surprise, also."

"But you're all right?" Relief, quick and precious, raced through her, driving knots from cramped muscles, making it possible to breathe again. "You're not just pretending?"

"No, I'm fine or will be as soon as I have a second cup of coffee."

For hours every nerve in her body had been tightly bunched. Now, realizing that he was safe, they uncoiled with a suddenness which left her weak and shaking. For a moment she thought she would be sick; nausea bobbled in her throat, and her face was damp.

"I didn't know what to think. We, I saw the afternoon Truro paper with the story." Her laugh was nervously uncertain. "After you didn't call I began to imagine they had you in jail."

"Not yet."

She grasped at the words. "Will, will it be bad for you,

Dan?" She hurried. "I know I sound stupid, but I don't know anything about such matters. The only warrants I ever saw were those around Coyne's carnival, and they always spelled trouble for someone. Is it going to be bad, as bad as it sounded in the papers?"

"A lot of folks will be disappointed if it isn't." He whistled softly; the sound was strangely close in her ear.

"Please don't joke, Dan. Don't you see, I have to know? If you won't tell me, who will? Can they, he, Titus really make trouble for you?"

"Not much more than has already been caused. Hereafter I better listen when you or Lute-Mae try to tell me something. Anyhow, don't worry. Everything will be straightened out, may take a little time."

She wondered if her imagination was tricking her again or if he really sounded dispirited, tired.

"You, you won't be able to come to Truro?"

"Not now, Lane. You sit tight. I'll keep in touch with you?"

He was gone. A brief click of the receiver, and then there was nothing. It didn't seem possible. She sat staring at the instrument. It was as though she hadn't spoken to him at all. The dull emptiness which had been filled by the sound of his voice was there, inside, again.

From the kitchen came the sound of Sarah moving about, arranging a breakfast tray. Lane remembered she had slept in her clothing and that she felt rumpled and frowzy. Sarah would think it funny to see her this way.

She hurried upstairs and into a shower. The rushing water made her feel better. After all, Dan must be all right. He would have said so if he wasn't.

Tingling from the bath she sent a surprised Sarah back downstairs with the tray.

"I'll have breakfast in the living room."

For reasons which she couldn't explain to herself she didn't want to stay alone in her room. Up here, there was a sense of being shut away, barred off from everything. It frightened her. That too, was a funny thing, she thought, while dressing. I was never easy to scare before. Maybe it's because everything I have means so much now. I'm afraid to lose it.

The commonplace, familiar things on the breakfast table had a tonic effect upon her. Bright yellow toast, freshly buttered, hot coffee a crisp napkin; other women might take them for granted. Lane had still to accustom herself to the service. Dan frequently laughed at her naïve expressions of

268

delight. He couldn't understand, she knew, how life on Flamingo Road seemed to a carnival kid.

Sternly she had forced herself not to look beyond the moment. To do that was to plan, and to plan was to invite heartbreak. She expected nothing more than this from Dan. Their life, she was certain, would always move through a back channel. Into his affairs away from her she never inquired. Mrs. Curtis and his children were of no substance, so unreal that she couldn't believe in their existence. All truth was centered here in this house on Truro's Heights, and she clung to it with the emotional fervor of a first love.

When Dan would come to her again, he would. It was enough to know nothing he was incapable of handling had happened. What plagued her was the conviction that Titus, failing here, would try again. He was not a man to be denied easily.

Once, shortly after the suicide of Field, she imagined that she had become an instrument of tragedy. Because of her, Field was eventually led to kill himself. Through knowing her, Dan Curtis was in trouble. That, she realized now, was nonsense. Nothing she did or failed to do could alter the set course of events. They moved, and she moved with them or was swept aside. It didn't make much difference since she was without choice. I just guess, she decided, I'm not cut out to be a tragically heroic figure. There was no greatness in only wanting to be left alone.

The telephone rang sharply, not in the short signals of long distance, but the regular local call. It couldn't, she knew, be Dan.

Unexpected as it was she felt no real surprise at the sound of Doc Watson's voice. After their talk yesterday she took his call as a matter of course.

"Mornin', Miss Ballou." No matter what he said Watson invariably conveyed the impression that he was laughing at himself. "This is the type-smeared father confessor of Truro. Got any troubles this morning?"

"It's still early." She was grateful for the concern.

"I'd take that to mean you've heard from Jacksonville?"

"Yes, he, Dan called half an hour ago."

She heard his cluck of approval, and then, in a monologue which grew increasingly pointless, Watson talked of the weather, the season, and a new bandshell the city was erecting in the park. He wanted to tell her something, of this she was sure, and her impatience mounted.

"Miss Ballou"—there was an almost unbearable pause—"I

269

was at City Hall this morning. In a way I'm editor, publisher, printer and reporter for my gazette." He made the explanation sparring with time. "Well, while I was there a committee, committee of women, was calling on the Mayor."

She waited for him to continue and, when he didn't prompted him.

"Yes?"

"Well, I'll swear but this is hard for me to say, they were there protesting to the Mayor about you."

"I don't understand." She didn't. In all of Truro she wasn't on speaking terms with more than half a dozen women, and most of those were employees in the stores or markets.

"Well"—Watson was having difficulty in talking—"it's this way, Miss Ballou. They call themselves the Mothers' Decency League."

No longer was it possible not to understand. "But they couldn't." It was a cry born of loneliness and desperation. "They wouldn't dare."

"I'm afraid they did, though, Miss Ballou." Watson's tones were grave. "You see, they didn't think of this themselves. I don't even know where they came from. They looked to me like women someone had recruited from around the railroad yards, you know: scrubbed with honest indignation and stinking of civic virtue. But they made a formal protest to the Mayor, Miss Ballou. It was a regular petition. Vice must be kept in the district, harlotry can't be allowed to invade Truro. It was all viciously simple and pretty dirty."

Something shriveled within her at the thought of the delegation with its hypocritical piety, bristling in excitement and mouthing filth for her public humiliation. She should have known that Titus wasn't finished. He had never really forgotten. With Dan away he had time for her again. The committee was his as surely as though he led it to City Hall.

"You see"—she only half heard Watson—"I know, you and a lot of people are going to know, this isn't spontaneous. The trouble is, the protest is on record, and it's going to make a nice hunk of rotten meat for the *Journal* and Truro's gossips to chew on. Miss Ballou?" He sounded worried.

"Yes." Her voice was small.

"Miss Ballou, it isn't going to be pleasant for you in Truro for awhile after this. The *Journal* will have it in the first edition. By night time every table in Truro will be serving it up as dessert."

"They didn't"—she was going to be sick in a moment—"they didn't mention my name?"

"Pretty near that, I'm afraid. Here, just a minute."

Waiting for Watson to locate whatever it was he wanted, Lane, for the first time, experienced complete spiritual exhaustion. She felt no anger, no desire to cry out against what Titus had done. Dead-eyed and nerveless, she waited.

"Here, I've got it." Watson read. "The mothers of Truro view with alarm the incursion of a former inmate of the notorious establishment conducted by Lute-Mae Sanders into Flamingo Road and the restricted residential district of Truro." There was a brief, sympathetic pause. "You see"— his voice was tinged with regret—"there isn't much chance you'll be overlooked, Miss Ballou."

"Thank you, Mr. Watson." She replaced the receiver gently, huddled into the chair, and stared at her hands.

What Titus Semple had done was so devastatingly plain, so cruelly unassailable. There was no defense against it. A committee of mothers protesting to the Mayor, who couldn't even if he hadn't been the Sheriff's man, ignore the petition. The women—Lane could imagine where they came from: Truro's poor whites, urged on by their husbands, who pocketed Semple's gifts of appreciation. It mattered little that they had probably never set foot on Flamingo Road or even knew of her existence until told. Here was outraged womanhood crying that the harlot be cast out. It was a crusade dear to the hearts of all self-anointed. The *Journal*, which must already have the petition in type, would need to make no editorial comment. The news story itself would mount the fury. She had been one of Lute-Mae's girls, and now she lived on Flamingo Road. Who could deny these facts?

With a gesture of weariness she leaned her head against the cushion's softness. In this, as in everything else, she thought the Sheriff displayed an uncanny ability to achieve his purpose while aligning himself in the ranks of the innocent spectators. Therein lay the unfailing accuracy of his sniping.

Even Dan, who should have known, had been tricked by this pose of slothful indifference. Dan and Field, Parker, Shelton, and all the others who persisted in clinging to the idea that the Sheriff was an agreeable, shrewd, but not dangerous fat man. One by one Titus picked them off.

What left her without the will to fight back now was the humiliating knowledge that she was unimportant to Titus. He hadn't needed to do this. Once, perhaps, when the house on Flamingo Road had achieved a certain significance through the gathering there of the men Dan Curtis ranged about him, the Sheriff might have considered her dangerous. At least, she was in a position to learn and understand a great many things and from this cover sap him. The threat was removed, though, when the organization broke away from Curtis. Now, Titus had simply gone back to beat her down. She was a minor detail which, for the sake of perfection, must be taken care of.

After today she would have no place in Truro. Already the house seemed no longer a part of her. She rose dispiritedly from the chair and walked about the room, regarding familiar objects as a stranger might. Yet, with an instinctively protective motion, her fingers would rest on a book, an ashtray, a leather covered humidor holding Dan's heavy black cigars. These were personal, intimate things charged with precious and ineradicable memories. They were the blocks which had built this home, a home erected on fragile unrealities.

Dan had meant that when he said, "None of it is real anyhow." She knew now they both must have felt it was not a house of stone, metal, and wood. It didn't even look like the houses which men with saws, hammers, and trowels built.

It was, she decided, the sort of a house a carnival kid might dream about, only a carnival kid would be old enough and wise enough to know it was a dream.

In the small, book-lined room which Dan used as a study and referred to as the Curtis Foundation Library for the Spiritual Advancement of Lane Ballou, she perched on a leather-covered stool. Knees drawn up to her chin she stared intently at the chair where Dan liked to sit. Of all the house this seemed to be the room most crowded with memories and the one she would hate to leave behind.

Thinking of this it occurred to her that she had no plans. Where am I going? How will I live? She posed the questions to herself and found no answer.

It would be impossible to remain on the Heights. She realized she could draw within the house, ignore Truro, Titus, Flamingo Road. No one could drive her out of town. Such defiance would be a hollow gesture without meaning or purpose.

Tomorrow or the following day Dan would come to Truro, or, in Jacksonville, he would hear the story. She knew he would rage against it and insist upon her remaining in her home. She realized, also, that his arguments would grow weaker, his determination less as the inescapable, simple truth of the situation intruded.

What then, she thought, of Lane Ballou and Dan Curtis? It was one thing for them both to have forgotten or ignored the existence of Lute-Mae's and another that the word whore

272

should be screamed on the corners. Something which had never existed before would inevitably stand mockingly between them.

Dan could take her away, but a new house, a different town would serve no better purpose than to remind him of what had happened. Pride could not stand against the assault. Sooner or later their relationship would become furtive, unclean, and loathsome. Of this she was certain. Neither she nor Dan would be able to endure against the odds.

You know, she thought, if I were really bad I'd know what to do. The irony of the notion was forced upon her, and she smiled for the first time.

Reluctantly she left the room, walking through the lower floor to the kitchen and standing there silently, watching without comment while Sarah picked and washed a head of lettuce. Even Sarah seemed a little strange. Either that or she, Lane Ballou, was the stranger in the house.

As though sensing something was wrong, the little colored maid kept her head averted over her task, and after a moment Lane walked away.

In her bedroom she idled by the bureau, studying herself in the mirror, regarding her reflection gravely.

"We came a long way from Coyne's Carnival," she said aloud, "just to walk back, didn't we?"

Impatiently she shook off the thought. That was an easy road to self-pity. You talked to yourself and began to ask why things happened the way they did. Then the first thing you knew you were blubbering and feeling sorry for yourself.

The branches of a giant mulberry tree brushed gently against the screens in the windows, making a hissing sound of rain on a wet street. That tree had always fascinated her. When the fruit was upon it she used to open the screens, picking and eating the black berries. Usually they had small bugs in them, and she didn't care much for the taste either; but the tree was hers, and it gave her a peculiar sensation of independence to taste its fruit.

Without a definite purpose in mind she drew out the bureau drawers, fingering the articles there. Then it struck her that she knew what she had to do. She'd get out of Truro this afternoon and go to Jacksonville. There, within the impersonal walls of a hotel room, she and Dan would be able to talk.

She packed without haste. Later Sarah could send the rest of her things. It was important now that she get away while her resolve was firm.

The open bag on the bed filled rapidly. Once, while she was

273

laying away neat folds of underwear, she raised her head at the sound of voices outside. Flamingo Road usually preserved a well-modulated dignity. The words rising to her window were strident, challenging. She listened for a moment and then went on packing. Grocery boys or truck drivers in an argument, she thought.

The suitcase was almost ready for locking when Sarah scuttled fearfully into the room. Her eyes rolled with excitement, and she teetered back and forth from one foot to the other.

"Miz Lane"—her mouth hung slightly open at the spectacle of her mistress packing so unhurriedly—"ain' y'u seen what goin' ahn outside?" She pointed jerkily at the front windows.

Puzzled Lane regarded the girl, and then she realized that the voices, heard awhile back, were no longer disjointed. They formed an irregular and subdued chant, ominous and deliberate.

With a quick stride she was at the window, brushing aside the light curtains and peering below. The back of her hand went quickly to her mouth in a defensive movement.

Marching resolutely up and down on the sidewalk before the house were half a dozen women. Clutching the rigid hands of an equal number of youngsters, little girls whose starched dresses stood out from spindly legs, they paraded. In free hands, raised aloft, were crude banners, painted oilcloth on wooden frames.

"Oh my God." The exclamation escaped from behind her clenched fist. "Oh, the stinking bastard."

It was impossible to hear what the women were saying, and Lane strained to read what was daubed on the signs they bore.

The marchers tramped resolutely, broad buttocks lumping up and down. They walked along the sidewalk from one end of the spotless picket fence to the other. Only when they turned could Lane read the placards.

WE DEMAND FLAMINGO ROAD
BE MADE SAFE FOR OUR CHILDREN

MR. MAYOR CLOSE THIS HOUSE
LUTE-MAE CANNOT ENTER HERE

She didn't bother to read farther. A couple of automobiles had stopped in the street, the occupants watching with delighted amazement and calling the signs to each other. All along Flamingo Road, Lane knew, people were coming from their houses to stand in silence.

The women and their cocky little brats. They didn't belong on the Heights. Their plain, greedy faces were varnished with fanatical indignation. Not only were they actually on Flamingo Road, but they were screaming imprecations at one of the residents. The triumph was almost too great to bear, and they turned to look at the little house now and then as though they wanted to hurl bricks through the windows.

Lane slumped against the window casement. For support one hand clutched flutteringly at the wall. She knew she was going to vomit; a terrible retching was already at her throat. Her body was drained of all strength, and she sobbed helplessly. The filthy swine. God damn them. God damn them to hell.

She realized it would be useless to call the police. They would laugh at her. This was what the Sheriff ordered, and every man on the force knew it.

Lane pressed her face into her arm. Hot tears scalded her eyes. She felt Sarah's hands on her shoulders and allowed herself to be turned from the window and heard it closed, blotting out the hideous noise from below but not the memory of what she had seen.

"Shuuh, now, Miz Lane. Don' cahry on so." Sarah tried clumsily to soothe her.

Lane lifted incredulous eyes to the concerned, pleading face. This couldn't have happened. No one, not even Titus Semple would do this. He must have known she was going or would go.

"Oh"—the cry was of anguished despair—"he didn't have to do it. He didn't have to."

"Now, Miz Lane." Sarah pawed ineffectually at her shoulder.

The quick, searing flame of hysterics extinguished itself. Bewildered, Lane glanced at the maid as though she had never seen her before. Then she shook her head, striving to clear it.

"I'm all right, Sarah."

Even her voice carried a strange quality. "I'm all right." She repeated the statement only for the sake of hearing this new note. It rang in her ears with the reverberation of a shout in a well.

Calmly she stood before the mirror, patted at the hair above her ears. Then without glancing at Sarah, who was watching her with wide-eyed interest, she walked into Dan's room.

Beneath her fingers the small drawer in an upper corner gave silently. She moved it out not more than half an inch at a time until its contents lay exposed. Deliberately and with a steady

275

hand she reached inside and felt the shock of the blue-black steel against her warm palm.

She drove leisurely through Truro's outskirts. With the roadster's top down the wind caught at her hair and flushed her cheeks. To a stranger she was only a remarkably pretty girl out riding by herself.

Her eyes, as they stared straight ahead, were untroubled, her features composed, almost masklike. Once, and then for just a moment, had her serenity, born of determination and the knowledge of what she was going to do, deserted her. That was when she ran the roadster from the garage, down the graveled drive, and past the marching women. One of them had yelled an unintelligible something, and the others laughed. For an instant she had been possessed of such a fury that black hell must have shown on her face, and the sight of it froze the cackling.

Driving now she tried to think, but ideas refused to shape themselves into recognizable forms. For reasons which she didn't try to explain she wanted to revisit certain sections of Truro. The light car bounced through the rutted Mill Road, halting briefly within the tangle of pine and oaks by the river. Later it was parked alongside the Apulca highway from where the scarred and seldom-used carnival or circus lot was visible. Still later it drifted with the traffic on River Street, slowing imperceptibly before the Eagle Café.

These were the way stops. It was as if they were marked with signs visible only to her eyes. Here Lane Ballou rested on her way to hell.

Only one place was left, Lute-Mae's in the district. Somehow she didn't want to go there. At the far end of River Street, near Cypress Avenue, she made a turn and retraced the course until she was downtown again.

Before the Palmer House she parked carefully, inching the car into a narrow vacant space. When this was done she shut off the ignition and locked it. On the curb she brushed and patted at her skirt and then closed the roadster's door. With bag tucked beneath her arm, she mounted the steps.

Titus didn't bother to look up at the sound of her step. He had heard the sharp click of high heels on the boards, waited as they paused, and listened as the sound advanced toward him.

In the creaky chair he rocked, a movement so slight it barely moved his body. He knew she was before him, by the railing where once she had stood, timorous and uncertain. He could

276

smell her, and the faint perfume was hateful. His nostrils twitched.

"I figured you'd be gone by this time, Miss Ballou." Through slitted eyes he could see the bright metal of the belt buckle at his paunch and beyond it the tips of her shoes.

Lane caught at breath which wouldn't come. Squatting there, enveloping and bulging over the chair. Titus made her think of a poisonous toad. There was the stench of implacable evil about him, as though his skin exuded venom.

"I told you once I wouldn't run." She attempted to shut her eyes against the sight of him, but they wouldn't close.

Something in her voice, bitter and unrelenting, made Titus lift his head, and the eyes which met hers were filmed and milky. His body stirred, and the rocking stopped.

"It would have saved a sight of trouble, Miss Ballou." He was watching her with the bright attention of a cat.

Lane had to suppress a cry of excitement. Titus Semple was frightened. She knew it. All of his instincts were warning him. His voice betrayed it.

"It wouldn't have saved Field Carlisle, would it?" She spat the question at him. "It wouldn't have saved Dan Curtis."

Titus's head seemed to settle within the glistening rolls of his neck.

"It sure enough would have saved you, Miss Ballou."

Titus must have realized instantly that he had said the wrong thing, for he made a squirming, ineffectual attempt to straighten up in the chair.

She might have been saved. The sweat and humiliation of the County Farm would not have been hers. The vindictive slatterns, hired by Titus and parading before the home Dan had built for her on Flamingo Road, would not be there. The rage enveloping her was a living thing. It had substance. She could feel it.

"Everything you have touched has been made filthy." The words tumbled over each other. "I don't care any longer what happens to me, but you don't deserve to live."

Titus saw the gun even before she was conscious of having drawn it from the bag. His eyes snapped outward like the white pulp of a squeezed grape, and a terrific yelp fuzzed within his throat.

The pistol jumped in her hand, once, twice, three times. The shots appeared to have no effect, and she screamed with horror at the notion that Titus couldn't be killed. Somehow this gross body was capable of absorbing the bullets without feeling them. Frantically she pulled at the trigger until the

277

bullets were exhausted and the hot gun hung loosely at her side.

Titus sagged in the chair, his enormous bulk alone keeping him in it. He coughed once with the empty sound of a drum, and blood flecked his lips. His head lolled stupidly, and his mouth dropped. As if at a great distance Lane was aware that people were screaming. There were heavy, running feet on the porch, and someone was pinning her arms. She continued to stare at Titus. He seemed to be wilting, collapsing before her eyes, and crimson was spotting the white silk of his shirt.

With a spasmodic jerk the head twisted in a half circle, and for a moment the Sheriff met her gaze. Brief recognition flared.

"You're still licked, Miss Ballou. You sure God are still licked."

As though the effort of speech unbalanced him, the unwieldy body leaned forward, and then, carrying the chair in which he was wedged, Titus rolled face down to the Palmer House porch.

CHAPTER TWENTY-SEVEN

SHADOWS DROPPING FROM THE SINGLE BARRED window high in the wall laid a grid on the bare stone floor.

Within the squares, from her seat on the narrow bed's edge, Lane could trace a game of ticktacktoe with the point of her slipper.

It was a silly contest, she thought, and one which always ended in a tie no matter how hard she tried to fool herself. Time and again during the afternoon she swept her foot over the lines as though to erase the entire pattern with one impatient movement. It was always there, moving imperceptibly across the stone, and after awhile she returned to the meaningless effort to outwit herself.

Waiting for Dan Curtis to come, listening for the sure sound of his footsteps, she had to do something. Walking was no good, and just sitting was worse. She hoped Dan would come soon and that there would be no others. Already there had been too many visitors. Doc Watson came first, almost as soon as they brought her in.

"It's too damn bad," he complained with an attempt at

humor, "that you couldn't have told me about this before you did it. I could have had an extra on the street."

He sat on the cell's one chair, hands swinging loosely between spread legs, eyeing her reproachfully, but there was concern on his face.

Lane had been grateful for his sympathy and for his honesty. Watson, when she asked him, hadn't attempted to wave aside the seriousness of her position.

"A lot of persons, Miss Ballou," he said, "are going to consider you as little short of an instrument of God in weighting down Titus Semple with lead like you did. Shortsighted folks, and there is usually a majority on a jury, are still going to think it was murder."

She had asked the question, wondering why as she did, and accepted the answer without flinching.

There was no regret at having shot Semple. Now it seemed almost as though she had finally brought herself to do a job which was given to her long ago. Everything she loved or cared for had been made hateful, foul by the man. There was no peace or decency with him alive.

From the beginning, on the night when he first spoke to her as she was walking from the Eagle Café with Field, it had been, between the two of them. She had sensed, if not understood, it then, and so, perhaps, had Titus. Anyhow, it was easier to think of it that way.

Watson hadn't stayed long. He must have realized she didn't need such comfort as he was prepared to offer.

"I'll be around if I can help, Miss Ballou."

Lute-Mae panting, excited, and flushed of face, came later, and after her Dan's lawyer, Jamieson.

Somehow she had felt sorry for Lute-Mae. The woman was so honestly upset and worried for her. Lute-Mae's vehement emotion filled the cell and crowded her in a corner. It was a relief when she left, protesting her determination to have the Governor himself take a hand.

Jamieson was different. Harassed but efficient, he told her first that bail for Curtis had been set in Jacksonville that morning and that he was already on his way to Truro.

"I don't mean to be such a world of trouble, Mr. Jamieson," Lane apologized after the man had introduced himself and explained who he was and why he was there.

"Well, you are." The words were harsh and impatient, but his smile belied them. "Hot-headed girls are always shooting someone, that's why I never interested myself in them or criminal law."

He softened after that, explaining about her arraignment, plea, and other technical and mysterious due processes.

"But"—Lane was really puzzled—"if I shot him and I say I did and a lot of people saw me do it, why must there be all this fuss?"

"Good God, girl," Jamieson protested, "how do you expect lawyers to make a living? Things like that would close half the country's courts. No, sir, it will all have to be done right with appeals, seals, and proper stamps."

On an impulse which seemed to surprise him the lawyer reached over, patted her hand, and winked quickly.

She felt a momentary loss when he left. For all his fussiness he was tactful, understanding, and wise. After he had gone the hours dragged into stretches of torment. She was restless and fired with an all-consuming nervous energy which could not be spent on floor-pacing. The childish game of ticktacktoe held her for awhile, but finally she slumped to the bed and lay there, lacking the strength to move to a more comfortable position.

Exhaustion held her, for there had been no sleep following her arrest. Throughout the long night she fought with her memory in an effort to repossess the scene on the porch of the Palmer House. It remained confused. She could remember only that Titus finally fell. He was dead. There was no sinister magic about him after all to deflect the bullets. He lay there, a sodden lump of meat stripped for all time of his power and evil. There had been a shuddering relief in that realization.

The shouting and screaming which seemed to have arisen from every side, once the noise of the revolver had been stilled, continued, boiling up from the ground while two men held her unresisting body between them and hustled her into the lobby. She could recall that they later went into an office presumably to await the police.

She also could recall how River Street looked, packed with a shifting block of curious men and women. Their mouths were open as the police knocked a path through their ranks, opening a way to the black sedan, and marched to it with their arms locked in hers. After that nothing was clear. One thing, though, was sharp. It was the not unmusical clang of a barred door closing upon her.

Now her toe halted its tracing, lifted above a square as a dancer's might be held.

"Murder." She spoke the word softly, feeling it with her lips. "Murder."

It was curious, she thought, that it should be such a gentle word for so violent a deed. The notion fascinated her, and she played with it, fitting other sounds to the acts they represented in speech and discovering how ridiculous many of them were.

There were footsteps in the corridor. She heard them after the door at the other end closed, and her nerves relaxed. It was Dan, no mistaking his tread. She waited without moving from the bed.

"Hello, Lane." He filled the doorway, looking down; and then he was inside, and a guard had relocked the door.

"Dan."

I don't have to say more, she thought a little wildly. I don't have to do anything but speak his name. He'll understand.

For a moment Dan considered the small chair, and then he came to her, sitting there where her fingers could reach him and there was no space between them.

"Dan, oh, Dan." The loneliness of the world was in the cry, and she crept within the strength of his arm.

He didn't ask any questions, and she was afraid to talk, fearful she would tell him how Titus had poured his filth upon their house on Flamingo Road. Of everything else that house seemed most precious at the moment. She didn't want him to know it had been defiled. Nervously, unsuccessfully she realized, she tried to pretend nothing was changed. Her eyes were shut against the cell confining them. She was some place with Dan, and soon they would go away together. The lights on Flamingo Road would be fluttering, warm the way a candle flame is. They would go inside and lock the door behind them.

"You saw Jamieson?" His arm tightened about her shoulders.

"Yes." She had to say something. Dan would want an answer. "Yes, he told me I was a damned nuisance." Her laugh was short.

"He's a good man."

She could feel the crispness of his hair as he bent down to lay his head against hers. Without opening her eyes she knew how he was looking, what he was experiencing.

What now of this man, this Dan Curtis? From this jail where will he go? Who will walk with him? The questions beat at her brain.

"You"—she must speak—"you're all right? Jamieson told me."

"Of course." Quick laughter died in his throat.

Lane understood what he had been about to say. He almost laughed and assured her that he was never in real trouble. Then he must have remembered Semple and thought she had killed the Sheriff because of him. It wouldn't do to tell her now that the murder had been unnecessary.

In a minute now he would begin to talk about Titus. Desperation drove her to chatter aimlessly about the visits of Lute-Mae, Doc Watson, what they had said. Dan musn't be given an opportunity to interrupt.

He listened gravely until a note of mounting panic was sounded, then he lifted her face and kissed her twitching mouth. He held his lips against hers until she was silenced.

"We don't have to talk, Lane." He pressed his palms against her cheeks, framing her face. "We don't have to talk or pretend, not now or ever."

He released her, and her face slid down to rest against his arm. Looking at the floor she saw that the shifting sun had spoiled her ticktacktoe game. It would be twilight soon and then night.

"I don't want you to worry, Lane." Dan's words were muted, his mouth was in her hair. "You know there isn't a thing, I, we won't do to get you clear. Everything will turn out all right."

There was no conviction in the assurance. Lane could sense that. He didn't want her to be afraid as he was.

"Of course, Dan. I'm not worried."

It's funny, she thought, I should be trying to comfort and shelter him. I know and he knows that it was murder, deliberate and premeditated. We can't change that, either of us.

"Jamieson will get the best men in the state."

"Yes, Dan. I know."

There didn't seem to be anything to say then. They sat in silence, and Lane felt herself growing smaller. She wanted to cling there within his arm, confident no one could find or touch her.

"Dan." She finally spoke his name in a whisper.

"Yes, Lane?" She felt him draw slightly away and knew he was looking down at her.

"Do"—the word was muffled—"do they hang people in Florida for murder?"

He held her out and slightly away from him at that. His hands were on her arms, quieting the sudden fit of trembling which raced through her body. She had to look at him.

"No, Lane." A tender smile of understanding dimpled one corner of his mouth.

"That's good." She laughed, a sharp, highly strung sound. "You know"—it was a crazy thing to think of—"in one of those books you gave me to read a woman said something."

282

She studied his face and then continued. "I didn't believe it when I read it because I didn't think a woman, not one in trouble, anyhow, would talk that way. Maybe you remember?" Her face had the seriousness of childhood upon it.

"Do you remember, Dan?" She seemed to be trying to recall the words. "Do you remember what she said when they were taking her away to have her head chopped off?"

With an unconscious gesture of self-protection one hand lifted and touched lightly at the side of her throat and then dropped to her lap.

"She said, 'I have such a little neck.' "

THE MEN OF DALLAS
by BURT HIRSCHFELD

Not even a gunshot fired by a jealous lover can keep J.R. down! He's back and he's more conniving and ambitious than ever. His appetite for power and carnal pleasure is unrelenting. And in the high-rolling game to dominate Ewing Oil, he'll stop at nothing to keep the others beneath his feet.

0 552 11844 3 — £1.35

PRINCESS DAISY
by JUDITH KRANTZ

She was born Princess Marguerite Alexandrovna Valensky.
But everyone called her Daisy. She was a blonde beauty
living in a world of aristocrats and countless wealth. Her
father was a prince, a Russian nobleman. Her mother was an
American movie goddess. Men desired her. Women envied
her. Daisy's life was a fairytale filled with parties and balls,
priceless jewels, money and love. Then, suddenly, the
fairytale ended. And Princess Daisy had to start again, with
nothing. Except the secret she guarded from the day she was
born.

0 552 11660 2 — £1.95

A NECESSARY WOMAN

by
HELEN VAN SLYKE

Two women sail into sunshine romances on board
an exotic cruiser. By the end of the voyage they have
both made decisions that will alter the course of
their lives – forever.

MARY FARR MORGAN

A successful radio personality in San Francisco,
wins a once-in-a-lifetime cruise. But as the ship sets
sail she realises that she has also gained a chance to
think over the pattern of her 15-year marriage to the
kind but weak Michael. Deep down Mary has
always longed for a man on whom she could rely
completely – someone who would not need her to
run their marriage with the same competence and
efficiency required by her demanding job. On the
cruise she meets just such a man. But will their
passion be the answer to her problems?

JAYNE

Mary's beautiful niece and companion is a girl of a
different generation. But self-sufficient, modern
Jayne needs this cruise as much as her aunt.
Recovering from a heart-shattering love-affair, she
stubbornly seeks a lover from amongst the passengers, ignoring Mary's warning that she is playing
with fire. . . .

When Mary and Jayne return home from their
cruise in the Far East, they both learn – the hard
way – how to be true to their own values, honest
with themselves and necessary women. . . .

0 552 11575 4 — £1.95

SISTERS AND STRANGERS

by

HELEN VAN SLYKE

Three sisters return home to celebrate
their parents' Golden Wedding
anniversary. Thirty years have passed
since they were together.

ALICE

had an illegitimate child at seventeen
Now, enmeshed in a nightmare marriage to a
brutal bully, she pines to find the son
she has not seen since he was born . . .

FRANCES

the oldest, had left home suddenly and
married an actor. Three marriages
later she has returned home, famous,
sophisticated, rich – and jaded . . .

BARBARA

the youngest girl, their father's favourite,
has wasted her youth as the mistress of
a famous congressman. Will he now reject
her to avoid the scandal that
would ruin his career?

Within a few days, the life of each of the
sisters will change dramatically . . .

0 552 11321 2 — £1.95

A SELECTED LIST OF CORGI TITLES

WHILE EVERY EFFORT IS MADE TO KEEP PRICES LOW, IT IS
SOMETIMES NECESSARY TO INCREASE PRICES AT SHORT NOTICE.
CORGI BOOKS RESERVE THE RIGHT TO SHOW AND CHARGE NEW
RETAIL PRICES ON COVERS WHICH MAY DIFFER FROM THOSE
ADVERTISED IN THE TEXT OR ELSEWHERE.

THE PRICES SHOWN BELOW WERE CORRECT AT THE TIME OF GOING
TO PRESS.

☐	11844 3	THE MEN OF DALLAS	*Burt Hirschfeld*	£1.35
☐	11660 2	PRINCESS DAISY	*Judith Krantz*	£1.95
☐	11730 7	PORTRAITS	*Cynthia Freeman*	£2.50
☐	11775 7	A WORLD FULL OF STRANGERS	*Cynthia Freeman*	£1.95
☐	11698 X	LOVE'S SWEET AGONY	*Patricia Matthews*	£1.75
☐	10494 9	LOVE'S AVENGING HEART	*Patricia Matthews*	£1.95
☐	10737 9	LOVE FOREVER MORE	*Patricia Matthews*	£1.95
☐	11181 3	LOVE'S MAGIC MOMENT	*Patricia Matthews*	£1.50
☐	11553 3	LOVE'S RAGING TIDE	*Patricia Matthews*	£1.75
☐	11149 X	IMOGEN	*Jilly Cooper*	£1.50
☐	10878 2	PRUDENCE	*Jilly Cooper*	£1.50
☐	10717 4	OCTAVIA	*Jilly Cooper*	£1.50
☐	10576 7	HARRIET	*Jilly Cooper*	£1.50
☐	10427 2	BELLA	*Jilly Cooper*	£1.50
☐	10277 6	EMILY	*Jilly Cooper*	£1.50
☐	11575 4	A NECESSARY WOMAN	*Helen Van Slyke*	£1.95
☐	11321 2	SISTERS AND STRANGERS	*Helen Van Slyke*	£1.95

*All these books are available at your book shop or newsagent, or can be ordered
direct from the publisher. Just tick the titles you want and fill in the form below.*

CORGI BOOKS, Cash Sales Department, P.O. Box 11, Falmouth, Cornwall.

Please send cheque or postal order, no currency.

Please allow cost of book(s) plus the following for postage and packing:

U.K. Customers—Allow 45p for the first book, 20p for the second book and 14p for
each additional book ordered, to a maximum charge of £1.63.

B.P.F.O. and Eire—Allow 45p for the first book, 20p for the second book plus 14p
per copy for the next seven books, thereafter 8p per book.

Overseas Customers—Allow 75p for the first book and 21p per copy for each
additional book.

NAME (Block Letters) ....

ADDRESS ....

....